AN ELEMENT
OF RISK

AN ELEMENT
OF RISK

A Jack Taggart Mystery

Don Easton

DUNDURN
TORONTO

Cover image: istock.com/InkkStudios
Printer: Webcom

Library and Archives Canada Cataloguing in Publication

Easton, Don, author
      An element of risk / Don Easton.

(A Jack Taggart mystery)
Issued in print and electronic formats.
ISBN 978-1-4597-4163-8 (softcover).--ISBN 978-1-4597-4164-5
(PDF).--ISBN 978-1-4597-4165-2 (EPUB)

      I. Title. II. Series: Easton, Don. Jack Taggart mystery

PS8609.A78E44 2018   C813'.6   C2018-900728-1
                                            C2018-900729-X

1   2   3   4   5   22   21   20   19   18

We acknowledge the support of the **Canada Council for the Arts**, which last year invested $153 million to bring the arts to Canadians throughout the country, and the **Ontario Arts Council** for our publishing program. We also acknowledge the financial support of the **Government of Ontario**, through the **Ontario Book Publishing Tax Credit** and the **Ontario Media Development Corporation**, and the **Government of Canada**.

Nous remercions le **Conseil des arts du Canada** de son soutien. L'an dernier, le Conseil a investi 153 millions de dollars pour mettre de l'art dans la vie des Canadiennes et des Canadiens de tout le pays.

Care has been taken to trace the ownership of copyright material used in this book. The author and the publisher welcome any information enabling them to rectify any references or credits in subsequent editions.

— *J. Kirk Howard, President*

The publisher is not responsible for websites or their content unless they are owned by the publisher.

Printed and bound in Canada.

VISIT US AT

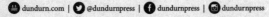

dundurn.com | @dundurnpress | dundurnpress | dundurnpress

Dundurn
3 Church Street, Suite 500
Toronto, Ontario, Canada
M5E 1M2

*For all the police officers who have lost their lives in service
of the people they were trying to protect*

Chapter One

Ana Valesi had no idea she was being spied on when she stepped out of the foyer of her office building. It was the last Wednesday in March and the rain, although not heavy, was decidedly cool. She opened a robin's-egg-blue umbrella and joined a sea of other workers intent on getting home. For the thugs who followed, her umbrella stood out like a beacon amongst a sea of bobbing black ones. It made their job all too easy.

As she walked toward the car park, her mind was focused elsewhere. She was a Crown prosecutor and today had been the opening salvo in what was scheduled to be a month-long murder trial.

The victim, eighteen-year-old Gerald Williams, was a member of a criminal gang based out of Mission called the United Front. Williams had been targeted and gunned down with multiple shots when he left a movie theatre. It was only by sheer luck that other movie goers had not been injured or killed as they fled in panic.

The accused, nineteen-year-old Ronald Forsythe, belonged to a neighbouring gang based out of Abbotsford called the Death Heads. The two gangs had been in a turf war for over two years and were vying for control of the lucrative drug and prostitution trade.

The gangs were primarily comprised of adolescent males. Approximately fifty members made up the Death Heads and there were perhaps a dozen less in the United Front. Even the leaders were younger than thirty years old.

It was their age that made them so dangerous. A lack of maturity, coupled with inexperience, decidedly limited their ability to reason, let alone envision the aconsequences of their actions or feel empathy for any unintended victims.

The wanton disregard for life exhibited by both gangs had been appalling. Drive-by shootings were occurring on crowded sidewalks, in restaurants, and in parking lots. Car chases with shots being exchanged had become outrageously common.

The trial was receiving a lot of attention from the news media and citizens, not to mention the gang members themselves. Security was tight, and those intent on attending the trial were subjected to the same intense screening one would receive at an airport.

During the preliminary trial, which had taken place months earlier, the defence lawyer, fearing that the presence of fellow gang members might have a negative influence on the judge, had strongly suggested to his client that he tell his fellow gang members not to show up in court. Any who did show had been requested to dress appropriately and try their best to look like choir boys. The same suggestion had been made by Ana for those who sided with the victim.

The gangs took the suggestion to heart and usually limited their support, sending only the leader of each gang along with one or two followers. When gang representatives did show, the two gangs were kept separate.

Harold Borman, the leader of the Death Heads, was delegated to sit on the right side of the courtroom, while Jarvis Thibault, leader of the United Front, sat on the left. Despite the heavy police presence, the tension was palpable.

Ana knew it wasn't only the tight security that aroused attention. The citizenry, stirred by media coverage of the ongoing shootings, were rightfully scared, angry, and keenly interested in the outcome of the trial.

Her case was also receiving rapt attention from her own superiors. She'd been selected to prosecute because she was a seasoned veteran with a reputation for being savvy, but she knew the respect she'd earned through years of dedicated work could vanish in an instant. Any slip-ups on her part would have serious ramifications for her future.

So far, the case was going as she wanted. The preliminary trial had gone well, but that being said, the real battle was yet to come.

Now, as she drove her white BMW out of the parkade, she went over the testimony she'd heard that afternoon and thought about the questions she'd ask when court reopened the next morning.

* * *

Twenty-three-year-old Aron Kondrat tapped the steering wheel of his blue Ford Mustang with a nervous energy when he stopped two cars behind Ana at a red light. Beside him sat twenty-two-year-old Jeremy Pratt. Both were members of the Death Heads, having joined the club when they were only twelve years old. The two had been close friends long before then.

Pratt spoke into his phone, using a conference call to update gang members in two other cars that were assisting in the surveillance. "Okay, the bitch is still on 99 but sittin' at a red light facin' Davie. Okay, the lights changed … we're goin' through the intersection and still headin' south on 99. Better scramble if you don't wanna miss the light."

"They made it," Kondrat stated. "Can see 'em in the rear-view."

* * *

Ana arrived at her mother's house and parked in the driveway before entering through the front door.

"Mommy! Mommy!" two-year-old Isabella shouted as she ran to Ana's outstretched arms.

Ana hugged and then kissed her, while her mother, Maria, retrieved her granddaughter's boots and jacket.

"How was she today?" Ana asked.

"A perfect angel … as always," Maria replied, while stifling a yawn.

Ana eyed Maria and thought she looked exhausted. "If you ever get tired, you'll let me know, won't you, Mom? We could always put her in daycare."

"Are you kidding? No way! I love looking after her." Maria paused and looked around. "Besides, I need something to do. I hate rattling around in this big house by myself. Issy gives me a sense of purpose."

"It's been a year since Dad died. Still no thought to moving? Pietro and I certainly have the space."

"Thanks, but I'm sure your husband doesn't want his mother-in-law moving in with him."

"Are you serious? Pietro adores you. He says you're simply an older version of me. He'd love it."

Maria smiled. "I know, I was teasing. The truth is, I'm not ready for that yet. All my friends live close by."

Ana nodded knowingly. She then glanced at Isabella. "Wrong foot, Issy. That boot goes on your other foot."

* * *

"Okay, the bitch is back out," Pratt reported excitedly, "an' she's got a little kid with her."

"This is fuckin' perfect," Kondrat stated. "It don't look like no fuckin' daycare, either. If that's the case, it'd be easy to do a fuckin' number on her right here."

"Maybe grab the kid or somethin'," Pratt suggested.

"Yeah, that'd be good. We'll have to run it past Borman."

"Figure he'll go along with it?" Pratt questioned.

"That fuckin' no-mind. Who knows what he'll want."

Kondrat gestured toward Ana's car. "She's backin' out. Tell everyone to get ready."

"We know where she drops her kid off," Pratt replied. "That's gotta be the best play. If we lose her, it won't matter."

"We won't lose her," Kondrat replied. "She drives like an old woman."

"Once we talk with Borman, how long you figure after that?" Pratt asked.

"If he likes our idea, we should confirm that she always drops the kid off here. We'll come back either tomorrow or Friday to make sure."

"So maybe we could do our thing on Monday," Pratt suggested.

Kondrat nodded in agreement, then said, "That'd give us time to pick up some wheels. I sure as fuck don't wanna use my own car."

* * *

For Ana, Thursday and Friday went well in court, but she still spent much of the weekend studying case law while Pietro took care of Isabella.

On Monday morning she drove Issy back to Maria's house. She thought it would be a day like any other. Instead, it was a day that would haunt her forever.

"Mommy, I see Gwama's house," Isabella piped up from her toddler seat in the back of the car.

"Grandmother's house," Ana replied, enunciating the words carefully. Besides taking law in university, Ana had also majored in English. Isabella was her only child and she was determined that she'd learn to articulate clearly and not use baby-talk.

"Gwama," reiterated Isabella emphatically.

Ana smiled and decided to let it go. A moment later, she opened the back door of the BMW and leaned in to unbuckle her daughter.

* * *

Kondrat and Pratt watched Ana from down the street. This time they were in a Honda Civic. It had been stolen the day before and had been swapped for Kondrat's Mustang, which was parked a few blocks away.

"Dis gonna be a day dat bitch ain't never gonna forget," Pratt said, gazing at the Glock 19 pistol he held in his hand. It had been fitted with a laser grip. "Man, I can't wait to see how dis baby works." He raised the weapon and rested it on the dash and looked out to get a fix on the laser dot. "Bet I could take her out from here."

"Fuck, Jeremy, put it down before someone sees you," Kondrat said.

"Ain't nobody gonna see me with this rain," Pratt replied, sounding annoyed.

"Yeah, well do it anyway. It's not her we're gonna —"

"Yeah, yeah, I know." Pratt lowered the pistol. "I was just sayin' is all. It'd be so easy to off the bitch. Fuck, you could pull right up an' I could do 'er when she stands up. I wouldn't even need to get out of the car." He eyed Kondrat. "You hear what I'm sayin'?"

Kondrat flexed his fingers inside his latex gloves, then glanced at Pratt. "Yeah, I hear ya', but what we're gonna do is better." He snickered. "Imagine how much she'll fuckin' freak when she gets the news."

Pratt grinned. "Yeah, it'll be so cool." He paused to stare at a passing car, then added, "Wish we were in court to see it when Borman looks her in the eyes and smiles."

"You an' me both." Kondrat gestured to the house. "She's taken the kid in."

"Yup." Pratt was silent for a moment, then laughed.

"What's so funny?"

"When Borman calls, you should tell 'im to video the bitch on his phone when she hears. What a fuckin' hoot that'd be to watch. Bet she bawls her eyes out right in court."

"Bor smilin' at her is enough," Kondrat replied. "She'll get the message. If he does any more than that, he's liable to get busted."

"Yeah, I know. It'd be so … like, cool to see it, though." He pointed. "The bitch is out."

Pratt glanced at his watch. "Seven thirty. Same as last week."

They watched Ana drive away, then Kondrat drove into an alley a couple houses down from where Isabella was dropped off and parked the car.

* * *

Sergeant Roger Morris was a Royal Canadian Mounted Police officer assigned to the Combined Forces Special Enforcement Unit, located in Surrey, about a thirty-five-minute drive from the RCMP headquarters building in Vancouver.

These days, a top priority for CFSEU was to try and get a handle on the street-level gangs who were actively trading shots with each other.

Roger, along with Detective Pete Davis, who was a colleague assigned to work with him from the Vancouver Police Department, were keenly interested in the gang trial taking place. They'd both played supervisory roles in the investigation.

Despite the security put in place, Roger's nerves were on edge as he and Pete took a seat in the back of the courtroom. Both gangs were striving to make a name for themselves — a name the gangs hoped would put fear in the hearts of everyone. That quest, coupled with an abundance of testosterone and juvenile thinking, made them unpredictable.

When Roger spotted Harold Borman, his suspicions were heightened. Last week Borman had sat in the last row of benches with his back to the wall. Today he'd moved closer and was sitting with one of his cronies directly behind the prosecution's table. *Okay, jerk-offs, what're you up to?*

The trial had barely restarted when Roger saw Borman nudge his buddy, then get up and leave the courtroom.

Roger elbowed Pete. "Keep an eye on the guy sitting behind Ana," he whispered. "I'm going to see what Borman's up to."

A minute later, Roger located Borman in a hallway using his phone. Not an unusual occurrence because phones had to be turned off in court.

Okay, time for me to quit being overly paranoid, Roger thought, before heading back to the courtroom.

* * *

Pratt waited anxiously as Kondrat spoke on the phone.

"Well?" he asked when the call ended.

Kondrat gave a grim smile. "Let's do it."

"Fuckin' Aye, man!" Pratt smirked as he snapped the latex glove on the wrist of his gun hand for effect.

Both men pulled the hoods on their jackets up over their heads before giving a tug on the peaks of their ball caps to lower them.

Kondrat then took his own Glock 19 pistol equipped with laser grip from his waistband and tapped the barrel on Pratt's like he was giving a toast. "Party's on, dude!"

Seconds later they hustled down the alley, opened the back gate to Maria Valesi's yard, and ran to her back door.

Pratt kicked the door, but the deadlock bolt held fast. He kicked a second time and the wood splintered, but the deadbolt remained in place.

"Come on!" Kondrat yelled in frustration.

Pratt kicked again. This time the door flung open and they burst inside.

Maria's screams and Isabella's frightened cry could be heard throughout the house.

Chapter Two

Corporal Jack Taggart and Constable Laura Secord were both members of the RCMP assigned to an intelligence unit in the headquarters building in Vancouver. Their mandate was to target sophisticated organized crime rings, particularly those who operated on an international level. At the top of their list was the Satans Wrath Motorcycle Club.

Satans Wrath operated in more than forty countries and included an overall membership of several thousand members worldwide. Most countries had numerous chapters, with larger cities being divided into more than a couple of chapters. Each chapter was overseen by a president, and a national president oversaw each country.

The club was responsible for a multitude of crimes, including murder, drug importing and exporting by the tonne, prostitution, corruption, identify theft, credit card fraud, and basically any other criminal activity imaginable.

Both Jack and Laura had been specially trained as undercover operatives, but their primary aim was to develop high-level informants. Undercover operatives, surveillance, and wiretaps could be important tools, but having someone on the inside was much more valuable.

Three months previous, Purvis Evans, who'd been the national president of Satans Wrath in Canada, was murdered after making a fatal mistake — he'd threatened Jack's family. A high-level informant Jack had cultivated within the club claimed that Evans had disappeared after meeting some Russian cocaine importers whose real identities were never discovered by the bikers. This informant was certain that Evans had been murdered. Jack was more than certain. He knew.

After speaking with his informant, Jack submitted an intelligence report advising what his informant had told him. The truth was that, unbeknownst to the informant or anyone else in Satans Wrath, Jack had assumed an undercover role and tipped off a small band of thugs who were about to be murdered on orders from Evans. He then arranged for these criminals to murder Evans and make it appear that Russian criminals were responsible — Russian criminals who did not exist.

Evans's murder, coupled with several arrests orchestrated by Jack and Laura from tips received from their informant, hindered some of Satans Wrath's criminal ventures within British Columbia ... but not all. Some crimes, regardless of how deadly, were allowed to continue to protect the identity of their informant.

Monday was the start of a new week and Jack took a sip of coffee and eyed Laura over the top of his mug. Her desk butted up to his and he'd noticed she'd been reading intelligence reports submitted from other parts of Canada. "You're quiet this morning," he noted. "Anything good?"

Laura frowned as she dipped a tea bag into her mug. "I don't know if you'd call it good. I'm reading a report from the Canadian Intelligence Service out of Ottawa about Italian organized crime in Montreal and Toronto." She took the tea bag out and gazed at it as it spun on the string before putting it aside. "It's been a long time since our unit has taken a look to see how much influence the Cosa Nostra has out west."

"Thinking we've stalled Satans Wrath a little and should take a look ourselves?"

Laura made a face. "You and I don't have the time. *Stalled* is the right word, but it won't take them long to recover. With our friend on the inside, we're still going to be busy. I don't see us getting the chance to take a long hard look at anyone else, which is the problem."

Jack put his mug down. "We're getting an increase in staff soon."

Laura's face brightened. "Yes, a new sergeant's position and two constables."

"That should help."

"The promotion board is supposed to sit next month. I'm certain you'll be the one selected to get your third stripe."

Jack pretended to eye her suspiciously. "You're hoping I am so you'll have an opportunity to move into my spot and pick up your corporal stripes."

Laura smiled. "I wouldn't turn down a 10 percent pay increase."

"Likewise," Jack replied. He took another sip of coffee as he thought about the possibility of Italian organized crime evolving in B.C. "I don't think we need to worry about the Italians at the moment. Our extra manpower, when we get it, could be used in other areas."

"What makes you think we don't need to worry about them?"

"What criminal activity do you think Satans Wrath is *not* involved in?"

"Is not involved in?" Laura appeared to think hard on the question. "None that I can think of. Drug trafficking, prostitution, not to mention corruption, infiltration of labour unions, elected officials, the judiciary, the ports…" She looked curiously at Jack. "Why?"

"In other words, anything that Italian organized crime would touch would also have to be in collusion with Satans Wrath. If they didn't, we'd be finding bodies, either bikers or Italians, or both."

Laura nodded. "And our friend would know about it," she added.

Jack was about to reply in the affirmative but stopped when their boss, Staff Sergeant Rose Wood, entered the office.

Looks ticked … what now?

"Hi, Rose. What's up? You look like you inhaled a bug."

Rose didn't bother to pull up a chair as she glowered at Jack. "I bumped into Lexton out in the hall a moment ago. She asked if our section has come up with any Russian organized crime factions in the city yet."

Crap! Assistant Commissioner Lexton was recently promoted to the position of being the criminal operations officer in charge of the Pacific region. She wielded enormous power and was someone whose attention he wished to avoid.

"Not coming up with anything doesn't exactly put our office in a good light," Rose said.

Damn it. I was hoping Lexton would forget about that.... He looked up at Rose. "I reported at the time that my informant believes the Russians were not from here and moved on after Evans disappeared."

"Alleged Russians," Rose retorted. "I get the distinct feeling that Lexton doesn't believe your informant."

"He's always been reliable in the past," Jack noted.

"Yes, I told Lexton that."

"How'd she respond?"

Rose stared at Jack a moment, "That perhaps your informant was fed misinformation and Satans Wrath only believes it to be true." When Jack didn't respond, her face hardened. "What do you have to say about that?"

That Lexton is a smart lady....

"Well?" Rose prodded.

"I suppose it's possible," Jack replied.

"Yes, it certainly is possible," Rose replied bluntly before trudging back out the door.

Jack stared after her.

And Lexton isn't the only smart lady.

* * *

Sergeant Roger Morris intended to return to the courtroom, but as he reached for the door he heard the order being given from inside for everyone to rise. Knowing an adjournment was taking place, he decided to wait.

Moments later, people started filing out, including Pete.

"Fifteen-minute adjournment," he said.

"Already? They barely started."

"It was the judge who wanted it. Probably drank too much coffee," Pete surmised. "What was Borman up to?"

"Just making a phone call," Roger said as he watched defence council approach the prosecution desk and speak to Ana. She stiffened, then looked around. Their eyes met. Immediately she grabbed her briefcase and made a bee-line toward him.

"Ana's ticked," Roger noted.

"What about?" Pete asked.

"I don't know. I think we're about to find out."

Pete turned to look. "Oh, yeah. She's angry," he agreed.

Roger smiled cordially when Ana arrived. "Good morning, Ana. What's up?"

"The three of us need to talk — privately," she snapped, gesturing with her briefcase for them to go to a witness room.

Once inside, Roger asked again, "What's up?"

"I just spoke with defence." Ava paused, her eyes studying theirs. "They gave me a heads-up that our murder weapon will be deemed inadmissible."

"What the hell! Why?" Pete exclaimed.

"They say they have proof that someone in CFSEU searched the car prior to getting a warrant."

"No way," Roger said firmly. "Uh-uh. I was in charge of that team. Do you really think I'd risk jeopardizing a case by doing something like that? There were plenty of grounds to get the warrant. Our people didn't mind waiting. We knew it would be signed."

"Defence claims that they're getting camera footage from outside the convenience store to prove it," Ana countered.

"Good, because there's no way anyone searched it without getting the warrant first," Roger replied adamantly.

"If it's true, I'll pull the case," Ana threatened.

"Everyone knows you would, which is why nobody would ever do it." Roger stared at her. "Defence is yanking your chain," he said confidently. "They're trying to rattle you, but of course once you find that out, they'll say they were only joking."

"Are you certain?"

"Yes, I'm certain. I was there that night from the time the car stopped until it was searched. The driver popped into the store and I had my team arrest him coming out. Nobody went inside the car until we had the warrant in our hands."

Ana sighed. "Okay, I believe you." She shook her head in apparent self-recrimination. "Damn him. I should have known he was —"

Rapid knocks on the door and the voice of the court clerk asking for Ms. Valesi interrupted their conversation. Roger opened the door.

"Ms. Valesi," the young woman exclaimed. "I received a call from the Vancouver City Police. You're to phone a Mrs. Maria Valesi immediately."

Ana's jaw slackened. She looked at Roger. "That's my mother! She babysits my daughter, Issy."

Roger had a sick feeling in his gut as he watched Ana fumble for her phone in her briefcase.

"I turned it … turned it off for court," she stammered, while placing the call. "Hello, Mom!" She paused and her eyes widened in panic, then she exclaimed, "They kicked in the back door! They had guns?"

Oh, fuck! Roger glanced at Pete, who looked ashen.

"Mom … Issy? What about Issy?" Ana pleaded. "Mother, please … quit … you're blubbering. Listen to me, damn it! Is Isabella okay?"

Roger felt like it was an eternity before Ana received an answer. For her, he knew, waiting for the answer was even worse.

"She is? She is? She's safe! Oh, God. Oh, God." Ana glanced at Roger and Pete. "She's safe. Issy's okay." She then took a couple of deep breaths in an apparent effort to control her emotions.

"Thank Christ," Roger said. "Where are they now?"

Ana spoke into the phone and said, "The police are there … yes, I'll talk to them." She then looked at Roger and Pete while holding the phone to her ear and said, "Two guys wearing hoodies and with guns kicked in the back door to my mother's house a couple of minutes ago. The police are going through the house now."

"Jesus Christ," Roger muttered.

"My mom saw them out the window when they were kicking the door. She grabbed Issy and ran out the front door as they came in. She heard one of them yell at the other to hurry. He said to get the kid and get out of there."

"Ana, I'm sorry," Roger said. "Would you like us to give you a ride over there? You probably shouldn't be driving until you've had time to calm down."

"They were after my Isabella." Ana looked confused, then added, "She's only two years old."

"Where are your mother and Isabella now?" Pete asked.

"At a neighbour's, and ..." Ana looked around, then sat in a chair. "VPD want to talk to me. I can't ... I need a minute. Pete? Will you?"

Pete took the phone and identified himself to the officer on the line. He then told the officer that Ana was prosecuting the trial between the United Front and the Death Heads. He listened a moment, then glanced at Ana. "Things are calming down," he said reassuringly. "Isabella is fine. She's already playing with the neighbour's toddler. Probably too young to understand. Your mom went to the washroom. She, uh, has to clean herself up and will call you back."

"Oh ... okay," Ana replied.

"They want to know if you saw anyone following you this morning or anything suspicious."

"No, I didn't," Ana replied. "Maybe I should have been watching. I didn't think —"

"It's okay," Pete said. "Who would even think that someone would do this?" He spoke into the phone a little more, then ended the call and gave the phone back to Ana, who put it away.

Roger saw Ana put her hand over her mouth and for a moment he wondered if she was going to be sick. Then she lowered her hand and took a deep breath. The fear was obvious on her face, but then she nodded to herself, perhaps coming to terms with what she thought happened.

"Initial results at the scene indicate it may have been done to scare you," Pete said.

"To scare me?"

"There are smears left from muddy tracks in the back entrance, but none leading anywhere else. Combined with them yelling to hurry and grab the kid — you'd think they'd have gone a little farther into the house if that was their real intent. Not to mention, if it was, why yell that out? They'd have already known what they were intending to do and wouldn't have had to say it. Also, there were no bad guys covering the front door, which would've been an obvious escape route."

Ana appeared to reflect briefly on what Pete had said. "I see," she replied. "You're right. That's logical." Anger had replaced the fear in her voice and on her face.

The court clerk then asked, "Should I notify the judge about what happened so you can get an adjournment?"

"No!" Ana said crossly. "Defence would claim that it would prejudice the judge and demand a retrial. If I try to get an adjournment for personal reasons the judge will ask questions and would likely clue in, which would still give defence grounds." She paused to stare at Roger and Pete. "Intimidation? Forget that! I'm going back in there and I'll pretend nothing happened."

"Are you sure?" Roger asked.

"Yes, I'm sure." She glanced at her watch. "We've still got five minutes." She looked at the court clerk. "Thank you for your assistance. You may go."

As the court clerk left, Ana said, "We'll likely adjourn again in about an hour for lunch. I'll call my mother now and tell her that I'll talk to her again later. I suspect it'll be past noon before the police finish getting a statement from her."

"I'm sure you're right about that," Pete replied.

Ana called her mother. When she didn't answer, she left a message to say that she was absolutely certain it was only meant to intimidate and that she'd talk to her at lunchtime.

"Ana, I am so sorry," Roger said as soon as she put her phone away.

"We both are," Pete added. "Believe me, we'll find out who did this."

Ana took a deep breath and appeared to reflect a moment. "Thanks. Come on. We better get back in there."

Back in the courtroom, Ana returned to the prosecution table and Roger and Pete decided to remain by her side until court was called to order.

Ana whispered, "Who would you call if this had happened to either one of your families?"

"VPD are good," Roger said, feeling embarrassed for his colleague.

Pete looked slightly perturbed. "I'd like to think we are."

"I know VPD are good," Ana replied evenly. "That's not what I asked."

Roger then saw Ana look past him and her face went cold. He turned and saw Borman smiling at them.

Ana's words seemed surprisingly calm. "So I'll ask again. Who'd you call if this happened to either one of your families?"

Roger glanced at Pete. They both answered simultaneously.

Chapter Three

Jack answered his phone and soon felt the rage roil within as he listened to what Roger had to say. Most people would be upset to hear that the prosecutor's family had been threatened, but for Jack it was more personal. For him it brought back memories of when his own family was threatened a few months earlier.

The effect it'd had on his wife, two sons, and him hadn't gone away. They'd all become hypersensitive to any noise around their home and were still having nightmares.

Mikey is only eleven and Stevie hasn't turned ten yet. To go through crap like that at their age isn't right ... and it sure as hell isn't right for the prosecutor and her family, either.

He thought of the long road ahead for both their families to put it all behind them. *How much time does it take to recover from something like that? Do you ever recover?*

"What's going on?" Laura whispered from across her desk.

Jack gestured with his finger to his lips for her to wait as he listened.

"I'm sure the Death Heads are behind it," Roger said. "Last week Borman sat in the back row, but today he sat directly behind Ana. I saw him slip out and make a phone call as soon as court started. After she received the news and returned to court he was smiling at her like some perverted sicko. I'm sure he was sending her a message."

"You're suggesting they did it to scare her?" Jack asked. "Maybe intimidate her enough that she'd purposely do something to have the case thrown out?"

"Possibly, but we don't know for sure. It took them a few kicks to open the door. Ana's mom heard the noise and looked out the window. When she saw two guys with guns in their hands she grabbed the kid and bolted out the front. Whoever it was might have heard them escaping and knew they were too late."

"Maybe lucky for her and the tot."

"There were no bad guys covering off the front of the house, but these guys are punks. They're not known for their brainpower. The United Front are also pissed off with Ana because she's subpoenaed a couple of them to testify … which they don't want to do."

"Thinking it'll make them look like wimps in the eyes of the other gangs. That they can't take care of business themselves."

"You got it. So I can't be absolutely certain Borman was behind it, but by the way he was grinning at us, I'm 99.9 percent sure."

"And one of the attackers yelled something about grabbing the kid?"

"Yes."

Jack felt his stomach churn. "The poor prosecutor. She must be sick."

"Ana supports the theory that it was meant to scare her — or maybe prefers to think that. If it was, they picked the wrong person. If anything, it made her angry. She was back in court moments later acting as if nothing happened."

She'll probably break down when she sees her kid.

"So what do you think?" Roger asked.

"Ana sounds like a gutsy lady," Jack replied.

"You've got that right."

"If you're so sure it was the Death Heads, or possibly the United Front, why are you calling me? Isn't VPD handling it?"

"They are, but it'd be appreciated if you'd help us out."

"The street gangs are your headache, not mine."

"I know, but both gangs get their dope from dealers who put out for Satans Wrath."

"So?"

"Your unit has been responsible for a lot of high-level busts involving those guys lately. My guess is you have someone talking to you from the inside. If you do, these punks might listen if they were to get a lecture on etiquette from the big boys."

Jack was silent as he thought about how to respond. Roger was someone he trusted, but admitting he had a high-level informant in Satans Wrath was not to his liking.

"I know you've never met Ana," Roger prompted, "but there's something you should know. When she got the news, she asked Pete and me who we'd call if it'd happened to our families — and she wasn't simply meaning the name of a good investigator. This lady's been around. She's sharp. She knows the game."

Looking for someone who isn't afraid to bend the rules or get a message across the hard way.

"I take it you're telling me I could trust her to keep her mouth shut," Jack said.

"Yes. She's a straight arrow and would readily toss out a court case or reject a warrant application if anything was amiss — but this is different."

"It's family," Jack said.

"For sure."

"You seem anxious to help her," Jack noted.

"I've known her a long time. Most prosecutors would've burned out, but not her. She stays at it, slugging away day after day. The truth be known, I look at her like she's my kid sister, but don't tell her that. She thinks of herself as being pretty independent."

"Until this happened."

"Yup." Roger paused. "That was a game changer."

"And you really do trust her?"

"Pete and I wouldn't have tossed out your name if we didn't trust her."

"You already told her you'd call me?"

"Yeah."

Jack took a deep breath and slowly exhaled as he came to a decision. "Okay … I do have someone on the inside, but it could be placing him at high risk to do what you want."

"I see." Roger paused, perhaps to reflect on what Jack had said. "Okay, I understand." His tone was polite, but sounded dismal. "Thanks for listening."

"I didn't say no," Jack replied. "I'll talk to my friend and see what he says. Maybe we can help you, but I'm not making any promises at this point."

Roger's tone lifted. "That'd be great. That's all I'm asking."

Oh, good. I thought maybe you wanted Borman dead.

When Jack ended the call he told Laura what had happened.

Her eyes flashed with anger. "Think our friend could help?" she asked.

"Let's find out."

* * *

It was early afternoon when Jack and Laura, each with open umbrellas to ward off the rain, walked through Pine Valley Cemetery on the outskirts of Vancouver.

Lance Morgan had arrived ahead of them and was standing at the usual spot, which was beyond a knoll where you couldn't be seen by passing cars. He peered out from under his own umbrella as they approached.

Jack fully appreciated the risk that Lance was taking by being their informant — particularly being the president of the Westside chapter of Satans Wrath in Vancouver. If the club found out, his death would be slow and painful. Added to that, Lance was married and had four grown children and a grandchild. Being an informant would place them at risk if he ever tried to enter the witness protection program. Past history verified that the club wouldn't hesitate to kill one or more of his relatives out of spite.

Jack and Lance had a long history together. Years prior, when Lance was a regular member in the club, Jack had obtained enough evidence to charge him and two other bikers with attempted murder.

At that time Jack offered Lance immunity to become his informant. Lance initially refused, but Jack played hardball. He told Lance that he'd arrest the other two, then ask for a reduced sentence on Lance and keep him in protective custody to make it look like he'd made a deal. Out of fear for the safety of his family, Lance decided to cooperate. In time, Jack had decided that Lance had repaid his debt and let him go.

A few months ago, Jack obtained evidence on Lance again. By then he'd become the Westside chapter president. Jack's evidence was also strong enough to convict Jake Yevdokymenko, or "Whiskey Jake" as he was known, who was the president of the Eastside chapter.

Jack had discovered that the two men owned a company registered in the Cayman Islands. Legal documents that he obtained proved that Lance and Whiskey Jake were laundering drug money from Canada and the U.S. The documents also revealed that each of them had five million in U.S. dollars stashed in those accounts.

Jack wasn't certain if Whiskey Jake would inform, but he believed Lance would because of their prior history together. He approached Lance and told him that in exchange for becoming an informant again, he'd be able to keep his money and that Whiskey Jake wouldn't know that their money laundering scheme had been discovered.

Jack also promised not to have Lance extradited to the U.S., where he'd likely spend the rest of his life behind bars. This time Lance found it easier to inform and readily accepted the offer. At that point, Jack let him know that he'd recorded their conversation and threatened to divulge the recording if Lance tried to move his money or renege on their deal. Lance wasn't happy about the recording, but understood the reason.

"Hey, Laura," Lance said cheerily as they approached. "We gotta stop meeting like this. My wife's getting suspicious."

"So's my husband," Laura replied, "and he's a policeman who carries a gun."

Lance grinned, then became serious when he caught the grim look on Jack's face. "What's up?"

Jack told Lance what had happened to the prosecutor, along with the reasons they believed Borman was behind it.

Lance shook his head and looked disgusted. "Fucking Christ. I can't believe how stupid they are. Makes me wonder if any of them are capable of thinking more than a minute ahead, let alone figure out what will happen to them down the road because of the way they carry on."

"How'd you feel about ordering someone from your club to approach them over it?" Jack asked. "These guys need to be taught the rules."

"Or the heat could come down hard on everyone," Laura added.

Lance took a deep breath and exhaled, "What you say makes sense, but to approach them on something like this means I'd have to discuss it with Whiskey Jake first."

"He's your equal," Jack noted.

"I know. It's not that I'd need his permission, but doing something like that could affect the future of everyone."

"Meaning that the Death Heads, if it was them, could be stupid enough to ignore your guidance and force you to take things further," Jack said.

"Yup … exactly." Lance shook his head again. "I knew they were stupid, but I'd no idea how stupid. Whiskey Jake and I've often talked about how they keep trading bullets and doing stupid shit. We've been okay with it because it takes the heat off us." He paused and appeared to think about it.

"The problem is that for me to appear to switch my way of thinking and suggest we tell them to smarten up will raise eyebrows."

"Then don't chance it," Jack said. "You know better than us what you can get away with and what you can't."

Lance's brow furrowed. "The thing is, if they do whack the prosecutor or her kid, you'll probably want me to stick my nose into it then."

"If the investigation into that stalled, I would ask you to help," Jack agreed. "It's not something we'd want to let slide past."

"Sticking my nose in then would draw more attention. The heat would be all over those guys and, if anything, we'd shut down business with them for a while and keep our distance. If I were to have someone approach them then, it would really seem odd. Especially if it involved asking questions about exactly who it was that did the hit."

"So what're you thinking?" Laura asked.

Lance paused to make a decision. "I'll talk to Whiskey Jake. I doubt he'll agree … but like you said, I'm a chapter president the same as him. We don't have a national president at the moment to give the deciding vote, so I could still get away with ordering it to be done."

"Another problem is how you'd know about it," Jack noted. "There's been no news release. I was told that the prosecutor didn't even want the judge to know."

"That's not a problem," Lance replied. "I'll tell Whiskey Jake that I heard what happened through the grapevine. He wouldn't question that."

"Grapevine?" Laura questioned.

"One of my guy's sisters works in the cafeteria at the courthouse. Whiskey Jake knows that and would presume that's how I found out. I'll tell him that if these idiots start going after prosecutors, it'll give the cops justification to get a bunch more manpower. I'll say that although it'll keep the cops busy temporarily, with extra manpower the street gangs would soon be behind bars. Not only would that have an adverse effect on our income because of all the dope they deal, but then the cops would use all that extra manpower to come after us."

"Actually, it sounds pretty logical," Laura commented.

"I think it's logical enough for me to get away with it," said Lance.

"As long as you're comfortable with it," Jack added.

"I am. I'll get on it right away."

"Thanks. Call me and let me know."

Lance nodded, then eyed Jack intently. "How heavy should I tell my guys to be with Borman?"

"If it was only meant to scare her, give him a warning. If it was something else they had in mind … give him more than a warning."

"How much more?"

"Whatever you think is necessary to ensure it never happens again."

Chapter Four

It was two days later when Jack strolled out of his bedroom and went downstairs to the kitchen. He was surprised to see both his sons already at the breakfast table. Usually it took more prodding to get them up.

They both appeared to be fidgeting while concentrating hard on their cereal bowls in an effort not to make eye contact with him. He glanced at Natasha as she poured him a cup of coffee and saw her smile.

Ah yes, it's April Fools' Day....

He slid back his chair and pretended not to notice the whoopee cushion as he sat down, then did his best to look embarrassed at the loud noise of what sounded like a gaseous explosion. "Excuse me! I'm sorry!" he exclaimed.

Mike and Steve squirmed in their chairs as they tried unsuccessfully to suppress their giggles.

"Must have been something I ate," he suggested.

That comment brought on a few more splutters as his boys tried not to laugh.

Jack hid his smile.

Great to see everyone so happy. It's how a family should be.

Then his phone vibrated. Lance. It was a harsh reminder of who he was and what he did for a living. He excused himself from the table and answered.

"I talked to Whiskey Jake and wanted to let you know it went about as I expected," Lance said.

"As you expected?"

"He gave me a puzzled look when I brought it up, like it wasn't any of our business."

"Puzzled ... or suspicious?"

"Both go together in our world. I gave him the reason we discussed, about how it could potentially affect us all. He still disagreed about warning them, but in the end we agreed to disagree."

"So? When?"

"Already done. I told you I'd get on it immediately. A few of my guys paid Borman a visit last night. He admitted it was his idea and said they only intended to scare her. He said it won't happen again."

"How was his attitude? Did your guys believe him?"

"Yeah, they believe him. He got the message loud and clear. They slapped him around a bit when he first admitted it, although it probably wasn't necessary. I'm told he was scared shitless. He said he'd put the word out to his guys, which I'm sure he will."

"Where'd this take place?"

"At his house," Lance replied. "Well, actually they went out to his garage behind the house in case you guys had his house wired."

"Was he alone?"

"A couple of his guys were there, but they didn't inter-fere."

"Good."

"Well ... sort of good."

"What do you mean?"

"I'm told that Borman's not all that respected by his guys. Being slapped around probably didn't help his rep, either, but I'd told my guys to ensure they got the point across."

"Sounds like the point was made."

"It was, and I think that prosecutor will be okay, but tell her to keep her eyes open. At least until the heat from the trial dies down. These idiots are totally undisciplined. I wouldn't put it past one of them to toss a rock through her window or something without Borman knowing."

"If that did happen and you found out, what would the consequences be?"

"We'd hold Borman accountable. If he, uh, disposed of the problem on his own, then everything would be okay. If he didn't, then he'd either be in traction for the rest of his life or end up in the place where you and I meet."

Except he'd be looking up at the grass in the cemetery.

"Okay, thanks for sticking your neck out."

"Hey, if it gives me one more step to get you off my back, I'm more than happy."

"It does, but you've got a long way to go yet."

"I know."

"Take care. I'll pass the message along that he's been warned."

After ending the call, Jack immediately phoned Roger.

After the initial greeting, Roger asked, "What's up? Early in the day to be calling."

"I figured your prosecutor would want to hear this sooner rather than later." Jack then told him about the meeting Satans Wrath had with Borman.

"Man, what a relief," Roger said once he heard the news. "I knew you were the guy for the job."

"Hopefully there won't be any more problems, but give her my number and tell her to call me direct if she has any further concerns or sees anything suspicious."

"Will do. VPD are making extra patrols past her house, as well as her mother's house."

"How long can they afford the personnel and time to do that?"

"They said they'd keep it up until a couple weeks past the trial."

"That's good of them." He glanced at his family at the kitchen table. "Listen, my coffee's getting cold, so have a good day."

Jack retrieved his coffee mug from the kitchen table and put it in the microwave. Before it was reheated, he received a call from Ana thanking him.

"No problem, but stay vigilant just the same," Jack warned.

"Roger mentioned we might still get a rock through our window. That I can handle."

I can see why Roger admires her....

"Call me immediately if anything like that happens."

"I will. Thank you."

Jack then wished her luck with the trial and said goodbye.

"So nice we can have these family times together," Natasha said facetiously when he put his phone back in his pocket.

"Sorry, Nat."

"Push the bread down in the toaster and I'll forgive you."

Jack pushed the button on the toaster and then returned to the table. When he sat down the noise caused his sons to howl with laughter.

"What the?" he exclaimed, jumping up from his chair before pretending to find the whoopee cushion.

* * *

When Jack arrived at work he submitted an intelligence report outlining the incident with the prosecutor and identifying Borman as the person who gave the orders. His report stated that his informant said that Satans Wrath used their influence to tell Borman to stop any further intimidation tactics against Crown prosecutors because of the ramifications it could have on other criminal ventures. He also noted there remained some concern that vandalism or some such threat could still take place due to the lack of respect Borman had with his followers.

Jack then entered Rose's office and dropped the report in her in-basket.

"Hang on a sec," Rose said. "Have a seat."

He sat, and raised an eyebrow.

"I want to talk to you about the upcoming sergeant's position. I'm optimistic that you'll get it and Laura will move into your position."

"It's nice to be optimistic," he replied. "I take it that you're one of those the glass is half full types?"

"What are you? The half-empty type?"

"No, I just say either way it's beer and slam it back."

Rose smiled, then became serious. "You're both well overdue for promotion."

"I wouldn't turn it down," he admitted.

"The thing is, space is tight and we're also getting two new constables. How about you and I share this office and we squeeze the two constables in with Laura?"

Jack frowned. "Laura and I are the only trained undercover operators in the office. It's nice to have her close to bounce ideas off of and vice versa." *Not to mention, she's my friend.*

"Maybe the two new constables will be operators, as well. If not, then Laura could check to see if they'd be suitable candidates when she's working with them."

"Laura?" Jack questioned. "What about me?"

Rose leaned back in her chair and appeared to study his face. "You'd still be involved to some extent."

"To some extent?"

"You've been through a hell of a lot in the last few years and have more than paid your dues. With your third stripe I'd expect you to start playing more of a supervisory role and a little less hands-on."

I like being hands-on.

"It would give you more time to spend with your family, too. How are they, by the way?"

Ouch. That's hitting below the belt. She's right, though, I couldn't even have breakfast this morning without working.

He saw Rose studying his face for a reaction. "My family's good … thank you." He made a face. "You're right, though. A little less hands-on would be okay."

"Good," Rose replied, then reached for his report to indicate that the meeting was over.

* * *

That afternoon Rose approached Jack in his office. "Assistant Commissioner Lexton wishes to speak to you about the informant report you submitted this morning."

Jack glanced at Laura, then at Rose. "When?"

"Right now."

"You coming, too?" Jack asked as he pushed his chair back. "Or Laura? She's his secondary handler."

Rose shook her head. "She said she wants to see you alone because it would give her a chance to get to know you better."

I don't want her to know me better....

Chapter Five

Jack entered Lexton's office and she gestured for him to take a seat across from her.

"I read your report with some interest," she said, tapping the file on her desk with a finger as he sat down. "I'm curious as to whether or not you know the actual names of the two perpetrators who kicked in the door?"

"I don't, and neither does my source," Jack replied. "There are about fifty in the gang. Any one of them would do it if ordered to. Satans Wrath's objective was to convince the leader of the gang to amend his ways and pass the word to the rest. Who actually kicked in the door wasn't of interest."

"The leader being Harold Borman."

"Yes. The only concern is he doesn't have the respect and total control of his people. My source thinks the prosecutor will be okay, but suggested she be cautious until the heat from the trial dies down."

"So you stated in your report," Lexton said absent-mindedly. Then her eyes focused on Jack. "I'm pleased that the matter appears to have been rectified in the manner it was."

"Hopefully it has."

"I'm curious that you were involved, considering that the matter fell under the jurisdiction of VPD and perhaps CFSEU."

"I was asked by Sergeant Roger Morris in CFSEU to lend a hand due to my knowledge of Satans Wrath in the hope that I could get them to use their influence. Which I did."

"Were you overt in your approach to Satans Wrath?"

"No, I have a high-level informant in the club. He's a chapter president and is the informant noted in the report."

"Chapter president?" Lexton exclaimed.

"Yes."

"An exceptionally valuable asset," Lexton noted emphatically.

"That's for sure. I had him order some of his men to pay Borman a visit and tell him to desist from any further such activity."

"Didn't that draw some suspicion on your informant from other club members? In reality, why should Satans Wrath care? It'd probably help deflect attention from them."

"There's always an element of risk for informants, but I discussed that exact possibility with him. He noted that approaching the Death Heads now would draw less heat than if the prosecutor was killed, and I then asked him to stick his nose into it."

"Good point," Lexton replied. "I take it that what you had him do didn't raise any suspicions with his peers?"

"He said he received a suspicious glance from another chapter president, but overall felt comfortable doing it. He noted that Borman's behaviour would bring heat down on everyone, including Satans Wrath."

"Dare I ask how you cultivated this informant? Turning a chapter president seems quite remarkable."

"I found out where he is keeping his retirement fund — several million in laundered money. It was incentive enough and he knows I recorded him providing me with information. If he screws me around or tries to move his money, I could burn him."

"In other words, have him killed," Lexton said dryly.

"That'd be a certainty ... which he knows better than anyone."

Lexton stared at him momentarily, then changed the subject. "So, if I understand you correctly, you're actually in a position to give orders to Satans Wrath, albeit indirectly."

"I'd say I'm in a position to nudge or influence them on occasion. My informant has control of his chapter, but there are other chapters, and sooner or later another national president will be elected. That person would have overriding authority when it comes to what the chapter presidents deem to be serious decisions."

"Things such as murder."

Jack shrugged. "Perhaps, but only if it involved someone's murder that could affect the club as a whole, such as a member of another gang, a member of the judiciary, or perhaps someone in law enforcement. For everyday drug dealers, prostitutes, and the like, killing them wouldn't require his permission. In fact, more likely than not, he'd be protected from knowing."

"I see." She appeared to ponder the situation, "Still, a nudge, orders, influence, or whatever you wish to call it … if instigated by you, could potentially have serious ramifications down the road."

Depends what you call serious.…

"What if Borman had not gone along with what he was told?" Lexton noted. "Satans Wrath may have killed him — all as a result of what you started."

Sure, but do you call that serious? I'd call that time to have a martini.

Jack opted to keep his thoughts to himself and cleared his throat. "I admit that approaching him to have his men warn Borman was a delicate matter, but I felt, as did CFSEU, that Borman would heed Satans Wrath's advice."

"Judging by your report, it appears he did — but, for a police officer to influence a criminal organization, an action that could potentially result in serious crimes being committed, makes me uncomfortable. These street gangs are obviously dangerous, even amongst themselves. Trying to control them with another gang could've had disastrous consequences."

"The street gangs are dangerous, but they don't fall in the category that Satans Wrath does when it comes to the more sophisticated crimes, such as corrupting government officials, the judiciary, or other assorted criminal acts which they commit on an international level."

"What does that have to do with it?"

"To me, that is the bigger picture, and my being able to exercise some influence on Satans Wrath might help us control or prevent more serious ventures from taking place down the road." He waited a beat, then added, "As far as what you label as a possible disastrous consequence goes, in this instance I think I made the right decision. The Crown prosecutor certainly thinks it was."

Lexton raised an eyebrow, perhaps as a gesture that he was being insolent, but then appeared to think about it. "Point taken," she said, then paused and looked deep in thought.

"Is there a dead dog lying on the living room floor that you don't wish to talk about?" Jack prodded.

"The dead dog being?" Lexton questioned.

"Are you concerned that my influencing Satans Wrath is not wise due to potential criticism from Ottawa?"

"Ottawa?" Lexton appeared irritated by the suggestion that her decisions were based on what Ottawa would think.

"Yes, Headquarters may not understand that any control we have is flimsy at best; they would blame us for something that could happen, despite the fact that we had no control over it. There is also the question of certain delicate matters ... such as what took place with the prosecutor. You have a fuller picture of that event because I've disclosed to you who my informant is. If Ottawa knew it was me who instigated Satans Wrath to do what they did, it could bring about criticism for the same reason which caused you concern."

"Are you suggesting I purposely hide what you did from Ottawa?"

"I respect the chain of command, but you are in a position of more understanding because I trust you and can speak to you in person." *Well, trust you about what I've told you so far at least.*

"Are you telling me you don't trust Ottawa?" Lexton asked.

"I'd hesitate to disclose any information in a report that could compromise any of my informants. Verbally confiding in you is far different than putting the information in a report which could pass through many hands. We've had leaks before by those who allowed themselves to become corrupted by Satans Wrath. Not only that, but there have been instances of judicial orders granted by judges to gain access to certain information. Usually we've been allowed to vet that information, but it's not guaranteed and sometimes the person doing the vetting doesn't have a clear picture of what they think is a minor detail — a minor detail that could actually be the difference between life and death."

"Yes, I understand your concerns. Back in the days when I worked in I-HIT, I had my own headaches with such matters."

Good. So you do remember your days with the Integrated Homicide Investigation Unit and what it was like to be a real cop.

Lexton paused, then continued. "You've also won me over with your argument that using your informant to control certain events is appropriate."

"Thank you."

"That decision could easily be revoked. I'll handle Ottawa, but be forewarned that you've placed yourself on a slippery slope. I'm putting my trust in you to be vigilant and use sound judgment."

Jack paused. "The trouble is what I consider sound judgment might not be considered sound by others. It certainly wasn't by your predecessor, Assistant Commissioner Mortimer." *That son of a bitch wouldn't let me do anything out of fear he'd be forced to make a decision that he could be criticized over.*

"I'm not him," Lexton replied coldly. She stared at Jack long enough to make him feel uncomfortable, then added, "If you're in doubt about a certain action … and time permits, discuss the situation with Staff Sergeant Wood. If there are still doubts, then the three of us could meet to discuss it." She paused as she looked at Jack, "I trust that would be satisfactory for you?"

"Completely. Thank you."

"Good." She appeared to study his face closely, "I wouldn't appreciate a biker hit team showing up at my house like what happened to Assistant Commissioner Mortimer."

Crap. She's definitely suspicious. She said that to see if I'd look guilty. Jack's face portrayed innocence. "I'd certainly use my influence if I was able to stop that from ever happening," he exclaimed.

Lexton looked slightly taken back.

I know you were implying I had a hand in it. I'm implying what you think happened would never occur to me. He then faked a frown. "My informant said it was the Russians who influenced the bikers to do that."

"Yes, the mysterious Russians. Strange that they appeared to arrive, be blamed for the disappearance of Purvis Evans, who was the national president of Satans Wrath, then disappear themselves without a trace."

"My informant believes they were connected to the Russian consulate," Jack noted. "No doubt they were professionals."

"So your report at the time said."

"Yes."

"Considering I raised the incident about what happened back then, I'm surprised you didn't mention that shortly before Purvis Evans disappeared he allegedly ordered his men to take photos of you and your family and leave them in your mailbox."

Still fishing for a response, are you? Jack glanced at her casually. "I don't like to make a big deal of that. In my mind it's like admitting that their intimidation worked." He waited a beat. "Besides, my situation was different than that of Assistant Commissioner Mortimer. It wasn't a hit team armed with weapons who went to my house. The photos left in my mailbox were on the cellphone of another informant of mine who was murdered."

"Three other people were also tortured and murdered that same day because Evans suspected one of them to be an informant."

You've done your homework.

"It is quite a coincidence that Evans then disappeared. Presumably murdered."

Okay, I can see where this is going. Are you expecting me to squirm? Jack maintained strong eye contact, "I strongly believe that he was murdered, which on a personal level makes me happy. The man was a violent psychopath who tortured and murdered innocent people. I truly believe that if someone in law enforcement did go after him it would be at the cost of putting their own families in extreme jeopardy. Even if Evans had been imprisoned, the power and prestige he had in the club would mean that his orders would be carried out regardless."

"I see."

Do you? I wonder if you have any idea what it's like seeing the fear on your family's faces or wake up in the night to the sound of your children crying out because of a nightmare about bad guys coming into their bedroom.

"How is your family?" Lexton asked.

For a moment Jack felt dumbfounded that Lexton seemed to have read his thoughts. "They're … they're fine," he stammered. *If I say anything else she'll probably suggest I be transferred.* "For my family, it was a simple act of intimidation. Meant to scare us is all."

"Like what happened to the prosecutor," Lexton mused.

"I suppose," Jack replied.

Lexton appeared to relax as she sat back. She appeared to be trying to stop herself from smiling. "I suppose with the influence you have over Satans Wrath, you could've given them a nudge to make Borman disappear?" Her tone was teasing, as if it would've been okay for him to admit to considering that.

Nice try. I'm not that stupid.

Jack's face hardened and his tone was harsh. "I don't think that would be using sound judgment."

Lexton stiffened. "You're right, it wouldn't." Her voice was cold. "You're dismissed … for now."

Chapter Six

Stan Irving worked as both a paramedic and a home renovator. The few hours he took off from work were precious to him, so he couldn't help but smile when he returned home after dropping five-year-old Emma off at school and proudly displaying a paper cut-out to his wife.

"She couldn't wait until the end of today to give it to us," he announced, holding up a white sheet of paper cut into a circle and glued to the top of a larger circle. Two more paper cut-outs glued on the smaller circle were supposed to be ears.

Rhonda looked up from where she sat on the sofa breastfeeding three-month-old Hannah and smiled. "The ears are hanging down. Shouldn't they be up?"

"Not if the poor Easter Bunny is standing in a downpour."

Rhonda looked bemused. "Quite an imagination our daughter has."

Stan smiled. "Emma's pretty proud of it. She told me she couldn't bring it home last night because the glue had to dry." He looked at it a moment. "I'm proud of it, too. I'm sure it was the best in the class."

Rhonda smiled. "Oh, definitely. She's a child genius. No doubt that's why she coloured one ear pink and the other green. She's showing her individuality."

"Oh, for sure. Anyone could have made one with two pink ears. This is more like a Picasso."

"And gluing a cotton ball for the tail where the belly button should be shows a sense of style, as well."

Stan chuckled as he went to the kitchen and used fridge magnets to display the work, then poured himself a cup of coffee and joined Rhonda on the sofa.

"Busy night last night?" she asked.

"Yeah, the glamourous life of being a paramedic. Spent half my shift in back alleys saving people from overdosing on fentanyl." He grimaced. "You wouldn't believe how tough some people have it out there. Wish I could do more than administer Narcan. All that does is revive them for the next fix. The situation leaves me feeling so hopeless."

"Tomorrow's Good Friday," Rhonda noted in an obvious decision to change the subject. "You're not working, are you?"

"No — on either job." He glanced at his watch. "I should get going. I promised the people I'd have their kitchen renovated before Easter. That only leaves today to get it done."

* * *

Aron Kondrat, with Jeremy Pratt beside him, slowly drove down the residential street. They were in a less prosperous neighbourhood than many, with small, box-like houses that were popular for first homebuyers or senior citizens wishing to downsize.

They stared at all they passed as they searched for a member of the United Front who they knew lived in the area.

At the end of the street, Kondrat cranked the steering wheel to continue looking in the next block. "This car's a piece of shit," he complained.

"It's a Chevy Nova. What's wrong with that?"

"We shoulda got somethin' bigger in case we gotta ram someone to get out of our way."

"Not like our guys always get a choice in what they can steal," Pratt replied.

"Yeah, yeah." Kondrat gave Pratt a sideways glance. "You sure he lives around here?"

"It was at night and Lorraine said she was smokin' crack and pretty fucked up when she went with him, but she's pretty sure. This is the area she pointed out to me on the map."

"Probably on her knees blowin' him the whole way. That's why she can't remember much."

"Yeah, maybe." Pratt twirled the Glock 19 pistol on his finger. "It's gotta be around here somewhere. His truck'll stand out."

They were quiet as they drove down two more blocks, before Kondrat decided to break the silence. "That fuckin' Borman. I still can't believe what we heard."

"Yeah, actin' like he was their bitch. Lettin' 'em get away with slappin' him around. What a pussy."

"All over that fuckin' bitch of a prosecutor." Kondrat glanced at Pratt. "Like it ain't none of their business. It's our guy who's lookin' at doin' time."

"Bor's a fuckin' embarrassment," Pratt stated. "We should all tell 'im to take a hike. You'd be a lot better at runnin' things than him."

"Anyone would be better than him," Kondrat muttered.

"All you need is the balls to stand up to anyone who tries to fuck with us." Pratt paused and moved the laser dot from the pistol around the dash. "Bam! Bam! Bam!"

"How much support do you think I'd get over Borman?" Kondrat asked.

Pratt looked at him intently. "A lot, man. A lot. Nobody wants to take orders from somebody who lets themselves gets bitch-slapped around. I bet you'd —"

"Fuck! There it is!" Kondrat exclaimed. "Red Chevy Silverado pickup! Parked in the driveway third house down on the left!"

Pratt eyed the truck. "That's his all right."

"Fuckin' Smolak," Kondrat said under his breath. "You're ours now, you motherfucker."

* * *

Stan Irving first kissed Rhonda goodbye and then kissed Hannah on her forehead before putting on his raincoat and heading out the front door. He fished the keys from his pocket as he approached his truck in the driveway.

Two shots were fired within a second of each other. One bullet tore through his lower jaw and his upper teeth before exiting out the side of his nose. The other shot missed him entirely.

He stumbled and it took a moment for his brain to comprehend. He automatically put his hand up to his mouth and looked back. When he saw two figures running toward him his brain kicked into gear and he flung his keys at them, then fled in terror around the side of his house. *Take my truck. I'd have given it to you. You didn't need to shoot.*

"You think you can get away from us, muthafucker?" one of his attackers yelled as they rounded the corner after him.

They're after me! Why? He heard Rhonda screaming from inside the house. *Oh, God! Lock the door! Lock the door!*

The sound of two more shots echoed between the houses. A bullet entered his back and lodged in his chest cavity near his heart, then he lurched around the corner into his backyard. He looked around in panic, then collapsed to his knees and crawled under some California lilac bushes.

Once there he lay on his side, hoping one lung would still work as the other filled with blood. Up until now, the shock to his nervous system had blocked the pain. That relief abruptly ended and he put his hand up to his jaw again.

"Think you can hide from us?" a voice said, startling him at how close it was.

He glimpsed the bottom of someone's jeans as they stopped, apparently looking around.

"It's gonna take more than growin' a puny beard to do that!" another voice said.

A branch was shoved aside and he stared up at their faces. Then they laughed and grabbed him by an ankle.

Stan gasped and then vomited as he was dragged out into the open.

Chapter Seven

Jack and Laura sat at their desks updating files and trying to discover which people linked to organized crime groups like Satans Wrath were working in areas where they could gain access to sensitive information.

Their search was routine in nature, often triggered as a result of police investigations from other sections or departments that had been compromised for unknown reasons. Sometimes it involved undercover operatives whose identity had unexpectedly aroused suspicion without explanation. Most of the investigations that had been compromised were drug-related. Hence, any investigations they examined that turned up possible links to Satans Wrath were of the utmost interest.

Jack and Laura looked at photos of people along with licence plates recorded at parties or bars primarily frequented by criminals and tried to find matches with those who worked in sensitive areas. Some of these included police departments, the Motor Vehicle Branch, courthouses, or other areas where criminals could gather intelligence which they could then use to identify and locate their enemies, police included.

Identifying them wasn't always an easy task. Some people had no idea that the persons they'd met were criminals. For some, it may have been a chance meeting and the person had not been corrupted. Others were unaware that they were slowly being groomed — or put in more compromising situations to gain control over them in the future. A common method used by criminal organizations like Satans Wrath was to send in women to work in areas to gain intelligence or use sex as a means to compromise certain individuals.

Then there were those who discovered that a family member or someone they loved was involved in a police investigation and either warned them or did so after being asked by that person to find out.

Sometimes computer records indicated when an undercover operative's identity or a licence plate had been queried by the police, but often that only identified the office the query was made from because the person who made the query may have obtained someone else's password. Many times it was a legitimate query, made when an officer didn't realize they were dealing with an undercover operative and thought they were checking on a real criminal. Due to potential corruption, undercover operatives usually maintained their cover even when dealing with the police.

Laura eventually sat back in her chair to take a break. "Hey, tomorrow's Good Friday. We've got four days off. Any plans?"

"Nothing much."

"Will you be hiding Easter eggs and candy for the boys? Or are they too old for that?"

Jack gave a lopsided smile. "I don't even think Natasha is too old for that — at least when it comes to chocolate." He paused. "You're right about the boys, though. They're getting older. Maybe I should hide ones filled with liqueur."

"Oh? I'm surprised. Being your kids, I'd have thought you'd be looking for ones filled with martinis," Laura said jokingly.

"I've looked for those, but I don't think they make them," Jack replied, keeping a straight face.

"That wouldn't surprise me." Laura pretended to give him a dirty look.

Jack grinned. "How about you? Any plans?"

"Staying home and saving our money. In a month I'll be on a beach in Hawaii and drinking Mai Tais."

"You should've gone over Easter break and saved some holiday time."

"No, that's when families go. I'm looking for peace and quiet. We rented a condo for two weeks. It's expensive, but not as bad as it is at Easter. Then when we come back it'll be the middle of May and we'll be into spring weather."

Jack nodded.

Laura stared at him for a moment and her face became serious. "Think you can stay out of trouble while I'm gone?"

"It's been pretty quiet." He faked giving a perturbed look. "I think I can manage to keep my nose clean. But thanks, Mom, for your concern."

* * *

Corporal Connie Crane from the Integrated Homicide Investigation Unit arrived at the Irving home and parked on the street. A colleague, Corporal George Hobbs, greeted her when she stepped from her car. Although he was the same rank as Connie, she was senior and in charge of the investigation.

"I've only been here twenty minutes, but something doesn't seem right," Hobbs said. "The victim's name is Stanley Irving and his wife's name is Rhonda. Neither of 'em have had as much as a speeding ticket in their whole lives. He was holding down two jobs. Paramedic and doing house renos on the side."

"House renos for who?" Connie asked. "He could've set up a grow-op or lab for someone. Maybe whoever it was got busted and suspected him?"

"I'll look into it, but I have my doubts." He gestured toward the house. "I'll give you the quick run-through. Irving left out the front door to go to work. His wife was nursing their baby when she heard two shots and jumped up to look. She saw her husband run around the corner of their house clutching his bloody face and two guys charging across the lawn after him. She called Emergency and, while still on the phone clutching their baby, went to the kitchen and looked out the window. She saw him being killed, then got scared and ducked back out of sight."

"Can she identify them?"

"No, they were wearing hoodies and had ball caps with the peaks pulled low over their faces. Come on, I'll take you through the front door and then out the back so we don't contaminate the scene."

"And she doesn't know who wanted him dead?" Connie asked.

"She says she doesn't have a clue as to why anyone would want to kill him. According to her, everyone liked him."

"It seems that someone didn't," Connie replied. "Where's Forensics?" she asked as they entered the house.

"On their way."

Connie trailed Hobbs into the house and walked past the living room, automatically taking in what she saw.

House is clean. Family photos — some not posed … everyone looks happy. Toddler smiling up from her doll-house…. Doesn't appear like the normal dysfunctional family or type of shit-rats I usually deal with.

As they passed by the kitchen to the rear door, Connie caught a glimpse of Rhonda sitting with an officer at the kitchen table.

Bawling and holding an infant. Tears accompanied by mucous shows her grief is genuine. She probably had nothing to do with it.

She glanced at Hobbs. *You're right … there's something wrong.*

"Here we are," Hobbs said, directing Connie out the back door where the victim lay on the lawn covered with a sheet.

Connie pulled back the sheet. *Sprawled on his back and shot multiple times in the face.* She eyed the drag marks smeared with blood and vomit. "Probably took one or two in the back as he was running. Looks like an entry wound through the lower jaw and out through the face, as well. Could've happened before he tried to hide."

Hobbs gestured to a kitchen window. "That's where his wife was watching from. She said they dragged him out of the bushes by the ankles, then each one shot him in the head."

Connie looked up at the kitchen window from where she remained crouched over Irving's body. "She had a front row seat, that's for sure. My guess is the perps were too busy to notice her, otherwise if they'd looked up, she may've had a better look at their faces. Probably lucky for her they didn't look up."

"She was on the phone to Emergency at the time," Hobbs continued, "but ran out as soon as the perps left. Her memory is hazy at that point. When uniform arrived she was sitting on the kitchen floor, rocking back and forth holding her baby."

"Try to get her to calm down and see if she remembers anything else," Connie said as she turned her attention back to Irving's face. "We'll need a statement."

Hobbs' face darkened. "There's one more thing you should know."

"Yeah? What's that?" Connie replied, not bothering to look up.

"His wife says they were laughing when they did it."

Connie looked abruptly at Hobbs. "Laughing?"

"Yeah, like it was all a big joke."

Connie felt her stomach knot.

Unbelievable. Just when I think I've seen and heard it all.... She shook her head in disgust. *Boy, was I wrong.*

"What're you thinking," Hobbs asked.

Connie pulled the sheet back over Irving's head, then stood up. "Gotta be gangbangers. They're the only ones that fucking stupid and callous."

Chapter Eight

Sergeant Roger Morris was in court watching the trial when he felt his phone vibrate. He knew Connie well and recognized her number on the call display. *I-HIT ... son of a bitch, we got another gang shooting.* As he left the courtroom he glanced at the representatives from the two gangs. *Who shot who this time?*

Connie was unusually terse. "Rog, I think I could use your help. I'm at a homicide."

"I figured that. What ganger bit the dust this time?"

"I don't think the victim was associated with any gangs, but thought I'd call you to double check. His name is Stan Irving."

"Doesn't ring a bell."

"He was married, had two kids, and was holding down two jobs. I think he was murdered by gangbangers. At least their behaviour and what they were wearing points to that. It happened in his backyard and his wife saw the whole thing from her kitchen window."

"Things are tense between the Death Heads and the United Front," Roger replied. "I'm at a trial now where one of them killed one from the other gang, but the name Irving isn't known to me."

"I know about the trial," Connie replied. "Some from my unit are testifying on that one. Let me tell you what I've got. Maybe the perps are from some other gang."

Roger listened as Connie spoke. When she finished he said, "It does sound like something the gangs would do, particularly the two gangs involved in this trial. That being said, I've never heard of the victim."

"My gut tells me that Irving was innocent, but maybe he was involved in drugs with your guys? He did home renovations. I'm wondering if he could've built something for them? Or maybe he was supplying them with dope. If he was higher up the chain, not having a record would be an asset."

"That's true," Roger noted. "Satans Wrath funnels drugs down to both these gangs. Some of the dealers don't have records."

"So it's possible he's dirty," Connie replied, glancing down at the corpse at her feet.

"Sure it's possible," Roger replied. "When it comes to Satans Wrath, Jack would be the guy to talk to. We don't have the manpower to go after the dealers. Too busy with the shooters."

"Taggart," Connie muttered. "I hate the thought of calling him."

"How come?"

Connie paused. "His methods aren't all that kosher in my mind."

"Maybe, but he sure helped us out earlier in the week," Roger replied. "Two guys from the Death Heads threatened our prosecutor on the trial I'm at. They had guns in their hands and kicked in the back door to her mother's house after she'd dropped her two-year-old daughter off for babysitting. One of them was heard yelling at the other to hurry and grab the kid. Luckily the mother was able to escape with the tot out the front door."

"Jesus!" Connie exclaimed. "I never even heard about it."

"Our prosecutor doesn't want word of it to get out for fear it will affect the trial."

"You said Jack helped. What'd he do? Find 'em and kill them?"

Roger chuckled. "No … and I'm only telling you because I know he trusts you."

"Which is funny, because I don't trust him. Not the way he operates."

"His job is different than yours. More proactive and less reactive." Roger paused. "In regards to our prosecutor, we never did find out who the two guys were, but Jack had enough clout to get Satans Wrath to put word out to the leader of the Death Heads to cease and desist."

"And did they?"

"It seems to have worked. The gangbangers who show up periodically to watch the trial used to enjoy glaring at the prosecutor and acting belligerent around her by trying to stand in her way when she came and went. That doesn't happen now."

"Maybe Jack did something right for a change," Connie said.

"My advice would be to call him and ask about Irving. If he's connected to Satans Wrath in any way, I'm sure that Jack will either know him or can find out if he's dirty."

"Yeah, I'll call him," Connie grumbled. "Any description of the two guys who kicked in the door to the prosecutor's mom's house?"

"Not really," Roger replied. "They wore hoodies tight to their faces along with ball caps pulled low."

"Exact same description as the two who did this murder," Connie stated.

"For these guys that's common attire," Roger replied. "We have a lot of them wired up, so if we hear anything I'll call you."

"That's good news. Maybe there'll be some chatter on the lines over what they did."

"I wouldn't get your hopes up. These punks are dumb but generally not dumb enough to talk on their phones."

Well, I can always hope. "They also tossed a couple of Glocks in the bushes. Both with laser-grip sights."

"That's new. Up to now they've only had Saturday night specials. Even those they sometimes hang on to after using them because they have trouble finding replacements."

"A sign of the times, I guess." Connie then thanked him and ended the call and told Hobbs what Roger had said.

"So what's wrong?" Hobbs asked. "You seem pretty morose."

"Morose? How long have you been waiting to use that one?"

Hobbs feigned surprise, then smiled.

"The truth is, I'm not happy and you know why," Connie continued. "You know his rep."

Hobbs gave a nod toward the body. "How bad do you want the guys who did this?"

"What do you mean, how bad? Look at this guy! In front of his wife and kid … then laughing about it? What kind of question is that?"

Hobbs stared at her in response.

"Yeah, I see what you're getting at," Connie grumbled, then tapped Jack's number into her phone.

"Hey, Connie," Jack answered cheerfully. "To what do I owe the pleasure?"

Believe me, calling you is no pleasure. "I'm at a homicide. The victim's name is Stanley Irving and he was gunned down in his backyard. Do you know him?"

"No, I've never heard of the guy."

"He doesn't have a record and was married with two kids. Besides being a paramedic he did home renovations on the side."

"Sorry, I can't help you."

"I suspect he was shot by gangbangers."

"If you suspect gangbangers, you should be talking to CFSEU. They deal with them."

"I did, and I spoke with Roger. He doesn't know the guy either, but told me that you helped him out a couple of days ago when the Death Heads threatened a prosecutor. He said you have some pull in Satans Wrath and suggested I call you."

"I wondered what prompted you to call. You must really be desperate to call me."

Connie wasn't in the mood for humour. "I want the guys who did this, Jack. I want them bad."

"You want them bad, do you?" His tone sounded ominous.

"I didn't call you to have them whacked."

"Whacked?"

"Quit jerking my chain. You know what I mean. I'd like for once for you to pass on whatever you can find out to me and then butt out."

"I'm sorry, but as I already said, I can't help."

"What if Irving was dirty? Maybe a dealer for Satans Wrath? Roger said you could tell me if that were so."

"I do have a high level source with Satans Wrath. If Irving was involved with them I'd know and would've already told you."

"Still, your source obviously has clout if he was able to get the gangbangers to back away from the prosecutor. Roger thinks there's a good chance the perps were from either the Death Heads or the United Front. Get your guy to find out."

"I'm sorry, but it's too risky for my guy to ask those sorts of questions. Giving guidance to the street gangs and telling them not to follow certain behaviour is one thing. To ask a pointed question about who killed someone is a different story. It's not something you ask. Especially when you're not even in the same gang."

Goddamn him.

"If you're not sure, maybe it wasn't even gang-related," Jack suggested. "I'd be putting my guy at risk for nothing. Maybe Irving was having an affair and somebody's husband paid for a hit ... or his wife is screwing around and wanted to get rid of him. Have you checked for insurance policies yet? Or maybe someone made a mistake and shot the wrong guy. Did he move into the place recently?"

"No, photos I saw of their oldest kid were taken in the yard I'm standing in. She looked to be learning to walk. The kid is in kindergarten now." Connie paused. "Jack, what happened here isn't right. This is a decent family. They dragged the poor guy out from under some bushes and took turns shooting him in his face while his wife was watching from the window."

"I'm sorry, Connie. Wish I could help. I really do."

"She heard them laughing as they were doing it. I want these guys arrested and charged ... and I mean that. Please, I'm begging you. Ask your source to nose around. These guys need to be caught."

"Laughing?"

"Yeah. Doesn't that sound like the sort of behaviour you'd expect from gangbangers? Maybe even high on the dope they get from Satans Wrath?"

Jack paused. "Connie, what you told me about is horrible and I hope you solve it, but my guy can't ask. You need to see the big picture. If it was someone connected to Satans Wrath, there wouldn't be a problem for my guy to nose around. Going to another gang to ask specifics would burn him."

Okay, how do I get this asshole to do it?

"You're good at what you do, Connie. I'm sure you'll find out who did it on your own sooner or later."

"Hang on," Connie said. "Hobbs spotted something ... what the hell? Jack! Maybe I'm wrong about them being punks. I'd like you to come here and see something."

"What?"

"What do you mean what? It's weird ... I don't work organized crime. It's better if you see it in person."

"Can't you describe it to me?"

"Jesus, Jack. I'm at a homicide. The wife is crying … so's her baby. I've gotta arrange for someone to pick up her kid from kindergarten. The news media is driving us crazy. What's with you? Are you too lazy to get off your ass and at least give me an opinion about something?"

"Okay, okay. Give me the address and Laura and I'll be over. Have someone meet us a block away with a couple of Forensic garments and then drive us in so nobody sees us or our vehicle. We're UC operators. I don't want to be on the front-page news."

"That's right, I forgot. The news you generate is usually in the obit section. No worries. I'll have someone meet you."

After giving the details Connie ended the call, then turned to Hobbs. "I can't believe it. In the past he's often butted into cases uninvited. This time I cringe at the thought of having him involved, then when I ask him he doesn't want to help."

"Sounds like he's coming over, though," Hobbs noted.

"Yeah, but if he does help we'll be damned lucky if we don't end up with more bodies."

"Then why'd you trick him into coming over?"

Connie sighed. "Jack has a source who could probably find out who did this, but being the asshole he is he doesn't want to risk having his source ask for fear it'll burn him." She gestured to the body. "Christ, look at this guy … his wife … kids … I'll do whatever it takes to solve it."

"You've proven that."

"What do you mean?"

"You called Jack."

Chapter Nine

After parking a few blocks away, Jack and Laura were met by a constable from I-HIT who supplied them each with forensic garments and then drove them to the scene. They were then escorted inside the front door where Connie met them.

"What is it you want us to look at?" Jack asked.

"Can you sit for a moment?" Connie asked, gesturing to the living room. "The mom is in the kitchen writing a statement. Hobbs is with her, but I need to make sure he asks her about something. Grab a seat and I'll be right back. Then I can show you."

Jack saw a uniformed policeman sitting on the sofa, unsuccessfully trying to soothe a baby. He opted to sit in a chair while Laura sat on the sofa.

"Here, let me try," Laura said, reaching for the baby.

"Be my guest," the officer said, seemingly anxious to give up his charge. "Her name's Hannah."

Laura cuddled and rocked Hannah and she stopped crying immediately.

"You got kids?" the officer asked.

"No, only wish I did," Laura replied.

Jack glanced around the room as he waited. He saw the photo Connie had mentioned, along with several others. *Seem like such a happy family. I remember when my boys were that young. Sometimes wish I could go back in time and enjoy them all over again.*

"Okay, ready," Connie announced. "Follow me out back."

Jack trailed along behind and caught the haggard, tear-stained face of the woman writing a statement as they passed through to the back door. *Connie mentioned they have one kid in kindergarten. And a baby.* He exchanged a look with Laura. By her face, he knew she was also saddened.

Once outside, Connie stopped beside Irving's body. She appeared to be thinking about something.

"So what do you have to show us?" Jack prodded.

"Hang on a sec," Connie replied. "I want to double-check something first." She then pulled back the sheet to look at Irving's face. "Yeah, multiple shots for sure." She looked at Jack. "How many do you think?"

Jack crouched down beside her for a better look. "Hard to tell. I'd say three or four. Looks like more, but they're probably exit wounds," he added, then stood up.

"Yes, his wife, Rhonda, said she heard two shots out front right after Stan left the house." Connie then rose and her voice softened. "She was on the sofa breastfeeding her three-month-old baby, Hannah, when it happened. She saw Stan stumbling as he ran past the front of his truck and around the side of the house. Two guys were chasing him."

You're using their first names. Personalizing it and you threw in the bit about the baby as an extra. Damn it, Connie. I know what you're up to.

Connie continued. "She then grabbed her phone and called Emergency. As she did she heard more shots and then voices in her backyard. She ran to the kitchen window, still holding Hannah in her arms, then saw them drag her husband out by the ankles and shoot him in the head."

"I don't need to hear those details," Jack said gruffly. "Show us what you called us over to see."

Connie lifted some branches on a California lilac bush. "Take a look," she said, "but don't touch."

Jack and Laura squatted and peered into the bushes.

"Two Glocks," Jack said. "Both with laser sight grips," he noted as they stood up. "So?"

"After it happened, a stolen Chevy Nova was located about ten blocks from here. It'd been torched and was still on fire when the call came in."

Jack shrugged. "Figures. What's it got to do with us?"

Connie gestured to the Glocks. "Two expensive weapons with laser sight grips? Come on! Does that sound like punks to you? Plus torching a car?"

"The gangers know to torch a car if they used it while killing someone."

"Okay, you're right. But guns with laser sights? Roger told me that most of the ones they've seized were Saturday night specials. He said even those were sometimes kept after a shooting because it was too hard for the punks to get guns. No guns of this quality have ever been found, let alone tossed away."

"Is this what you wanted us to look at?" Jack replied. He didn't like being conned and let his anger show. "You could have said that over the phone."

Connie stood her ground and her tone reflected Jack's. "You're telling me you're not interested in where they got the guns? I'd think that'd be part of that big picture you're always talking about."

"It sparks my interest, but as far as who did it goes, you said yourself you believe it was one of the street gangs. They're not our problem."

"No, but Satans Wrath are."

"What have they got to do with it?"

"What if it was Satans Wrath who supplied them with the guns? Your source would know or could find out who they sold them to."

"For your info, Wrath funnels dope to the gangs — not guns. The bikers look at them as not only being idiots, but also a potential enemy. I've no idea where the street gangs get their guns and as I said before, it would jeopardize my guy to ask."

"So you're refusing to help?"

"Maybe down the road people might talk about it and he might hear something, but that's different than going out and asking questions at this point." He stared at Connie. When she didn't respond, he added, "You've wasted our time. We're done."

"Okay, come back inside," Connie pouted. "I'll have someone give you a ride back to your car."

Once inside, Connie glanced at Hobbs, who was sitting with Rhonda while reading her statement. "Wait in the living room," Connie whispered. "Looks like he's almost done. The others are busy. I'll get him to give you a lift."

Jack and Laura returned to the living room. Connie's voice was audible from the kitchen, asking Rhonda if she had someone who could pick Emma up from kindergarten.

A moment later Connie reappeared and looked at Jack. "She finished her statement. Hobbs did a quick analysis and it suggests she's telling the truth."

Jack had taken a course in statement analysis, as well. Often it wasn't what a person said, but when they said certain things in their statements that were of importance. Mathematical formulas were then used to analyze the statements and had been proven to be surprisingly accurate at separating truthful statements from ones that were fabricated.

No surprise Hobbs thinks she's telling the truth. Everything I've seen indicates that. So what if she is? It's not my concern.

"Hobbs is taking us back?" he asked.

"Yes, but first there's one thing I'd honestly like your opinion on. It's her description of the killers."

"Description?" Jack asked.

"With all your undercover experience, maybe you'll be able to flush out some more information from her in that regard. Come and listen to how she describes them," she added, turning on her heel.

Jack and Laura followed her into the kitchen where Connie picked up Rhonda's statement, then skimmed through it, apparently looking for a particular segment. As she did, Jack took in his surroundings. *Easter Bunny on the fridge. I can remember my boys making one like that when they were in kindergarten. It hung on our fridge for about —*

"Rhonda, this is Jack and Laura," Connie said, breaking the silence. "They're experts when it comes to gangs."

Rhonda's expression said she was confused as to why Jack and Laura would be there or any reason that her husband could have been targeted by a gang.

Connie cleared her throat. "Rhonda, I've read your statement, but before Jack and Laura leave, let me read back what you said and see if there is anything, anything at all, you could add."

Jack saw the tears stream down Rhonda's face as she relived her nightmare while Connie read the statement.

Come on, Connie. Do you really have to do this?

After getting to the end of the statement, where it described what the shooters were wearing and the fact that they were laughing, Connie lowered the statement and looked at Rhonda. "Are you sure that's everything? Think hard about what you saw and heard. Is there anything else at all?"

"No," Rhonda cried, then between sobs, said, "I was phoning ... I ... no, that's all I can remember. I'm sorry."

"Jack," Connie said, "is there anything you'd like to ask her? Anything about their clothing that is significant to you at all? Perhaps related to a specific gang?"

"No," Jack replied, making a conscious effort to keep the ire he felt for Connie out of his voice due to the empathy he felt for Rhonda. "Lots of people wear that clothing. It doesn't mean they're even gang-related."

"I see," Connie replied. She then caught Jack's eye and gestured to the fridge. Her words oozed sarcasm. "I suppose, as the bunny on the fridge likely exemplifies, this family doesn't fit into that big picture of yours. Thank you so much for your help. I'm sorry if you found coming here a complete waste of your time."

Jack caught the horrified, disgusted look that Rhonda gave him.

Chapter Ten

Neither Hobbs, Jack, nor Laura spoke a word as they were driven back to where they'd parked their SUV. Jack's anger manifested itself when he slammed the door to Hobbs's vehicle as he got out.

"I feel the same way," Laura noted as Hobbs drove off. "That was one of the worst experiences I've ever had in my life. Did you see the look Rhonda gave us?"

"I saw," Jack replied as he opened the door to their SUV and got in. Once there he didn't start the engine. Instead he clenched his fists while taking a deep breath. When he exhaled he slowly opened his hands in a vain attempt to relieve the stress.

"It was all a set-up," Laura seethed. "Hoping we'd take pity on the woman and help out."

"Of course it was."

"Connie could've told us about the guns over the phone. As far as what she said to us before we left, that … that was plain nasty." She paused. "I used to respect Connie. Not anymore."

"I told her when she phoned that I wouldn't risk our source," Jack said. "I would if it was viable, but to send him out on a fishing expedition like she wants would get him killed."

"No kidding," Laura snapped. "You'd think she'd appreciate that."

"Maybe she's never had an informant. Most members haven't."

"Whether she has or not, she should still respect what we tell her and not pull a stunt like that."

"It pisses me off. I don't think she understands the situation. Every time we use him, we put him at risk. It was bad enough getting him to help the prosecutor. To ask him for help over this wouldn't be right."

"Definitely not. I agree."

Jack started the engine, then turned to Laura again. "Connie's good at what she does. If it was someone from the street gangs, she'll be able to solve it without our help."

"I thought the same thing," Laura replied. When Jack continued to stare at her, she said, "So, back to the office?"

Jack scowled. "I'm so frustrated I don't know what to do."

"What do you mean?"

"I don't know if I'm angry at Connie or at life itself." He stared out the windshield a moment, but didn't put the SUV in gear. Then he turned back to Laura. "You saw what Connie was going through. Personally, I don't know how she can handle it. I felt so bad for the wife. It was horrible."

"I know," Laura said. "I had to clench my jaw most of the time to keep the tears out of my eyes."

Jack grimaced. "The truth be known, on one hand I'm ticked at Connie for trying to con us, but on the other hand I don't begrudge her for trying. It's her job to solve the case. It was pretty damned emotional in there. You and I'd have probably done the same thing if we were in her shoes."

"Maybe," Laura admitted.

Jack hit his forehead with the palm of his hand. "Damn it! I can't get the image of the bunny rabbit out of my head."

"Thanks, now it's in my head, too."

"Sorry."

"Maybe it's better than the image I have of holding their baby."

Not an image I want to remember, either. His mind raced. *What to do? What to do?*

"What're you thinking," Laura asked.

Jack took in a deep breath and slowly exhaled. "Let's talk to our friend and run things past him. See what he says. Maybe he'll have an idea that we haven't thought of."

* * *

"For the amount of time I've been in this graveyard, I'm starting to think it might become my permanent home," Lance said dryly. "And I don't mean above ground. This is the second time in a week."

"I know, we're sorry," Jack replied, "but something happened a couple of hours ago. We want to tell you about it."

"Okay … shoot. I mean, I'm listening."

"I don't expect you'll be able to help … at least, not at this stage, but I want your thoughts on the matter."

"I'm good at giving free advice," Lance replied. "It's apparent from being caught by you guys that heeding good advice is where I have a problem." He shook his head in apparent self-recrimination. "You warned me years ago that you'd be watching me. I should've listened."

"It is what it is," Jack replied. "Now let me tell you why we called."

After hearing the details of what happened, Lance's jaw slackened, then he said, "They were fuckin' laughing?"

"Yes," Jack replied.

"Christ, for sure that sounds like kids. Bet they were high."

"Kids with Glock 19 pistols equipped with laser grips," Jack added.

Lance appeared to think about it. "Yeah, it's gotta be one of the punk gangs. Maybe screwed up and got the wrong guy. You can tell I-HIT they're probably on the right track."

"The thing is," Jack said, "I-HIT asked for our help." He stared silently at Lance.

"Me? Are you serious?" Lance replied.

"Like I said, we're only running it past you as an after-thought. I already told I-HIT we couldn't help them."

"You don't even know for sure if it was a punk gang behind it. For me to start asking questions would make me sound like a cop."

"I understand," Jack replied. "There's something else, though. What about your hit squad?"

"The three-three? What about them? That story you spread about one of them being a rat worked. They're no longer active."

"I was thinking about the gun angle," Jack replied. "Two expensive pieces were tossed. If it was one of the street gangs, is there any chance they got them from your guys?"

"No way they'd have gotten them from us," Lance said firmly. "Not a chance. That'd be like giving a potential enemy a gun to shoot you with."

"Do you have any ideas who'd be selling those kind of weapons?" Laura prodded.

Lance gestured with his hands to indicate he didn't know.

"Where would you get weapons if the need arose?" Jack asked.

"We've had our own gun connection from our U.S. chapter in Frisco long before these wannabe gangs were formed. There's no way the punks get their pieces from any of our people. Not in Canada or any other country."

"The ones you guys have … I presume some are military grade?" Jack asked.

"Some," Lance replied. "We're not really at war with anyone at the moment, so our arsenal is small. A few AR-15s and assorted pistols. If things ever heat up, then we'd be getting more, including grenades and explosives."

"Would you happen to have any info I could pass on to ATF?" Jack asked.

"You wanna get the U.S. Bureau of Alcohol, Tobacco, Firearms and Explosives involved?"

"Might be necessary."

Lance paused, apparently thinking about it. "No, not really. The last acquisition for us was years ago. I don't even know who was involved."

"Do you have a piece yourself?" Laura asked.

Lance cast each of them a suspicious glance. "Makes me wonder if you already know," he said.

Jack and Laura stared back at him poker-faced.

Lance made a face, appearing to brood about what they knew. "Last week we had a member visiting us from Germany. He gave me a Walther PPK as a goodwill gift."

"How'd he get it in?" Jack asked, giving no indication if they already knew he had the pistol. If Lance thought they did know, it would ensure he was more open and truthful in whatever he told them.

"The guy who gave it to me has a brother who works for a company that exports car parts globally. Guess it wasn't difficult, although a little risky. The parts are often checked at Customs." He paused, then added, "The gun is new, right out of the box. Same type as James Bond uses."

"You have it with you?" Laura asked.

Lance gave a wry smile. "No, I'm not the James Bond type of guy. I don't even like having it around." He eyed Jack. "I'll give it to you if you like."

"What would I want it for?" Jack responded.

"I don't know. You could have it as a throwaway," Lance suggested.

"You've been watching too much television," Jack replied. He glanced at his watch. "Okay, until next time then."

"Hang on a sec," Lance replied. "About this guy getting whacked in front of his wife. If it was a case of mistaken identity and it came out in the news that way, I could put the word out to warn both gangs to be more careful. Shooting an innocent person is about the same as when they hassled the prosecutor. It could justify the cops getting more manpower." Lance looked to Jack for a reaction. When he didn't get one he added, "Who knows, maybe we'd hear something about who did it that way."

Jack frowned. "Even if it did come out in the news, would you be telling the gangs to smarten up if it wasn't for the fact you're working for us?"

Lance's eyebrows furrowed.

"Exactly," replied Jack.

"Yeah, but the more I can do to get this monkey off my back the better. I hate being a rat."

"It's better to have a monkey on your back than being dead," Jack cautioned, then glanced at Laura. "Or in our case, a pair of monkeys."

"Hey, speak for yourself," Laura said.

Lance appeared to be too deep in thought for humour. "If it came out on the news that it was a case of mistaken identity, then I could get away with it. I'd approach it as basically being an extension of the same shit they pulled on the prosecutor. At least, that's what I'd tell Whiskey Jake. I'd go at it about them inflaming the public and scaring the citizens. Hell, Whiskey Jake might even agree."

Jack paused for a moment. *Two times in a week … will it arouse suspicion? Or will it work in our favour because Whiskey Jake might think Lance has a burr up his ass about how stupid the gangs are and think that this has simply aggravated him more?* He glanced at Lance. *You do know how to take care of yourself.*

"So? Should I go for it?" Lance prodded.

Jack nodded. "I'll talk to I-HIT. If they're convinced it was an innocent person being shot down in front of his family I'll get them to do a press release. I'm sure it'd garner a lot of attention with the media."

"Okay," Lance replied. "If it hits the news I'll meet with Whiskey Jake and get the ball rolling."

"If you do, would it be any more risk to ask the gangs where they get their guns?" Jack asked. "Maybe suggest to Whiskey Jake that it'd be a good idea to know so if you ever needed to back one gang, or more importantly, went to war with either gang, you'd know who to wipe out to stop their flow of weapons."

Lance chuckled.

"What's so funny?" Jack asked.

"Sometimes it surprises me how much you think like we do."

"Knowing how you think doesn't always mean that's how I think," Jack replied. He waited a beat. "So, would that scenario work for you?"

"Yeah, I'd be comfortable doing that. The Death Heads are dumb and usually trying to impress us. A lot of them are spoiled kids who were left at home with both parents working. They look at shooting people like they're playing video games. If I had my guys ask them if they tossed the guns after the hit, they might say something that'll lead to talk about where they get them from."

"And the United Front?" Jack prodded.

"As far as those boys go, they're a smaller gang. A lot of them are from the rez — no lily-white spoiled brats there.

Most of 'em know how the game is played. They're far more experienced and tend to be more tight-lipped." Lance shrugged. "I can still try."

"That's all a mule can do," Jack replied. "Let me know."

As they walked back to the SUV, Laura sighed audibly.

"What's wrong?" Jack asked.

She gestured toward Lance, who was walking in the opposite direction. "Think he'll come through for us?"

"Hope so."

"I feel like Connie. I want these guys caught."

"If he doesn't, I'm sure Connie will catch them sooner or later."

Laura's face darkened. "Providing that later doesn't mean another innocent person gets killed."

There's always that possibility....

The image of the paper bunny rabbit on the fridge played in Jack's head as he unlocked the SUV and got inside. He then thought about the danger he'd placed Lance in and recalled a picture he'd seen a few months previous. It was of Lance and his wife along with their grandson, who was then a year old. *Hopefully if that kid makes a bunny rabbit, Lance will still be alive to see it.*

Chapter Eleven

Jack was blunt when Connie answered her phone. "Okay, you win," he said.

"I thought I would," Connie replied. "I saw how angry you were and knew it wasn't all at me."

"You played us like you were an operator. Not a good one, mind you. It was rather obvious."

"I knew you'd clue in. You're not stupid … but you are emotional. My only concern is that you're too emotional and not pragmatic enough to accept the proper course of the judicial process."

"Believe me, this homicide is all yours." Jack paused. "I'll give you credit. What you deal with can be gut-wrenching. I've got enough things keeping me awake at night as it is."

"As callous as it sounds, you do get used to it," Connie replied. "You become like a surgeon and try not to personalize things too much … but sometimes you can't help it."

"I take it this is one of those times," Jack said.

"That's for sure. It'll help, though, if I get a chance to slap the cuffs on whoever did it." She paused. "Are you going to speak to your guy and see if he can find something out?"

"Already did."

"Oh, Jack … thank you."

"I'm not making any promises. If he does comes up with something that can give you a nudge in the right direction, then the rest is up to you. For Laura and me, we'd then be done with that end of it."

"That end of it?" Connie questioned.

"I'd like to find out where they're getting their weapons from and put a stop to it."

"You and the FBI both," Connie replied.

"The FBI?"

"Both guns we found at the scene were reported stolen from a gun shop in Alabama. A place called Live Free Guns. It was cleaned out entirely and the father and son who owned it were murdered."

"Sounds like the store should have been called Live by the Gun, Die by the Gun."

"Trust you to think of that. Two brothers, Zachary and Luke Coggins, were identified as suspects but fled before the arrests."

"There's money to be made smuggling them into Canada," Jack noted. "Legally you could purchase a Glock in Canada for a grand and maybe tack on about four hundred dollars extra for a laser grip. Buying hot ones could easily double the price."

"Yeah, well … guns aren't what I'm interested in. I want to find out who pulled the triggers."

"Oh, you're one of those people."

"One of what people?"

"Guns don't kill people, people do."

Connie gave a snort. "Don't even get into that shit with me. I've been to too many murders to listen to that crap." She paused. "Do you honestly think your guy will be able to help?"

"Do you have anything to support that it was a case of mistaken identity? Other than they seemed like a decent family?"

"I know for sure it was a case of mistaken identity. Roger came up with something. Irving's truck is the same make, model, and colour of a truck owned by a United Front member by the name of Barney Smolak. He lives two streets over from the victim. There's no doubt in my mind that the Death Heads hit the wrong guy."

"Son of a bitch," Jack swore.

"Here you go getting all emotional. I've seen that movie before and —"

"I'm not in the mood for a lecture," Jack said harshly. "If you leak it to the media that it was a case of mistaken identity, then I'll get my source to nose around. Also, include a blurb about the police being concerned about the laser-sighted handguns being found at the scene."

Connie paused. "It'll be on the news by suppertime," she said, then ended the call.

* * *

The following day was Good Friday and Jack was barbecuing hot dogs for lunch when his phone vibrated. He put the tongs down and looked at the call display. *Okay, Lance, what do you have for me?*

"So, to make it look good, 'cause the news didn't say which gang, I had my guy visit the United Front and they denied it was them," Lance announced. "Also brought up the topic of guns and all they said was they shop around and got 'em here and there."

"What about the Death Heads?" Jack asked. "I-HIT thinks they're the ones who did it."

"Borman is visiting someone on the Island and won't be back until tomorrow afternoon. One of my prospects is scheduled to meet with him Saturday night."

"Which prospect?"

"Buster Linquist. We don't show these punk gangs any more respect than we need to. Sending a prospect for something like this is enough."

"I understand. How hard will Linquist be on him?"

"I ordered the easy approach. No need to spank 'im. Linquist deals with them on occasion as it is, so Borman should feel more relaxed. I didn't want to come on strong because it might scare him into lying about it."

"Probably the right play," Jack replied. He waited a beat. "I really want these guys. The guns found at the murder scene were stolen in Alabama. An entire gun shop was cleaned out and the father and son who owned the store were both murdered. Two brothers are wanted by the FBI over it."

"So this connection is important to you," Lance noted. "It might lead you to the two brothers."

Jack raised an eyebrow. "Meaning would it be a big check mark toward helping get me off your back?"

"I was hopin' so," Lance replied.

"Somewhat, but my focus is on whoever is bringing them into Canada. I've got enough to deal with that I don't need to go poaching down there. The two brothers are the FBI's problem, not mine."

"Yeah, okay. I understand. No worries, I'll get on it."

"Good. Make damn certain you don't do anything to jeopardize yourself." When Lance didn't respond, Jack added, "You hear me?"

Lance's tone sounded stark. "I'll look after myself."

Sounds like there's no doubt about that. Now I have to worry. Is that a bad thing?

Chapter Twelve

It was 6:30 a.m. on Easter Sunday when Jack was roused from his sleep by another call from Lance. He mumbled an apology to Natasha, then reached for his bedside table and answered.

"Hope I didn't wake ya," Lance said.

"It's okay. I had to get up to answer the phone anyway." Jack stifled a yawn. "How come you're up so early?"

"On our way to see our grandson look for candy."

"Isn't he only about a year-and-a-half old?"

"He can crawl," Lance said, sounding defensive. "Anyway, I've got something for you. Linquist paid Borman a visit last night."

"And?"

"This should make you happy. He admitted it was his guys. Linquist then told him that if his guys were dumb enough to kill the wrong guy, then they were probably dumb enough to talk if caught. Borman then said they call them the two rats, but there's no way they'd ever rat. He swore that they were solid."

"Any idea who the two rats are?"

"Yes, Linquist was at their place once. Their first names are Aron and Jeremy. They live with two other guys, one whose name is Pete. We don't know the other guy's name. I was also told that they live in PoCo, but it wouldn't have been appropriate for me ask for an address. I don't talk to Linquist direct because he's only a prospect. Everything I get is second-hand, so to have him ask questions about things that shouldn't concern me would raise suspicion."

"I know someone who'd probably know who they are," Jack replied.

"CFSEU no doubt," Lance replied.

"You got it."

"We also found out they get their pieces from some guy they call Zombie."

"Zombie? As in someone who crawled out of a grave?"

"Yeah. I tell ya', we're dealing with kids. Even Borman has the mentality of a teenager. He offered to introduce Linquist to him if he wanted to score some pieces."

"When?"

"Linquist said he'd get back to him on that. He's still prospecting and he figured that wasn't a decision he could make on his own."

"Is Zombie an American?"

"Don't know."

"I'll get you to follow up on placing an order, but wait a few days and I'll talk to you about it later. I want to see how things pan out with the two rats first."

"Fine by me. I'd be putting myself in hot water if the two rats and the gun dealer were all busted right after I sent my guy over asking questions about 'em."

"I'll look after you on that. The last time I nailed people with illegal handguns was when two warring gangs met to discuss turf issues in a lounge full of innocent people. I attended and each side thought I was with the other side. While the bosses met at one table, many of the gang members sat nearby holding their guns under the tables so they'd be ready to start shooting if things went wrong. Others were posted with guns outside. Talk about a powder keg. I had the tactical team swoop in and make arrests and it ended with them all getting two hundred and fifty dollar fines."

"I bet that taught them all a lesson," Lance said facetiously.

"I told you because I want you to keep in mind that from my point of view guns aren't worth risking your life over. When it comes to dealing with Zombie, I'll maintain control. If he's arrested on anything linked to you, it won't be until I give the okay. As far as the two rats go, I-HIT won't have grounds for any immediate arrests, so there are no worries there."

"Good. I imagine I-HIT will get a wiretap on them if CFSEU doesn't already have one."

"You're likely right, but it could still come out down the road as to when I-HIT learned the information."

"That's only if the two rats get arrested and if it does go to trial … which would be at least a year from now at best."

"We're required to give defence a copy of everything we have long before trial."

"Yeah, but that'd still take time. By then they might not remember when I ordered the questions … or if they do, Linquist would be suspected before me."

"For this, perhaps, but later there could be other things that Linquist isn't involved with and you are. We need to be careful."

"I hear ya. No worries, I wouldn't be chapter president if I didn't know how to take care of myself."

Jack ended the call and put his phone back on the bed-side table.

"Is this how our Easter Sunday is going to be?" Natasha murmured, not bothering to open her eyes.

The two rats.... How long before these goofs or their buddies kill another innocent person? He glanced at the clock. *Early, but this shouldn't wait.*

Natasha sat up in bed. "You didn't hear a word I said, did you?"

"I thought you were mumbling in your sleep," Jack replied. "It'd be rude to listen."

Natasha made a face. "You've always got an answer."

Jack leaned over and kissed her. "Sorry about waking you. I have to make one or two calls, then I'm done."

"You better be. I hear the boys. They won't want to wait long."

As Natasha put on her housecoat and left the bed-room, Jack phoned Roger and started his conversation by apologizing for calling him at home and for calling so early in the morning.

"It's okay," Roger replied. "At my age I get up early. I've already had two pots of coffee, six eggs, couple of pork chops, and ten slices of bacon."

"You lyin' dog. You're not that much older than me."

Roger chuckled. "What's up?"

"Have you heard of any gang members in the Death Heads with the first names of Aron and Jeremy?"

"Sure. Aron Kondrat and Jeremy Pratt. They call them the two rats because of how their surnames are spelled."

"That's them!" Jack smiled to himself. "You made my day. For sure you made Connie's day."

"Christ! They the ones who murdered that poor sap in front of his wife?"

"Yes."

"Man, that's great news. I wondered why you called so early. Especially on Easter Sunday."

"I found out through an informant. Knowing isn't the same as proving it," Jack noted.

"No, but it's a hell of a good start. Connie told me you were trying to help."

"You'll need to keep this under your hat. It's strictly on a need-to-know basis. My informant stuck his neck out and I don't know how many people know it was them. Any arrests could put him in jeopardy."

"Understood." Roger paused. "But you are going to call Connie?"

"Yes, I trust her enough that she won't run out and arrest the guys immediately."

"Then let her know that we've already got Kondrat and Pratt named in a wiretap. They live in a basement with two other gangbangers in PoCo. One by the name of Peter Jones and the other is Ronald Pierce. We have them both named, as well. It's a dump and they only have mattresses or foam cushions on the floor for beds."

"They sound like typical shit-rats. I'll pass the info on to Connie."

"They're obviously stupid, but not stupid enough to talk on anything other than a disposable phone." Roger paused, then swore before saying, "Maybe the little assholes are smarter than I thought. They've been keeping such a low profile that they were way down on our priority list. We've been following other gang members around."

"Not your fault. We can only do so much with the manpower we have. Prioritizing a few selected targets and ignoring the rest is the norm."

"Yeah, but it sucks to think if we'd been on them that poor guy might still be alive."

"Let's not go there. It's too depressing," Jack responded.

"You're right," Roger muttered. "Back to the two rats. Even though they're already named in a wiretap, Connie will have to get a new one."

"Specifically naming them as suspects in Irving's murder, otherwise the evidence could be tossed in court. Connie will know that."

"I know, but what I'm trying to say is that it will take time for her to do that. Maybe that will help your source."

"It will, but her getting a wiretap also makes me nervous. I'll want to proofread what she says when it comes to my informant. I'll also want to talk to whichever prosecutor is handling it so there won't be any surprises down the road when it comes to disclosure."

"Connie will need you to help her regardless because you'll have to document his reliability."

"You're right. I've got another question. Have you heard of someone connected to these guys who goes by the name of Zombie?"

Roger paused, then replied, "Nope, don't know that one."

"He supplies the guns to the Death Heads."

"No kidding? Man, you really made my day finding that out! You're better than the Easter Bunny."

Not an image I want to remember.

"Will your guy be able to identify him properly?" Roger asked.

"Yes, it's already in motion. It concerns me that these punks have access to such high-grade weapons."

"It concerns you?" Roger exclaimed. "Think how we feel in CFSEU. They're better armed than we are."

"I want to take complete responsibility when it comes to investigating Zombie. I'll be using my informant and need to control what happens along with who knows what."

"Be my guest, but if I can help out with surveillance teams or something, let me know."

"I appreciate that."

"I take it Connie told you about the double murder in Alabama," Roger said. "Where the father and son were murdered?"

"Yes, she said the FBI are looking for two brothers for that. Zachary and Luke Coggins."

"Someone from the FBI emailed me a list of the guns stolen in that robbery. I'll send you a copy."

Jack was surprised. "The FBI and not the ATF sent you the list of stolen guns?"

"The FBI may have linked it to another gun store robbery in Arkansas. Something to do with bad guys crossing state lines and all that. I imagine both the FBI and ATF are involved." Roger paused. "Wait until you see the list of what was stolen. You won't believe it."

"Why not?" Jack asked.

"Each store was cleaned out for about five hundred weapons. Many of them were military-type assault rifles."

"Okay."

"Along with laser sights, silencers, and ammo."

"Silencers?" Jack was astounded. "They sell silencers to the public?"

"Yup. Wait until you see the list. You wouldn't believe what they get away with selling down there. I doubt that even our military has the quality of some of these weapons."

"That's insane."

"I know. If you can put a stop to whoever is supplying the assholes up here, I'm all for it. Our priority is on the active shooters because of the threat of harm ... and loss of life to innocent people. We don't have the manpower to look much beyond that."

"I'll make it my priority," Jack said assuredly. "My hunch is they're being smuggled in from the States a few at a time. I'll contact someone in the ATF office in Seattle to liaise with."

"If it leads to the two brothers wanted for the murders in Alabama, you'll be working with the FBI as well," Roger noted.

"You want the weapons pipeline closed and the two murderers? Guess it doesn't hurt to dream."

"Yeah ... well, you never know. I was sent mugshots of the Coggins brothers. I'll send you copies of them, as well. You never know where it could lead."

"Thanks. I also may need a hand with surveillance once I identify Zombie."

"If he's supplying the punks we're working on, that won't be a problem."

Jack ended the call, then paused to listen to the excited voices of his sons from their bedroom as they spoke with

Natasha. It made him feel good that they weren't so old yet that they were no longer excited about hunting for Easter eggs. "I'll be right there guys!" he yelled. "Only one more call. Ten minutes tops."

"We know your ten minutes, Dad," Mike complained.

Jack quickly punched Connie's number into his phone. Her excitement at what he told her outmatched that of his sons.

"My God," Connie said. "This is absolutely fantastic. You really came through for me."

"My source came through for you," Jack said. "He's stuck his neck out twice in the last few days. I don't want any immediate action. It could burn him."

"No worries there," Connie replied. "I'll need evidence. If CFSEU hasn't got anything on their wiretaps yet, maybe I'll have better luck with a room bug."

"That's the route I figured you'd take. I'll want to review your wiretap application in regards to my informant. He needs to be protected."

"Of course. Better yet, you write that part yourself. You know what could burn him when it comes to disclosure and what won't."

"Great."

"It'll be an easy application to get because mostly all I'll have to do is piggyback your info onto the one Roger's team did. That and outline why we believe they killed the wrong guy."

"How long will that take?"

"You need to document reasons why you believe your guy is telling the truth."

"I know. I can show them good info he's given me that

goes back years. It might take a while, but I'll have my end ready for you by Friday at the latest."

"Good, then hopefully I'll have it completed by next weekend. Once it's signed, I'll work on getting a bug in the house where they live."

"Okay, we'll talk later. I have to go."

"Sure, but, uh, Jack?"

"What?"

"Thank you. I mean that from the bottom of my heart."

"You're welcome. Believe me … I want these guys caught, as well."

"I know. Still, with what you've done to help … it makes me think maybe I've misjudged you sometimes."

"No … you haven't misjudged me."

"What? You ass! I'm holding out an olive branch here and —"

"Yeah, olives do go well with martinis. Have a good day." Jack smiled as he terminated the call.

A moment later he stood with Natasha and watched Mike and Steve eagerly take apart the living room in their search for candy. Watching them scramble about and listening to their excited laughter, Jack hugged Natasha and they exchanged smiles.

Then his thoughts went to the Irving household. *What are they doing this morning? Is their five-year-old looking for candy? I bet not. Any laughter Rhonda hears from now on will remind her of her husband being murdered.*

Chapter Thirteen

On Tuesday morning Jack and Laura arrived at work and reviewed the information that Roger had sent them.

"Did you see this?" Laura asked, her face registering shock as she scanned the lists of weaponry stolen from gun shops in Alabama and Arkansas. "It's appalling."

"Scary, isn't it?" Jack replied, while studying mug shots of Zachary and Luke Coggins. Both men were in their midtwenties, tall, and had long red hair pulled back in ponytails. They were clean-shaven, with sharp facial features. He decided that each looked as sullen as the other.

Laura glanced over at the mugshots. "Those the ones wanted by the FBI for the murders in Alabama?"

Jack nodded.

"They look like twins," Laura noted.

"I thought the same, but if they are, Zachary arrived fourteen months ahead of Luke."

He tossed the mug shots over for Laura to have a better look as he answered his office phone. The call display listed the caller as being from within the building.

"Jack Taggart?" a woman asked, sounding like she was on the verge of tears.

Jack had already identified himself when he answered, but it appeared that the caller had been too distraught to listen. "Yes, this is Corporal Jack Taggart. How can I help you?"

"This is Bonny Wright," she sniffled.

"Sorry, have we met?"

"No. I, uh, work for Chief Superintendent Quaile in Staffing."

"My condolences," Jack said.

"He's an awful man," she spluttered. "He really doesn't like you."

"The feeling's mutual. I don't know if you know but he was my boss several years ago, and let's just say that we didn't see eye to eye. Then, one day things came to a head — something he didn't like about one of my files. Fortunately, no one else sided with him. Let's see, how did the brass put it at that time … ? right, I was told that some people's abilities were more suited for administrative duties. And that's what happened. He was transferred within a few months when it became painfully obvious that he wasn't qualified. Some might suggest that his continued rise in rank would prove he had a talent for such work. He's such a brown-noser that I suspect he uses more toilet paper to clean the end of his nose than he does his own ass." Jack paused. "Sorry, I got carried away. Why are you calling me?"

"He —"

Jack waited patiently as she blew her nose.

"I'm not sure what I'm supposed to do," she whimpered. "He's been sitting on your last performance evaluation for four months."

"Four months!" Jack exclaimed.

"Yes. I went over it the day we received it to ensure all the appropriate categories were filled out. All he's supposed to do is read it to ensure that your score is justified by appropriate examples outlined by your boss. I know it was. Staff Sergeant Wood was thorough in that regard."

"How long does it take him to review other evaluations?" Jack asked.

"Most times it takes him less than five minutes."

"So he's purposely holding it back to stop me from being promoted," Jack said decidedly.

"Definitely. The competition is so tight that, without it, you won't have the points you need to be on the short list of candidates. If it was included, I know you'd qualify. I keep reminding him to hand it in."

"What does he say?"

"He used to say he'd get around to it. Now he tells me it's not my concern." She paused. "I don't know, I ... it's not fair. Every day he manages to clean out his basket of everything else that comes in, but leaves your evaluation laying there."

Jack listened to her blow her nose again and thought about how much he respected her strong sense of justice and appreciated the risk she was taking by telling him. Trying to comfort her, he said, "Don't worry about it."

"Don't worry about it? How can you —"

"Quaile is pompous, petty, obtuse, and vindictive. It is the vindictive part that concerns me. If he knew you'd called me he'd either make up an excuse to have you fired or treat you so badly that you'd quit."

"I know, but it's not right!"

"No, it's not, but I don't want to jeopardize your job over it."

"Nobody in this office can stand him."

"I'm sure, but I don't see anything we can do about it."

"Your section is getting two new constables, as well."

"Good, that'll help."

"Not with the two he picked. One of them's spent most of his career on medical leave for a bad back and the other's morbidly obese and can only handle administrative duties."

"Wonderful," Jack lamented. "I'm sure Quaile is delighted, but don't worry about it. If I retire a corporal, so be it. I'm happy with the work I'm doing and to me that's more important than climbing the corporate ladder."

"Really?"

"Really. I appreciate you telling me, but I know how important your job is to you. Obviously you looked and can't find anything else."

"How do you know I've already looked?"

"You wouldn't be as upset as you are otherwise, let alone work for a man like that. Again, thank you, but to me it doesn't really matter."

"Are you sure?"

"Yes. I'm sure. Take care of yourself and don't worry about me."

When Jack terminated the call, he saw Laura staring at him. "You heard?" he asked.

"Quaile is holding back your last performance evaluation to keep you from being promoted?"

"Yes."

Laura's face revealed her anger. She opened her mouth to say something, then closed it and started again. "It's been what? Seven years since he was our boss? We were working on that human smuggling file. We couldn't prove it, but I'm certain that if he hadn't interfered that kid would still be alive."

"Guess he blames me for exposing his incompetence."

"He's been carrying that anger around with him all these years," Laura sighed, shaking her head.

"Yes. In a way that makes me feel like I've won. To me, the promotion isn't all that important ... but that's just me. For yourself, I'm sure you want to get above the rank of constable."

Laura screwed up her face. "I expected to."

"If you're offered a corporal's position somewhere else you might want to take it. Obviously my spot won't be coming open."

Laura seemed to contemplate his words for a moment, then shrugged. "Thanks, but like you I'm happy where I am."

Jack gave her a smile of appreciation.

Laura paused. "So," she said cheerily, "what do you want to do today? I can find out what car Quaile drives if you want to head home to your garage and make a pipe bomb."

Jack was about to play along with the joke but saw the dark look on Rose's face as she strode through the door.

"Quaile? Car bomb? What the hell is going on?" she demanded.

Jack rolled his eyes. "Pull up a chair and I'll tell you as long as you promise to keep it to yourself."

"Not if you're going to kill Quaile," she said, perhaps jokingly.

"No, I won't kill him," Jack replied.

Rose eyed Jack momentarily, then rolled a chair over from across the room and sat down. Her face darkened further as he told her about the call he'd received. When he finished, she said, "That's absolutely despicable. What a wretched —"

"There's nothing we can do about it," Jack stated. "Quaile would either fire her or make her life a living hell if he found out she told. As far as the alleged constables we're getting, it's not a promotional move for them so he has the power to do that on his own."

"He doesn't have the power to be vindictive and purposely screw our section!"

Yes, but knowing that and proving it are two different things. Especially with someone of his rank. He eyed Rose and saw how furious she looked. *Okay, settle down. We can't fix what we can't fix. Learn to live with it.*

"He's obviously been carrying his anger all these years," Laura noted. "I'm seriously beginning to question whether he's mentally ill or has some type of personality disorder."

Ouch. That didn't help. Rose looks like she's about to come unglued. Time for a little humour. "I guess the good news is that space in the office won't be a problem," he said. "By the sounds of it, one person won't be here and the other could share the office with our secretary to help with the clerical duties."

"This isn't funny," Rose snapped.

"I know," Jack replied quietly. "The thing is, I couldn't

stand it if my promotion cost the secretary her job. Let it be. I'm happy where I am."

"Likewise," Laura added.

Rose shook her head then abruptly got to her feet. "I came in to see if you wanted to go for coffee but I don't think I could keep it down. This really sucks."

"You promised not to say anything," Jack reminded her.

"I know," she replied, "which is why it really sucks." She viciously shoved the chair and sent it flying across the room and stormed out.

"She's taking it worse than we are," Laura noted, raising her eyebrows.

"She'll get over it. She's probably more angry that you and I will still be a team," Jack added jokingly.

"I bet you're right. She once said that the two of us would send her to an early grave."

Jack grinned, then became serious. "Speaking of graves, I've arranged for another walk amongst the tombstones at noon."

"Going to flush out a Zombie," Laura quipped.

"That's my plan. Who knows, maybe he'll end up back in a grave."

* * *

Jack nudged Laura when he saw Lance ambling toward them in the cemetery. As Lance neared, he paused and appeared to be studying a couple of the tombstones carefully.

"What're you doing?" Jack asked as Lance neared.

"What do you think of this one?" Lance replied, gesturing to a tombstone. "I figure you should buy me one like that." He paused. "Considering the number of times I've been meeting you, I'm sure it'll only be a matter of time."

Jack ran his hand across the smooth marble finish. "Yeah, it does look nice." He looked at Lance. "Sure, we'll spring for the cost of one like this for you. No worries."

Lance glared. "You're a prick, you know that?"

Jack chuckled.

"So what is it this time?" Lance asked. "Zombie?"

"It's about Zombie. We want to find out who he is."

"That won't be hard. Borman offered to introduce Linquist to him. I'll get him to meet Zombie and order a couple of pieces." He paused, then added, "You could've told me that over the phone. We wouldn't have had to meet."

Yes, but I want to read your face to see how worried you are about doing it.

Jack glanced at Lance and shrugged in response. "I'd like it set up so Laura and I can watch."

"Do you plan on busting him once he delivers the guns?" Lance asked.

"No, I want his source," Jack replied. "Zombie may not even be charged in Canada if his connection is in the States. If he does go to the States and ends up leading the investigators there to the two brothers who are wanted for murder, so much the better."

"If he's busted in the States it'd be better for me," Lance noted. "Any heat could be deflected as having come from down there."

Jack studied Lance's face. "Speaking of heat, how safe do you feel about it? Do you need to discuss it with Whiskey Jake?"

"It'd be better to let him know in advance so it doesn't look like I'm hiding anything in case the shit hits the fan later. I already mentioned to him that it would be good to find out who they're getting their guns from, so it won't be a surprise to him that I'm ordering some pieces."

Good, he seems calm about doing it.

"How soon can you talk to him?" Laura asked.

"He's visiting relatives in Regina but will be back in a week. I could go ahead and do it without talking to him if you're in a rush."

"No, wait until he comes back," Jack said. "Your safety is the first priority." He then gestured to the tombstone and looked serious. "But if things do go sideways, would you want one with the RCMP crest engraved above your name?"

Lance's jaw slackened momentarily, then he snickered. "Yeah, and I want my wife to get survivor benefits, too!"

* * *

Over the next couple of days Jack worked on his part of the wiretap application. As the only direct evidence to support the application came from his informant, he had to list how many times the informant had supplied information in the past, coupled with how many times the information provided had proven to be reliable or corroborated from independent sources.

It was a sensitive document and one that would have to be censored later before being given to defence council prior to trial. Some prosecutors left the censorship entirely up to whoever was handling the informant, while others balked if they felt the investigator was censoring too much material.

Late Friday afternoon Jack met with Connie at her office and they went over the information he supplied.

"This is great," Connie said after she read what Jack had provided her. "I won't need to change a word."

"I'll want to be there when you meet with the prosecutor," Jack said. "I need to ensure that if it is given to defence later on that I have full control over what is released and what isn't. If a judge decides to override what I'm willing to give, then there needs to be no misunderstanding with the prosecutor as to what will happen."

"No ... I hear you. I'll be happy to have you with me. All of the information from the previous wiretaps obtained by Roger's team has already passed scrutiny. If there are any questions, it'll be over what you've written. It's best you're there."

"Good, as long as we're clear on that."

"We're clear."

* * *

Jack returned to his office and saw Laura raise an eyebrow at him from behind her desk.

"Done," he said, wiping his hands together for show as he strode to his desk. "Connie said she'd finish preparing it this weekend and then take it to a prosecutor on Monday."

"Good," Laura commented. "It's also Friday and quitting time. Up for an olive soup?"

"No martinis today, thanks. I want to get home. It's Steve's birthday. He's turning ten."

Laura smiled. "That's an excuse I'll accept. What do you get a ten-year-old boy these days?"

Jack gave a lopsided grin. "As a present, he wants to be taken out to a really high-end restaurant." He paused. "Seems funny to me that a kid that age would want that."

"That's good that he does," Laura commented. "If he likes that he'll have to work hard in school so he can get a good job to afford it when he's older."

"Right, along with being able to afford expensive vacations, like lying on a beach in Hawaii," Jack chided.

Laura frowned. "Three weeks to go. I feel a little bad about leaving when things are busy."

"Nah, I won't be all that busy. I-HIT will follow up on Irving's murder and CFSEU will keep tabs on the street gangs. I'm sure before you leave we'll find out who is supplying the guns and pass that info on to either the FBI or ATF." Jack smiled. "No worries. Enjoy your holiday."

Laura eyed him suspiciously. "With you, there are always worries."

Chapter Fourteen

It was Monday afternoon when Connie called Jack. "You available tonight?" she asked.

"Available for what?"

"I finished the wiretap application and dropped it off this morning at the Department of Justice. Ana Valesi has it. She's busy with the trial but said she'd review it at home this evening and asked that we come by at eight thirty p.m."

"Why didn't you take it to another prosecutor who wasn't so busy?"

"I tried, but it got shuffled back to her. She looked after the wiretaps that Roger's team got and my application has all of that info in it. She's already familiar with most of it."

"Okay, what's her address and phone number?"

Connie gave it to Jack. "Want me to pick you up instead?" she asked.

"Thanks, but no. She only lives about twenty minutes away from my place. I'll see you there."

* * *

Jack arrived at the Valesi house precisely on time. A tall, thin woman with plain features met him at the door and introduced herself as Ana. Somewhere within the house a toddler was crying.

Ana glanced behind her. "Sorry about that. Isabella was supposed to be in bed an hour ago. She's running a bit of a fever. Maybe teething."

"No problem," Jack replied. "My wife and I have two sons. They're older, but I do understand."

Ana eyed him briefly and a sparkle appeared in her eyes. "So you're the famous Jack Taggart. The one to call when things get rough."

Jack rolled his eyes. "I think infamous is a better adjective."

Ana grinned. "Either way, nice to meet you in person. I want to thank you again for what you did when my mother's door was smashed open."

"Any time."

"I'd like to thank you, too," said a man who appeared in the foyer holding Isabella.

Ana introduced him as her husband, Pietro. He was a short, slim man with black wavy hair. He shook Jack's hand, saying, "I teach English Literature at the university. It is not a profession noted for its violence unless you count a verbal tongue lashing over a dangling participle." He eyed Ana. "Something I'm more likely to receive at home."

"So you should be," Ana replied with a wink directed at Jack. "It's not the sort of language you should use in front of Isabella."

Pietro chuckled then his face became serious. "The whole matter left us really shaken. I really do thank you for your assistance. Ana told me you played a key role helping to ensure it doesn't happen again."

"I spoke to someone who assisted in passing the word on to the gangs that what they did was inappropriate. Hopefully there won't be any further incidents," Jack replied.

Ana pointed out the door. "Looks like your partner in crime has arrived."

Jack saw Connie arriving and moments later he and Connie were ushered into a den where they sat across from Ana as she flipped through the wiretap application on her desk.

"You did a good job, Connie," Ana said, not bothering to look up as she studied the application.

"Don't give me any credit," Connie responded. "I copied what Roger's people wrote in their applications, then copied and pasted in the informant information that Jack supplied."

Ana's eyes focused on Jack. "It would have been better if your informant hadn't received the information second-hand, but you did a good job explaining that the prospect either directly or indirectly works for your informant, who is a full member of Satans Wrath."

Jack nodded.

"So, your informant has provided info that's proven to be true or has been corroborated from independent sources."

"Yes."

Ana appeared to study his face closely, "And he's never lied to you."

"No, he hasn't," Jack replied and returned Ana's gaze who stared stone-faced at him. Then she gave a nod, possibly to indicate she was satisfied with his response. Her question of doubt as to what he'd stated in the application irritated him. "If he did, it would cost him his life," he added bluntly. "And he knows it."

Ana looked at him sharply. "I'm glad you didn't decide to note that as his incentive to tell the truth."

"Some things are best left unsaid," he replied.

"So it would seem." Ana looked at Connie. "I don't see any changes that need to be done except for one minor error." She leaned over and gestured for Connie to look at a particular paragraph. "See where you quoted part of a previous conversation overheard on a wiretap? You ended it with three periods and there should be four."

Connie glanced at it. "I'll take it back to the office and have it back to you by tomorrow morning."

Jack tried to maintain a poker face to hide his thoughts. *Really? You're going to make her take it back for that? Couldn't you dot it in with your pen and have her initial it?*

Ana appeared to have read his thoughts. She pointed her finger at him and said, "Maybe you don't think that a missing period is important, but let me tell you that defence —"

Jack held up his hands for her to stop. "It's okay," he said. "I know how important it is. Once, when I was little, my older sister missed a period and all hell broke out in our house."

Connie chortled while Ana appeared to be momentarily caught off guard. She then smiled and glanced at the application again and her face became serious. "There is something you need to understand," she said, looking at Jack. "If the investigation is successful, I won't be able to censor everything relating to your informant. You could be called to the stand and cross-examined."

"Yes, I realize that, which is why I wanted to meet you in person," Jack replied. "I'll need to keep some of these details secret."

"I understand that, but once on the stand, the judge may order you to disclose something you don't want to disclose. Naturally I'd object, but that doesn't necessarily mean the judge would agree."

"If the judge orders me to disclose something I feel will jeopardize the informant, I'll refuse."

Ana looked shocked. "You can't refuse an order from a judge like that!"

"Just watch me," Jack replied firmly.

Shock turned to alarm. "You'd be found in contempt! Perhaps sent to jail!"

Jack gave her a hard look. "So be it. I'd go to jail before disclosing something that'd result in my informant being murdered. I'd view that as partaking in a conspiracy to commit murder."

Ana took a moment and her face revealed her angst.

Is she upset with me personally, or at the possibility of what might happen to the trial? Maybe both.

He cleared his throat. "Should I be sent to jail, my first phone call would be to the media. It would be interesting to find out what the public would think.

I'm optimistic that I'd get some support. Perhaps even enough to bear pressure on the judge and bring about my release."

Ana appeared to think about it for a moment then her face became noncommittal. "There is another possibility we could be faced with. You might not be ordered to disclose certain information, but by not doing that, defence may succeed in having the wiretap tossed out of court, leaving us with insufficient evidence to proceed."

"I'd rather that than have my informant murdered." Jack looked at Connie and saw her face darken, but was pleased when she made eye contact with him and gave a nod of agreement.

"Hopefully it'll never come to that," Ana said. "I simply wanted you to be aware of the different possibilities that could arise."

"I appreciate that," Jack replied. "Thank you."

Ana's eyes shifted between Jack and Connie. "Then we're done. I wish you luck on bringing this to fruition."

"There is something else," Jack said. "I might be applying for a wiretap in regards to who is supplying guns to the Death Heads, which I suspect are coming in from the States. I'm still in the early stages of investigation, but perhaps I might be looking at applying for one in a couple of weeks." He looked at her and raised an eyebrow.

Ana gave a quick smile. "Once you've finished the application I'll be glad to take a look at it."

I was hoping you'd say that. Periods or not, you are thorough.

"It shouldn't take much work if you are using the same informant," Ana continued. "With the information contained in Connie's application, all you'd have to do is add whatever new information you obtain."

"Good. Thank you," Jack responded.

"If there's anything you're unsure of then don't hesitate to call me. It would save time, rather than having you run back and forth."

"That would be great."

"Not a problem. Whatever I can do to prevent guns from coming into Canada, so much the better." She paused a moment, "I'd never allow one in my house." She then looked at Jack and Connie before giving a pert smile. "Present company excluded, that is."

"Situations do arise where I've needed one," Jack noted. He glanced at Connie. "You, too, for that matter."

"I appreciate that they're needed in your line of work," Ana said, "or for the military, but outside of trappers or ranchers, I don't see a proper use for them when it comes to the general public. Far too many people are killed or wounded to justify the people who claim to have them for self-protection or for entertainment."

"Despite having your mother's door kicked in by two armed men, you still think that?" Connie questioned. "Personally, I'd think you'd fall into the category of someone who should be armed."

"I've taken a stand on that issue," Ana said firmly. "I entrust my safety to people like you who are properly trained. I don't believe in giving in to the perpetuation of fear so often promoted by certain organizations or gun companies to increase their revenue."

"A lot of people would disagree with you," Jack said.

"A lot of people need to be better informed," Ana replied.

"The odds of a citizen having a gun for protection and actually using it to defend themselves is minuscule compared to the number of weapons stolen in home break-ins and used by criminals to kill or injure innocent people."

"Can't argue with you there," Connie said. "I deal with the victims at work often enough. Then when I'm off duty I can't escape it because it's on the news."

"Which, with the sensationalism generated by the media, perpetuates more fear, which equates to more people buying guns," Ana said.

"I think part of the problem is that many people are gullible enough to believe the fake media that has become so popular on the internet," Jack stated. "People are becoming enraged or scared over things that aren't factual or never happened."

"Don't get me started on fake media," Ana said with disdain. "At one time it was tabloid trash you'd find in supermarket checkout lines. No sane person believed it and may have only looked at it as entertainment. These days it's better disguised and has gone viral. The motive for much of it is the same as the tabloids, to make money, but not all of it is intended for profit."

"You mean it's propaganda," Jack said.

"Exactly."

"Which promotes irrational thought because humans tend to absorb what they first believe," Jack noted, "and disregard any subsequent facts that'd negate their original belief. They're more inclined to believe the fake media if it coincides with their original thoughts."

"You've got it." Ana eyed Jack for a moment. "It would appear that you and I share some common beliefs."

"In some ways, but living in fear is hell," Jack stated. "Having a gun gives me a sense of protection. My wife, too, for that matter."

"For the general public it is a false sense," Ana retorted. "Statistics prove it." She paused. "Yes, I'm scared over what happened, but somebody has to draw a line. Mine is not to own a firearm."

Jack's gaze fell upon a family portrait on her desk, then he saw Ana glance at what he was looking at, before making eye contact again. He swallowed. "You're an extraordinarily brave person."

"I don't think so," Ana replied. "I'm sure there are a lot of people who feel the way I do."

"I'm not so sure. People like to think they'd be brave, but until they've faced something like you've faced, lived with what you've lived with on a daily basis, they've no idea what being brave really means." He glanced at Connie. "People tend to think police officers are brave, but you and I carry guns. How brave would we be without them?"

"In our circles, not having a gun wouldn't be called being brave; it'd be called being suicidal," Connie replied.

Ana turned to Jack. "Roger told me about Satans Wrath taking pictures of you and your family. I'm sure you appreciate how it feels to have your family threatened, but for me the answer is not to buy a gun. Am I supposed to get one for every member of my family and carry it everywhere I go? You might, but I doubt the rest of your family does."

"I'd be more concerned if I didn't have a good informant who gives me the inside track," Jack replied. "I'm pretty sure that the photos they sent me were only meant to intimidate, and they didn't kick in my door. It wasn't as bad as what happened to your mother and the effect I know that has on you and your family." He gestured at the wiretap application on her desk. "Both are examples of why informants are a vital tool and need to be protected."

Ana glanced at the application. "You've made your point about the need to protect informants." Her eyes drifted back to her family portrait. "When things become personal, you appreciate it all the more." She then looked up. "Looks like we're done."

A moment later Jack opened the front door and saw a Vancouver Police Department patrol car slowly driving past. It stopped and the officer waved at Ana. She gave a friendly wave back and the car continued on.

"They've been making regular patrols past our house," Ana noted. "I really appreciate it. We sleep better knowing they're around."

Jack nodded. *It helps, but the stress is still there. I know all about that.* He eyed Ana. *At least I've a gun. What you have is guts....*

Chapter Fifteen

Three days later Jack and Laura were at their desks when Lance called.

"Things are happening like you want," he said after greeting Jack. "I met with Whiskey Jake and told him I think we should take the opportunity to have Borman introduce us to who is supplying the Death Heads with weapons. He agreed it would be a good idea."

"Great," Jack replied.

"He said if they're stupid enough to make an introduction, we should jump on it before something changes."

"You didn't have to work hard to convince him?"

"No, I suspect he wonders why I've taken an interest in the Death Heads all of a sudden, but he readily went along with it."

"When can you set it up?"

"I already did. Linquist contacted Borman, who arranged to introduce him to Zombie tomorrow morning.

Also found out that Zombie lives up here someplace, so is presumably a Canadian."

"That's super. If we follow Linquist, he'll lead us to wherever the meeting is."

"You won't need to. The meeting's out in PoCo at a place called the Aquatic Centre Café. It's scheduled for ten a.m."

"Didn't your guys wonder why you asked?" Jack asked. "Normally you wouldn't be involved in trivial details like that."

"I mentioned I might assign a surveillance team to follow Zombie after."

"Will you?"

"No, I think if I did and Zombie was busted later it'd have the potential to draw more heat my way." Lance paused. "Why, do you want me to?"

"No. Laura and I'll handle it."

"Just the two of you?"

"I don't want word to get out that we knew about the meeting. If it does end up in court, someone might let it slip. The fewer from our side who know, the better."

"I see." Lance paused. "Thanks for looking after me."

"I figured I should for now. I submitted an expense claim for that tombstone you wanted and ran into some flak. Until that clears up, I better try to keep you alive."

Lance chortled. "Aw shucks. I thought maybe you were becoming emotionally attached to me. You know ... that Stockholm thing."

"Forget Stockholm Syndrome. I'm a realist. What's being ordered?"

Lance became serious. "Four Glocks with laser grips."

"Four?" Jack replied. "Let me guess. You're looking at it like a dope deal. If you only ordered one, he might have it on him. This way there's a better chance of us following him to either his source or his stash."

"You got it."

"Price?"

"To be negotiated. I'll get word on that after they meet and let you know."

Jack said goodbye, then placed a call to the Bureau of Alcohol, Tobacco, Firearms and Explosives in Seattle. After being passed around on the phone by two different investigators, a third person came on the phone.

"Hello, Canada," a jovial voice said. "I'm Special Agent Glen Ferguson, but you can call me Ferg. Everyone else does, even Betty, and she's my wife."

Jack introduced himself. "I'm investigating a case where some high-end pistols stolen from a gun shop in Alabama are turning up on our doorstep."

"That's what the person told me who forwarded your call. Speaking of which, sorry for the way they bounced your call around our office. I'm based out of Seattle, but I recently bought acreage about an hour drive north of here, near a place called Burlington."

"Burlington," Jack repeated. "I've heard of it, but can't quite place where it is."

"It's an easy forty-minute drive south of Canada." Ferg paused, then noted, "They like to give me cases close to the border to save them the drive up. I'm glad, because then I'm closer to where I live and it justifies taking a company car home. Gotta enjoy all the perks I can before I retire."

"Let me outline all the details as to why I'm calling," Jack said.

"Go ahead. Got my pen in hand."

Jack told him about Irving's murder and the pistols found at the scene that had been stolen in Alabama and the circumstances of that robbery. He also told him that the FBI had issued warrants for the Coggins brothers and suspected them of having cleaned out another gun store in Arkansas.

"Maybe the Coggins are in Seattle," Ferg suggested.

"Maybe," Jack agreed. "I've got an informant who says that the guy supplying the guns to the Death Heads goes by the name of Zombie. That's all I know about him at the moment, other than he lives up our way, so he's likely a Canadian."

"I'll run the name on our system anyway. You never know what'll pop up."

"I might have more info on him tomorrow."

"What's happening then?"

Jack decided to lie. "My informant is being introduced to him in the morning and will be ordering four Glocks with laser grips." *If there's ever a leak, the finger will point to Linquist instead of Lance.*

"What time?" Ferg asked.

"Ten a.m. I'm hoping to identify him then and do surveillance to try and find out where he goes to get them. I don't know if the guns are being smuggled in from your side of the line or if they're already here."

"My hunch is they'd be coming from here," Ferg said.

"Mine, too, which is why I called. If the same people did rob two stores, then we're looking at about a thousand weapons. That's more than our local market could handle, so I think the bulk of them are still in the States."

"That's a hell of a lot of firepower, by my standards as well. Seattle's the biggest and closest city to where you are. If the rest of the arsenal is still together, it'd make sense that the sons-of-bitches would have them stashed here."

"That's what I'm thinking. If they are down your way, then hopefully Zombie will lead you to whoever is supplying him. If you have to bust Zombie, go ahead, but if he leads you to someone else, I'd be happy if he wasn't busted, to make it look like he was the informant."

Ferg was silent for a moment. "Yeah … I guess that'd be all right, although I hear that Homicide is a little busy these days."

"My guess is he'd make it back into Canada before they decided he was the informant."

"You're probably right. I also bet you haven't discussed this with your Homicide people," Ferg said wryly.

"It's what I call 'a delicate matter.' No need to rock the boat at this point."

"I hear ya. No worries. Do you expect Zombie to go get the guns right away?"

"I don't know. I'll find out tomorrow."

"I'll have a team ready at the border, so let me know."

"Will do."

"If Zombie decides to head down some other day, make sure you call me direct and I'll take it from there. Day or night, I'll be on it."

"Much appreciated. Thanks."

"Hell, it's me who should be thanking you," Ferg replied. "If we can take that many weapons off the street, it'll be me who owes you big time."

"If this goes down the way I hope, we'll meet over a beer and decide then who pays for the round."

"Perfect! You and I are going to get along really well there, partner."

Jack smiled and ended the call.

* * *

The next morning Jack and Laura took separate vehicles and arrived outside the Aquatic Centre Café at nine thirty. Laura went inside so she wouldn't look suspicious by following Linquist in, while Jack watched from a surveillance van.

At ten Jack called Laura when he saw Linquist park his car and walk toward the café. "You're about to have company. Linquist has arrived. How're you fixed for cover?"

Laura kept her voice low. "Lots of people in here. Blending in isn't a problem." Laura paused. "Okay … I've got eyes on him. He's taking a seat halfway across the room from me. Will be too noisy to pick up any conversation."

"That's okay. We know what they'll be talking about." Minutes later Jack called Laura again to report that Borman had arrived and parked his car.

"Okay," she replied after Borman entered the café. "I can confirm Linquist and Borman are seated together. All we need is Zombie."

A few minutes later Jack saw a man walking toward the café. He was glancing in parked cars and looking intently at passing vehicles as he approached.

Jack was glad that he'd parked far enough away that the van he was in didn't receive any scrutiny. He called Laura. "Okay, we've got a guy approaching on foot and acting kinky. Put him to be about thirty years old, shaved head, wearing jeans and a black leather bomber-style jacket. He's coming in now."

"I see him. He's standing inside the door looking back toward the street."

"Checking for heat, I bet."

"Okay ... it's probably Zombie," Laura said. "He came inside and Borman is introducing him to Linquist. Did you happen to see what vehicle he arrived in?"

"Negative. From what I could see he walked. Give me a heads-up when he's leaving and I'll see if I can follow."

"Will do."

The next twenty-five minutes passed uneventfully, then Laura called Jack. "Get ready. They've all stood up. Looks like they're leaving together ... confirmed. They're out and I've lost the eye."

"No worries," Jack replied. "I've got glass on them now. Stay put. It looks like they're saying goodbye out front."

"Gotcha."

A moment later Jack gave her an update. "Zombie is loitering around the entrance, but Borman and Linquist are each getting in their cars."

"Zombie waiting for someone?" Laura wondered aloud.

"Could be. Hang tough." Jack continued to watch, then said, "He was only waiting for Borman and Linquist to leave. Now that they've left, he's crossing the street and walking west on Princess Crescent. I'm going on foot."

"Want me to follow on foot or grab my car?" Laura asked.

"Grab your car," Jack replied as he bailed out of the van.

A moment later Laura called. "I'm in my car. Where do you want me?"

"He's entering a path that connects at the end of Princess. According to the map on my phone it comes out on Lasalle Place."

Seconds later, Laura said, "I see it on my map. I can get to it by driving down Guilford and up Johnson."

"Go for it." A moment later Jack said, "Confirmed. We're walking north on Lasalle. I have to stay way back. Nobody else on the sidewalk but him and me."

"I'm on my way."

A moment later Jack said, "Okay, he turned west at the next block. Visual contact broken."

"According to my map, that's Durant," Laura replied. "Where do you want me?"

"Maybe at whatever main exit Durant leads to but use your judgment. I'm too busy trying to get to the corner to pull up the map again."

"That'd be Johnson," Laura replied. "A couple blocks to the west of you. I'll be there in three minutes."

As Jack rounded the corner on Durant, he saw Zombie spin around halfway down the block. *Shit....* "I see him ... he's doubling back. I'm going to have to veer off or we'll be face to face. You better pull over and wait."

Jack walked up to a nearby house, opened a gate to the rear yard and entered. *Good, no dog.* He then peered through the wooden fence and saw Zombie pass by on the sidewalk. "Okay, I may be out of it for a bit. Visual contact broken. I don't want to heat him up."

"What do you want me to do?"

"Stay put. I'd rather lose him than get burned. I don't know how far he'll backtrack. I'm holed up but will stick my head out for a look in a second. He could be planning to take that path back through to Princess."

"Copy."

Jack crept out of the yard and peeked around the corner of the house. He saw Zombie walking toward the end of the block while continuing to peer all around. Then when he reached the corner he looked both ways on Lasalle before doubling back on Durant. *Here we go again.*

Jack took up his location behind the fence but this time saw a set of keys dangling from Zombie's fingers when he passed by. "Laura, you near that exit off of Durant you mentioned?"

"I can be there in about two minutes."

"Hustle!" Jack left the yard again and peered around the corner of a house and saw Zombie getting into a vehicle parked on the street. It was one Zombie had walked past earlier before doubling back.

Jack's voice was tense as he spoke to Laura. "He's getting in a black Ford F-150 pickup with a silver tool box in the back. Can't see the plate. That'll be up to you."

"Copy."

Jack continued to relay what he saw. "He's westbound on Durant ... slowing ... stopping at a set of lights and has his left indicator on. Light's changed ... okay, he made the corner. Southbound. I'm VCB."

"That'd be Johnson," Laura stated. "I'm northbound on it now. He should be coming right at me ... yup, I see him. Okay, I've got the plate."

"Perfect. Swing by and pick me up."

Moments later Jack got in Laura's car and saw her grin.

"Guess who the plate is registered to?" she said, then answered for him, "A fellow by the name of Derek Graves."

Graves? Zombie? Jack smiled. "Perfect!"

"His address is listed as an apartment about a ten-minute drive away."

"Good. First drop me off at the van and we'll go check it out. If he doesn't live there, at least we know what he drives. Next time he meets I'll borrow one of Roger's surveillance teams and find out where he does live."

As Laura drove him back to where he'd left the surveillance van, he called Ferg and updated him on Zombie's real name along with the vehicle description and plate number.

"That's great," Ferg replied. "You hear from your informant as to a delivery schedule?"

"My informant is with someone," Jack lied. "As soon as he's free he'll call me and I'll let you know."

"No problem. I'll have my team stay at the border in case he's coming our way. Let me know if anything changes."

Jack retrieved the surveillance van and ten minutes later he and Laura both arrived at the address. It was an older wooden apartment building in dire need of paint. Graves's truck was parked in a stall behind.

Laura parked beside Jack and lowered her window. "What now?"

"We'll watch him until we hear from our friend. I'll take the front of the apartment in case he leaves with someone. You watch his truck."

"Will do."

Twenty minutes later Jack saw Graves and called Laura. "He came out the front door carrying two large garbage bags."

"The garbage bins are in the back," Laura noted.

"He's walking north on the sidewalk."

Ten minutes later Jack and Laura watched as Graves entered a laundromat. They realized the bags probably contained laundry.

"Okay, doesn't look like he's in any hurry to go anywhere," Jack noted. "Let's go back to the office and see what we can find out about him."

On his way back to the office Jack gave Ferg another update. He said he'd continue to keep his team at the border until Jack heard back from his informant.

Once back at the office Jack and Laura learned that Graves didn't have a criminal record, but he did have his own website. It contained racist literature along with conspiracy theories about different ethnic groups plotting to control the world. The website had a photograph posted of him.

"Looks like we've got ourselves a white supremacist," Laura noted.

"Yes, I wonder if he's got eyeholes in his pillowcase," Jack replied. "Love the photo."

In the photograph Graves stood in front of what appeared to be a cardboard cut-out of a black swastika on a wall behind him. His shirt was open and pulled back to reveal the butts of two pistols sticking out of each side of his waistband. Assorted tattoos on his chest included an eagle clutching a swastika over his heart and *SS* near the base of his neck.

"Skinny little guy," Jack noted.

"Explains the sneer on his face," Laura commented. "He's trying to show attitude and look tough. Instead he comes across as insecure." She shook her head. "What a pathetic loser."

Jack gestured to the pistols. "Too bad we weren't there when the photo was taken."

Laura gave Jack a sideways glance. "So we could reach over, pull the triggers, and shoot his balls off?"

Jack chuckled. "You know me too well."

He felt his phone vibrate.

Chapter Sixteen

"The meeting went well," Lance reported. "The four pieces are to be delivered a week from Monday and they're to meet at the same coffee shop at ten a.m."

"Good. It went well for us, too. We ID'd him, but I won't tell you his name in case you say it by mistake."

"Yeah, there's no need for me to know."

"Today's Friday, so that'd make the next meeting ten days from now," Jack noted. "It doesn't sound like the stash is close."

"He was bitching about not being able to do it sooner because he has to drive to Winnipeg tomorrow and won't be back until next Thursday."

"For his job?"

"Nope. Apparently he does drywall, but he's been out of work for a while. The trip is for some family thing."

"Then it'd appear that he'll be getting the guns on the weekend right before the next meet."

"Probably."

"What's the cost?"

"For the four, it works out to three grand each."

"Twelve grand seems a little pricey when you're getting that many," Jack stated. "I figured you'd get them for about ten."

"The guy seemed keen that Linquist was prospecting for us. He said that the price would come down if we did more business down the road."

"Makes sense," Jack replied. "Twelve g's is probably a lot of money for a low-life like Zombie. Especially if he's not working. I bet he'll have to get the guns on credit and pay his supplier after."

"Yeah, you might be right. If they're being fronted to him you might be able to follow him after Linquist pays him to see who he hands the cash to."

"My thoughts exactly."

"You'll need to watch yourselves," Lance cautioned. "I was told that he's super paranoid. Zombie cautioned Linquist to be careful and said that he crawls under his truck to check for trackers before doing any business and also changes phones frequently." Lance paused. "Maybe he was trying to impress us, but that's what he said."

"I suspect he's telling the truth. He was doing heat checks before and after the meeting."

"Okay, so on that note, there's another thing. He said he usually leaves his phone at home and gets the messages off it later."

"So his movements can't be tracked. He probably has another one he uses for his own supplier. Either that, or he uses computer chat rooms or something."

"Probably."

"Did Linquist get a phone number?"

"Yes, but Zombie made it clear that no business is to be discussed on the phone. All that can be talked about is when to meet for coffee. I've got the number if you want."

"How'd you get it?" Jack asked in surprise. "What reason would you need to know it?"

"I said I wanted it for comparison to see if it matched any number we might get from the United Front or any other group later on. No worries. I look after myself."

Right. No worries. Jack took the phone number from Lance, then ended the conversation.

"Do I take it that everything went well?" Laura asked when Jack put his phone away.

Jack told her what Lance had told him.

"Too bad Graves is such a paranoid little weasel," Laura said. "A tracker would've been nice."

"He might be tough to follow. Hopefully we'll be in a position to watch him search his truck and see how thorough he is when he looks for a tracker."

"If only they made one that looked like a swastika," Laura said wryly. "We could send it to him and he'd probably hang it from his rear-view mirror."

Jack thought about the mentality of the man they were dealing with. *Making that asshole look like the informant could make the world a better place.*

"Do you want me to check with Roger to see if he's ever heard of Graves?" Laura asked.

"Sure. Have him check the phone number we were given as well, and see if it ever came up on any of their lines. Also, let Connie know who Graves is and give her the number. Tell her to call us if he or his number shows up on her wiretap. While you do that, I'll update the ATF so they can break off their surveillance."

Jack then called Ferg and told him what they'd learned.

"I find it interesting that Graves is a white supremacist type," Ferg said. "We have a lot of white supremacists living in the northwest of the good ol' U.S. of A. That, and assorted other racists, survivalists, conspiracy types, and those who have an absolute hatred for anyone connected to government."

"Have our share of kooks in B.C., as well," Jack replied.

"After you called me yesterday, I did some checking on the father and son who were murdered at that gun shop in Alabama. They were both black, and coincidence or not, the Coggins brothers were proud members of the Klan. Maybe they do know Graves."

"Possible," Jack agreed. "Judging by Graves's website, they seem like birds of a feather."

"Any chance you can wire up his phone and pull his phone records?"

Jack saw Laura end her call with Roger. "Hang on a sec, Ferg." He looked at Laura. "Did Roger know Graves?"

"Nope."

Jack turned his attention back to Ferg. "We have wire on some of the people he sells his guns to, but there haven't been any calls to the number we have for him."

"Maybe switching phones," Ferg suggested. "The number you have could be a new one."

"Could be. I might get wire down the road, but with our justice system you can't get it except in emergency situations or unless you prove that you've tried all other avenues of investigation first — surveillance, informants.

Either that, or you have to have a damned good reason why those steps can't be taken or are likely to fail. The courts here look at invasion of privacy as a last resort."

"By the sounds of it, he isn't saying much on the phone anyways."

"No, from what I've been told he only uses it to plan face-to-face meets. My source says he's super paranoid and routinely does heat checks and crawls under his truck to check for trackers."

"Try to give that evidence in court and he'll say he was checking for oil leaks."

"For sure."

Ferg paused a moment, "My office has quite a few files and loads of pictures on people who belong to the groups I mentioned. I only live forty minutes from the border. How about we meet and I'll give you the lists of names and photos? Maybe the Coggins brothers are hiding out in Canada. Some of the good ol' boys from down here might show up where you are and maybe lead you to them."

"That would be great. Do you have any plans tomorrow? My family and I often go down to Bellis Fair on the weekend for a little cross-border shopping. Seeing as you live so close, maybe we could meet?"

"Hell, Bellis Fair is only twenty minutes from where I live. Betty and I often go there. We usually go during the week, because on a weekend it gets busy. Actually, on weekends I think there are more Canuck plates in the parking lots than American; but sure, tomorrow would be okay. What say we meet there for lunch?"

"Great idea."

"How old are your kids?"

"Mike is eleven and Steve is ten."

"I've got two sons myself, but they're grown up and live in California. Also have two granddaughters, aged three and five."

"Nice."

"Red Robin at twelve? I'll be the guy carrying a file box."

* * *

Jack and Natasha, along with Mike and Steve, arrived at the entrance to the restaurant at the same time as Ferg and Betty.

Ferg appeared to be in his early fifties. He was Jack's height, but with a huskier build, and had a horseshoe pattern of short grey hair. Ferg's warm smile and hearty handshake told Jack that they'd likely become good friends.

Betty was a short, plump woman with curly black hair. She seemed full of life, particularly around Mike and Steve, who she joked with by telling them they were handsome and pretending to guess how many girlfriends they had. Jack saw Natasha smile and knew the two women would hit it off, too.

They found a booth that offered privacy and took a seat. The conversation through lunch was lighthearted, but when the meal was over Betty and Natasha gave each other a look and then, as if on cue, rose from the table.

"Time to let the men talk," Betty said, looking at Mike and Steve. "Come on, guys, I bet you want to go to a video game store."

Natasha smiled as the boys' faces lit up. "How'd you know?" she mused.

Once Jack and Ferg were alone, Ferg reached for the file box and dug out reams of paper held together with large metal paper clips, along with manila envelopes stuffed with photos.

"You can take the whole box when you leave," Ferg said. "These are all copies, so you can keep 'em after, but I'll go over some of the stuff with you." He handed Jack one of the stacks of documents. "Take a look at these assholes. They're all white supremacists."

Jack flipped through the pages and saw that they were criminal records complete with mug shots of the various individuals. Many of the convictions involved violent assaults and weapons charges. "Looks like they have anger management issues," he said facetiously.

"Yeah, you might say that. They're ones to be particularly careful about. There are lots more who don't have any records, and many who we simply don't know." He gestured to an overstuffed legal-sized manila envelope. "Dump that puppy out and take a look."

Jack did as instructed and looked through the photos.

"We've got a few group shots where they posed for the photo," Ferg said when he saw what Jack was looking at. "If you flip the photo over, you'll see that we've written some names on the back, but most are unidentified. A lot of these photos are copies of ones we found in the homes of some of the people we did have run-ins with. Others, as you can see, are surveillance shots."

"I really appreciate this," Jack said. He picked up one photo showing a group of about forty men in a room giving a closed-fist Nazi-style salute. There was a speaker at the front of the room, a balding man of about sixty, but it was someone in the audience who caught Jack's attention.

Ferg glanced at Jack's face, then pointed to the man Jack was looking at in the audience. "Yeah, made me sick, too, when I saw it."

"Is it a security guard or a policeman's uniform?" Jack asked.

Ferg grimaced. "That's a county sheriff." He shook his head. "I support our First Amendment under the Constitution of free speech … but using that as an excuse to instigate violence and hatred, uh-uh. I've a real problem with that."

Jack studied the photo. "Not the usual types."

"What do you mean?"

"Most of the white power types we see are skinheads. Basically punks, misfits, and losers in their late teens or early twenties — but most of these aren't kids."

"These groups attract those types, but as you can see, a lot of 'em are older. Some are self-proclaimed anarchists. Others are simply radicals or nut cases with a passion for violence. I really have no sympathy for those types."

What the hell? "You have sympathy for some of them?" Jack asked.

"There are some who are simply ranchers or farmers who've fallen on bad times. Most of them haven't had any conflict with the law, but all it takes is for someone to blame their woes on some minority group and get them all worked up. These days, with fake news stories and all the other crap on the internet that people take as gospel … well, some people aren't smart enough to see through it."

"Funny, I was talking to one of our prosecutors the other day about the same thing." Jack paused. "I find it depressing that people are so gullible."

"Yeah, they're gullible, but I don't really hold that against them."

"I would once they go so far as to join a white power group."

Ferg shrugged indifferently. "It's easy to blame them and be judgmental, but if you look at it from their perspective they've worked hard all their lives. It's hard for them to understand why everything you've worked for is going down the toilet because of the economy. I've been fortunate and never had to walk in those shoes. I think when you do, the frustration you feel makes it easier to hate." Ferg paused, then added, "Yeah, they're dumb and they frustrate me, but those types I do tend to feel sorry for."

Jack looked at Ferg for a moment as he thought about what he'd said.

"What're you thinking?" Ferg asked.

"That you're an exceptionally understanding guy."

"Yeah, well, not always," he replied gruffly. "Especially not with assholes who wear a badge and do things like that," he said, stabbing at the county sheriff's picture with his finger.

"They all seem so angry and full of hate," Jack noted. "I wonder what was said to get them to do that? This isn't Second World War Germany."

"I don't know, but it'd be a load of one-sided bullshit that nobody would dare question. These meetings don't leave much room for open discussion. Their attitude is, you're either with 'em or you're against 'em." He eyed Jack.

"How many people in your unit do you have to help you with this case?"

"I've got one partner, but she's leaving on vacation for the first two weeks of May."

"That's it? One? And she's leaving?" Ferg looked aghast.

"I can borrow people from another unit to help with surveillance on occasion."

"Man! I don't want to tell you how to do your job up in Canada, but I can't emphasize how dangerous these people can be. Some are super paranoid … heavy into conspiracy theories and hostile when it comes to anyone representing the government or law enforcement."

"They do look crazy," Jack admitted as he glanced at the photo again.

"Yeah, but keep in mind that being crazy doesn't nec-essarily mean they're stupid," Ferg stated. "These guys can be deadly."

Jack nodded, then, in an effort to ease the mood, he tapped the photo with his finger and said, "Ah, maybe they just need to hear a good joke to get them to lighten up."

Ferg cast Jack a serious look. "What some of these boys would laugh at would turn your stomach."

Chapter Seventeen

Starting Monday Jack and Laura tried to cross-reference the lists of names that Ferg had given them with police data in Canada to see if they could find a connection. Many of the more common names they had were without dates of birth, and it proved to be a difficult task to confirm whether or not it was the same person. It was time-consuming work, and by late Tuesday afternoon they were only halfway through the lists and hadn't had any success.

Jack took a call from Connie. "Hey, you, how're you doing?" she asked, with an unusually friendly tone. From the background noise, he could tell she was in a vehicle.

"Hi," he replied. "What do you want?"

"What? I try to be nice to you and you automatically presume I want something?"

"Yes."

"Well, it so happens that I called to let you know that last night we got a room bug in the bachelor suite where Kondrat and Pratt are staying."

"That's good."

"I've got my fingers crossed. They share the place with two other goofs, Peter Jones and Ronald Pierce. Since they all sleep and eat in one room, it makes for a lot of chatter. It's easy to make out what they're saying, provided they don't have their headbanger music going."

"Let me know if there's any chatter or contact with Zombie."

"I will." Connie paused. "Hey, any chance of getting your informant to stir up some conversation between Kondrat and Pratt about Irving?"

"Forget it," Jack replied firmly. "My guy couldn't do that without burning himself. I've told you before. There are certain things you don't talk about."

"Yeah, I guess you'd know about that, wouldn't you?" she replied.

"Come on, Connie. I already gave you the names on a platter. Now you want me to risk someone's life by doing your whole job for you?"

Connie's sigh was audible. "Yeah … I'm sorry." She paused. "I met with Rhonda a few minutes ago. It got me feeling so damned worked up and anxious to clear this file that I acted on impulse and called you."

"Don't try to sucker me back in by using her to —"

"No, no. I wasn't. My heart really goes out to her … but I know you're right. At least this time you are. A moment ago she was questioning me about whether or not we had any leads. I said no, because, well, you know why."

"You can't afford to risk word getting out."

"Exactly. I'm sure she thinks we're not doing anything. It's frustrating having to keep her in the dark."

"How's she doing psychologically?"

"Not good. Victim Services are involved. Her doctor's prescribed sedatives, but she says she still can't sleep. She's also too freaked out to live in her house, so she's moved in with her sister who lives in Burnaby."

"Sorry to hear that, but I know it won't take long for you to wrap it up. I bet next time it's on the news it'll prompt the idiots to talk about it."

"If they're home for us to listen," Connie grumbled.

"With four of them living together, the odds are good that they'll talk about it there at some time or another. Especially with the trial taking place. That should promote some chatter."

Connie's tone brightened. "Actually, Roger told me that the trial is expected to wrap up in the next few days if defence doesn't take too long. The Crown is expecting a conviction, too. I bet you're right. That should get them talking."

"For sure it will," Jack replied. "Are you or any of Roger's teams following Kondrat and Pratt around?"

"No, we don't want to take a chance on heating them up. If they think we're on to them, they might suspect we've bugged their place. If they're relaxed, it might loosen their tongues more."

"If their guy goes to jail, they may seek revenge against the United Front," Jack noted.

"Good point. Maybe we'll hear them planning something. Perhaps talk about making sure they shoot the right guy."

"Exactly."

"Hope so." Connie paused. "Anyway, you've really helped me out. I can't thank you enough."

When Jack ended the call, he told Laura about his conversation.

"I bet you're right that things could heat up if there's a conviction," Laura said.

"Yes, and if so they might be looking for more weapons," Jack stated optimistically.

"That'd be nice," Laura replied. "Between us, Roger's teams, and ATF, we could have it wrapped up soon."

"Hopefully, but speaking of Roger, I'd like him to lend us some surveillance teams for this coming weekend. Graves is supposed to deliver the guns on Monday."

"Right. That," Laura said, looking concerned. "I don't like the idea that we're responsible for four more handguns on the street. Laser-grip, even."

Yeah, I don't like it either. "I don't feel we have much choice. We can hem and hah and philosophize about it, but my feeling is that I'd rather Satans Wrath have a few more weapons in their arsenal than allow the street gangs to become better armed."

"Guess you have a point there," Laura replied.

Jack reached for his phone.

Roger listened as Jack told him he suspected Graves would be obtaining guns over the weekend and then asked for help doing surveillance, starting Friday afternoon.

"Sure, I'll send some teams your way," Roger said. "The only thing is the trial is expected to end this week. If we get an indication that any of the gangers are heading out to kill someone, we may have to pull off from helping you."

"I understand. Laura and I will each work different shifts over the weekend and hopefully pair up with your team. I'd like to get a tracker on his truck, but I'm told he checks for one every time he heads out to do something of a criminal nature. If your crews are watching him when we're not around, I'd like to see how thorough he is when he searches."

"We'll see what we can do."

"I also don't want any heat. I'd rather lose him on surveillance than let him know we're on to him."

"You're the boss."

* * *

Late the following day Jack received an update from Connie. "The trial's over," she announced.

"That was fast. It's only Wednesday."

"Apparently, defence decided not to call any witnesses."

"And it was only yesterday you wanted me to risk my informant," Jack noted.

"I know. Sorry about that. I got emotional."

"Gee, isn't that what you accuse me of?"

"Yeah, well, I don't go overboard about it."

Overboard … guess that's a nicer word than implying I murder people, like you usually do.

"Anyway," Connie continued, "the good news is the punk from the Death Heads was convicted of first degree and sentencing is set for a week from today."

"Perfect," Jack said. "That should stir up some conversation. You going to spend tonight in the monitor room listening to the room bug?"

"You bet I am. The monitors are working until midnight, but if Kondrat or Pratt are home shooting their mouths off, I'm not going to wait until morning to find out what they're saying. I wouldn't be able to sleep regardless."

"Hope it works out. Also, thanks for letting me know. Give me a call to tell me how it went."

"You got it."

* * *

Connie was good to her word. When Jack arrived at work Thursday morning, Connie had left a message. He noted that it had come in at 4:40 a.m.

"Things are hot," Connie had said. Then he heard her yawn. "But nothing that helps me. The four of them went to bed a few minutes ago. They're really pissed off over the trial and said they needed to do something, but didn't suggest what. Other than that, they're also pissed off at Borman, saying what a pussy he is and that it's time they got rid of him. By that, it didn't sound like they were think-ing of killing him. I think they just want him replaced. Anyway, time for bed. Maybe next week after sentencing we'll get something."

Jack deleted the message, then ruminated about it. He recalled Lance's words for the prosecutor to be wary, with mention that she could get a rock tossed through her window.

If Borman's no longer in charge, will they decide to do something more than throw a rock through Ana's window? He subconsciously bit his lower lip as he thought. *How stupid are they?*

Chapter Eighteen

It was approaching suppertime when Buster Linquist parked the moving truck behind the storage company he worked for. He was tired and hungry, but he knew his day wasn't over yet.

It was the third Thursday of the month. Church night. The monthly meeting would take place at the clubhouse, and he had to be there.

As a prospect, he wouldn't be allowed to take part in the meeting. His job was to cater to the whims of the members, such as washing their bikes, perhaps providing security where needed, and most definitely cleaning up the clubhouse after.

He was in a hurry to leave work, but when he rounded the side of the building where he'd parked his new ride, he stopped, his mouth gaped open in shock. Kondrat sat side-saddle on the seat of the Harley, staring at him. Behind him Pratt had tilted one of the rear-views up and appeared to be squeezing a pimple on his face.

"What the fuck?" Linquist roared as he broke into a run. "That's my hog you're messin' with!"

Pratt stepped back, but Kondrat remained seated. When Linquist was within striking range, he pulled his fist back to take aim at Kondrat's face.

"I wouldn't do that if I were you." Pratt barked. He leered at Linquist as he held a pistol in his hand, waving the muzzle from side to side as an added warning.

Linquist hesitated then lowered his fist. "What the fuck you doing? I'm not in the mood for games!"

Kondrat smiled and slid off the bike, leaving his jacket open to show he also had a pistol tucked in the front of his waistband. "You see, the thing is, we ain't nobody's bitches."

"You won't get away with slappin' us around like that little asshole-suck Borman," Pratt chipped in.

"What do you want? Why're you here?" Linquist asked, making a conscious effort to control his rage.

"Now that's better," Kondrat said. He grinned and spoke over his shoulder at Pratt. "I told you these guys would be reasonable."

Pratt smiled and folded his arms across his chest, which would conceal his pistol from any passersby.

Linquist glared as he locked eyes with Kondrat.

"What we want is respect," Kondrat stated. "You an' your other guys won't be dealin' through Borman any-more. We gave him his walkin' papers today."

"You're telling me that Borman's no longer boss?"

"That's right," Kondrat replied. "The Death Heads are officially under new management. You can pass that on to whoever."

"Under new management," Linquist repeated. "Who?"

Kondrat looked taken back. "Me," he stated, sounding irritated that the question was even asked.

"You?" *Fuck me, you gotta be kiddin'.*

"That's right. From now on, you'll be dealing through me."

"I see."

Kondrat stared at him.

If you're looking for a reaction, I'm not going to give you one. I'll be the good little messenger boy like you've asked me to be. Then, when I get the okay, I'll rip your nuts off and shove 'em down your throat. After that I'll gut the both of you.

"Also, tell your guys there's gonna be some changes," Kondrat stated firmly.

"Such as?"

Kondrat paused, loudly inhaling mucus from his sinuses before spitting.

Is that supposed to impress me?

"Such as, you won't be tellin' us how to run our business," Kondrat continued.

"In what way?"

"In every fucking way," Pratt said, coming around from behind the bike. "Yesterday that bitch prosecutor convicted our bro. He'll be gettin' sentenced next week."

"Yeah ... so?"

"So seeing as she's gonna put him away, we're gonna put her away," Kondrat stated.

"Yeah," Pratt said. He gestured at Kondrat with his thumb. "Last time the two of us only kicked her fuckin' mom's door open. This time it's gonna be different. *A lot different.*"

"And it ain't none of your fuckin' business," Kondrat stated, pointing his finger for emphasis.

Linquist sneered. "Sure, no skin off my ass. I'll pass the word. Anything else?"

"Yeah, one more thing," Kondrat said. "Tell your people if they don't show us the respect we deserve, then we'll swing over to the Asians. See how much coin you'd lose out of your piggy banks then."

"I'll tell them." He then moved close enough to Kondrat that their faces were almost touching. "Now get the fuck away from my bike," he snarled. "Come near it again and you're dead."

Kondrat let out a snort then glanced at Pratt before the two slunk away.

Chapter Nineteen

At 8:30 p.m. Jack was watching TV with Natasha when his phone vibrated. He recognized the number as belonging to Lance. "What's up?" he asked.

Lance was unusually terse. "Quite a bit. We need to talk."

"Has the deal with Linquist been postponed?"

"No, so far that's still a go. That's not why I called. We need to meet in person as soon as possible."

Okay, about the only thing he doesn't like to talk to me about over a phone is murder. Who, when, and why? "I'm available, but isn't it church night?" He saw Natasha make a face.

"I'm outside the clubhouse now," Lance continued, "but I'm skipping it."

Okay, I don't like the sounds of that. "Usual place?"

"You at home?" Lance asked.

"Yes," Jack replied, feeling uneasy. *You're not dropping in for a beer....*

"How about someplace halfway to save time?"

"There's a parking lot on the west side of Crab Park off of West Waterfront Road. It's between the park and the Pan Pacific Hotel, close to where the Helijet lands. It'll be empty at this time of night."

"I'll be there. Twenty minutes."

"I'll be waiting."

* * *

It was dark when Jack saw Lance's van pull in and skid to a stop. Seconds later they met outside their vehicles. There were certain conversations that neither one of them ever wanted to discuss inside a car, building, or over the phone.

Jack listened as they strolled through the lot while Lance told him about Linquist's confrontation with Kondrat and Pratt.

"You know we can't let this sit," Lance said when he finished.

"I know," Jack replied. "Wait a sec while I make a call, then we'll talk."

"There ain't a lot of time," Lance noted.

Jack motioned with his hand for him to calm down while he walked out of earshot then made a hasty call to the monitoring room. "Nicole, I'm glad it's you working tonight," he said.

Nicole was good at her job, and despite the fact that Jack's phone was blocked she identified him by his voice. "Hey, Jack. Dare I ask why?" she replied.

"Do you know if the two rats, I mean Kondrat and Pratt, are home?"

"They are, along with both roommates."

"Is Connie with you?"

"Not tonight. She was in last night. What's up?"

"I heard a rumour that Kondrat and Pratt could be up to something. Anything to indicate that on your end?"

"They got home about an hour ago and were bragging to their roommates about telling someone off. They had music on and with the noise it was hard to tell, but they mentioned a name once. It sounded like Buster. Something along those lines. Other than that, only the usual crude and juvenile behaviour you'd expect from their calibre."

"Call me if they leave tonight, will you?" Jack asked.

"You got it, but there's nobody working in here after midnight."

Jack glanced at his watch. "That's fine." He then ended the call and returned to where Lance waited.

"So, these two punks had to be dealt with," Lance stated while giving Jack an angry look, perhaps expecting him to object.

"Makes sense to me," Jack replied indifferently. He eyed Lance curiously. "Had to be dealt with?"

"The hit is in progress as we speak. I gave the order to —"

"I don't need names," Jack said, "only details."

Lance looked puzzled.

"It's easier if I don't know the names for later on if I'm questioned. Provides you more protection in the event someone in my outfit gets the idea to arrest them. Saves me from having to lie."

Lance frowned. "Okay, the job was given to two club members, one of whom is good at picking locks."

Picking locks ... that narrows it down to about three that I know of. Better tell Nicole to take her headphones off before she gets a broken eardrum ...

Lance looked concerned. "Besides those two, only me, my vice-prez, and Whiskey Jake know about it."

"I understand."

"Good." Lance paused. "I can tell you who won't be involved. We told Linquist to go to the hospital emergency tonight and put blood in his piss to fake a bladder infection or something."

"In other words, an alibi," Jack noted.

"He'll know it's goin' down tonight, but not how or by whom."

"With so few knowing about it, there'd be serious heat if your two guys were caught."

Lance looked startled. "Of course there would!"

"Relax. I said I understand. Don't worry, I won't interfere. Simply thinking out loud."

"Oh ... okay, good." Lance took a deep breath, then continued, "My idea is to give the Death Heads an idea of how professional we are."

"Professional? Are you thinking a car bomb?"

"No, with that there's always a chance we'd kill the wrong person or some citizen walking past."

"You're going to shoot them?"

Lance nodded. "Yes, but anyone could walk into their place and blast them. If we did that, they're liable to think someone in the United Front did it. My plan won't leave any doubt it was us and probably prevent retaliation."

"What's your way?" Jack asked.

"They live in some one-room dump with two other guys," Lance said.

"I'm listening."

"I want to have them taken out after they all go to sleep."

"The four of them?"

"No, only the two rats." Lance smirked. "My guys will use silencers. The other two kids won't be disturbed."

"Oh, shit," Jack said as he imagined waking up and finding the person beside you had been murdered while you slept. He looked at Lance. "I'm pretty sure they'll get the message."

"That if you decide to fuck with us, you won't sleep well," Lance stated.

"Your two-man team knows what they look like, I presume?" Jack said.

"Linquist said the other two have beards, so the two rats will be easy to identify. The idea is to sneak in quiet ... real quiet if you guys have the place bugged, get the job done, and slip away."

Jack noticed Lance studying his face when he spoke. "I couldn't tell you if it was bugged," he replied.

Lance shrugged. "Doesn't matter. I doubt anything will be heard until the other two wake up. Ought to make their assholes pucker once they see what happened when they were in la-la land."

"I'm sure it'll give them something to talk about over their Fruit Loops," Jack said. "Same for everyone else in the gang."

"That's the idea."

"You'll know as soon as it's done?"

"Yes, I'll give you a call." Lance paused, appearing to think about something, then shook his head. "Kids these days … seems like they've never been taught to respect anyone or —"

Jack held up his hand for Lance to stop as he answered his phone.

"Jack, it's Nicole. Kondrat and Pratt left the house."

"Any indication why?"

"No, Kondrat said … 'that's it.' Then they left. The other two are still home. Sounds like they're playing video games."

"Keep me appraised if you find their whereabouts," Jack said as he sprinted toward his car.

"I take it we're done!" Lance yelled.

"Call me when you hear," Jack replied. *That's if I don't kill them first.…*

Chapter Twenty

"Laura," Jack said tersely when she answered. "I want you over at Ana's house ASAP. Wear your vest. I'm on my way there now."

"Ana?"

"The prosecutor who had her mother's door kicked in by the Death Heads. I just spoke with our friend. Kondrat and Pratt were the ones who did that and it sounds like they're planning to kill her. They both left their place about a minute ago and we don't know if they're going to Ana's or not."

"Oh, man."

"No worries. Even if they drive straight there it'll take them at least forty-five minutes. I'm fifteen minutes from my house, but if I hustle I've still got time to go there and grab my vest and the shotgun. We've each got time to be there ahead of them."

"Where does she live?"

"I'll give you the address. From your place you're maybe thirty minutes away. We'll probably arrive at the same time."

"You calling VPD or backup?"

"Can't. It'd throw too much heat on our friend if they were arrested and it went to court. Defence council would be all over us. If Kondrat and Pratt are planning this on their own, it'd be obvious that our source was in the bikers. Only a few people know, and it wasn't mentioned on the room bug."

"So it'll only be you and me," Laura said.

"This is only for tonight in case they show up. There's more happening that I'll tell you about when you get there."

"I take it that if they do show up, you don't plan on arresting them?"

Jack paused. "You ready to copy her address?"

"Oh, man ... yeah, go ahead."

* * *

Jack had retrieved a shotgun from his house and was nearing Ana's house when he decided to call her. She answered over the background noise of Isabella crying.

"Ana, sorry, I hope I didn't disturb you. It's Jack Taggart calling."

"Oh ... hi. Give me a moment. Issy woke up screaming and Pietro's at a seminar in Ottawa. Hang on a sec."

Jack listened as Ana tried to soothe Isabella. It was met with partial success.

"I'm back," she announced. "No, you didn't disturb me. I was about to pour myself a glass of wine and run a bath. You heard there was a conviction, right?"

"I heard. Congratulations."

"Thanks. I take it you've got that authorization ready that you spoke about?"

"No, this is something else. I'm pulling up to your house now. We need to talk about something."

A moment later, Jack parked on the street. He then hid a Bushmaster shotgun with folded stock inside his jacket and clamped it in place with his arm. He then took in the surroundings as he approached Ana's house, noticing which cars were already parked nearby, what bushes planted near the house could be used to conceal someone. He was glad to see that the drapes in the living room were already closed.

The front door opened when he neared and he saw Ana holding Isabella in one arm.

"That was quick. Come on in," she said cheerily.

Jack entered the foyer and closed the door behind him. He smiled at Isabella, who briefly hid her face in her mother's neck before turning to peek at him.

"Let me take your jacket," Ana said. "We can sit in the living room."

"Hello," Isabella said, pointing her finger at him.

"Hello," Jack answered back.

"Well, your mood has brightened," Ana noted as she looked at Isabella before turning her attention back to Jack. "You said you have two boys. Do you think children can get nightmares when they're this young?" She stood bouncing Isabella in her arms.

"I'm not sure. Did you ask her?"

Ana flashed a smile. "That sounds like the appropriate thing to do, but she doesn't articulate that well yet."

"My boys are ten and eleven. They definitely have nightmares on occasion." *No thanks to me.* "I can't remember how old they were the first time," he added, trying to ignore the pang of guilt he felt about the stress he put his family through.

"I guess it's all part of growing up," Ana concluded. "Coffee?"

"Uh, no thanks," Jack replied, hesitating with his arm clamped over his jacket.

Ana noticed and gestured to his arm. "Did you hurt yourself?"

"No, I'm fine. It's in relation to what I want to talk to you about."

"Oh?"

"I don't want you to be alarmed, but, uh, I'm carrying this." He reached inside his jacket and retrieved the shotgun.

"Oh, fuck," Ana blurted out.

"Oh, fuck," echoed Isabella in a high-pitched voice that caught their attention.

Ana stared open-mouthed at her daughter.

Jack hid his smile. *She cares more about what Isabella said than the fact that I'm holding a shotgun.*

"Pietro is going to kill me," Ana said.

"I've slipped up with my own sons when they were that age. I think the best approach is to ignore it and not give them any attention."

"Oh, fuck. Oh, fuck," Isabella repeated.

For Jack, the sound of a car rapidly approaching from the end of the block brought an immediate sense of urgency. "Get back out of sight," he ordered, while flicking off the foyer and front porch lights.

Ana's gasp was audible as she retreated with Isabella while Jack opened the door a crack and peered out.

The car slowed as it neared, then Jack felt the tension ease from his body. "It's okay," he shouted as he turned the lights back on. "False alarm. It's my partner."

Ana peaked from around a corner. Her face and her voice betrayed her fear. "What's ... what's happening?"

"A threat was made against you, but now that my partner's arrived, everything's under control."

"A threat?"

"Yes. It may have only been false bravado, but we need to talk."

Without taking her eyes off the shotgun, Ana said, "What should I do with Isabella?"

"You can put her back to bed if you want. Really, I'm not going to let anything happen to you ... or her. Trust me, you'll be safe."

Ana swallowed nervously. "I'll be right back."

"Before you go, is your back door locked and any shades or curtains closed?"

"Yes. All my outdoor lights are on, too. I always make sure I do that when Pietro's away. I also have an alarm system."

"Great. This looks and sounds worse than it is. Everything is going to be okay. The problem is only temporary and I expect it will be cleared up overnight."

Ana took a deep breath and slowly exhaled. "Okay, I'll put her to bed and be right back."

Jack watched Ana go up the stairs to the second floor, then let Laura in. A moment later Ana returned without Isabella and introductions were made. They then went to the living room.

"Okay, let me begin," Jack said, from where he sat in a chair with the shotgun laying across his lap. "Laura and I have a high-level informant, one that you're familiar with from Connie's wiretap application."

Ana nodded.

"Tonight he told me that Kondrat and Pratt said they were going to kill you."

"They actually said that?"

"I believe their words were that they were going to *put you away*. In their language, that means to kill you."

"Did they tell your informant for sure that it was me they were after? Last time —" Ana couldn't bring herself to finish the sentence, opting instead to look up the stairs to where she'd put Isabella to bed.

"The threat relayed to my informant was only about you. Nobody else."

"Relayed?" Ana questioned. "This isn't first-hand?"

"No, but —"

"Was there anything on the wiretap to corroborate what your informant told you?" Ana asked anxiously.

"No. If it hadn't been for my informant we wouldn't know about it. He'd also be in jeopardy if the bad guys found out we know, which is why I haven't notified anyone other than Laura at the moment."

"Still, your informant is getting this second-hand," Ana noted, grasping on to hope. "Perhaps it isn't as accurate as —"

"It's accurate," Jack said. "The person they told works for my informant. It's the same prospect and the veracity of what was said would be the same as what I presented in Connie's wiretap application. I can assure you that what

Kondrat and Pratt said to the prospect would have been repeated to my informant word for word."

Ana went from feelings of denial to anger — at Jack. "You told me to maybe expect a rock through my window," she said harshly.

"I know. We discovered that the person who was controlling the Death Heads was replaced by Kondrat. Things change. I'm sorry."

Ana pursed her lips, perhaps in an attempt to control her emotions. It didn't work and tears formed in her eyes.

"I can assure you that you will not be in any danger," Jack said firmly.

Ana gave him a look of exasperation. "How can you say that?" she demanded. "What do you plan to do? Provide round-the-clock protection for God knows how long?"

"That won't be necessary. I'd like to stay in your house tonight while Laura monitors from outside. I'm confident that the threat against you will be taken care of by morning."

"Taken care of? Like you did last time? How do you know they won't change their minds again?"

"No, it won't be taken care of like last time. Kondrat and Pratt did something tonight that for them was far more dangerous than threatening to kill you."

"They killed someone else?" Ana blurted. "They're going to be arrested?"

"No, what they did wasn't a criminal act. What they did was show disrespect."

"Disrespect?" Ana repeated, looking puzzled.

"Disrespect in the world my informant lives in is viewed as a serious matter."

Ana's mouth gaped as she stared at Jack. When she recovered, she simply said, "Oh … I see."

Do you? You realize that I didn't say they'd be murdered to protect you if something is made of this later? Jack cleared his throat and continued. "I can tell you that I-HIT was successful in getting a room bug in where Kondrat and Pratt live."

"Are they home now?" Ana asked.

"No, that's why we're here. They left their place about forty-five minutes ago and we don't know where they went. That was at the same time I found out that they'd made a threat against you earlier in the evening." Jack did his best to give a reassuring smile. "We are here likely in an overabundance of caution. In my mind, if they were going to come after you, they'd wait until after their guy was sentenced, but I can't be sure."

"No disrespect, but with only the two of you, it doesn't seem like you're using an overabundance of caution to me."

"There are only two of them, and they won't be expecting anything." Jack tapped the shotgun. "Trust me, if they show up, they'll be leaving in body bags."

"A pleasant thought," Ana said disdainfully. "Wouldn't that then jeopardize your informant because it would be obvious you had advance knowledge?"

"It might cause some suspicion, but the blame could be directed at Kondrat and Pratt for having done or said something to have alerted us."

"Particularly if they're not alive to refute it," Ana said, while casting a hard look at Jack.

Now you're getting the picture. "With luck, they won't even show. The people who were disrespected are taking immediate action."

"You're talking about Satans Wrath."

"Yes."

"By immediate action, you mean tonight?"

"Yes, tonight."

Ana took a deep breath and slowly exhaled.

Is she relieved that the assholes are going to be murdered? Or concerned that she knows about it and could be in trouble for not stopping it?

"Again, I cannot stress how important it is for my informant's survival that our knowledge of this not get out," Jack said firmly.

Ana appeared to mull things over, then asked, "This disrespect you talk about, is it because Satans Wrath told the Death Heads to leave me alone and they're not?"

"Basically, that's what prompted it, but, again, if word got out it would jeopardize my informant."

"So, what is going to happen tonight is because of me? All because Kondrat and Pratt are disobeying the order to leave me alone?"

You sound like you're blaming yourself. "Only partially," Jack replied, emphasizing his words. "They both showed a lack of respect with not only how they delivered the message to Satans Wrath, but by telling them that their advice would no longer be heeded."

"How they delivered the message?" Ana questioned.

"They weren't polite enough."

"I knew I should have gone into corporate law," Ana stated, sounding less angry and scared. She looked at Jack a moment. "Do you have any thoughts on how Kondrat and Pratt intend to kill me?"

"My guess is they would wait for you to back your car out of the garage in the morning, then block your exit and run up and shoot you."

"That'd be far easier than trying to kick in the door to your house, wondering if you had a gun because of what they did before," Laura added. "Not to mention, you live in an upscale neighbourhood. These gangs have a lot of experience when it comes to breaking into homes. I'm sure they'd figure your place was alarmed and worry about you hitting the panic button. They'd know your call would be treated with priority."

Providing they don't know how to dismantle the alarm from the outside. He looked at Ana. *Guess she doesn't need to hear that.*

"You're thinking of something," Ana said as she stared back.

"Yes, if they don't return home tonight, we'll play it by ear, but I've got a couple of options. Tomorrow morning I may get Laura to back your car out of the garage with me hiding either nearby or in the back seat."

"What if they're waiting at my mother's place?" Ana asked.

"That brings me to another option. If they're lurking around your mother's place, then I might contact my informant and mention where they are, simply to confirm with him as to whether or not Satans Wrath has changed their minds on doing to Kondrat and Pratt whatever it is they intended to do."

"Satans Wrath would then know where they were and ..." Ana stopped talking and stared at Jack.

"As I said, we'll have to play it by ear. Things could

change by —" He felt his phone vibrate. "Hold on, incoming call." The room became silent as Jack reached for his phone.

"Jack, it's Nicole. Kondrat and Pratt are back. Sounds like they made a booze run and picked up a pizza."

Perfect. Jack felt instant relief. "Thanks, Nicole. If they take off again before you go, let me know."

"Will do. I suspect they're in for the night, though. Sounds like they're sucking on a pipe, as well. Don't know if it's pot or crack."

"Good," Jack replied. *It'll make it easier to kill them.*

"Good?" Nicole asked.

"I meant that I know where they are," Jack replied. He then ended the call and told Ana and Laura what he'd been told by Nicole.

Ana swallowed. "Are you both leaving, then?"

Jack shook his head. "We'll still be your bodyguards tonight. If they're getting drunk or high, it's still possible they'll decide to do something stupid."

"Likely more possible," Laura noted.

Jack tried to give Ana a smile of assurance. "I'll stay inside and Laura will cover from outside."

"The disadvantage of being junior," Laura quipped.

Ana's face looked grim, but she kept her thoughts to herself. "Anything I can get either of you? Coffee, tea?"

"A coffee would be nice," Jack replied.

"I'll put a pot on in the kitchen and you can help yourself," Ana replied. She eyed Laura.

"Nothing for me," Laura responded. "I don't want to be running in to use your bathroom. If you have a spare blanket, though, that'd be nice."

Jack smiled to himself when he saw Ana frown.

Laura quickly added, "Not for sleeping. Simply to keep warm. I can't sit in my car with the engine on because the exhaust would give me away."

"Oh … I'll get you one," Ana said, getting to her feet, "then I'll put the coffee on." She eyed the shotgun on Jack's lap before leaving the room. "Please try not to shoot up my place too much. I taught Isabella one bad word. I think that's enough for one day."

Jack grinned.

* * *

It was 6:00 a.m. when Ana plodded into the living room wearing a housecoat. "Long night?" she asked.

"Probably longer for you," Jack replied.

"I didn't get much sleep, that's for sure," Ana admitted. "I'll put on a fresh pot of coffee if you'd like some more."

Jack gestured for her to wait as he answered his phone.

"It's done," Lance said.

"Any problems or collateral damage?"

"No," Lance replied, then terminated the call.

Jack saw Ana looking at him with raised eyebrow. "You can rest easy," he said, getting to his feet. "There won't be any further threats coming your way."

"Kondrat and Pratt, they're …"

"Yes."

Ana's jaw slackened briefly. "You're sure?"

"Positive. Nobody knows yet, outside of us and those who, uh, dealt with the problem."

Ana was quiet as Jack put his coat and shoes on in the foyer, then she placed her hand on his arm. "Thank you."

"You're welcome. Any time."

"I hope there is never another time," she said seriously.

Jack nodded. "Take care." He then stepped outside and saw Laura watching from her car.

He felt good as he walked over to where she was parked. When she unrolled the window, he said, "It's done."

"Our friend called to confirm?"

"Yes. You can go home. Count last night as your shift for today."

"Did it go as planned?" Laura asked.

"Apparently it did. He didn't say much."

"You heading home, too?"

Jack grimaced. "No, my day is just beginning. I need to put in a report and see how Lexton handles it."

Laura looked surprised. "You're going to tell her? I don't think Ana will say anything."

Jack made a face. "Satans Wrath's fingerprints will be all over it. In fact, they want them to be. I need to nip this in the bud and convince Lexton that I wasn't involved." He paused. "Well, sort of not involved."

"Oh, man." Laura gestured toward Ana's house. "Maybe you should go back and ask her if she could recommend a good lawyer," she said wryly.

Jack sighed.

Chapter Twenty-One

Jack arrived at his office and prepared a short informant debriefing report outlining what had taken place. He kept it brief. In part, it said:

20:50 hours — The writer was notified by the informant that Aron Kondrat and Jeremy Pratt, both members of a street gang called the Death Heads, told Buster Linquist earlier in the evening that they planned to murder Ana Valesi, who is a Crown prosecutor. Buster Linquist is a prospect for Satans Wrath and is subservient to the informant who is a full-patch member.

Linquist also told the informant that he was told that it was Kondrat and Pratt who, while armed with handguns, kicked in the door to Valesi's mother's home less than a month ago as noted in a previous debriefing report dated April 1.

Kondrat and Pratt did not reveal their plans to Linquist as to when or how Valesi was to be murdered. The informant expressed concern that few people knew about Kondrat and Pratt's plan and that his life could be in jeopardy if immediate action was taken to arrest them or have them brought in for questioning.

The informant further reported that Kondrat and Pratt showed disrespect toward Satans Wrath when they spoke with Linquist. As a result, Lance Morgan, who is the president of the Westside chapter of Satans Wrath, and Jake Yevdokymenko, who is the president of the Eastside chapter, conspired to have Kondrat and Pratt executed for what they perceived to be bad manners. They then assigned two as yet unidentified club members to carry out the order. With the exception of these two, only three other Satans Wrath members (including the informant) know the details, so again, any action taken by the police would jeopardise the informant.

It should be noted that Kondrat and Pratt are the primary suspects in an ongoing murder investigation and their threat to murder Ana Valesi was taken seriously. As a result, the writer took immediate steps to ensure the safety of Ana Valesi and her family.

At 06:00 hours this date, the informant advised that the aforementioned club presidents indicated that both Kondrat and Pratt had been murdered in their sleep within the last couple of hours. Two *associates who lived with Kondrat and Pratt by the names of Peter Jones and Ronald Pierce were unharmed and apparently asleep when the murders took place.*

It is the writer's opinion that Ana Valesi is no longer in danger.

As soon as Rose arrived at work, Jack strode into her office. "Good morning," she said jauntily, while taking off her coat.

"Good morning to you, too," Jack responded in kind. "Beautiful day." Then his tone became serious. "Hopefully it'll stay that way."

Rose gave him a hard look, then took a seat behind her desk. "What's up?"

Jack handed her his report and sat across from her. "Laura and I worked all night. I sent her home, but thought I should give you this report and be around in the event any questions arise."

Rose read the report, then looked intense as she viewed him over her glasses. "In the event any questions arise?" She glanced at the report. "Christ, couldn't you have waited until I'd had my morning coffee?"

"Your morning coffee? I've been up since *yesterday* morning."

"What did I-HIT say about this?"

"I don't think they know yet. The two roommates probably haven't woken to discover the bodies."

"You haven't told them?" Rose's eyes flashed with anger. "Call them immediately!"

Jack gestured with the palms of his hands for her to calm down. "Okay, no reason to give me the stink eye. I was only told they were dead this morning. I barely finished the report when you arrived. I was about to call I-HIT, but thought you'd like to know first."

Rose stared open-mouthed at Jack, then appeared to become more agitated. "Okay, so now I know! Call them!"

"I'm sitting right here," Jack said calmly. "No need to yell." *There's that stink eye again.*

Rose paused to take a deep breath. "With this report, you better get used to it." Her tone was stilted as she made an apparent effort to control her ire. "It's not only me who'll be yelling," she warned.

"Okay, I'll go call Connie," Jack said as he stood up.

"No, sit! Call her from here, damn it."

Jack gave his wide-eyed look of innocence, then sat and took out his phone.

Rose took a deep breath and exhaled audibly, then her voice returned to normal. "I want to listen. If you're passed off to Inspector Dyck, I may need to handle the flak. Also, we're going to have to meet with Lexton. No doubt I-HIT will want to be in on that as well."

Jack tapped in Connie's number and put his phone on speaker so Rose could listen.

"So, you've heard," Connie said, sounding both pleased and excited when she answered. "I'm almost there. Heading down the hall right now."

This doesn't sound like Connie. What the hell? Did she overdose on happy pills? "Heard what?" he asked.

"The room bug! It worked. We got 'em!"

"Kondrat and Pratt?"

An Element of Risk

"Of course, Kondrat and Pratt. Who else would it be?"

"I hadn't heard that you got them," Jack stated. *Someone else ... yeah.*

"Sure did! I got a call this morning to say that they listened to a recording made last night. Both Kondrat and Pratt talked about killing Irving by mistake. Can you believe it?"

"Well —"

"Wait, there's more." Connie's voice became grave. "Apparently they're planning to kill Ana Valesi next week right after their buddy is sentenced."

"You got that on the wire, too?"

"That's what I was told. I tell you, these guys are going down big time! And Jack, I owe it all to you."

"Actually to my informant," Jack replied. "Hopefully you understand why I need to protect him." He glanced at Rose, who looked irked at his comment. *Come on, Rose, that was a good line. Might as well prime her when I can. She'll be hearing it again when we talk to Lexton....*

"He definitely came through for us, that's for sure," Connie said.

"Did the monitors happen to mention if Kondrat and Pratt talked about Satans Wrath at all?"

"No, but hang on, I'm entering their office as we speak. I'll ask."

Jack listened to some background conversation and then Connie came back on the phone.

"Apparently they did talk about telling someone off by the name of Buster and the need to stand up to those guys." She paused, and when Jack didn't reply, she asked, "Is Buster with Satans Wrath?"

"Yes, his name is Buster Linquist and he's a prospect for the club."

Connie let out a snort. "I'm surprised Kondrat and Pratt didn't get punched in the face. From what I've heard, Satans Wrath doesn't take well to being told off."

"Yeah ... I've heard that, too," Jack replied. *Okay, Rose, no need to roll your eyes.*

"So why'd you call if it wasn't over this?" Connie asked.

"Well, Connie, the thing is, I received some information from my informant at six o'clock this morning. He told me that Kondrat and Pratt were murdered last night. Both shot while they slept."

"What!" Connie exclaimed, then paused. "Nice going, Jack ... trying to rattle my chain. Obviously, we'd have heard if that had happened."

"Do you have a phone number for either of the two roommates?"

"We have a number for Peter Jones, why?"

"Give it a wrong number call and then have the monitor turn the volume back up."

"Are you serious?" Connie asked.

"I was told that, so let's check it out."

"You better not be joking around," Connie warned.

Jack didn't reply. He then listened to Connie muttering in the background and a moment later he heard her apologize to someone for calling the wrong number.

"I did it," Connie said, when she came back on the phone.

"Good. Let's wait a moment," Jack said.

A minute passed and Jack and Rose sat in silence, then Connie said, "This is bullshit. I woke him up and it sounds like he went to the can. I can hear him coming back into the room. There's nothing to indicate anything's wrong. Looks like your guy is way off on —"

Jack heard the screaming emitting from the recorder in the monitor room and understood why Connie hadn't finished her sentence. When she spoke again, Jack held the phone away from his ear.

"You did this!" Connie yelled. "You bastard! You —"

Jack put his phone away and turned to Rose. "I detected a hint of annoyance. What do you think?"

"I think I better call Lexton before they do."

"Hopefully she doesn't think I'm a bastard, too," said Jack.

Chapter Twenty-Two

Jack plunked himself down at his desk and called Roger. After exchanging greetings, he said, "I called to let you know that Kondrat and Pratt were murdered last night by someone from Satans Wrath."

"From Satans Wrath? Holy shit! Why?"

Jack then told him about Kondrat and Pratt's meeting with Linquist.

"Those bastards," Roger replied when he heard that Ana's life had been threatened. "Good news then that they're dead."

Jack yawned. "I think so. Let me tell you the rest."

"Christ," Roger said, when Jack told him that he and Laura had spent the night at Ana's house. "You could have called me. I'd have helped."

"I'm not sure how this will pan out with the brass. I figured the fewer who knew the better. No use all of us getting in trouble. Besides, I had Laura with me. Taking care of Kondrat and Pratt wouldn't have been a problem."

"Or worrying if you called backup as to what someone might say if you were, uh, forced to kill them yourself," Roger commented.

"That, too," Jack admitted.

"When it comes to protecting Ana, you could've trusted me," Roger said. "As far as the brass go, if they didn't like how the situation was handled, I wouldn't give a shit. I'm due to retire anyway." When Jack didn't reply, he asked, "How was Ana when you left?"

"Her husband's in Ottawa at a conference, but she seems okay. Tired, but okay."

"The poor woman. I'll call her later. So, tell me, how were the two rats killed?"

"It happened when they were asleep."

"Asleep? Were Jones and Pierce killed, too?"

"No." Jack then related how the murders took place.

"Holy shit," Roger repeated. "Remind me to buy a guard dog."

"They wouldn't be averse to shooting it either," Jack stated.

"Have you talked to Connie yet? She'll probably be ticked off after going to all the work of getting a wiretap and putting a bug in their place."

"I called her a couple of minutes ago. She's more than ticked. It turns out that last night they got Kondrat and Pratt on wire talking about killing Irving by mistake. They also heard them planning to murder Ana."

"No kidding? Wow. Sounds like Connie was a day late and a dollar short. At least it'll save her a lot of work preparing for trial."

"Yes, you'd think she'd be happy, but for some reason she figures I had a hand in what happened."

"I suspect you two have a bit of history," Roger noted.

"A bit," Jack admitted.

"Still, she shouldn't blame you. Seems to me what the two rats did was an act of suicide. It's not your fault. I told you they were dumb."

"Do me a favour and tell Connie that when she calls you."

"I will." Roger paused. "Do you still want us to follow Graves today and on the weekend?"

"Please. I've been up all night and I expect I'll be tied up here until late in the day. I'm sure he'll be getting the guns sometime over the weekend. I'll come in tomorrow, but if you could get your teams started on their own today it would be greatly appreciated."

"No problem. Considering what happened last night, I imagine the Death Heads will be running home to their mommies. At the very least it'll take their minds off attacking the United Front."

Jack ended the call as Rose stuck her head into his office and waved a copy of his report. "I spoke with Lexton. She wants me to drop this off immediately."

"Maybe you should've waited until she had her morning coffee," Jack noted.

Rose made a rude gesture with her finger, then left. Twenty minutes passed before she returned.

"I take it that she had you wait while she read it?" Jack asked.

"Yes."

"And?"

Rose shook her head. "I don't know."

"You don't know? Give me a hint. Did you have to perform CPR?"

"I think she was too gobsmacked to know what to think. Inspector Dyck also called her when I was there. We're all scheduled to meet in an hour."

"Great. That gives us time to have a coffee."

Although an olive soup would be better.

* * *

Jack and Rose entered Assistant Commissioner Lexton's office and saw that I-HIT had already arrived and were sitting with Lexton in a cluster of chairs around a coffee table.

Jack nodded cordially to the group. He received a curt response from both Lexton and Dyck, but Connie chose to cross her arms over her chest and ignore him.

Lexton gestured for them to take a seat. "Okay, let's get started, shall we? First of all, Corporal Taggart, would you object if Inspector Dyck and Corporal Crane read the informant debriefing report you submitted this morning?"

"I don't object to them reading it, provided they never disclose the information outside of this office," Jack replied. "My informant is connected to Satans Wrath and they've managed to corrupt officers before and gain access to secret information. If word got out that I'd an informant amongst them, it could be fatal for my source."

"I agree," Lexton replied, turning to Dyck and Connie. "I will allow both of you to read the report and we will discuss it after, but the contents of the report are never to be repeated outside of this room. Understood?"

Dyck and Connie each agreed. Lexton then handed Dyck a copy of the report while Connie leaned over to read it.

"So, you did know before they did it!" Connie blurted out, scowling at Jack.

"Yes, as noted in the report, I was told about it at 20:50 hours last night."

"Told about it?" Connie scoffed. "Or was it your idea because you acted on the spur of the moment when you first gave me Kondrat and Pratt's names? Then later became afraid that your informant might get burned so you conspired with him to do it!"

All eyes turned to Jack.

"I put a lot of thought into whether to help you when you first asked me for assistance," Jack said firmly. "As I did when I told you that my informant identified Kondrat and Pratt as the ones who murdered Irving. It wasn't something I did on the spur of the moment. Did I ... and do I have doubts? Yes, a little. I always worry about my informant's safety, but I decided prior to giving you any information that what I was going to give you was an acceptable element of risk for my informant."

"Really?" Connie said skeptically.

"Yes, really," Jack replied calmly. "Kondrat and Pratt were killed because they showed a total lack of respect to a criminal organization that exists, in good part, based on fear. Allowing someone like them to get away with what they did would seriously jeopardize that factor."

"Can you elaborate as to how Kondrat and Pratt exhibited disrespect?" Lexton asked. "Or 'bad manners' was how you worded it in your report."

"Basically, I was told that when Linquist finished work, he found Kondrat sitting on his motorcycle while Pratt was playing with the rear-view mirror. Linquist was going to punch Kondrat, but Pratt waved a gun in his face. Kondrat then told him that they were going to ignore the advice given earlier by Satans Wrath to leave the prosecutor alone and said they were going to kill her."

"Yes, I could understand why Satans Wrath would view that as disrespectful," Lexton stated.

"Where were you last night?" Connie asked.

"Corporal," Dyck stated sternly, "an accusation like that is uncalled for."

"It wasn't an accusation. I'm just curious if he witnessed what took place," Connie replied. "It wouldn't be the first time he stood by and watched someone being murdered."

"I wasn't there," Jack replied. "Me and Constable Secord spent the night at Ana Valesi's home, protecting her and her two-year-old baby — a sweet little tyke by the name of Isabella." Jack eyed Lexton. *Did that soften you up and bring you over to my side a little?*

Lexton's face hardened and she stared at Jack and gave a subtle shake of her head.

Ouch. She saw through that one.

"So you allowed the murders to take place to protect the prosecutor?" Inspector Dyck stated.

"I view that as a favourable outcome," Jack admitted, "and obviously it crossed my mind, but as noted in my report, the objective was also to protect my informant."

"Your report doesn't say who murdered Kondrat and Pratt," Connie stated.

"That's correct," Jack replied. "My informant didn't tell me the names."

"I bet," Connie said sarcastically.

"To help you understand," Jack said, "when my informant first came to work for me, I promised that I'd never burn him over information he gave me, but at the same time I told him that he's not immune from prosecution should some other officer catch him. In regard to this event, I didn't need to know the names."

"You're telling us you didn't need to know the names of two professional killers who belong to an international organized crime syndicate?" Lexton questioned.

"When I spoke with my informant, my concern was for his safety. I planned to submit a report on what he told me, but I'm not in a position to know where the report will end up as that decision is made above my rank level. I believed that if the killers were named, they could conceivably be arrested or questioned, which would greatly endanger my informant."

"I see," Lexton replied, looking disgruntled.

"Further to that, all members of Satans Wrath could be viewed as killers when it comes down to it. Anyone of them would murder if ordered to by the club, and there are many in the club who have committed murder."

"I suppose you have a point," Lexton conceded.

Jack turned to Connie. "I know that identifying who did these murders is important to you, but you have to look at the big picture from my perspective."

"I'm sick of hearing about the big picture," Connie stated. "We heard them mention Linquist's name on the wiretap as the person they told off, so obviously he was in on it. You can tell your source that we discovered that on our own!"

Jack looked at Connie calmly and said, "I will tell you that I know that Buster Linquist wasn't involved. From what I heard, he was at the hospital all night and was likely diagnosed with a bladder infection. If you do decide to pick him up, he'll call his lawyer immediately and you'll be wasting your time. He also wouldn't know who did it because not only is he still a prospect, but there is no reason for him to have been told. Everything would've been kept on a need-to-know basis."

"He had a bladder infection?" Inspector Dyck asked.

"No, he was told to fake one so that he'd have an alibi," Jack said, "in the event his name surfaced in the investigation."

"So Satans Wrath has anticipated that they'll be suspected of these murders," Lexton noted.

"They wanted to be," Jack replied. "The method they used was to instill fear amongst the criminal element about who they are and what they're capable of. It was also intended to scare the Death Heads, to prevent them from attempting any type of retaliation."

Connie made a face and pointed her finger at Jack. "If you'd told us, we could've set up on Kondrat and Pratt's place," she stated. "The Death Heads are often under surveillance. Roger's teams follow them a lot; not to mention they were subject of a wiretap. It'd make sense that we were watching. Then we could've caught the bikers in the act before they killed them."

"Then what, arrest two guys for possession of guns and burglary tools?" Jack asked. "Then have to provide twenty-four-hour protection on the prosecutor, not to mention Kondrat and Pratt?"

"We had them. I'd have arrested them this morning," Connie replied.

"Which we didn't know until this morning," Jack stated. "Even if Kondrat and Pratt had been arrested last night as soon as they made the admission, would that have stopped the Death Heads from sending someone else to kill Ana?" He waited a beat. "It would also jeopardize my source if they knew you were there in advance. It wouldn't take a defence lawyer long to figure that out. How many other nights have you watched their house?"

Connie's silence answered the question.

"Exactly, so to try to convince them that the night Satans Wrath sends a hit-team in is the same night you decide to conduct surveillance wouldn't be believed. Especially when a defence lawyer would bring it out that you'd already worked all day. The bikers would know they had a leak."

"It doesn't seem right," Connie lamented.

Jack shrugged. "As it happened, Ana is safe, and word will be out not to mess with her again. That seems right to me."

"And no doubt to Ana," Rose noted.

Jack was pleased to see Lexton give a slight nod of agreement.

"But I-HIT is faced with two more murders," Connie stated. She then turned to Jack. "We're expected to bust our butts to find out who did it when you could tell us. I don't believe for a second that if you asked your informant that he wouldn't tell you —"

"Hold it," Lexton said. "We can dance around this all day, but quite frankly I've heard enough." She turned her attention to Inspector Dyck. "I want you to assign someone, other than Corporal Crane, to investigate these murders to their fullest ability and without Corporal Taggart's help."

Connie's face expressed the anger she felt.

Lexton's face softened. "I appreciate how frustrated you must feel, but I do sit in a position that allows me to see the bigger picture. I feel it best for all concerned that you remain clear of this particular case."

Jack caught Lexton's glance. *Good. The big picture. My words exactly.*

"Corporal Taggart is on an intelligence unit," Lexton continued. "He wouldn't receive the information he does without the trust of his informants. If it were not for his informant, you likely wouldn't have known who killed Irving and you may well have been investigating the murder of a Crown prosecutor next week, as well."

The anger drained from Connie's face and she nodded glumly.

"Unless anyone has anything they feel they need to add, this meeting is over," Lexton stated.

Everyone shook their heads and started to rise.

"Except for you, Corporal Taggart," Lexton said. "I'd like a word with you."

Crap … I knew this was too easy. He caught a glare from Rose as she left. *Yes, Rose, I'll behave….*

* * *

Lexton studied Jack's face as soon as they were alone. *He must wonder why I'm making him stay, yet there are no outward signs of anxiety or fear. Then again, he's an operator.* She cleared her throat. "The national president of Satans Wrath has not yet been replaced, is that correct?"

"That's correct," Jack replied. "It may be another month or so."

"I find it interesting that your report names the two chapter presidents as conspiring to commit the murder. Someone reading the report would think that your informant was the third party, as you noted in your report that three bikers knew about it in addition to whichever two did the murders."

"Yes, I wrote it that way intentionally to provide another layer of protection for my informant in the event my report was ever compromised."

"This is what I was only able to conclude because I know from what you told me earlier that your informant is, in fact, one of the chapter presidents." Lexton glanced at the report. "The wording indicates to me that you really do think things through and do not act on the spur of the moment as suggested by Corporal Crane."

"Actually, it was my informant who took the lead in deciding Kondrat and Pratt's fate because Linquist is attached to his chapter. My informant's discussion with the other president was more of a courtesy."

Wow, that was straightforward. Lexton waited a beat while maintaining eye contact. "I'm glad to see that you're honest."

"If given the opportunity, I am."

What the hell? "If given the opportunity?"

"If you hadn't agreed with my decision and ordered me to disclose information to I-HIT, I must admit I would've been tempted to blame the other chapter president as being primarily responsible. Hypothetically speaking, of course."

Well, aren't you smug? I can't accuse you of being insubordinate because you didn't say you'd lie to me, simply that you'd be tempted. You're also warning me that if pressed, then you might lie. "I see," she replied, conscious of the icy tone she used.

Jack gave what appeared to be a meek smile. "How's that for honesty?"

Lexton scowled. "I'd say that was being too candid."

His eyebrows pinched and he appeared to be thinking about what she'd said. "I agree. I guess there are times when being overly candid is not advisable."

Of all the gall! The cocky bastard is playing with me!

"Is there anything else?" he asked.

"No, that's all." Her tone was harsher than she intended and his dismissal faster than she wanted, but for the moment she didn't know what else to say.

She stared after him as he walked out of her office. Remaining calm and solving issues with intelligence gave her a sense of pride, yet there was something about him that brought raw emotion to the surface.

Okay, Corporal, if you wanted to attract my attention, you've succeeded. Let's see how well you handle it!

Chapter Twenty-Three

It was early Saturday morning when Roger called Jack. "Did you get your beauty rest last night?"

"Actually, I did," Jack replied.

"So, if you weren't gnashing your teeth all night, I take it that the meeting you had yesterday with I-HIT and Lexton went okay?"

"Connie wasn't happy, but Lexton went along with what I did."

"Good."

"I was about to call you to let you know I'm ready to head out to join up with your surveillance team," Jack said.

"You may not need to," Roger replied. "You missed out on some action with Graves last night."

Jack felt his adrenalin rise. "You identify his source?"

"No, but we know how he's getting the guns in from the States."

"That's half the battle. What happened?"

"My first team set up on his apartment around noon

yesterday, but he wasn't home and didn't show up until six p.m. My second team came on shift then and hung in there most of the night because his lights were on. They decided if they wasted that much time, they may as well put him to bed and get the next team to set up on him in the morning. It was a good thing they waited, because at two a.m. he got in his truck and drove off."

"Did they see him check it for a tracker?"

"They spotted a flashlight beam under it before he left, but it was too dark to see how thorough he was. He then went to a residential area in Langley and drove slowly down a street like he was looking for an address."

"In Langley," Jack noted.

"Yes, but I think the location is incidental to what he was doing. He then braked near a house where there was a Chrysler Pacifica parked in the driveway before continuing on to the end of the street, where he parked and got out. He then snuck back and crawled under the engine block of the Chrysler Pacifica. When he returned to his truck, he was carrying some items dangling from inside a pair of socks. After that he went home and my people broke off."

"You check out the owner of the Chrysler?" Jack asked.

"The registered owner is a guy who is seventy years old and has no record."

"Sounds like Graves is using GPS and planting it along with the guns on people's vehicles who don't know he's doing it."

"That's what I'm thinking," Roger responded.

"I'll have uniform approach the owner on the pretext of looking for a similar vehicle involved in a hit and run, then call you back."

"There won't be any damage to the Chrysler to warrant many questions."

"I'll get uniform to say someone's dog was run over when they were walking it on a leash. Damage wouldn't be expected. Uniform could simply glance under it on the pretense of looking for blood or hair and ask whatever questions are necessary."

Roger chuckled. "I forgot I was talking to an operator. Let me know."

Jack then called uniform and told them what he wanted. Two hours later he got the answer he was expecting and called Roger.

"We were right," Jack said. "The owners of the Chrysler Pacifica are a retired couple and were both schoolteachers at one time. They said that yesterday they'd been cross-border shopping down at Bellis Fair and offered to show some sales receipts as proof."

"They don't sound like the criminal type," Roger said.

"No, I'm told the woman was in tears to think that someone had their pooch run over and that the guy was pretty emotional about it as well."

"So, I think we can say for positive that's how Graves is bringing them across." Roger paused. "Bellis Fair ... lots of Canadians go there. All he needs to do is stuff a sock or two with a gun and a GPS, then crawl under someone's vehicle who has B.C. plates and hang it inside the engine compartment. After that, he uses the GPS to find the vehicle when it's back in Canada."

"I was at Bellis Fair a week ago myself," Jack said. "Guess I should've checked under my own car before I left."

"Makes you wonder, doesn't it?" Roger paused. "What's next? I have a team that could go back on him at noon if you like?"

"Thanks, but no. The next step involves my informant. Laura and I will handle it for now. I appreciate the help and will keep you appraised."

"Any time. If you need a hand again, call me."

Jack put his phone away and mused about what to do next. *Tomorrow Graves is to deliver four Glocks with laser grips to Linquist. We know how they're being brought in, but who is he getting them from?*

Briefly he recalled the lists of military assault rifles and laser accessories that were stolen in Alabama and Arkansas, then he thought about the 9mm Smith & Wesson pistol that he carried. *Obviously it's someone a hell of a lot better armed than I am.*

Chapter Twenty-Four

On Monday morning Jack and Laura arrived at the Aquatic Centre Café in separate vehicles. Their aim was to follow Graves after he delivered the weapons to Linquist. If Jack was right in his belief that Graves had received the guns on credit, then he'd have to pay whoever supplied him with the guns afterward.

Jack chose to drive an SUV, as they were more common and less obvious than trying to follow someone in a van. He parked in a location where he could watch the entrance through binoculars while Laura parked her car and went inside.

At 10:00 a.m. Jack saw Buster Linquist arrive and phoned Laura. A moment later she confirmed that he'd taken a seat by himself in the café.

As the minutes ticked past, Jack used his binoculars to scan other cars parked in the area to see if anyone else was watching. Counter-surveillance by bad guys was not uncommon, both for protection from the police and from other bad guys intent on robbing them.

He didn't see anyone suspicious, but did notice a car slowly driving past for the second time. *Someone looking for a parking spot, or checking for surveillance?*

He took a photo of the car and licence plate as it passed, then realized they were dealer plates. *Okay ... test driving a new car.*

Then someone caught his eye. A man exited the café and immediately used his phone while looking intently all around.

Jack took a couple of photos, then called Laura. "You see a guy with a black jacket, dark grey pants, about forty, leave?"

"Yes. He was by himself. Eyed me up and down, but I thought he was only being a guy. Maybe he was looking for heat. Why? Do you think he's the connection? Maybe hanging around for the money?"

"Could be. He's standing outside the entrance and using his phone and gawking all around."

"Gotcha."

Jack took a few more photos, but the man had the phone close to his mouth and he wasn't able to get a good facial image.

He then saw Graves carrying a backpack and walking toward the restaurant.

Jack eyed the man with the phone again. *Did you just give him the all-clear call?*

Graves walked past the man without any obvious sign of recognition and Jack told Laura what he'd seen. A moment later Laura reported that Graves had joined Buster at his table.

Jack then saw a woman pull her car over to the curb. The man he'd been watching put his phone away and quickly got in.

Jack photographed the car and licence plate, then saw the man give her a peck on the cheek. A toddler's seat in the rear told him that his suspicions were likely unfounded.

"Okay," Laura whispered into her phone. "Graves handed Linquist the backpack. He's unzipping it ... peeking inside ... Linquist is reaching under the table ... Graves is glancing down. Okay, I suspect Linquist handed him the money under the table."

"Good."

"Linquist is standing up. Looks like he's leaving."

"Stay put to see if Graves hands cash off to someone else in there."

"Will do. I bet they were fronted. I don't see a goofball like him having ten grand or whatever amount he'd need to pay for them. Okay ... hang on, guess if he is handing the money off it's not in here. They're leaving together."

Jack watched Graves and Linquist part company out front. He and Laura then followed Graves back to his apartment. Once there Jack positioned his SUV to watch Graves's truck from the rear of the apartment building while Laura parked her car to watch the front.

There was no activity until 5:00 p.m. when Jack next saw Graves. He quickly phoned Laura. "He's going to his truck. Hang on ... he's leaning over." Jack thumbed the dial on his binoculars. "Maybe getting something from the glovebox. He's back out of the truck. Yes! We're in luck. He's got a flashlight and is crawling underneath."

"Good, I was getting bored. Hopefully he's getting ready to meet his connection and not deliver guns to someone else."

"My guess is it's his connection. Roger's team was on him. He only retrieved two socks from one vehicle. I'm sure all the guns he had were what he passed on to Linquist. Okay ... he's popped the hood and is looking inside the engine compartment."

"Monday night at the border shouldn't be much of a wait," Laura noted.

"He closed the hood and is looking under his seat ... wait ... no, the asshole has his own set of binoculars. I've got to duck. He's scanning the area."

"He is one kinky puppy."

Jack peeked over the dash and saw Graves using the binoculars to scan the sky.

Looking for aircraft surveillance, jerk? No worries. I know where you're going.

Graves then got in his truck and drove away.

"Okay, he's on the move." Jack said, smiling to himself. *You're not as thorough as you think you are.*

"Head for the border?" Laura asked.

"You got it. I'll get ahead of him and wait while you follow him through. I'm calling ATF now."

Jack then called Ferg and told him what had transpired.

"Good timing," Ferg said. "I'm already on my way home. Leaving the Seattle city limits as we speak. I could be in the vicinity of Bellis Fair within forty-five minutes."

"That's where he brought the guns to be delivered to Canada," Jack noted, "but who knows where he goes to pick them up ... or pay for them, if my guess is right. He might be going to Seattle."

"Either way, he's coming my way. We'll have him between us."

"I think I can confirm he's heading to the States. I just spotted him ahead of me, southbound on the 99. I'll pass him and wait on your side of the border so I don't get caught up waiting at Customs."

"See you soon, amigo."

Twenty minutes later Jack crossed into the U.S. and waited near the border while Laura followed Graves. Ten minutes after Jack crossed the border, Graves also cleared Customs and Laura followed two minutes later.

Jack then called Ferg. "We've cleared Customs and are southbound on the I-5."

"Perfect," Ferg responded. "That puts you about thirty minutes away from Bellis Fair, which I'm almost at. I'll set up north of it on the I-5 and wait to join the parade."

"Good. I'll call you when we're about fifteen minutes away."

As Jack followed Graves south on the I-5 he noticed he was checking the side mirrors on his truck continually. Jack glanced in his own rear-view mirror and saw that Laura was behind him. Jack picked up the phone again.

"We better drop back out of sight, Laura," Jack said. "He's driving slower than most everyone else and is checking his rear-views continually. You and I are beginning to stand out like a couple of sore thumbs."

"We'll risk losing him," Laura replied.

"I'd rather do that than heat him up. He's only about fifteen minutes north of where Ferg is. I'll call him and tell him to keep his eyes peeled. With luck, the three of us can then follow him without being made."

Jack then called Ferg and kept him abreast of the distance between them as he drew nearer. Any hope he had of discovering Graves's connection vanished when he drove past Ferg, who was still waiting on a side ramp.

"Sorry, amigo. He didn't come by," Ferg said.

Damn it! The son-of-a-bitch turned off.

"Maybe he took the Bakerview Road exit north of here," Ferg suggested. "It's not the shortest way to the mall, but it still takes you there. Let's check the mall regardless. He could still be meeting someone there."

Jack felt disheartened, but agreed. Minutes later he was driving through one of the mall parking lots when he knew his troubles were not over.

Oh shit!

He swung the wheel hard, but the sound of grating metal and his SUV being knocked sideways told him he was too late.

Jack came to an abrupt stop and stared out the window. *Oh yeah. I'm in it now. Right up to my ears....*

Chapter Twenty-Five

The following morning, Jack and Rose were summarily called to Lexton's office and each took a seat in front of her desk.

Lexton gave Jack a look of contempt. When she spoke, her tone was calm but her words were cutting. "Going down there like a renegade cowboy and smashing up a police vehicle — let me guess. I bet you were also wearing your sidearm?"

Jack sighed. "There wasn't time to leave it at the office."

"You didn't have authorization to go to the U.S. Carrying a weapon into a foreign country is a second offence — regardless of whether you had authorization to enter their country."

"Yes, I realize that, and I'm totally to blame."

"Did it never occur to you to seek Ottawa's permission?"

"I didn't get confirmation until Saturday that Graves was crossing the border and planting guns on inno-cent cross-border shoppers. Yesterday I was tied up on surveillance, but it was my intention to apply for permission this week."

"What about Constable Secord? Did she cross the border?"

"Yes, but under my orders."

"Your orders don't override policy."

"Perhaps she thought I had permission," Jack suggested.

Lexton ignored the comment. "No doubt she was also armed," she stated.

"Would you believe she turned her weapon over to me?" Jack asked.

"No, I would not," Lexton replied crossly.

"I guess I wouldn't either," Jack replied.

Lexton raised an eyebrow. "Do you think this is funny, Corporal?"

Jack paused to take a deep breath. "No, I don't, but you must realize that it wasn't done out of malice. Our hearts were in the right place."

"Obviously your brains weren't." Lexton paused. "Don't look to the Force to cover the damages sustained to either vehicle or for any civil litigation that may follow."

"The other driver backed out of a stall and hit me. He admitted fault and our police unit should be out of the body shop in one or two days. The fender was bent into the tire, but it's mostly cosmetic. It's only the fender that needs replacing. The other driver was insured, so there —"

"I'm not interested in the details! That will be between you, the other driver, and whatever lawyers may become involved."

"I understand. I used my own credit card to pay for it to be towed to the body shop."

"You better understand, because if it ever happens again, let me assure you that the next border you'll be looking at will be from Baffin Island across Davis Strait to Greenland. Tell Constable Secord that goes for her, as well."

Jack nodded.

"How is the vehicle being returned to Canada?"

"The ATF agent I was working with will deliver it to the border."

Lexton paused. "Then we're done. Get out of my office."

As Jack and Rose got out of their chairs, Lexton pointed her finger at Rose. "You stay."

Jack glanced at Rose and discreetly mouthed the word *sorry* as he left.

* * *

Rose tried to look calm as she faced Lexton.

"I take it you didn't know he'd entered the United States until after?" Lexton asked.

"I wasn't aware of it until he called me after the accident."

"Perhaps he doesn't respect you, either," Lexton noted. "It's obvious he has no respect for commissioned officers."

"That's not necessarily true. He held Assistant Commissioner Isaac in high regard," Rose stated. "I think if you get to know and understand him a little —"

Lexton acted as if she wasn't listening. "He acts like

everything's a joke," she fumed. "What's even worse is that he exhibits a superior attitude to those above him." She paused to glare at Rose, then said. "His attitude needs to be documented and should be reflected on his annual assessments."

Okay, how do I reply to that without having you flip out at me? Ah, what does it matter? It's not like I'm expecting to be promoted above the level I'm at.

When Rose didn't immediately respond, Lexton said, "You're his boss. Bringing him into line and documenting his atrocious behaviour is your job. Start doing it!"

Rose took a deep breath and slowly exhaled. "Yes, I'm his boss. As such I feel obligated to protect him from false accusations."

Lexton looked startled. "False accusations? There's nothing false about his insubordination! If you allow that to continue, it will become like an infectious disease."

"I agree that insubordination cannot be tolerated. However, what you perceive as insubordination may be a sign of the frustration he has in regard to a recent incident involving another commissioned officer. I don't believe that he's intentionally disrespecting you."

"Another commissioned officer?"

Rose hesitated. "May I talk to you off the record about Corporal Taggart? It's not something I ask lightly. He asked me to keep what he told me secret, and if he found out I told you it could seriously affect the trust he has in me. Trust which, when it comes to sharing intelligence, is an essential component to a good working relationship."

Lexton sat back in her chair and appeared to study her face carefully. "Okay, you have my curiosity. Go ahead. What you say to me will remain between us."

Rose waited a beat. "First of all, let me lead up to it by addressing your concerns, starting with his respect for commissioned officers. You believe that the rank of commissioner should automatically grant respect."

"It should."

"Corporal Taggart has good reason not to blindly follow that assumption. Your predecessor —"

"Assistant Commissioner Mortimer."

"Yes. He basically tried to shut down our office. He didn't want any criminal organizations to be targeted. At one point he ordered all undercover operations to cease and for Corporal Taggart to turn over any informants he had to someone else. He wanted our office to collect statistics or look at drug smuggling trends instead of going after the groups responsible."

Lexton's brow furrowed. "What was his rationale?"

"He didn't provide any rationale to me, but warned Corporal Taggart that his career would be finished if he submitted any reports that would force him to make any decisions that had the potential to bring about criticism from Ottawa."

Lexton looked skeptical. "Was this alleged interaction between Assistant Commissioner Mortimer and Corporal Taggart witnessed by anyone else?"

"He held his meeting with Corporal Taggart in private. There was nobody to corroborate what was said. If Corporal Taggart had said anything, it would have been his word against the word of a commissioned officer."

"Yet you believe what Corporal Taggart told you?"

"Yes. I also had conversations with Assistant Commissioner Mortimer. His orders support what Corporal Taggart told me as far as redirecting our office to collect statistics and cease investigations like the ones we had targeting Satans Wrath."

Lexton put an elbow on her desk and stroked her chin with her fingertips as if in deep thought. When she lowered her hand, she said, "Years ago when I was stationed on I-HIT, there was a situation where Corporal Taggart was accused of wrongdoing by a Superintendent Wigmore. Are you familiar with it?"

"No, it must have been before my time," Rose replied.

"At that time, before downsizing, Superintendent Wigmore was in charge of the intelligence units throughout the province."

"I don't even know the man," Rose replied.

"The allegations that Superintendent Wigmore made were discredited. In fact, he was institutionalized for a thirty-day psychiatric assessment after threatening the assistant commissioner."

God, Jack. What did you do to the guy? Is that where I'll end up?

"While he was in the psych ward, his replacement discovered that Superintendent Wigmore was into child pornography. It was rumoured at the time that the reason he wanted to get rid of Corporal Taggart was because he'd been investigating a child pornography case."

"I never heard about it," Rose stated.

"Later on, Superintendent Wigmore admitted to consuming child pornography, but strongly denied the accusations and circumstances that first led to him being sent to the psych ward. He claimed he'd been framed by Corporal Taggart in a series of events to make it look like he was mentally unbalanced."

Should I act surprised? Rose opted to remain stoic instead. "I don't understand why you're telling me."

"You don't think it more than coincidental that Superintendent Wigmore went after Corporal Taggart and was committed to a psychiatric ward and then Assistant Commissioner Mortimer tried to shut Taggart down and a squad of biker hit men showed up at his house?"

"I'm not one to deal in rumours," Rose stated. "I deal in facts, and the facts of the matter regarding Assistant Commissioner Mortimer indicate that Satans Wrath and some Russian drug dealers were responsible. There's nothing to indicate that Corporal Taggart had any involvement whatsoever. In fact, the opposite was true. Corporal Taggart's own family were threatened by Satans Wrath."

Lexton appeared to ponder her words for a moment. "This problem that Corporal Taggart and you had with my predecessor is what you wish to keep secret? I'd hardly think it necessary seeing as Assistant Commissioner Mortimer has retired."

"No, what I am about to tell you is what I wish to remain between us. It's in regard to another commissioned officer. Chief Superintendent Quaile."

"In charge of Staffing."

"Yes, but years ago he was a staff sergeant in charge of the intelligence unit. He only lasted a few months and was transferred due to his incomp … I mean, inability to handle operational duties. His inability was exposed in part by an investigation headed by Corporal Taggart." Rose paused, wondering how deep a hole she was getting herself into.

"Continue," Lexton said. "Inability … incompetence, whatever it is, don't dance around the issue. Tell me what you have to say."

"Recently it came to Corporal Taggart's attention that Chief Superintendent Quaile is holding back his performance evaluation to prevent him from being shortlisted for promotion. I submitted it four months ago and it's remained in his basket ever since, despite repeated reminders by his secretary."

Lexton appeared taken back. "He's holding it until after the promotion board sits in two weeks."

"Exactly."

"How does Corporal Taggart know this?" Lexton questioned.

"The secretary called him because she was so upset at what she perceived as being wrong."

"It is wrong," Lexton stated. "Why haven't you or Corporal Taggart reported it?"

"Because Corporal Taggart knows it would jeopardize the secretary's job. Considering Chief Superintendent Quaile's personality, I'd have to agree."

"So he is willing to forgo his own promotion to protect the secretary?"

"Yes."

"I take it they're friends?"

"No, he's never met her. I presume she's someone with a strong sense of what's right or wrong." Rose paused, and when she didn't get a response she continued. "Corporal Taggart holds some commissioned officers in high regard, but for him, that respect doesn't come automatically and perhaps for good reason."

"I see."

"As you are likely aware, I have my masters in psychology. I am well acquainted with people's behaviour patterns and have known Corporal Taggart for a number of years. You mentioned he acts like everything is a joke. Were you to consider the number of attempts on his life and the severe stress he has endured, you might be surprised there is any humour left in him."

"You may think of it as humour, I don't. I didn't find it humorous when he asked if I'd believe that Constable Secord turned her firearm over to him, then acknowledged that he wouldn't believe it, either." Lexton leaned forward in her chair and her face darkened. "He was playing with me. I had the same experience when I spoke to him last Friday. He backed me into a corner to make it sound like I told him that being overly candid was not always advisable."

"Overly candid?"

Lexton ignored the comment. "He was being intentionally provocative to judge how I'd react."

"I think *judge* is the wrong word," Rose said. "To assess how you'd react, perhaps, without being judgmental."

"Judge … assess … whatever. I felt as if he were treating me like I was a lab rat."

"That doesn't surprise me about him. Little doubt he was assessing your cerebral level, personality … and perhaps sense of humour."

"Exactly!" Lexton replied as she slapped her desk with the palm of her hand. "How dare he! I'm a commissioned officer. If anything, I should be the one assessing him."

"Did you consider his motive behind what he did?" Rose asked calmly.

"His motive?" Lexton sat back and looked puzzled.

"Corporal Taggart's intelligence reports are second to none. He has a proven track record of developing high-level sources. With that comes responsibility. Responsibility to those who have placed their lives in his hands."

"What does that have to do with it? Everyone understands, or should understand, the need to protect their informant's identity. I've backed him on that."

"Yes, but you know how much protection is needed. We've had previous cases where groups like Satans Wrath developed their own sources within our organization, as well as other police bodies."

Lexton made a face. "Highly disturbing, I admit, but that is not a reason for him to be flippant with me."

"There's no doubt in my mind that how much Corporal Taggart reports, verbally or otherwise, has a direct correlation with the amount of trust he has in those who he passes the information on to. Obviously his trust and respect for you has risen considerably since you backed him on protecting his informant over the Kondrat and Pratt murders."

"Hold on a second. Are you telling me he holds back information? I find that unacceptable. He should report everything of any significance to his superiors and let them decide what should be passed on and to whom."

Lexton eyed Rose suspiciously. "Or is it less of an issue of protecting his informants than it is of something else?"

"Something else?" Rose questioned.

Lexton's words were blunt. "Has Corporal Taggart been breaking the law?"

Breaking the law? I can't imagine how many times. He carries a small set of lock picks in his wallet, for Christ's sake. Rose locked eyes with Lexton and her words were firm. "I do not believe that Corporal Taggart would ever commit a criminal act for his own benefit."

"That is not what I meant. Would he break the law in his own blind quest for what he perceives to be justice?"

Rose paused to take a deep breath and give herself a moment to compose a response. "There have been several Internal Affairs investigations involving Corporal Taggart over the years, including the use of wiretap and surveillance on him. They've never come up with an iota of evidence to say that he has ever broken the law."

"So are you saying he hasn't broken the law, or could it be that he's smart enough to never get caught?"

"He is highly intelligent, but —"

"So that's it."

"I'm not implying that he has ever broken the law by that comment."

"No, but that might explain why he's never been caught."

Rose felt the tension rise in her body. *I feel like a mother bear trying to protect her cub.* She made a conscious effort to keep her tone one of reason and not of anger. "Would it make you feel better if you had a less intelligent person working for you? Perhaps a sycophant so that you'd never need to challenge your own cerebral output?"

"That's —"

"Or someone who has a keen sense of justice and is highly intelligent — who, granted, may be challenging at times over some of the delicate matters he brings forward?"

The irritation showed on Lexton's face, but then she appeared to reflect on what was said.

Was that a hint of a smile?

Lexton's face became passive and her tone was matter-of-fact. "It would appear that backing people into a corner is a common tactic in your unit." She paused. "Out of curiosity, when did Corporal Taggart discover that Chief Superintendent Quaile was holding back his evaluation?"

"About three weeks ago."

"Interesting that out of two previous commissioned officers who crossed paths with Corporal Taggart, one was institutionalized in a psych ward for thirty days and the other retired after a Satans Wrath hit team showed up at his house. It makes me wonder what the future might hold for Chief Superintendent Quaile."

"I'm sure it was a coincidence," Rose scoffed, in a tone and manner as if to say that any other conclusion would be ridiculous.

Lexton stared at her. "Trust is a two-way street. You and I have had an enlightening conversation. Don't spoil it by trying to be deceptive."

Rose swallowed, then acknowledged her guilt with a nod. *Okay, you're good....*

"You may go. Be sure to remind Corporal Taggart that if he plans any more forays across international borders ... to obtain written authorization first."

Chapter Twenty-Six

Rose slid the chair back from her desk and plunked herself down. A moment later Jack entered and took a seat. She moved her feet uncomfortably under her desk as he stared at her.

"I thought you'd have stuck your head into my office to call me in," he said. "Is everything okay? I'm hoping that my accident in the States didn't cause you to get into trouble. I told her I was entirely responsible."

"No, she's not angry with me," Rose responded.

"Good."

He crossed his legs and sat back in his chair.

Damn it, you look like you're settling in. I wish you'd leave.

"I presume you were told to keep an eye on me and document any further transgressions?" he said.

"She has her eye on you, that's for sure. I'd suggest you be extra polite in any future dealings you may have with her. She's also perceptive and doesn't appreciate being conned."

"Yes, I clued into that in the meeting when I tried to soften her up by talking about the prosecutor's two-year-old daughter. She gave me the hairy eyeball then."

"So you know she's not someone you should mess with."

"What did you talk about after I was dismissed?"

"She made it clear she doesn't like your sense of humour and feels you show a lack of respect for her rank."

"I see. What did you say?"

"I told her I'd speak to you about it, so consider yourself spoken to."

"Was that all?" He glanced at his watch. "You were gone a long time."

Damn him. Reminds me of the time I interviewed some inmates over a murder. The other inmates timed how long the interviews took to try and figure out who was saying something they shouldn't. Rose shrugged. "What else was there to say?"

He looked at her curiously.

"What else was there to say?" Christ, how could I make such a rookie mistake? He knows I'm holding something back. "She also said to tell you to submit a request through channels if you plan to cross the border again."

Jack studied her face briefly then rose to his feet. "No problem. I'm working on it now," he said.

She found herself staring blankly at her doorway after he'd left. It was the first time she'd broken her word to him. *Why do I feel so upset? I had his best interests at heart.* She busied herself straightening out the items on her desk, and then straightened them again. A haunting feeling remained. *He knows I lied to him....*

* * *

Late that afternoon Jack submitted the request seeking permission to authorize him and other investigators, if need be, to enter the U.S. to work with investigators there on the gun smuggling investigation.

He knew that the bureaucrats in Ottawa would have to approve the request, then contact their counterparts in the U.S., gain permission, then send documentation back. He was optimistic that the process would be completed by the following week.

In the meantime, Laura prepared a warrant allowing them to place a tracking device on Graves's truck. At noon the following day Laura walked into their office with the warrant in her hand and waved it at Jack. "Got it signed," she said. "Good for sixty days starting today."

"Perfect," Jack replied.

"Tonight?" Laura asked as she sat down.

"Sure, I'll pick you up at your place at eleven. Shouldn't take long."

"It better not. That'll take us into Thursday. I'm off to Hawaii Friday morning. Don't you dare get me into something to screw that up."

"Me? Never!" Jack exclaimed, hamming up his surprise. "How could you even think that I would ever —" He stopped talking to answer his office phone.

"Jack! It's Bonny … from Staffing," she added.

"You sound chipper," Jack noted.

"I am. I have some unbelievably good news," she said. "I wanted to phone you earlier but had to wait until you-know-who left for lunch."

"My dear friend Chief Superintendent Quaile," Jack replied.

Bonny's voice spilled over with excitement. "I wish you could have been here this morning to listen to the lambasting he received from Assistant Commissioner Lexton."

"Oh?"

"She showed up this morning asking for him and when she discovered he wasn't in, she went to his desk to drop off something and write him a note. Then she saw your performance evaluation in his basket. Well! I tell you! Quaile arrived a moment later and the proverbial you-know-what hit the fan."

"I bet Quaile put the blame on someone else," Jack said.

Bonny snickered. "You're right. First he tried to say that he received it late, but she noted the dates beside the initials of those who'd forwarded it to him. Then he changed his story to say it must have been inadvertently misfiled and only recently located."

"What did Lexton say?"

"She didn't swallow any of his malarkey. She told him off in no uncertain terms, then stormed out." Bonny giggled. "Honestly, his face was so red that I thought he was going to have a coronary."

"Too bad he didn't," Jack said. "It would have been the first real service he did for his country."

"Nobody I know would have called Emergency if he had," Bonny replied.

"Out of curiosity, do you happen to know what Lexton was leaving for him?" Jack asked.

"It was an invitation to a social gathering, but that subject never came up again."

Jack thanked Bonny, then told Laura.

"Oh, man! That is super!" Laura exclaimed. "Glad to see someone put that jerk in his place."

"Wish we could have been there to see it," Jack replied.

"Hey, maybe you and I will have a shot at promotion yet," she said, her face beaming. "Let's go tell Rose. She was pretty upset about it."

Jack frowned. "She may already know."

"Oh?"

"Yesterday I think Rose went behind my back and told Lexton. She was with her for quite a while, then acted funny when I asked her what they'd talked about."

"Acted funny?" Laura questioned.

"Evasive. You know that most people don't like to lie."

"Right, they use terminology to evade the question."

"When I asked her what else they talked about besides giving me an attitude adjustment, she said, 'What else is there to say?'"

"Maybe she was busy and wanted you to leave," Laura suggested. "Her way of dismissing you."

"I didn't get the feeling she was busy. Then for this to happen so soon after — I'm not buying it. Lexton could have even left the invitation or message with the secretary. She wouldn't have had to go into his office."

Laura pursed her lips. "I don't know. If Lexton was standing right there, why interrupt the secretary? It would be easy enough for her to drop it off. Maybe it was a coincidence."

"Coincidence? That's what we say about ourselves when something happens — and you know how much truth there is there," Jack said wryly.

Laura rolled her eyes. "You're right about that."

"We'll tell Rose about Quaile catching hell," Jack continued, "but study her reaction. It could be interesting."

"Are you going to accuse her?"

"No point. She'd be concerned that it'd affect the trust I place in her, which will later translate to suspicion that I'm holding stuff back from her."

Laura gestured with her hands. "You do anyway."

"Exactly, so there'd be no benefit to channelling her mind in that direction and promoting more suspicion."

"If she did tell Lexton, it would've been because she wanted to help you," Laura noted.

"I know. If she did do it, she must trust Lexton to some degree or else she wouldn't have."

"What do you think about Lexton?"

"Time will tell. If Rose did tell her, then I'm impressed with how she handled it." Jack paused. "Let's go find out."

A moment later, Jack saw Rose's eyes briefly widen with surprise when he started to tell her about the latest call he'd received from Bonny. That was followed by a slight flicker of concern ... then her face became passive as she listened.

As Jack talked, he saw that Rose was studying his face. *Looking to see if I suspect something and am angry?* His tone and expression gave the impression that he was pleased as he related what Bonny had told him.

Rose smiled when he finished. "That's wonderful! It sounds like he got what was coming to him."

"I'll say," Laura replied. "It puts Jack and me back in the running again."

"That's fantastic," Rose replied. "I really hope the both of you get promoted. I can't imagine anyone else being more qualified."

After a little more chatter, Jack and Laura returned to their desks.

Jack then eyed Laura. "Diagnosis?"

"She initially looked surprised. She didn't know what Lexton was up to," Laura concluded.

"I agree. What else?"

"I saw some concern. She was checking you out to see how you were reacting."

"Meaning?"

"She told Lexton, but wasn't aware of the action that Lexton took."

"Exactly."

"And you didn't give even an iota to suggest you'd clued in."

Jack gave a lopsided smile in response.

Laura stared at him. "You're going to toss it back at her someday, aren't you?"

"What do you mean?"

"You know damn well what I mean. You're going to wait until she's giving you hell for having done something without telling her. Then you'll let her have it with both barrels and use this as an excuse."

Jack shook his head in mock disbelief. "It saddens me to think you've become so cynical and devious. Whatever happened to that nice young woman I first met?"

"I met you, is what happened."

Jack chuckled. "Sounds to me like you should be promoted."

Chapter Twenty-Seven

It was approaching midnight when Jack and Laura arrived in the alley behind Graves's apartment. His truck was parked in the usual spot, but his apartment light was on and they could see the glow from a television.

Jack glanced at Laura. *Okay, I know what you're thinking.*

She caught his glance and appeared to read his mind. "Yes, it shouldn't take us long," she observed as she squirmed and slouched in the seat to make herself comfortable.

"Probably watching a movie. Bet he goes to bed in an hour," Jack said, trying to be optimistic.

"Either way, I'm off to Hawaii soon. Hot sun. Warm beaches."

"You'd rather be lying on a beach in Hawaii with your hubby and drinking piña coladas than sitting in an alley with me?" He let out a loud sigh. "Obviously, I've lost my charm."

"Yeah, well, what you call charm, others call B.O."

"I stink?" He sniffed under his arm.

"Not yet, but give it a few hours."

"After a few hours we both will." He stared up at the apartment. "I'm sure he'll be going to bed soon."

"He doesn't work, remember?"

At 3:00 a.m. Laura glanced at her watch. "He'll be going to bed soon, will he? Wished I had bet you."

"His window overlooks his truck. I don't want to chance it. If he finishes watching television, it'd be too easy for him to glance out on his way to bed."

"I know."

"If you want to get some sleep, go ahead. I'm okay."

"No thanks. Last time I did that with you on surveillance I woke with a kink in my neck that lasted for three days. Mind you, I think this car is more comfortable than the SUV."

"Better than what happened to me last time I fell asleep on surveillance. When I woke up my underwear was on backwards."

Laura tittered, but by 5:00 a.m. they'd both run out of humour and patience.

Jack tossed the binoculars to Laura. "That's it. I'm going in. Either he fell asleep on the sofa or is stoned. Let me know if you see movement."

Laura glanced at her watch. "In exactly twenty-four hours I'm heading to the airport. If you haven't picked the lock by then you're on your own."

"If I'm not done in twenty minutes you can walk over there and kick me in the ass."

"Don't think I won't."

In the seven minutes that followed, Jack picked the padlock on the toolbox in the back of Graves's truck and hid the GPS unit inside. It was one place that Graves had not thought to search, and the whereabouts of his truck could now be fully monitored from a laptop computer.

Laura yawned as Jack climbed back into the SUV. "Too bad you didn't do that five hours ago."

"I know, I feel the same way," he replied, then glanced at his watch.

"What are you thinking?" Laura asked.

"About calling Ferg and meeting him to give him one of the GPS locators. It's a little early, so if you like I'll drop you off at your place and do it myself. You can call last night your shift for today and officially be on vacation."

"Didn't you tell me he lives an hour north of Seattle?"

"Yes."

"We're halfway to the border already. You're tired, too. Call him. I bet he's an early riser if he has to drive to Seattle."

"You sure?"

"No problem. If we do that, by the time we're done I can call home and sweet talk my better half into making me breakfast before I go to bed."

Jack reached for his phone.

Ferg sounded cheery and didn't seem to mind being woken up. "Actually, my alarm would have gone off in another fifteen minutes," he said. "I've got a couple of horses I need to attend to before going to work. Also, I was about to phone you."

"Horses? I didn't know you had horses."

"Sure do. I'm looking forward to when my grandkids are old enough to ride. Your boys are. You should bring the family down sometime. Being a Mountie, I imagine you know a thing or two about horses."

"Me? No way. I'd probably fall off and break my neck."

"And you call yourself a Mountie. That's sad," Ferg kibitzed.

"I keep my horses under the hood."

"Speaking of that, I've got an SUV parked in my yard with a shiny new fender."

"It's ready?"

"Yes. I picked it up last night. That's why I was about to call you."

"What do I owe you?"

"Nothing. The guy who backed into you paid for it and gave me cash to reimburse you for the tow bill. He doesn't want his insurance company involved for fear his rates will go up."

"That's great news. Is there any chance you could have it brought to the border? My partner and I managed to get a tracker on Graves's truck a few minutes ago. The reason I was calling was so we could give you a locator for the GPS."

"No problem. I'll drive it and have Betty take our truck. There's a coffee shop a little south of our Customs office if you'd like to meet there," Ferg suggested.

"Hell, no," Jack replied. "I'm lucky to still have a job from last time. I think Ottawa is still considering whether or not to charge me with theft of auto."

"I thought you might have gotten your ass reamed out," Ferg mused.

"I did, but a couple of days ago I put in a formal request for permission. With luck, I'll be able to come your way next week if need be."

"No worries," Ferg replied. "We'll meet you at the border in an hour. If you're not allowed in, you can chuck the locator over the fence."

"What I'd like to chuck is our policy."

"Ours isn't much different, amigo."

* * *

Jack introduced Laura to Ferg and Betty at the U.S. Customs office, but kept their meeting brief as they were both exhausted and wanted to get home.

After handing Ferg the locator, they each drove back to the office. Laura dropped off the car and got into the newly repaired SUV with Jack.

A short time later Jack parked in front of Laura's house. "Think of me when you're getting laid in Hawaii," he said.

Laura cast him a sideways glance. "Don't you wish."

"What do you mean?" Jack asked innocently.

"How are you spelling 'laid'?"

"L-E-I-D," Jack replied.

"Sounds to me like you L-I-E-D."

"That's good," Jack replied. "I'm so tired I think it's funny."

Laura leaned over and kissed him on the cheek, then reached for her door handle. She paused and her face became serious. "Can I really trust you to behave yourself while I'm gone?"

Jack gave his usual lopsided grin. "No worries. There's not a lot left to do. Next time Graves makes a move, I'll notify Ferg, and they'll take him to his source."

"Hopefully that'll be the Coggins brothers and they'll nail their butts."

"That'd be nice. Either way, I'll be pretty much out of it."

"You're never out of it," Laura said dryly. "Hip-waders should be part of your daily attire."

Chapter Twenty-Eight

Over the next couple of days Jack monitored Graves's pickup truck movements over his laptop, but didn't see anything to arouse his curiosity. A trip to a grocery store that Graves made confirmed that the GPS was working properly.

It was noon on Sunday when Roger called Jack at home.

"The name Zombie came across our wiretap," Roger said. "Two of the Death Heads were chatting about him."

"What are their names?"

"Lyon Downes and Jimmy Ferris. In the call Lyon said he just got back from meeting Zombie."

"A couple of days ago Laura and I managed to get a tracker on Zombie's, or I should say Graves's, pickup. I can tell you that it hasn't moved all morning."

"Maybe Downes met him at his apartment or someplace close to there."

"Maybe," Jack agreed.

"Downes told Ferris that Zombie would bring them a six-pack of beer to the party in the next day or two. I'm betting they ordered six guns."

"I'd say so," Jack replied. "That's great news. Love it when a plan comes together."

"The thing is, I can't spare anyone to watch Zombie at the moment. We think two from the United Front are going out to waste someone today."

"Their targets wouldn't be Downes and Ferris, would they?"

"We don't know. It sounds like they're planning to scout out a few places that the Death Heads frequent. Restaurants and the like."

Jack briefly imagined the potential carnage for families having Sunday brunch at some restaurant. He took a deep breath and exhaled. "Sounds like you're busy. No worries as far as I go. I've got the tracker on and a bunch of ATF agents who are eager to take over south of the border. I'll set up on Graves. If he goes south he might not be coming back — or if he does, he'll be labelled a rat."

"Either way would be great. If my people get free, I'll send them over to lend you a hand, otherwise let me know, will you?"

"You got it. Thanks for the info."

Jack immediately called Ferg and gave him the details.

"Good chance he'll be heading down to Seattle to pick 'em up," Ferg noted.

"Very good chance," Jack agreed. "That's only about an hour and forty-five minutes south of the border."

"I'll contact my guys in Seattle to have a team on standby to head north and meet up with him at a moment's notice.

Who knows, he might lead us to the Coggins brothers."

"That'd be perfect. It'd be nice if they were all busted down your way."

"What do you want done with Graves? Let him go, or bust him?"

"He met with a member from a gang called the United Front this morning. It would be okay to bust him. I think the heat would go to someone in the United Front and not my guy."

"Sounds good. We'll play it by ear. If we catch him red-handed doing the deal we'll take him down then. Otherwise, we may jump him as soon as he heads north again and take him down with the six he came to get. That would also give us grounds for a warrant to search wherever or whoever we figured he got them from."

"Good. Thanks."

"Any time, amigo. Any time."

* * *

An hour later, Jack parked his SUV where he could watch Graves's pickup. Except for when Graves made a short trip to a drive-through for fast food, there was no other activity for the rest of the afternoon.

At 6:30 p.m. Roger called. "I've some rather interesting news," he said. "My team took down the United Front boys ... Downes and Ferris. Caught 'em each with a Kel-Tec 9mm pistol."

"The ones the Death Heads were using were Glocks," Jack noted.

"I know, but guess what; the Kel-Tecs we seized were stolen from the gun shop in Arkansas. The same store the FBI thinks was robbed by the Coggins brothers in Alabama."

"No kidding!"

"It looks to me like Graves is playing both sides of the fence," Roger noted.

"Pretty dangerous thing to do," Jack replied.

"No shit. I'd be tempted to let the gangers on both sides know. They'd probably take care of him for us."

"Except some innocent schmuck might get killed."

"That's the problem. So ... give my people a couple hours to do the paperwork and then I can send them your way if you like."

"Thanks, but it sounds like they're busy enough. Except for grabbing a bite to eat, Graves hasn't moved his truck all day. The tracker is working good. If he does head to the border, I can handle it myself."

At 8:00 p.m. Graves went to his truck. Unlike when he went to the restaurant earlier, this time he crawled underneath first.

Stay out of your tool box, jerk....

A moment later he finished his search and drove away.

Jack felt the adrenalin surge as he called Ferg to tell him what happened.

"I'm on it!" Ferg exclaimed. "Grabbing my coat as we speak."

Jack heard Betty's voice in the background say, "Again? You better not be making this up to keep from doing the dishes. If you come back with beer on your breath you'll be sleeping in the barn!"

Jack smiled to himself, then ended the call. He then used his laptop to follow Graves, and thirty minutes later called Ferg to give him an update.

"Graves is in the lineup to cross the border," Jack reported. "Looks like he'll be about fifteen or twenty minutes judging by how many people are ahead of him."

"Not bad for Sunday traffic," Ferg noted. "My team's on their way. I'll call them and let them know. We'll talk again once he clears. By then, I should be there."

Fifteen minutes passed, then Jack called Ferg again. "He's cleared Customs. You watching on laptop?"

"You betcha," Ferg said, then muttered, "That's right. Come to papa, baby, come to papa."

"Good luck, hombre," Jack said. "Wish I could be there to join in on the fun."

"No worries. My guys are leaving the outskirts of Seattle as we speak. With the tracker, we'll be able to gift wrap him for you."

"He's your gift, and I have a no return policy."

Ferg chuckled.

"Happy hunting, and let me know how it goes."

Chapter Twenty-Nine

Twenty-five minutes south of the border Ferg's laptop revealed that Graves had exited the I-5 and was entering a small town called Ferndale.

He immediately notified his team, who were about an hour away, then narrowed the gap between his vehicle and Graves's truck so that they were only a block apart.

Graves slowly drove past a bar called the Main Street Bar and Grill. It was the second-last building on the block. He made a right run onto a side street.

Ferg followed and saw that the street was wide enough for vehicles to be parked nosed to the curb. He then spotted Graves getting out of his truck and continued past before parking farther down the street.

Graves walked back toward the main street.

Ferg quickly updated his team and followed Graves on foot. As he approached the corner, he noticed a bearded man sitting in a blue Ram crew cab pickup truck nosed up to the curb. The truck had a winch on the front and a canopy on the back.

As he passed the front of the truck he was conscious
of the man staring at him. *Coincidence?* He nonchalantly
glanced around and memorized the plate. *The buildings
are commercial and closed for Sunday. Odd place to be
waiting for someone.*

A moment later he rounded the corner where Graves
had gone, but could no longer see him. The only place
open was the bar, so he paused to quickly jot the licence
plate number of the pickup on his wrist, then headed
toward the bar. As he opened the door, Graves literally
brushed past him on his way out. He was with another
man — clean-shaven with short brown hair, Ferg noted.
He looked to be about thirty years old.

Ferg continued inside the bar, then glanced around
briefly to make it appear to anyone watching that he may
have been looking for a friend. He then went back outside.

The door to the bar was slightly inset from the building and he was able to peek around the corner in time to
see Graves and the other man turn right at the side street
where Graves had parked his truck.

Okay, the guy in the Ram … is he a lookout or not?

Ferg kept to the shadows and crept up to the corner
and took a peek. The man with the beard was still in his
truck, but Graves and the clean-cut man had continued
on past his truck, as well as Graves's own truck.

Do I follow or stay put and risk losing them? He grimaced
as he looked at his wrist, then called in the licence plate
number to the truck. The answer he received told him
he couldn't walk past the Ram again. The plate was registered to a red Chevy sedan. *Oh yeah, they've got counter-surveillance.*

Ferg's next call was to his team, who reported that they were thirty minutes away. "We don't have thirty minutes," Ferg replied. "The deal is happening now." A flash of light caught his eye. "Hang on, the yahoo in the Ram flashed his headlights. Wait … yup, it's what I figured. The guy in the Ram gave them the all clear. Graves and the clean-cut guy are walking back toward him."

Ferg watched as the man with the beard got out and went to the back and opened the rear door on the canopy as Graves and his associate joined him. *Perfect.*

Ferg then whispered into his phone. "I gotta go. The deal is happening right in front of me." As he pulled out his weapon, the bearded man handed Graves a backpack from out of the canopy. While the three men were distracted looking at the bag, Ferg scooted up the street toward them — his soft-soled rubber shoes not betraying his approach.

"Don't move!" he yelled. "You're under arrest!"

Three faces turned and gawked. He partially crouched behind them in a shooter's stance, levelling his pistol straight at them. "All of you! Hands in the air!" He motioned Graves with the muzzle of his pistol. "Drop the bag! Do it!"

The bag landed with a clunk from the guns inside, and all three raised their hands.

"Lace your fingers over your head and drop to your knees!"

The three men slowly started to comply.

Ferg's aim was steady. He'd made many arrests in his career and hadn't become complacent when it came to maintaining an acute focus of every eye movement or unspoken signal that their faces might portray.

It was only at the last second that his thoughts were diverted by a truck rapidly approaching from behind. By then, it was too late.

Ferg's body was impacted with the grille first and then flung in the air. His first instinct was to protect his head and cup his arms around his temples, but he was too late. The back of his head hit the windshield and he heard the crunch of glass as it spider-webbed out from the back of his skull. Next came the squealing of tires as the driver applied the brakes. The momentum sent his body flying off the hood and tumbling down the road.

Despite multiple broken bones he was still conscious, and, for a moment, still in shock as his brain started to process the pain. He heard the driver get out and run toward him. For a brief moment he thought … or hoped … it was an accident.

A balding man of about sixty looked down on him. *His face … I've seen it before.*

Another man, also sporting a beard, appeared beside the older man.

"Where the hell were you?" the older man asked the new arrival.

"Across the street like I was supposed to be. I only had one car to hide behind and, as you can see, it's a little farther down."

"Too far to get a good shot in," the older man surmised.

"Yeah, I seen he had his gun out. I was gonna wait until he was busy handcuffin' them, then make my move."

The three other men's faces appeared over him and the older man looked at them. "He's still alive," he stated, then looked down at Ferg.

Christ, he's holding a pistol with a silencer. He's going to kill me. Betty, I'm so sorry. I love you so —

The older man spoke to him. "Y'all didn't think I'd let you arrest my boy now, did you?"

Ferg didn't reply. His breathing was laboured and came in shallow, painful gasps.

The man then looked at Graves and gestured to him with the silencer on the muzzle of his gun. "You led 'im right to us." His words sounded matter-of-fact.

"I did everything I was supposed to," Graves protested.

"They obviously know about you," the older man stated.

Graves shrugged and looked at the others. "I don't know how," he replied.

The older man cleared his throat. "You understand that a man has to protect his family, don't you, boy?"

"What? No! I'd never tell —"

A hole appeared in Graves's forehead and blood squirted out the back of his skull. His body landed with a thud beside Ferg. The older man stared down at the body. "May the Lord have mercy upon your soul."

He then looked at Ferg. "And may he have mercy upon your soul, as well."

Chapter Thirty

At 10:00 p.m. Jack was about to watch the evening news with Natasha when he received a call. "Washington area code," he said as he grabbed his phone.

"Finally," Natasha said. "You've been antsy ever since you got home."

"Ferg!" he answered.

"This isn't Ferg. It's Ray Schneider. I work for Ferg." There was a long pause before he asked, "Are you Jack Taggart?"

"Yes."

"Where the fuck are you?" he asked angrily.

"Home … in Canada. What's going on?"

Ray spoke to someone in the background. "He's safe. Sitting at home in Canada, if you can believe it. Left Ferg high and dry all on his own."

"What the hell happened?" Jack asked.

"What happened?" Ray repeated. Then he screamed into the phone. "What happened is Ferg is dead!"

No … oh no. Please no.

"He got run over, then shot in the face … no thanks to you!"

No. Please tell me this is all a stupid joke. Put Ferg on the phone.

"Christ, Ray, give me that," a voice in the background said. The man identified himself as Special Agent Wayne Dawson. He was polite, but the gravity of the situation had reduced his voice to a robotic-sounding monotone. He explained that they had found Ferg and Graves lying on a side street in Ferndale, about a twenty-five-minute drive south of the border.

Jack felt numb, not wanting to believe what he was hearing. Wishing he'd wake up and discover it was all a dream. His stomach sloshed bile up his throat like white-caps hitting a beach. He swallowed repeatedly to get rid of the acid, only to be hit by another wave.

For Jack, Wayne's narration never seemed to end, out-lining grisly details that he wished weren't true — but wishing didn't change the truth.

"Honey? What is it?" Natasha asked with concern.

"Ferg was murdered," he whispered. He saw the shock register on her face and wished he could say more to com-fort her. Instead, he gestured with his finger to his lips for her to be quiet so he could listen to Wayne. As he did, he took slow and moderate breaths, hoping to calm his nerves and his stomach.

"We believe whoever ran him down was parked across an intersection from the main drag on the same side street Ferg was on," Wayne continued. "We found Ferg's weapon lying on the street. It hasn't been discharged, so it wasn't him who killed Graves."

"Any witnesses?" Jack heard himself ask. *My voice sounds like a stranger's.*

"Nope." Wayne paused. "There's bits of windshield glass embedded in the back of his head. Our theory is that whoever did it came barrellin' through the intersection and nailed him from behind when he was trying to make an arrest."

Less than twenty-five minutes from the border ... I should have been there. Not sitting at home.

"We're presuming he was still conscious after," Wayne continued. "That'd explain why they shot him in the face afterward."

Jack's brain replayed an image of Ferg's jovial face and big smile. Then the image was replaced by something much more horrific.

"We have roadblocks up everywhere," Wayne advised. "Graves's truck is still here. Maybe they clued in that there's a tracker on it."

"I put the tracker inside his tool box. It's inside a rolled-up black plastic pouch which has pockets for tools," Jack offered lamely.

Wayne acted like he hadn't heard. "So, we're looking for a vehicle with considerable damage to the windshield. So far that's our only real obvious clue. Ferg had written a licence plate number down on his wrist. He'd told us there was a guy with a beard in a Ram truck who was doing the deal, but the plate turned out to be stolen. The owner didn't know it was gone until our officers went to his house."

Jack took the pause that followed to ask, "Has Betty been —"

"Two from our office are on their way to see her. She needs to know before she hears something on the news."

"I'm sorry," Jack said. "I don't know what to say."

"Yeah, well, being sorry can come later. Right now we need to catch the son-of-a-bitch who did it."

"Of course. Is there anything I can —"

"We'd appreciate it if you could search where Graves lives. See if you can find anything that might link him to someone down here. There's no phone on his body, so they must have taken it. We're grasping for anything we can get at this point."

"I ... I'm on it," Jack said. "Give me your contact details and I'll call you back in a few hours."

Jack had wanted to sound firm and professional, but his words were shaky and anything but firm as he fumbled for his notebook.

A minute later he ended the call and looked at Natasha. She seemed at a loss for words. He hugged her and said, "It looks like Ferg was making an arrest when someone drove into him and then shot him." His words seemed blunt and without feeling. It wasn't how he felt, but he had work to do and was making a determined effort to keep his emotions in check.

He felt Natasha tremble as she clung to him. "That's so awful," she said. "His poor wife ... Betty ... I —"

"I know." He patted her on the back and held her a moment longer. "I have to go." He gently pushed her back and his eyes met hers. "Don't worry. I'll be careful."

Chapter Thirty-One

Jack obtained a search warrant and rounded up three members from the Major Crimes Unit, who would be assigned the investigation on the Canadian side of the border. It was 3:00 a.m. when he buzzed the apartment manager.

"It's the middle of the bloody night," the manager complained as he let them into the building. "I'd like to know what's so damned important that you couldn't wait until morning."

"An officer was murdered tonight," Jack said harshly. "So was Derek Graves, who lives in this building. Is that important enough for you? 'Cause it sure is for me."

"Uh, yes, sir. Sorry."

"We have a search warrant for his place," Jack stated.

"I, uh, don't have a key to let you in to his place," the manager replied.

"Not a problem. Do the tenants have storage lockers?"

"No."

"Good. Go back to your own apartment. I'll let you know when we're done."

A moment later Jack approached Graves's apartment door and pulled out his pistol. He then glanced at his three colleagues, who did likewise.

Some of Jack's fury was channelled into the kick he gave the door. It crashed open with so much force that it imbedded the door knob into the drywall on the wall behind. A quick check told them the apartment was deserted and they holstered their weapons.

Jack then paused to scan what he saw. Near the entrance was the kitchen, which had a sink full of dirty dishes. The kitchen table held a laptop, and two mismatched chairs were pulled up to the table.

Bordering the kitchen was a living room, which consisted of a television set, a sofa, and two stacks of cement bricks with a plank on top to make a coffee table.

The back of the sofa appeared to have been used by a cat or cats as a scratching post, but there were no cat dishes or anything to indicate he had a pet. It left Jack with the impression that Graves had likely retrieved the sofa from the garbage. A large cardboard swastika that had been blackened with shoe polish adorned the wall behind the sofa.

While one member from MCU took an interest in the computer, another started to search the kitchen. Jack and the remaining officer went to the bedroom, which contained an unmade twin bed and a dresser.

Two photos were propped against empty beer bottles on top of the dresser. In one, Graves was smiling from the driver's seat of a vintage model Corvette Stingray. Jack thought Graves may have looked more impressive if it hadn't been for a tall potted plant beside an array of windows to indicate the car was in a showroom.

The second photo was the one Jack had seen on Graves's website — the one where he was leering at the camera with two pistols stuck in his waistband. It was obvious from the swastika in the background that the picture had been taken in the living room.

What murderous piece of shit would deal guns to an idiot like you?

The search didn't take long and there was nothing obvious to connect Graves with anyone in the United States. Hate literature, which appeared to have been copied from various internet sites, was found in his dresser.

The photos, hate literature, and laptop computer were seized by MCU, who would turn the laptop over to Forensics when their office opened in a few hours.

It was 5:00 a.m. when Jack returned to his office and called Wayne Dawson in Washington to tell him what, or, in reality, what they had *not* found.

"Nothing on our end, either," Wayne said, sounding depressed. "We still have roadblocks set up, but after this length of time I'm doubtful we'll get anything. Forensics is still on the scene, but I haven't heard if they found anything or not."

"Maybe the laptop we seized will reveal something," Jack said.

"Let's hope so. I'm the lead investigator, so let me know."

"I will as soon as I hear." He heard a wavering female voice in the background. "Where are you?" he asked.

"At Ferg's … uh, Betty's place."

"Can I talk to her?"

"Just a moment." Jack heard a murmur of voices, then Wayne came back on the line. "She's, uh, resting."

"Tell her I'll call her later," Jack replied.

"I think it best you wait until she feels up to calling you."

Jack sighed. *Yeah, I get the message.*

*   *   *

Rose was starting work a few minutes earlier than usual, but it was the first Monday of the month and that meant more administrative work needed to be completed to appease the bureaucrats.

She looked in and greeted her secretary before continuing down the hall to her own office. As she hung up her coat she realized she was being watched. "Wow, you're in early," she said when she saw that it was Jack.

Jack swallowed, then held a report toward her while hoarsely announcing what he had to say. "Read this. It'll explain what happened better than I can articulate at the moment."

Oh Christ ... what happened? Rose took the report from his hand, sat down, then stared at him as he took a seat across from her. She'd seen him looking tired and depressed before, but never like this. His face was sallow and dark shadows made his eyes look sunken.

He gestured to the report. "Read it."

She stared at the report but couldn't immediately bring herself to read it. She felt sickened that whatever was in it had affected Jack that much. Then she inhaled deeply and let her breath out slowly as she focused on the words.

When she finished reading, she felt worse than she'd imagined. The report was strictly factual. No room for the emotion or trauma that went with such an event. Emotion and trauma that she knew Jack was trying to deal with.

"That pretty well sums it up," Jack said, gesturing toward the report with a flick of his hand. "A factual account of what my investigation and actions have achieved."

"Jack, what happened isn't your —" A flash of anger in his eyes told her to stop. She bit her lower lip. *Okay, I'll try to keep emotion out of it for now.* She swallowed. "This is international. I need to advise Lexton pronto and give her a copy."

He stared at her silently in response.

Rose took another deep breath, then called Lexton's secretary and made an appointment. When she ended the call she looked at Jack. "We can see her at nine o'clock."

He didn't respond.

Rose glanced at her watch. "Gives us twenty-five minutes. Do you want a coffee?"

He shook his head. "I'll wait in my office."

As he got to his feet their secretary arrived with the mail. Rose glanced at the first item on top of the pile. *Oh God, no. Not now.*

Jack read her face. "Permission granted allowing me to cross the border?"

She nodded.

His jawline hardened and he briefly squeezed his eyes shut in an apparent attempt to control his own emotions, then he left.

Chapter Thirty-Two

Lexton read some of the incoming mail in her basket, then glanced at her watch. *Two minutes to nine....* She pondered over what the meeting could be about. All her secretary had said was that Staff Sergeant Wood had said it was urgent.

Does it have something to do with Quaile? Did he figure out it was his secretary who first spilled the beans? She shook her head. *Doubtful. That dolt continually thinks of himself, but he doesn't have the capacity to think for himself.*

"Your nine o'clock meeting has arrived," her secretary announced.

Lexton gave Rose a polite smile as she entered her office, then saw Taggart trailing behind. *What the hell has he done this time?*

As they dutifully took a seat across from her desk, she glanced at a piece of correspondence she'd received earlier that morning. "I see permission has been granted for investigators to work in the U.S. on your cross-border gun smuggling file. I'm glad to see it. That's good."

"Yeah ... real good," Taggart said. His voice cracked and he looked like he hadn't slept in a week.

Hungover, perhaps?

Rose glanced nervously at Taggart. "There's, uh, been an incident," she said, as if in explanation. "Perhaps it'd be better if you read this first," she added, handing her the report.

"Oh?" Lexton replied. She couldn't help glaring at Taggart as she accepted it. *So that's why you look the way you do. You did something, got caught, and it's time to pay the piper.* She flipped to the last page. *Submitted by Taggart.* She looked at Rose and scowled. *Yes, he's done something.*

"It's better to read the report first," Rose suggested. "Then we can discuss the issue."

Yes, the issue ... whatever that is. She started reading. "Oh my God," she heard herself say when she read about Special Agent Ferguson's murder. It was as if someone else had blurted out the words. Someone from another dimension. Certainly not a dimension she wished to be part of.

She felt her stomach knot and swallowed, then snuck a peek at Taggart. He was staring at her stone-faced. She then took a deep breath and continued reading. When she was finished, she put the report aside and stared quietly at him, hoping for a moment to collect her thoughts. She didn't get that moment.

He leaned forward, his face distorted and seething with rage. "The important thing is you can rest easy knowing I didn't violate policy by going into the U.S. without permission! I left him, to use the words of one of his guys, high and dry on his own!"

"Corporal Taggart!" Rose said sharply in an attempt to shut him up. Her attempt failed.

"Yup, we can all be proud that on this side of the border we respect our policy. Mind you, his wife, Betty, might disagree."

"Corporal Taggart! That is no way to address a superior off—"

Lexton silenced Rose with a gesture of her hand. "It's okay ... I'm upset as well."

"Upset?" Taggart snarled. "A law enforcement officer is murdered and all you feel is ... upset?"

She stared at him, hoping to give him a chance to calm down, then continued. "I heard you use the phrase that people need to see the big picture. Policy is part of that big picture."

"Yeah, some policy," he retorted.

"I happen to agree with this particular policy. We can't have law enforcement officials from two different countries, who are trained differently and operating under different judicial processes, hopping back and forth across the border without permission. Yes, I'm upset. I'm upset because I don't see a better solution to that policy. As far as the perpetrator or perpetrators who ran down the officer and then killed him in cold blood, I feel sickened by it. No doubt how you felt when you first received the news."

Taggart swallowed and his face paled when he appeared to reflect back.

Lexton decided to continue. "Undoubtedly, like most people, I will also feel the emotions that follow, such as grief and anger." She waited a beat. "It may interest you to know that I did not rise to this position easily. I've earned my way, and for your information this is not the first murdered officer I've encountered in my career."

He looked at her and his face softened. "Mine either," he said glumly.

"I want to do everything within our power to help the U.S. in their investigation. But we will do that while obeying policy and following the letter of the law." She paused, then asked, "Do you feel you're capable of performing your duties as I've described?"

"Yes," he replied. He looked into her eyes. "I apologize for my outburst. Directing my anger at you was totally uncalled for."

Directing it at me? My guess is you're angry with yourself for following policy and not crossing the border — which next time could make you a loose cannon. She cleared her throat. "I presume, from your report, that MCU has taken the lead on our side of the border?"

"Yes, as per policy, I turned the brunt of the investigation over to them ... although it is remotely possible I may be able to assist with the help of an informant."

As per policy? Was that another dig at me? "Corporal, it would appear that you are too emotionally distraught at the moment to act in a professional manner. If that persists, then I will see to it that you're removed from the investigation entirely."

He looked puzzled, then appeared to understand why she'd said what she did. "Sorry, my comment about policy was not intended as a barb."

Wasn't it? She stared at him. *He seems genuine. Perhaps too tired to choose his words carefully? Then again, he's an*

operator whose ability to deceive comes as easy as breathing.
"How long has it been since you slept?"

"Since I slept?" He glanced at his watch. "Uh, I guess about twenty-six hours."

"Then you need to go home and get some sleep. It doesn't appear that there's anything you can do at the moment."

"I have an informant who might be able to nose around," he suggested lamely. "It's a long shot, but maybe down the road someone else will contact the gangs to sell them guns."

She nodded indifferently. "It will take a few days to download Graves's computer. In the meantime, go home, get some rest, and we'll discuss the situation in a couple of days."

She thumbed through the daily diary on her phone. "Ten o'clock Wednesday morning." She stared at Taggart, then added, "At that time I'll be making a decision as to whether or not you remain involved in any way."

He stared at her blankly without any sign of emotion.

No anger or surprise? Perhaps the trauma coupled with exhaustion has left him numb. Either that or he knows I'm right and that he should be removed from the investigation entirely.

Chapter Thirty-Three

As Jack and Rose walked back to their offices she looked at him and opened her mouth to say something, then appeared to change her mind and continued on.

"What is it?" he snapped.

Rose gave him a hard look. "I figure I don't need to tell you that you came off as anything but professional in there."

"You really think I don't know that?" he replied harshly. *Okay, calm down.* "I did apologize," he added matter-of-factly.

"She's not a person you give the tone to."

"The tone?"

"You know exactly what I mean. You have a habit of changing the tone of your voice so that the words you say may not be construed as offensive, but your tone implies sarcasm. She's not a person you should be messing with like that."

I know. I was angry. I couldn't help myself. I'm still angry.

"She means it when she said she's thinking of taking you off the case. You'll need to present a different attitude to her on Wednesday."

That's if she hasn't already made up her mind. I was such an ass in there I deserve to be taken off.

"Go home and pull yourself together," Rose continued, not unkindly. "Get some rest."

"I'm too upset to go home and sleep."

"Maybe it'd be a good idea for the both of us to get out of here. Perhaps we could go to a coffee shop? Give you a chance to decompress before going home."

"Your version of a psychiatrist's couch?" Jack asked.

Rose shrugged. "If you're feeling like you need to talk, that'd be fine. If not, that'd be fine, too."

He gave her a pat on the back as they walked. "Thanks. I know you care, but maybe I should just go home and get some rest. I know I need to calm down and get my act together. I'm going to grab my coat and head home."

"Okay … good. Stay home tomorrow and I'll see you Wednesday."

Jack entered his office and put on his coat — but Rose's suggestion of a coffee shop played with his memory. *Did I miss something at the coffee shop when Graves met Linquist?*

He paused at the door, then pulled out his phone and thumbed through the pictures he'd taken that day and studied the photos of the man who'd come out of the coffee shop and used his phone. Another photo showed him being picked up by a woman in a car with a toddler seat in the back. *You're grasping at straws. Go home and get some rest….*

Then another picture caught his eye. It was one he'd taken moments before the man came out of the coffee shop. It was of the car with dealer plates that had circled the block a couple of times. The driver looked to be in his late twenties with a bristle of short blond hair.

Dealer plates? He felt a surge of optimism. *Could it be?*

He hustled back to his desk and made a call to check the ownership of the dealer plates and discovered they were registered to Johnny's New and Used Cars. The business was about a twenty-five-minute drive from the coffee shop where Graves met Linquist.

Long way to go for a test drive....

When he left his office, he glanced down the hall toward Rose's office. *Do I tell her about my suspicions?* He stifled a yawn. *She'll say I'm acting in desperation and order me to go home.* He gave a snort. *Maybe I am.*

Forty minutes later he walked into the showroom at Johnny's. The convertible Corvette Stingray he'd seen in the photograph at Graves's apartment was not there. What he did see, however, was the same potted plant in front of the same array of windows that were in the photo. He felt the adrenalin pump through his veins. *Okay, who are you, you son of a bitch?*

A dozen framed photographs of the salespeople adorned one wall. Each person's name was under the photo and he recognized the person with the bristle of short blond hair as being the driver of the car outside the coffee shop. The name under the photograph identified him as Erich Vath.

Gotcha, asshole!

As he gazed at the photograph his thoughts went to whoever had murdered Ferg. *Okay, you bastard, whoever you are, I've picked up your scent. The U.S. border be damned. You and I are going to have a face to face!*

He brushed off the advances of a salesman who approached and returned to his car. He then placed a call to the RCMP Telecommunications Centre to check Vath's name for a driver's licence and any vehicle registrations. There was only one Erich Vath listed and his address was a basement suite not far from the dealership. A white Hyundai was registered in his name.

Jack's next call was to Wayne Dawson. By the sound of his groggy hello he knew he'd awakened him.

"It's Jack Taggart. Sorry to wake you."

Wayne became instantly alert. "You got something for us off the computer?" he asked excitedly.

"Nothing back on the computer yet. That'll take a few days, but I do have a possible lead that I'll follow on this end."

"A lead! Who?"

"A Canadian by the name of Erich Vath. He did counter-surveillance when Graves was selling guns to someone a couple of weeks ago, but I didn't find that out until a few minutes ago. I've an idea for an undercover approach, but first need to meet with an informant to arrange an introduction. If it works, Vath might introduce me to who his gun supplier is."

"Undercover?" Wayne paused, then said what was on his mind. "Uh, I expect with what happened that they'll be pretty damn cautious about meeting anyone new. If you scare Vath away, he may never go to his source."

"I'm aware of that, but the approach will be through someone Vath will trust completely and who he knows has already bought guns from Graves. If his supplier has shut things down, my plan might not work, but at the same time, it wouldn't heat anyone up."

"I see. If Vath already knows him, then there's nothing to lose by you trying it."

"Exactly." Jack waited a beat. "First, though, I need your guarantee that if I do get Vath to lead me to his connection, that he not be arrested, and if need be, my identity and profession also remain a secret."

"You want to make it look like either you or Vath are informants? Or maybe both?"

"Yes. It would take the heat off the real one."

"We can work with that," Wayne said quickly. "We'll go along with anything if it'll give us who killed Ferg."

"Good. It might take a couple of days, but I'll be in touch."

"Baby Jesus, if this works … thanks."

Jack was about to end the call. *There's one more thing.* "I received permission allowing me to enter the States. It came through this morning."

Wayne was silent for a moment. "The funeral is scheduled for next Monday. Thought you might want to know that," he added, then terminated the call.

And how welcome would I be at that?

Chapter Thirty-Four

Jack felt the kick from Lance's boot on the sole of his shoe and opened his eyes. He felt a shiver go through his body and didn't know if it was because of the cold marble tombstone he'd had his back against or whether it was from a lack of food and sleep.

"Are you dead?" Lance asked. "Should I get a shovel and bury you? Maybe with one of them fancy tombstones you were talking about getting me with the cop crest?"

"I'm alive," Jack responded, getting to his feet.

"Were you sleeping?"

"I'm not sure. Maybe I was. It's been a long day."

Lance glanced at his watch. "It's only two p.m."

"My day started yesterday with the guy you call Zombie. His real name was Derek Graves."

"Was?" Lance asked.

The surge of adrenalin Jack had felt earlier after discovering Vath had long since vanished. Knowing what he was about to say and ask made talking seem like an effort.

An Element of Risk 261

Not to mention depressing. "I managed to get a tracker on his truck. He went to the States last night and I had an ATF agent follow him. Both the agent and Graves were murdered less than an hour later in the middle of the street in some little town called Ferndale. At the moment there are no witnesses and no suspects."

"Holy fuck. So that's why you look like shit."

"I feel like shit."

"You weren't there when it happened?"

"No, I wasn't fucking there," Jack replied angrily.

Lance paused. "I was just asking."

Jack made a face. "Yeah … I know. Sorry. You rubbed a sore spot."

"Can you tell me what happened?"

"It appeared that the agent was making an arrest when someone drove into him from behind. After that he was shot in the face while lying in the middle of the road. Graves's body was beside his and we think he was killed to stop any chance of the police using him to get to his connection."

"You want me to put the squeeze on the Death Heads to see if they know anything?"

"No."

"Good, because doing that would really make me look bad."

If you think that's risky, wait until you hear this....

"Besides," Lance continued. "I doubt that they'd know anything. From what I was told, they only knew Zombie, and if he's dead, then —"

"I'm a step ahead of all that. I've identified someone who acted as a lookout for Graves when Linquist met him. A fellow by the name of Erich Vath."

"Okay …" Lance replied, sounding confused. "I've never heard of him," he offered.

"We also learned that the United Front are getting weapons from a robbery in Arkansas that the FBI suspect was done by the same people who did the murders and robbery of the store in Alabama."

"The one where the FBI is looking for two brothers," Lance noted.

"Yes."

Lance eyed him warily. "So why're you telling me?"

"I want to do an undercover scam. My theory is that Graves was selling weapons to the Death Heads and his buddy Vath was selling to the United Front."

"Yeah, probably."

"Vath is a car salesman. It'd be easy for me to meet him on the pretext of buying a car and see if I can scam him into selling me a gun, but I don't think it'd work."

"I doubt it would either," Lance replied. "Not after what happened. You being a new face showing up — hell, they'd make you in a second. Not to mention, everyone involved has probably gone to ground. The heat is on, obviously."

"Exactly."

Lance looked more agitated. "So?"

"How'd you like to earn your freedom?" Jack asked.

Lance gave a snort. "I take it that question isn't rhetorical, so what do you have in mind?"

"I need to bait the trap and spark their greed."

"It would take a lot of bait after what happened last night."

"You're right … it will. Forget about buying a couple of guns. I'm going to ask for five hundred."

"Five hundred! What the fuck? If you came askin' for my advice, I'm tellin' ya, that's way over the top." He shook his head in admonishment. "What are you going to say? Tell them you're purchasing them for some army in South America? They'll never believe —"

"They will if I'm introduced to them by somebody they'd trust as genuine. Someone who is an executive officer in a crime family that has that many members and associates in Canada alone."

Lance looked taken back. "Fuck, you want me to introduce you to him?"

"That's my plan."

Lance took a deep breath, then let out a low whistle. "Sure, I want to get you off my back and earn my freedom — but not if I end up here," he said, gesturing to a tombstone.

Jack grimaced. "Hear me out first. I won't push you into this if you don't want to do it. Believe me, I'm already worried that you'll agree to do something you shouldn't. I want you to think long and hard about the potential consequences of what I'm about to suggest."

"Meeting in this place, I'd have to be pretty fuckin' stupid not to realize the consequences," Lance said dryly.

Jack glanced around at the cemetery then turned back to Lance. "I've got a couple of thoughts, but I'm so bloody tired I feel like my brain is in a fog. If what I suggest doesn't make sense or feel right to you, I wouldn't be totally surprised and we'll drop the idea."

"All right. Let's hear it."

"What if you introduced me to Vath and I convince him to introduce me to his connection in the States? I'd then meet the connection, maybe set up the purchase, and then I'd leave. The Americans would then arrest whoever the connection is, and with luck, seize the weapons. I've already got them to promise they'd never identify me in court. It'd make it look like I was the informant."

"Uh-uh. That wouldn't work because it would've been me who vouched for you. When word got out what happened, it wouldn't take my guys long to figure it out, especially when you weren't even known to them ... or at least whatever name you used wouldn't be known to them. Not to mention, if they did find out it was actually you, I'd be dead. Maybe someone in my family, too."

Jack sighed. "I wondered what the ramifications would be for you vouching for someone that supposedly turned out to be an informant, but thought I'd ask. As I said, my brain is in a fog, but what you said makes sense. Particularly the last bit."

"It'd be the same thing if you tried to make Vath look like the informant when it came out that the weapons were for Satans Wrath. Even if you remained anonymous, once it was discovered that it was me who introduced you to do the deal, everyone in our club would wonder who the hell you were. Same thing if we left you out of the scenario and I placed the order myself so you could follow him. There's no way our club needs five hundred pieces at the moment. Even if we did, we'd go through our chapters in the States."

"Yeah, that figures."

"Plus, I'm a president," Lance noted. "If we ever did contact Vath, we'd send a prospect or someone other than exec level. It sure as hell wouldn't be me talking to him."

"Okay, okay," Jack said. "I still have one last plan to run past you."

Lance looked skeptical.

"What if you introduce me to Vath in a way you could deny having introduced me later on?"

"What are you thinking?"

"As long as I was never identified in the U.S., and neither Vath nor I were arrested, it might make it look like we were both informants to whoever was busted in the States. Vath wouldn't know what to think. Maybe he'd think I was the informant, but if he said anything, you'd have the option of saying he was the informant and denying ever having introduced him to me."

Lance stared at the ground while running his tongue along the inside of his upper lip as he thought.

"In the end, your word would be believed over his," Jack prodded. "If he'd half a brain, he'd know that." He paused as he eyed Lance, then added, "Not to mention, it'd probably get him killed if he accused you of setting him up."

Lance raised an eyebrow. "*Probably* get him killed?" he questioned.

Yeah, I'm tired. Guess there'd be no doubt.

Lance stared silently at Jack for a moment. "The thing is, if he did say something, trying to squelch what he said later would be like trying to put the toothpaste back in the tube. Yes, my word would initially be believed over his. At least officially it would, but unofficially there'd be suspicion. Particularly if Whiskey Jake discovers that the lawyer's files from Mexico on our money laundering scam have disappeared. He might put two and two together and clue in that you have them and used them to turn me."

"Meaning there'd still be an element of risk," Jack stated.

Lance gave him a hard look. "It's an element of risk I'd deal with — if you're telling me that you and I would then be finished, that I'd be free to go on with my life without having you hanging off my back."

Jack swallowed as he thought about what he was asking. *Is my logic blinded by my need to catch Ferg's killer? Ferg had a wife, children, and grandchildren. Lance has a wife, children, and a grandchild. Is it right to have him risk his life, too?* He studied Lance's face. *No longer friendly and easy-going like he was a moment ago. Dangerous ... his eyes calculating ... yeah, he'll do what it takes to survive, but that in itself raises a question. Is it right?*

Lance raised an eyebrow. "So? Is it a deal?"

There are grey areas and there are black. This is definitely black.

Jack stuck out his hand. "Yeah, it's a deal. You'll be able to take your money and retire for all I care — providing whoever it was who did the murders last night is caught."

Lance engulfed Jack's hand like it was a child's, gripping it tight and giving a solitary shake. "Good," he said, before letting go.

"Yeah, good," Jack replied.

Lance looked at Jack curiously. "Now, my worry is that part of the plan will hinge on whatever string of shit you're going to tell Vath to bait the trap."

"I'm confident I can pull that off."

Lance seemed surprised. "Are you?"

"Graves was a racist. I'm betting his buddy Vath is, too. Birds of a feather type of thing."

"How does that help?"

"Racists are gullible when it comes to believing things that aren't true as long as it fits into what they want to believe. Couple that with greed, and I'm sure I'll achieve the results I want."

Lance stroked his chin and stared at a tombstone. Then he looked at Jack. "How do you want to go about it? For me to introduce you without my guys knowing about it, yet still seem believable to Vath? It might not be easy. Especially when I've never even heard of him and I doubt any of my guys have."

"I've got an idea for that," Jack said.

"I expected you would," Lance replied sardonically.

"My idea will also plant a seed amongst your guys that Vath is an informant. It'll help if they ever do get wind of it later on."

Lance gave a begrudging smile. "You really do cover all the bases."

Jack scowled. *I didn't last night....*

Lance was quick to read Jack's face. "What's wrong?" he asked.

"Nothing," he replied automatically. He then locked eyes. "I'll have your back on this right to the end," he said solemnly. "That I promise."

Chapter Thirty-Five

As he left the cemetery, Lance called André Gagnon, who was the vice-president of his chapter, and said, "I got a call at my amusement centre from some guy by the name of Erich Vath who wants to meet me. Said he has a real interesting deal to discuss, but will only talk to me."

"Erich Vath?" Gagnon repeated. "Never heard of him. How'd he get your name or know where you work? It seems suspicious."

"He said he got my name and where I work from someone we do business with, but didn't want to say who it was over the phone. At first I was skeptical, but he did give me a number to call him back at a car dealership where he works. I checked that part out and it's legit. He wants to meet me tomorrow night when he gets off work."

"You want him grabbed?"

"Naw, he sort of piqued my interest. I don't want to scare him off until I hear what he has to say. I'll meet

An Element of Risk   269

with him, but instead of meeting him after work tomorrow, I'm going to pay him a visit at the dealership when he's still there."

"Catch him by surprise."

"Exactly. I also want to show the patch to make sure he gets an up-close feeling for who he's fuckin' with. Round up half-a-dozen or so of the guys and tell 'em to wear their colours. We'll take a little ride tomorrow around noon."

* * *

As tired as Jack was, that night he had a fitful night of sleep. His brain played havoc and left him fighting for his life in his dreams. When the nightmares did wake him he'd lie there and worry about how successful his plan would go with Lance.

At 5:30 a.m. he got up to use the washroom, and when he came back to the bedroom he saw Natasha returning from the living room with her pillow.

"Not again," he said.

She nodded. "The sofa was safer than the risk of being punched and kicked."

"I'm sorry. You should've woken me and I'd have slept on the sofa. When I got up a minute ago I hadn't even realized you'd left."

"I didn't want to wake you. I knew you needed to sleep." She looked at him curiously. "Speaking of which, did you get any?"

"Get any?" He pretended to think about it, then replied, "Sleep or sex? I'm too tired to remember."

Natasha eyed him scornfully. "If you'd had sex with me last night you'd remember." She tried unsuccessfully to keep a pert smile off her face.

"It's been that long, has it?"

She wrapped her arms around him, then kissed him passionately before murmuring, "You tell me how long it's been."

"Uh …"

She whispered in his ear and said, "It'll take your mind off of things and help you get back to sleep."

"Doctor's orders?"

"Yes."

* * *

The rumble and vibration of eight Harley-Davidsons pulling up in front of the showroom at Johnny's New and Used Cars caught everyone's attention. Even more so when they realized all the riders were full-patch members of Satans Wrath.

The bikers parked their hogs in a cluster, then milled around on the pretext of looking at some cars that were for sale. Soon a salesman appeared from out of the showroom and hesitantly asked if he could be of assistance.

Lance stepped away from the group. "I'm interested in that van," he said, gesturing to a van parked at the end of a long row, farthest from the showroom. "I want to deal with a guy by the name of Erich Vath."

"He's inside," the salesman replied, looking relieved. "I'll send him out," he added as he scurried back into the showroom.

Vath appeared a moment later and Lance met him out of earshot of the rest.

"You looking to buy a van?" Vath asked.

Lance noticed Vath checking out his colours, including the emblem on his chest which identified him as president. He glowered down at Vath, then turned and walked toward the van.

"You want us to wait, boss?" Gagnon yelled.

"Yeah. We won't be long."

"I was told you asked for me," Vath said, sounding friendly as he hurried to keep pace.

Lance kept walking.

"Have we met before?" Vath asked.

Lance gave him a hard look. "No," he said in a manner that didn't invite further conversation.

When they arrived Vath fumbled to open the van door, but before he could Lance shoved him against the side of the vehicle and held him in place with one hand on his chest.

"Wha ... what's going on?"

"I'm not here to buy a van," Lance stated. "I'm here because we know you deal with Derek and —"

"Who?" Vath asked nervously.

"Derek Graves ... or do you call 'im Zombie?" Lance questioned.

"Uh ... uh ..."

"Don't fuck with me," Lance replied.

"No, sir, but —"

"But what? We know you stood six for him last week when he met our guy."

Vath's mouth flopped open.

"Can you imagine what would happen if someone

tipped off the Death Heads that you're doing business with them and the United Front at the same time?"

"You … you know that?"

"Of course we fuckin' know that. We've been keeping tabs on you for some time. The United Front and the Death Heads don't know what you're up to, but if you try to bullshit me, that'll change."

"Please, no, don't do that," he begged.

"I'll decide on that after we're done talkin'."

Vath's eyes widened and he glanced back at the other bikers. "So you were there when Borman introduced your guy to Zombie? That's how you know about me?"

"No, I wasn't there myself. I'm president, for fuck sakes. I send my guys to do that shit." He shook his head as if in disbelief. "Why are you surprised? Did you think you were dealing with amateurs? That you're the only guy smart enough to do counter-surveillance?"

"No, I … no, I, uh, of course. Your guy's reputation is, uh …"

"Is what?"

"Is … is solid," he stammered. "Everyone knows that."

Lance glared at him, then lowered his hand from his chest. "You're fuckin' right it's solid. Speaking of which, me talking to you is a one-time thing. I don't normally get involved on a personal level with this shit. The only reason I showed up is so you and your people will know that we're serious."

"My people?"

Lance stared in response.

"I … I see." Vath swallowed as he straightened his sports jacket and adjusted his tie, then asked, "What do you want with me?"

"Something urgent has been decided and we can't seem to get hold of Graves, but we know you can. We have a business proposition for him. A very profitable one."

"Uh, I, uh, I guess you don't know. Uh —"

"Know what?"

"Zombie, uh, Graves … he's dead."

"Are you shitting me?"

"No, sir."

"If you are then I'll tell you that you're making a huge mistake."

"No, I'm not. He went down to the States on Sunday night and got shot."

"Got shot?" Lance paused. "Huh. I guess that explains why my guy can't get hold of him." He looked at Vath curiously. "So who shot him? Was he robbed?"

"No, it wasn't a robbery. I, uh, don't know for sure what happened. It was on the news this morning. A cop was killed, too."

"Have the cops been around to talk to you?"

"No, they don't even know that I know him."

"Oh … that's good." He eyed Vath long enough to make him squirm. "Looks like we're dealing with you, then. You're off work at five p.m., right?"

"Yes."

"I'll send a guy over to that basement suite you live in at six p.m. He'll have a chat with you and explain what we're looking for."

Vath's face paled, perhaps with the knowledge that the bikers knew where he lived. Then he said, "Uh, if this is about you wanting guns, we, uh, aren't doing that —"

"What the fuck?" Lance roared while grabbing him with both hands by the front of his sports jacket and slamming him against the van. He then held him pinned with his feet dangling. "Don't ever say shit like that to my face! You got it?"

"Yes — yes, sir," Vath replied quickly.

Lance saw some of his guys approaching, so he let Vath slide to the ground and waved them back. He then looked at Vath. "If you got something to say to me, choose your words carefully before you shoot your yap off. Treat me like the honest, respectable businessman that I am."

"Yes — yes, sir." Vath swallowed again. "All I was trying to say is, uh, this business thing isn't up to me. There's someone else who calls the shots."

"Whatever, but you can pass the message on. All you gotta do is listen to what my guy has to say. If you or whoever you work for doesn't like it — we'll go elsewhere."

"And that's it? If, uh, things don't work out, then, uh, you'll go elsewhere?"

"We'll go elsewhere. You … I'm not sure where you'll be going. That might depend on how genuine we think you're being with us."

"Oh."

"Make sure you're home on time," Lance ordered. He then left Vath staring after him and returned to his group.

"What was that all about?" Gagnon asked as Lance got back on his hog.

"The fucker says he has a line on some guns he wants to sell. I don't know if he's stupid or trying to set me up to the cops."

Gagnon snorted. "Either way he's stupid."

"Yup," Lance agreed.

Chapter Thirty-Six

It was 2:00 p.m. when Jack was awakened from a deep sleep by the sound of his phone vibrating on the bedside table.

"You're on," Lance said. "His place at six p.m."

"How'd it go?"

"I did what you told me. That part was easy. He said that Graves was shot and killed, but told me he didn't know any details other than it wasn't a robbery and that a cop was killed, too. He said it was on the news this morning. He also said there was no heat on 'im."

"Good."

"It's up to you now."

"I know. I'll be in touch."

* * *

Jack parked a block from Vath's basement suite and walked the rest of the way. The entrance was alongside the house, but he hadn't reached it before the door opened and Vath beckoned him inside.

"I don't discuss business inside buildings," Jack said.

"Of course," Vath replied nervously. "I'll … I'll grab my coat."

"Relax, will ya? Mind if I borrow your can first?" Jack asked.

"Uh, yeah, no problem. Straight through the living room. It's at the end of the hall past my bedroom."

Jack scanned the living room. A Confederate flag adorned the wall above a sofa. "You an American or been to the southern U.S.?" he asked.

"I'm Canadian. Haven't been down there yet. Some day."

"Why their flag?"

Vath looked surprised at the question. "I respect them for what they stand for and represent."

"And what is that?"

"Well, uh, you know."

"Maybe I know, but I'd like to hear it from you."

"They're rebels and think and act for themselves." He paused and eyed Jack. "They're like you guys. They don't put up with any shit. Especially from people who don't belong."

Don't belong? We were talking about the U.S. Confederate flag, which is from an area you've never even been to, let alone belong to yourself.

"Is that what you think, too?" Vath asked.

Think, too? You don't have the ability to think. "Yeah, I hear ya, man," he replied, then went down the hall. A glimpse at the bedroom didn't reveal anything significant so he entered the bathroom, waited a moment, then flushed the toilet and returned to where Vath was waiting at the door.

"Okay, raise your fuckin' hands up over your head," Jack said, gesturing with his hand. "I'm gonna check you for a wire."

"A wire?"

"I'm the cautious type." He gave a hard look and added, "You got a problem with that?"

"No, uh, yeah, sure ... okay."

"Don't take it personal," Jack said as he began to pat him down. "This afternoon you weren't expecting us. Now you are. I need to be sure."

"I understand."

Jack took his time and had Vath pull his shirt up to expose his chest, as well as having him drop his pants and take his boots off for examination. "Okay, get dressed and we'll go outside."

A moment later, they walked down the alley behind Vath's home and Jack said, "What I'm gonna tell you isn't to be spread around. It's strictly on a need-to-know basis, got it?"

"Of course. I'm not going to do anything to piss you guys off."

"Okay, then here's the scoop. We're —"

"Your guy told you that this isn't up to me, right?" Vath blurted.

"My guy?" Jack questioned.

"Your president. The one who visited me at work today."

"Yeah, he told me, so listen to what I have to say. If whoever you deal with isn't interested, we'll go elsewhere and you'll forget this conversation ever took place."

"I was worried after talking to your president that you guys would come down on me if I couldn't come through."

"If you're straight with us, do your best, and don't fuck us around, then you got nothing to worry about."

"Good, okay." Vath gave a weak smile. "I'm listening."

"We're looking to arm all our chapters across Canada."

"The whole country?" Vath replied.

"We're going to war from coast to coast. The Somalis, East Indians, Chinese, Viets in the lower mainland … Jamaicans in Toronto, blacks in Halifax. We've had enough."

"Holy fuck!" Vath exclaimed. "Would I love to be a part of that," he murmured, more to himself than Jack.

"I take it you're not a fan of them, either?" Jack replied.

"Are you kidding? No way! They're invading us from all sides." Vath's face revealed his disgust. "None of our politicians have the guts to step up and do what's right!"

Jack made a face. "Ain't that the truth. Not only that, but when it comes to business those parasites don't care who they deal to. Whether it's to young white kids on school grounds or messin' with our women, they seem to feel they got the right."

"I know," Vath exclaimed. "I've said exactly the same thing."

"We've decided enough is enough."

"Man, I hear you."

"We're looking for at least five hundred weapons to start with."

"Five … did you say —"

"Right, five hundred to start with. Likely more later. It's not like we'll be hanging onto them once they've been used.

Vath looked astounded, then mumbled, "That's … that's a lot. To try and bring that many across the border …" His words trailed off and he looked at Jack.

"We'd look after that part. We bring in merchandise by the tonne, not to mention smuggling in immigrant whores or whatever else we want. We've got several pipelines back and forth to the States. For us that part is easy."

"And you want five hundred," Vath uttered quietly as if thinking out loud. He looked in deep thought.

"If you can't handle that much then say so. If you can't come up with at least fifty, it isn't worth our while dealing with you. We've got other suppliers we can approach state-side and we're shopping for the best price."

"The, uh, thing is, I'm supposed to be laying low, but for that many, I think I should call someone."

"Laying low?"

Vath swallowed. "Because of Graves getting killed."

"Yeah, I was told something about that, but you said there was no heat on you."

"There isn't."

Jack looked suspiciously at Vath. "What's him gettin' killed got to do with anything? All I heard was that a cop was killed and we presumed they shot it out with each other and both died."

"Maybe that's what happened. I'm not sure. My buddy wasn't all that forthcoming about how it went down. All I was told was that I'm to lay low for a few months."

"Your buddy … you mean your contact for getting guns? He was there?"

"Yes," Vath replied hesitantly.

"Wish you'd said so, 'cause that changes everything. We don't need the heat, especially with the amount of money we're talking about." Jack gestured with his hands up in the air. "Sorry, man. I don't know what your profit would've been, but if you only made, say, three hundred dollars a gun on your commission, multiply that times five hundred and you'd be making one hundred and fifty g's."

"I'd expect to make five hundred dollars a gun," Vath said.

"Yeah, whatever. Guess your profit then would've been a quarter mil." Jack gave a sympathetic smile and patted him on the shoulder. "That's life. Sorry, but we don't want to do business with someone who's got that much heat on 'im, and a dead cop means a lot of heat."

Vath looked agitated as Jack turned and headed back down the alley.

"But there's no heat on me," Vath said as he hastened to catch up. "The only guy the cops know about was Graves."

"No heat on you, but what about your buddy?"

"No, the cops don't know about him either. It was Graves who was being followed. They were probably hoping he'd lead them to Jerry." Vath frowned, perhaps upset that he'd let the name slip. Then he continued, "The cop was alone and he was killed as soon as Graves met up with my connection — that's Jerry. From how it happened, the cop wouldn't have had a clue who Jerry was, so he couldn't have told anyone."

"So you're willing to swear to me that this Jerry is cool?"

"For sure. The cops woulda come looking for him if he wasn't."

Jack stroked his chin as he appeared to think about it, then focused on Vath. "That's good, I guess, but either way, we're not waiting a few months or for however long Jerry wants you to lay low. We won't even wait a few weeks. If you can't do it, we'll get them somewhere else."

"Let me contact him," Vath pleaded. "For the amount you want, I think he'll make an exception."

Jack pretended to mull it over. "How long will it take you to find out?"

"I'll call them right now!"

"Them?"

"I deal with Jerry, but sometimes there's another guy who's with him. I don't know his name."

"All right," Jack replied. "Go ahead. Talk to Jerry."

"All I have to do is pop out and get a new phone because I was told to throw my other one out when Graves was killed. If I do that I can talk wide open, and we won't have to worry about our call being bugged."

"I see."

"Can you meet me back at my place in an hour?"

"How about I wait at your place and order in a pizza? You might need me to field a few questions once you contact him."

Vath's face lit up. "Great. I've got beer in the fridge, so you can help yourself."

They returned to the basement suite, and Vath ordered a pizza before leaving. Jack watched him drive away in his white Hyundai, then used the opportunity to search the premises in the hopes of finding names or phone numbers. The fact that he didn't have a warrant didn't bother him. He knew he wouldn't be going to court.

He discovered a laptop, but it was password protected. In the end his search came up empty, and when Vath returned thirty minutes later, Jack was sitting on the sofa sipping a beer.

Vath held up a phone. "Got it," he said.

"Good. The pizza hasn't arrived yet."

"Okay, give me a sec." Vath paused at the entrance to the hall and grinned at Jack.

"What's so funny?" Jack asked.

"These guys are gonna shit when I tell 'em who you are and what you want."

I bet they will....

Vath went to his bedroom and Jack could hear the murmur of his voice. At one point he heard Vath excitedly exclaim, "Damn right, I'm sure! The fucking president and a bunch of his guys came to visit me at work today. They were all wearing their colours. This is the real deal, man."

Minutes later, Vath returned to the living room while still speaking on the phone. He then gave Jack a thumbs up, lowered the phone slightly, and said, "We can do five hundred immediately, all sorts of different makes and types. Got full autos, rifles with silencers ... you name it, we probably got it."

"Cost?" Jack asked.

"Cost to you would be roughly 1.25 mil." He studied Jack's face for a reaction. When he didn't get one, he hastened to say, "But that's negotiable depending upon what models and types you select."

"I see. That works out to about twenty five hundred dollars a pop. Seems a little steep in my mind for an order that big. Especially since I'm assuming you're talking U.S. dollars."

"Hang on." Vath put the phone back to his ear. He then looked at Jack and said, "That price would also include ammo and lots of accessories like scopes and silencers and shit."

"That sounds more reasonable," Jack replied. "Make it clear that I'll want to see and examine what we're buying before toting 1.25 mil across the border."

"Uh, hang on … okay, he heard you. Yup, that won't be a problem." Vath listened to the phone, then added, "As long as you're not armed and you come alone."

"Of course," Jack replied.

"Of course," Vath repeated into the phone. He turned to Jack and asked, "Once you check 'em out, how long would it take you to get the money?"

"We have that much on hand," Jack replied.

Vath repeated what Jack said, then listened for a moment and ended the call. Once he put the phone in his pocket he looked at Jack and smiled broadly as he sat in a chair facing him.

"So?" Jack asked.

"I'm to take you across the border into Washington this coming Saturday around seven p.m. You're to pack an overnight bag for a two-day trip."

"Two days? Where the hell we going?"

"I don't know where they're taking you. All I was told was I'd be dropping you off and that you'd then go with them while I return to Canada." He waited for a response. When he didn't get one, he asked, "Is that okay with you?"

"Yeah … no problem."

"Good. That's it then." Vath then settled back in the chair.

"Jerry and his buddy, how long have you known them? Do you trust them not to try to rip me off?"

Vath leaned forward, looking worried. "To be honest, I only met Jerry a few months back. He was introduced to me by Graves."

"How'd Graves meet him?"

"Over the internet. Graves has, uh, had a website, and Jerry reached out to him through that."

The white supremacist website.... Jack studied Vath's face. "So, you don't really know Jerry well," he noted.

"Not really. He's a short little guy. He doesn't look tough, but to be honest, something about him freaks me out sometimes."

"Freaks you out?"

"Maybe that's the wrong word. He seems like he's always angry or pissed off at something. I don't like being around him any longer than I have to. I get the feeling he doesn't like me, either."

"What about the other guy?"

"Him ... I don't even know his name. He usually remains in the background and hangs on to the pieces until Jerry knows it's safe, then we meet up with 'im."

"Does he look like he could handle himself in a fight?"

"For sure. He's a big guy. It wouldn't surprise me if he rode a chopper."

"Oh?"

"He's got long black hair and a bushy beard to match."

Too bad, the Coggins brothers are tall, but have red hair and were clean-shaven.

Vath shrugged, "Guess that doesn't mean he rides a bike, though. I mean, look at you guys. Most of you look like guys who'd wear suits."

Because Satans Wrath doesn't need to look tough. Everyone knows they are.

Vath was silent for a moment. "I know it doesn't sound good what I said about Jerry and his buddy, but they've always been straight with me. If they're going to show you the guns first, then you know that they got 'em and aren't blowin' smoke."

"That's what I figure, too."

A look of suspicion crossed Vath's face and he looked at Jack. "That being said, they're not somebody I'd dare screw with either."

"I don't intend to screw them around," Jack replied. "We've got the money."

Vath nodded, but didn't appear convinced.

"So I meet them Saturday night," Jack stated.

"Yes."

"Want me to meet you here before we leave?"

"That'd be good. Come over about six."

"Not a problem. I'll get my ol' lady to drop me off."

"Okay, but if there's a change, do you have a number I can reach you at?"

"Yeah, grab a pen and paper and I'll give it to you. I'll also reverse the last four numbers to be on the safe side."

"Got a pen and paper in the kitchen. You want another beer while I'm at it?"

"Sure." He watched as Vath went to the kitchen and rummaged around in a drawer before retrieving a pen and piece of paper. He then took two bottles of Lucky beer from the fridge and set them on the counter. Jack saw him furtively looking at him before opening them.

Vath's hand trembled when he passed Jack the beer along with the pen and paper. After he sat down his face twitched and he turned his head and raised his own beer to his mouth in an apparent attempt to hide his nervousness.

"What's wrong?" Jack asked.

"What do you mean?"

"Don't give me that shit. Something's on your mind. You look like a kid in a drugstore working up the courage to buy his first box of condoms."

Vath set his beer on the coffee table and looked intensely at Jack. "I know these guys will kill you if you mess with them," he said bluntly. "Maybe kill me, too."

Second thoughts? This isn't the time to fuck with me, asshole.

Jack took a sip of beer, then glared at Vath. "Likewise," he snarled.

Chapter Thirty-Seven

Jack was backing out of his garage to go to work the following morning when his phone vibrated. He stopped and glanced at the call display. *Washington area code. Sorry, Wayne, I was going to call you when I got to the office to bring you up to date.* He answered.

"Hi, Jack. It's Betty." Her tone revealed how depressed she felt.

Betty? He tasted the black coffee he'd had moments before rise to the back of his throat. "Hi, Betty. Uh —"

"I'm sorry it took me so long to call you," she said. "I know you called and wanted to speak to me the night Ferg was killed."

He breathed a sigh of relief, then said, "When I called then I was told you were resting and to wait until you called me. I've been thinking about you a lot."

"I know. I'm sorry. I was there when you spoke to Wayne, but I wasn't up to it then."

"I understand."

"I hope you forgive me. Emotions were running pretty high with the guys and I was in a mess from hearing the news. I thought it best to wait. Then things got busy with family and people dropping in."

"I wanted to tell you how sorry I am," Jack said. "I feel sick that I wasn't there when —"

"No, don't do that," Betty said sharply. She paused and her tone softened. "Please don't blame yourself. Ferg told me when you called him that night that he had to skedaddle up to the border. He mentioned you didn't have permission to enter the States, but he wasn't upset. He really liked you. He understood where you were coming from. The morning he drove your SUV up to the border for you he told me that you'd gotten in trouble for crossing the border. He felt bad about that and would've really gotten worked up if you'd done it again."

Jack was conscious of the pause that followed, but didn't know what to say.

"I'm sure you were frustrated over not having permission" Betty continued. "You wouldn't believe the number of times Ferg bellyached to me about policy or the law, for that matter. Still, when it came down to it, I know he respected both."

"You have no idea how much your call means to me," Jack said. "It really helps to hear you say that."

"I don't want you blaming yourself. Not in the least."

Thanks, but it was me who let a piece of policy get someone killed. For that, I'll never forgive myself.

"I mean that, Jack. We were married for twenty-nine years. I knew the risks involved in the work that Ferg

An Element of Risk

did, and so did he. What happened … happened. It was through no fault of yours."

"Thank you so much," Jack said emphatically. "You've lifted a heavy burden off my heart."

"Good. That burden should never have been there to start with." She paused. "Anyway, I want you to know that the funeral is on Monday and I hope you'll be there."

Crap, I might be busy meeting whoever killed Ferg, yet I can't tell her that and give her false hope. What will you think of me if I don't show?

"I'm serious, Jack. I don't care that you're from another country. When it comes to this, we're all family. Same for Natasha. You're both welcome."

"I know Natasha would like to attend and offer her condolences, but she won't be able to because she works at a small clinic and is covering for another doctor who is away. Plus she's juggling that with being home to look after our sons."

"I see, but you'll come?"

"I promise I'll do my best."

* * *

When Jack arrived at work he avoided Rose and went straight to his desk and called Wayne.

"How'd it go?" Wayne asked as soon as the salutations were over. "Any luck getting your source to meet Vath?"

"Yes. Good news. The intro was made and I met Vath last night on the pretext of buying five hundred guns."

"Five … holy shit. You asked for a lot."

"If I only ordered a few they might not have gone for it."

"So what —"

"Vath called his source when I was with him and his source went for it. Tentatively they think I'll be paying 1.25 mil U.S. for them."

"Oh, man. That's great. The money won't be a problem. I'll arrange to get it in case you need to flash it. How soon is it going to happen?"

"I don't think it'll be necessary to show the money. Vath is bringing me down to the States Saturday night. I'm then supposed to take a look at the guns and decide which ones I want, then return to Canada and get the money."

"Sweet baby Jesus! We're gonna get 'em!"

"Vath also told me he deals with two guys."

"The Coggins brothers?"

"Doesn't sound like it. One guy is named Jerry, who he described as short, and the other guy he doesn't have a name for, but said he's big with long black hair and a bushy beard."

"It doesn't matter. It's who killed Ferg that's important to me. Oh God, this is fantastic!" Wayne exclaimed.

"I'm not sure how long it will take. Vath is supposed to drop me off and head back to Canada, but I was told to pack an overnight bag for two days."

"Two days?"

"I've no idea where they're taking me."

"It won't matter. I don't care if they take you all the way to Alabama. We'll be there to cover you. Don't worry about that. It won't be like last time."

Yeah … last time.

"It'll be like we're in you hip pocket," Wayne continued. "That's guaranteed."

"The hip pocket is a little too close," Jack replied. "These guys obviously run counter-surveillance. You'll need to give me some distance. They had no qualms about murdering Graves to sever the connection to them. They wouldn't hesitate to do the same with me and Vath."

Wayne's voice became solemn. "We also don't want the same thing happening because we weren't there to back you up."

"I'm not too worried about needing protection. They think I'm with Satans Wrath and —"

"Satans Wrath! How the hell did you pull that one off? Steal a set of colours?"

"Don't ask, and keep that detail to yourself," Jack replied. "The point is that I'm sure whoever I'm meeting will respect me enough not to piss me off. They might be worried that I'll try to rip them off, but I doubt they'll ever suspect I'm a cop."

"But you'll still need protection. You'll have a phone, right? We could keep a safe distance and track you through that, providing they don't make you turn it off."

"I doubt they would make me turn it off because of who they think I am. If I was really a biker and intent on ripping them off, my fellow bikers wouldn't have the access to the phone companies along with the sophisticated technology needed to track me by phone. I'll probably be treated like royalty. At this point they expect me to check out the merchandise and decide on what I want to buy. After that they think I'll be returning to Canada to talk to my people and get the money."

"So once you've seen the guns and are clear, we could arrest them," Wayne noted.

"Exactly, but I still don't want Vath charged or arrested later on. It would bring too much heat on my informant. I want to keep my identity as a police officer secret, as well. It'll muddy the water enough that the bad guys won't know whether both Vath and I ratted them out or only one of us."

"Yup, you mentioned that before. I confirmed it with our district attorney. It's not a problem. Vath isn't who we want."

Jack felt his anger rise when he thought about the nameless killer he was after. "You got that right," he said vehemently.

Chapter Thirty-Eight

After ending his call with Wayne, Jack strode into Rose's office and took a seat to wait while she was talking on the phone. When she ended her call she peered over her reading glasses at him.

"Good morning," he said.

"Good morning to you, too. You're looking a little better than you did two days ago," she noted.

"I feel a lot better," he said emphatically, then gave her a lopsided smile.

"Have there been some new developments south of the border?"

"They don't have anything yet. They're relying on us at the moment."

"Oh." Rose looked disheartened. Then she eyed him curiously. "You seem awfully chipper. We're to meet Lexton this morning. Aren't you concerned she'll remove you from the case?"

"She won't," Jack stated.

"*Humph.* I wish I had your confidence. She was seriously thinking about it when we last spoke to her. I think whatever she's decided will be anybody's guess."

"Things have changed since then," Jack said.

"How? I thought you said there weren't any new developments?"

"There aren't down in the States. It's up here that things have progressed."

Rose's face brightened. "That sounds promising. Did MCU get something off of Graves's computer?"

"No ... nothing to do with MCU." He paused as he decided what to say. "Maybe I better start from Monday when you told me to go home."

Rose took off her glasses and sat back in her chair. Her eyes narrowed as she regarded him suspiciously. "You didn't go home?"

"Not immediately."

"Damn it, Jack." She folded her arms across her chest. "Out with it. What did you do?"

"I discovered someone who was acting as a lookout for Graves when he sold guns to Satans Wrath last week. I pulled a quick UC on him and last night he called his connection in the States and arranged for me to meet him."

"Are you serious?"

"I wouldn't be this ... chipper, as you put it, if I wasn't."

"That's ... I ... How?"

Jack told her how he'd identified Vath as Graves's colleague and then used his informant to arrange an introduction. Then he told her about his meeting with Vath and the arrangements that were made for him to go the States.

Rose shook her head, seemingly irate. "I should've known you'd be up to something. Why didn't you tell me what was going on? You also should've had a proper UC plan in place with someone to cover you."

"Laura's on holidays." He paused. "I wasn't worried. I was packing my piece last night when I went to meet him."

"I'm not on holidays. I would've covered you."

"I was afraid you'd give me hell for not going home right away. I was too tired and upset to deal with you. Having Vath on my plate was enough."

"What makes you think I won't give you hell anyway?"

Jack grinned. "Don't give me that malarkey. I bet you're thrilled with what happened."

Rose tried to look stern, but then capitulated and flashed a smile.

"I thought so," Jack said, feeling smug.

"You still should've called me out last night."

"You're right. Not having cover wasn't a smart move." He paused. "Next time I will."

"Good."

"Can we get back to talking about the bad guys?"

Rose nodded.

"I contacted the lead investigator with the ATF in Seattle a few minutes ago — Special Agent Wayne Dawson. They'll provide a cover team for when I cross the border. Basically, all I have to do is see the weapons and then leave. The U.S. team has agreed not to identify me or arrest Vath, so when they scoop in and make the arrests the bad guys won't know who to blame."

"You don't think your evidence will be needed in court?"

"I'm sure once we find the vehicle that hit Ferg, his DNA will be all over it. Not to mention that more than one bad guy was involved. One of 'em will probably flip for a lighter sentence." Jack thought for a moment. "If my evidence is needed in court, they might still be able to keep my real identity secret. Either that, or I'd find a way to put the heat on Vath."

"Your informant go along with that?"

"He acknowledged that there's an element of risk, but nothing he can't handle."

"Good, then except for not keeping me in the loop, congrats on what I think is a job well done." She glanced at her watch. "It's almost time to meet with Lexton. Let's hope she agrees."

"She'll *have* to go along with it," Jack said.

"She doesn't have to go along with anything," Rose stated.

* * *

Jack was conscious that Lexton was studying his face closely as he and Rose took a seat across from her at her desk. He gave her a polite smile.

No smile back … avoiding eye contact … she looks grim. She's planning on dumping me.

"Corporal Taggart has come up with an important lead within the last two days concerning the murder investigation in the States," Rose said. "I'll let him explain."

Jack caught Lexton's look.

Okay, maybe you have a right to be suspicious….

He told her what had transpired while attempting to read her face for a reaction as he spoke. He learned that she'd be a great poker player.

When he finished, Lexton eyed him long enough to make him feel uncomfortable, then asked, "After you left my office Monday morning, did you hasten to arrange this because I was considering removing you from the investigation?"

"It was after I left that I discovered Vath was a link to Graves. My primary objective then was to catch whoever murdered Special Agent Ferguson. I knew that my informant wouldn't have trusted anyone else to do what followed next, so I took action on my own accord. Yes … I was conscious of the fact that you were contemplating removing me from the case, but I felt that was incidental compared to actually solving the murder."

"So you went ahead with your plan and assumed that I'd be so impressed with your abilities that I'd simply allow you to continue?"

That sounds a little nasty. He felt Rose nudge his foot with hers. *No, Rose, I won't give her the tone, but it is time to go on the offence.*

He looked Lexton in the eyes. "I was confident you'd allow me to continue because you recently proved to me that you also have a strong desire to see justice."

"A strong desire to see justice?" Lexton paused. "On what basis did you form that idea?"

"The immediate action you took when you found out my performance evaluation was being held up in Staffing." He then turned to Rose, gesturing openly with the palms of his hands as if to say it was time to come clean. He turned back to Lexton. "Personally, I think it's better if you know I'm aware of what you did so I can express my gratitude."

Lexton looked at Rose. "So you went and told him," she said, sounding irritated, presuming Jack's gesture and comment indicated that Rose had told him.

"I didn't tell him anything about our talk," Rose replied, sounding peeved.

Surprise registered on Lexton's face. "Oh," she said, upon realizing she'd been duped.

Hope that didn't piss you off, but I'd rather risk that than have you think I'm a fool for not figuring it out.

Jack cleared his throat to catch Lexton's attention. "I want to thank you for intervening in the manner you did," he said in a tone that conveyed his sincerity. "I appreciate and respect how you protected the person who confided in me."

Lexton paused, seemingly to contemplate the situation. "You're welcome."

"May we get back to the ... proposed undercover investigation with Vath? If I am allowed to continue, there's little time to get everything in order. I already have fake identification on file with the undercover coordinator, but I'd still need to arrange for cover teams and authorization from Ottawa. As it stands now, I'm to meet the bad guys Saturday night and plan for a two-day trip."

"Yes, about that," Lexton said. "I didn't see an operational plan for your initial undercover meeting with Vath — let alone any approval for it."

You're throwing policy in my face over that! We're dealing with a murdered cop! He felt a kick on his leg and glared at Rose. *Yeah, Rose, don't do that again or I will explode.*

Lexton continued. "I take it no plan was submitted because your informant arranged the meeting unexpectedly and you were caught off guard. Considering the gravity of the investigation, you felt forced to step outside the bounds of policy to take advantage of an opportunity that may not have presented itself later on."

"My informant introduced me, but he did so on —"

"His own initiative. Yes. Thank you, Corporal Taggart. As you noted, time is of the essence. There's no reason to waste it by being ... overly candid about every little detail."

Overly candid? Jack saw the hint of a smile in Lexton's eyes. *Okay, lady. I'm beginning to like you.*

"I understand," he replied.

"I'm sure you do." Lexton paused. "I think the actions you took were admirable in response to what was an unexpected situation and I will certainly inform Ottawa of that should there be any negative feedback."

Thank you for having my back

Lexton's face then hardened. She momentarily pointed her finger at him and warned, "That being said, the circumstances of this case are unusual and involve a murdered law enforcement officer from another country. You might not find much sympathy or understanding with any opportunistic episodes that might arise in the future."

"I understand." *Message received loud and clear.*

Lexton turned to Rose. "Is there anything else?"

"I've nothing further," Rose stated.

"Then I suggest you get on with it. If there's anything I can do to assist your office or speed up the process, feel free to contact me."

After leaving Lexton's office, Jack saw Rose giving him furtive glances as they walked down the hall toward their respective offices.

Eventually she couldn't contain herself. "When did you figure it out?"

"That you'd told Lexton about Quaile holding up my chance for a promotion?" he replied innocently.

"Yes. That."

"I was suspicious when you returned from talking with her after I was dismissed. My suspicions were confirmed the next day after I heard what Lexton did and Laura and I came in to tell you."

Rose sighed. "I felt awful. I figured you were suspicious."

"Is that why you felt awful? Not for betraying my trust but out of fear you'd be found out?"

Rose looked appalled. "No! Not that. It was because I went against my promise."

She doesn't realize I'm toying with her.

After a few steps where neither talked, Rose broke the silence. "Are, are you really angry with me?" she asked hesitantly.

Jack stopped and turned to face her. "No ... not angry. Perhaps a little disappointed. You were someone I trusted and respected."

"At the time I felt like I was supporting you," she pleaded. "Lexton was furious with you for not showing enough respect for the commissioned rank. I wanted her to know that you had your reasons."

Her eyes had watered and Jack realized that his comment affected her more than he thought it would. "Oh, hell, I won't do this."

"Do what?" she asked.

"Make you feel bad so that you'll suck up to me and maybe owe me one for down the road."

Her face registered shock. "You were doing that?"

"Yes. I'm neither angry nor disappointed. From what I've seen, I think your trust in Lexton is warranted ... at least to a certain degree."

Rose's face darkened. "You can be a real asshole sometimes," she fumed and started walking again.

Jack fell in step. "Is that your clinical diagnosis? All those years to get your masters in psychology and that's what you come up with?" he chided.

"It sure is! That label was made for you," she replied adamantly.

"Would an olive soup after work cause you to reconsider your diagnosis?"

Rose stopped and took a deep breath, then gave him a perturbed look.

"Come on, Rose, let's put it behind us."

She made a face. "Okay ... sure. I think today a martini would go down good."

"You're buying, of course," Jack stated.

"Me?"

"To help make up for the emotional trauma you've caused me. It's like I don't know who to trust anymore. I can't eat. I can't sleep. It's affected my sex —"

"Can it, asshole."

Chapter Thirty-Nine

By Saturday officers from the Major Crimes Unit had been arranged to supply cover for Jack north of the border while a team of ATF agents led by Wayne Dawson were detailed to take over on the U.S. side.

Once Jack crossed into the U.S., two MCU investigators by the names of Corporal Geoff Frisby and Constable Kate Willisko had then been authorized to accompany the ATF agents in their vehicles.

It was 3:45 p.m. and Jack was on his way to the MCU office for a last minute debriefing when he received a call from Vath.

"There's been a slight change of plans," Vath said.

Jack groaned inwardly. "What the fuck?" he said angrily. I've already got my bag packed and my ol' lady's made plans for after she drops me off."

"No, no. Everything's still like we talked about, but instead of you coming to my place we, uh, need to meet at a restaurant."

Need to meet at a restaurant? Sounds like you were given orders.

"Sure, I know a good spot not all that far from —"

"No, we need to meet at the Eagle's Perch Restaurant out in White Rock. It's, uh, close to where we have to go and less chance we'll be late crossing the border in case there's lineups."

Yup, you were given orders.

"Same time?" Jack asked.

"Yeah, yeah. Everything else is the same."

Okay, let the games begin....

* * *

Jack arrived at the Eagle's Perch at precisely 6:00 p.m. after being driven there in a car by Corporal Tina Chan, who was an undercover operative borrowed from Drug Section. When they arrived, she double-parked near the entrance.

For an hour prior to Jack's arrival, two members from MCU had been watching from inside a surveillance van parked in the restaurant lot. Their objective was to see if they could spot anyone doing counter-surveillance. None had been spotted, but it didn't mean they weren't there.

Two other MCU vehicles, one containing Corporal Frisby as a passenger and the other Constable Willisko, were positioned a couple of blocks away to conduct a loose surveillance on Jack when he was taken to the border. At that time Frisby and Willisko would then join the ATF agents in their vehicles.

Jack eyed the parking lot. "No sign of Vath's white Hyundai," he noted. He then reached over the back seat and grabbed the backpack he'd stuffed with two days' worth of clothing and toiletries.

"Forgetting something?" Tina prodded, leaning toward him.

"Hell, no." Jack leaned over and embraced Tina before kissing her. "I knew there was something about working undercover that always attracted me," he whispered, giving a husky tone to his voice.

Tina snickered. "And a kiss and a hug is all you get," she said, sitting back.

Jack chuckled. "Obviously your nickname, Asian Heat, isn't all that deserved."

"Well, I'll tell you, Bubba, my husband, sure thinks it is."

"Bubba?"

Tina grinned. "With the guys you'll probably be dealing with, that name sounds appropriate."

Jack gave her his usual lopsided smile. "You're right. Come to think of it, if someone pulls out a banjo, I'll run for the hills." He reached for the door handle but Tina placed her hand on his arm.

"Be careful down there." Her eyes and her tone conveyed her worry.

"Always."

"You sure I couldn't come along as your ol' lady?"

"As much as I'd like you to, real bikers wouldn't allow a woman along at this point. The bad guys might smell a rat."

Tina appeared to reflect on what he said, then replied, "Yeah ... you're right. They really are a chauvinist bunch of assholes." She then kissed her fingertips and touched his lips. "Good luck."

Jack got out of the car, tossed his backpack over one shoulder, and entered the restaurant as Tina drove away. A quick look around confirmed that Vath wasn't there. He took the only window seat available in the hope of remaining visible from the surveillance van, but the location did not afford that.

Moments later, Jack saw Vath arrive in a taxi.

We're not taking a taxi into the U.S. What's going on?

He knew the observers in the van would be wondering the same thing.

Vath entered the restaurant and quickly approached Jack, but he didn't sit down. "You ready to go?" he asked.

Jack lifted his backpack and said, "Ready whenever you are."

"Good, once you pay for your coffee we're on our way."

"I saw you arrive in a taxi," Jack noted as he remained seated. "How're we going?"

"I parked my wheels here earlier," Vath replied, looking uncomfortable.

"Oh? I didn't see it. You drive a white Hyundai ... right?

"I traded that in yesterday and bought a Nissan Rogue. We'll be taking it."

"So why'd you arrive in a taxi?"

"Yeah, uh, listen. Don't get pissed off. I trust you, but my guys in the States ... well, they've heard stories."

"Stories?"

"Of guys being ripped off dealing with bikers. Not Satans Wrath, but I'm sure you understand. They're nervous and want me to jump through a few hoops to make sure you're alone."

"I'm alone," Jack stated. "Also not carrying any weapons. If you want to search me, go ahead. We can go to the can."

"Naw, that's okay." He gestured toward the coffee mug. "You done?"

Jack took the hint and went to the till. After he paid for his coffee he turned to head for the exit, but Vath tapped his arm.

"No, this way," Vath said. "Follow me."

So that's your plan. Jack did as instructed and was led through the restaurant's kitchen and out the rear door. By the surprised looks of the kitchen staff, he knew Vath wasn't known to them.

The Nissan Rogue was parked nearby and moments later they drove away via a back alley.

Jack glanced at Vath.

You're not smart enough to pull a stunt like this. Obviously your source is.

He took a long, slow breath.

Too bad, I was hoping you'd all be dumb.

Jack thought about his cover team still back by the restaurant, but told himself that within seconds the GPS in his phone would alert them to his movement.

I've got nothing to worry about.

Twenty minutes later they cleared U.S. Customs without incident. After that they were southbound on the I-5. It was then that he saw Willisko in the passenger seat of a car as it passed them. *Thanks, Kate, for the reassurance. All is well, now make sure everyone backs off and gives us lots of space.*

Twenty-five minutes south of the border, Vath exited the I-5 into Ferndale.

"Where we going?" Jack asked, feeling a sense of foreboding as Ferg's murder came to mind.

"This is where we're to meet them."

Jack nodded, then quietly stared out the passenger window at the side streets as they drove past. *Which street were you murdered on? Wish I'd asked. Was it this one ... or this one? Does the murderer live here? Maybe in one of the houses we're passing?* He viewed a row of houses. *It all seems so peaceful ... like a place everyone would like to live.*

Moments later, Vath parked at a restaurant called Jack in the Box. Jack wondered if the restaurant name foretold his fate, then he thought, *Naw, I want to be cremated when my time comes. No coffin for me.*

Once inside, Vath ordered a hamburger. Jack did the same. They'd almost finished eating when Jack saw Vath glance at his watch. He seemed worried.

"Something wrong?"

"Jerry isn't usually late," Vath explained. "He said they'd be here half an hour ago."

"That's only a little late. I wouldn't worry."

Jack excused himself to go to the men's room. After checking to ensure he was alone he went into a stall and phoned Wayne.

"What's happening?" Wayne asked anxiously. "We followed you to the restaurant."

"It's where Vath said we're to meet Jerry and his sidekick. He told me they were supposed to be here thirty minutes ago and that it was unusual for them to be late."

"Maybe they're like dope dealers. Those guys are never on time, no matter what they say."

"Maybe, but Vath seems concerned. Anyone on your team think they might have been burned?"

"No, if they had they'd have mentioned it. Nobody is in sight of the restaurant. In fact, both your people are insisting we don't come within a couple of blocks of you. Personally, I think that's a little too far away."

"Did you hear about the stunt Vath pulled at the restaurant in Canada before I left?"

"Yeah … okay, I hear you. I'll keep my people well back, but be warned that you're strictly on your own in there."

"That's how I want it." Jack paused. "Hopefully everything is okay. If they do show up, it might be a while before you and I talk again."

"You're packed for a two-day trip. Still no idea where you're being taken?"

"No, Vath doesn't have a clue. At the earliest, I won't find that out until Jerry arrives."

"When he does, it'd be good if you could let us know or at least call us each time you stop at a gas station or something."

"I could fake having food poisoning, but I think these guys are too kinky for me to be running back and forth to washrooms. Even if … or when they do show up, I might not be told. It wouldn't surprise me if I was blindfolded."

"Guess we'll have to wait and see."

Jack ended the call and headed back to the table. As he approached, he saw Vath talking on his phone while writing on a napkin. His face looked tense and he looked up to eyeball the other customers.

Damn it, something has them heated....

As he sat down, Vath glanced at him and shoved the napkin in his pocket while continuing to talk on the phone. "He's back. I'll ask him." He then looked at Jack and said, "They want your phone number. Is it okay if I give it to them?"

"Fine with me. Same number you used to call me earlier. I'll give it to you again."

As Jack gave the number, Vath repeated it into his phone, then said, "Okay, we're on our way."

Jack looked around to give the impression he was suspicious, then leaned forward and whispered, "What's going on? Why'd they want my number?"

Vath frowned. "He said it was in case we get split up. I'm supposed to take you some place and drop you off, then go meet them for a chat. I think they want me to assure them once more that you're okay."

"Why don't they come here?" Jack asked. "I can see them not trusting me, but if they have concerns they should meet me face to face so we can talk."

"It's not only you," Vath replied. "All of a sudden I get the feeling that they don't trust me, either." He shrugged. "I dunno. Maybe I'm wrong. It was Jerry's friend I was talking to and he seemed pissed off and suspicious-like. Could just be his personality."

If they don't trust you either, perhaps you should be thinking about what happened to Graves.

"But as far as them not coming here," Vath continued, "they told me they're introducing you to someone and he doesn't want to risk being seen."

"Being seen?" *Like perhaps one of the Coggins brothers?* "Do you mean being seen with me, or being seen by anyone? It's not like I'm wearing any colours."

"I don't know the reason. I didn't ask. I think because of what happened they're being extra cautious." Vath paused. "Anyway, after I meet 'em and have a talk, I'm to take 'em back to where you'll be waiting. Then you'll go with them and I'll head back home."

After you meet them and have a talk? Damn it, they've either spotted surveillance or are checking to see if one of us is being followed through the GPS on our phones.

He eyed Vath. "Still no idea where they'll be taking me after you go back?"

Vath shook his head. "I've no idea. I've only met them in restaurants or bars." He waved to the waitress to get the bill. "Let's pay, then we're on our way."

Jack trailed behind Vath toward the till. *Should I dump my phone ... or am I too late and our executions have already been planned?* He thought of Ferg. *Do I really have a choice about going along with this?* He swallowed. *Guess not. Not if I want justice....*

Two men wearing heavy coats and work boots were paying their bills at the till ahead of them. When they turned to leave, Vath stepped forward to pay.

I'm going to have one pissed off cover team, Jack thought, as he brushed past one of the men and slipped his phone into the man's coat pocket.

A moment later Jack followed Vath outside where he saw a man and woman with two boys heading to the restaurant. It left him with a lump in his throat.

Wonder if I'll ever see my family again.

Chapter Forty

Vath flicked the key on in the ignition then turned to face Jack. "I sure hope you're the real deal."

"What the hell? What kind of comment is that?" Jack replied.

"I mean that you're being straight with us. Not trying to rip us off or anything?"

"Believe me, with the amount of cash we're talking, your friends aren't the only ones who're feeling tense. All I want is for everyone to go away happy and safe."

"Exactly. I'll tell 'em that." He smiled and gave Jack a thumbs-up before fishing the napkin from his pocket.

"You've got a map?" Jack noted as he peered over.

"To where I'm to drop you off and then meet them. It's not far." He glanced at the napkin, then put the vehicle in gear.

Jack casually checked the side mirror after they'd driven away from the restaurant. *Yeah, it looks like I'm on my own, for better or worse.*

Vath glanced at the napkin in his hand periodically as he drove. A few minutes later they travelled down a quiet residential street that led them into a forested park that appeared to be deserted.

Wonderful. Perfect place to murder someone.

Vath stopped in a parking lot and pointed at a picnic table. "You're to wait there while I go talk to them. It shouldn't take long; then we'll all come back and go from there."

Is that what you think? Guess now isn't the time to remind you about Graves....

Jack got out. Somewhere in the darkness he heard the sound of a river. He watched Vath drive away, then eyed the picnic table. It was in the open and behind it was a path that disappeared into the woods toward the river. He sighed, then took a seat and waited.

Soon a light rain started to fall. He zipped up his jacket and pulled his collar tight to his neck before seeking refuge under some nearby trees. The sound of the river didn't do anything to calm his nerves.

I wonder how far my corpse would float downstream.

Twenty minutes later Jack saw Vath's Rogue return, followed by a Ram crew cab pickup with a canopy on the rear. His adrenalin kicked into high gear. *A Ram ... same type of truck Ferg saw before he was murdered.*

The vehicles parked side by side in the lot, so Jack left his shelter from under the trees and walked toward them. It was then that he heard someone walk out from the bushes behind him and turned to look.

"It's all right," a man said as he neared. "I'm with them." He gestured toward the vehicles.

"Okay," Jack replied and fell in step with him. Once they stepped into the illumination from the headlights, he caught a better look at his companion. The man had shoulder-length hair and a full beard. Despite having dyed his hair black, Jack recognized him immediately. *Luke Coggins — wanted for murder in Alabama.*

Vath and the driver of the pickup emerged from their vehicles. The new arrival was someone who'd also grown a beard. *Zachary Coggins ... wonderful. You two boys come to a decision as to whether or not you're going to kill us?*

Luke went over to his brother and Jack heard him say, "Didn't see anyone, and he didn't call anyone." They then spoke in hushed tones.

Vath approached Jack. "You okay?"

"Sure. Why wouldn't I be?"

"Uh, I don't know. Just that it's raining."

"Right, like that's what's on my mind," Jack replied angrily. "Who are these two guys? I take it one of them is Jerry?"

"No, I left Jerry a few minutes ago. The guy with the pickup is the other guy I deal with. I asked him his name tonight and he told me it was Bammer, or something like that."

Bammer ... as in being from Alabama.

"I've never seen the other guy before," Vath stated. He then looked around and said, "I don't see his car. Did someone else bring him?"

"He was waiting when I arrived," Jack replied. "I presume Bammer dropped him off earlier."

"That's strange, they didn't tell me there was someone else here," Vath replied.

It's not strange. They didn't trust you either.

The Coggins brothers then approached and Luke looked at Jack. "Hope y'all don't mind, but I need to search ya."

"Be my guest," Jack replied, raising his arms over his head.

"Y'all got some luggage, too?" Zachary asked.

"I've got a backpack on the back seat," Jack replied, gesturing toward the Nissan. He then stood patiently as Luke searched him while Zachary removed his backpack from the back seat and rifled through it.

"He ain't packin'," Luke declared, after patting him down.

"Nothin' here, either," Zachary stated. He tossed the backpack at Jack. "Y'all are comin' with us," he added.

"You finished with me?" Vath asked.

"Yup," Zachary replied. "Go back to the land of the Eskimos. We'll get hold of ya once the deal is over and figure out your cut."

"Wahoo!" Vath exclaimed. "Lookin' forward to that!" He then returned to his vehicle and drove away.

Jack locked eyes with Luke and gestured to the bush where the man had been hiding. "What the hell was that all about? You do know who you're dealing with, right?"

"Yeah, we know," Luke replied gruffly. "But the thing is, a car with two guys in it was parked a block away from the restaurant we was supposed to meet you at. We figured it was the cops, so we separated the two of you to see if they was followin' one of you."

"And?" Jack asked.

"'Bout then we seen that car take off and go south on the I-5."

"So then you knew it had nothing to do with me."

"Yeah, we know that now." He smiled apologetically. "Looks like we got spooked for nothin'."

"Why'd you hide in the bush?"

"To see if ya called anyone." Luke gave him a serious look, then opened his jacket and patted the butt of a pistol stuck in his waistband.

And if I had, I'd be taking a river cruise without a boat....

Chapter Forty-One

Jack sat in the back seat of the crew cab, and Zachary and Luke sat in the front. Once Zachary started the ignition, Jack leaned forward to memorize the mileage on the speedometer. If he was later blindfolded, at least when they arrived at their destination he'd have an idea how far they'd driven.

"What you doin'?" Luke asked suspiciously.

Jack stuck out his hand. "My name's Jack Bryson. I figure with the amount of money and merchandise we're going to be swapping, it'd be better if we show a little trust and introduce ourselves."

Zachary and Luke looked at each other. Zachary reached back and shook Jack's hand. "I'm Zach. This here's my brother Luke."

"I didn't catch your last name?" Jack replied, while shaking Luke's hand.

"Uh, it's Bammer," Zach stated.

Jack hid his smile. *So you decided you'd half trust me. Bammer, my ass. Do I look that stupid?*

Zach drove east out of Ferndale, crossed the I-5, and continued east. Soon the countryside was mostly farmland with few roads and no traffic. After twenty minutes Zach pulled over to the side of the road.

"Everything okay?" Jack asked.

"Hope so," Luke replied.

"Waitin' to hear from someone," Zach said. His tone indicated that further comment wouldn't be appreciated.

Ten minutes passed and the only noise was the sound of the windshield wipers. Jack stared out into the rain reflected in the headlights, then peered into the darkness around them. He didn't see any other lights or signs of habitation.

Zach's phone rang. As he answered, Luke turned in his seat and looked intently at Jack while slipping his hand inside his jacket toward his pistol.

I really don't care for your attitude....

"Good. Yup," Zach said into his phone. He then glanced at Luke and said, "It's okay."

Luke appeared to relax and removed his hand.

Zach refocused on the phone. "We'll wait till ya go by." He paused and glanced out the window. "Yeah, for sure. Comin' down harder. Gonna be slippery headin' up the mountain tonight." He then ended the call.

"You're expecting company?" Jack asked.

"Yeah, the boss man is about five minutes behind us."

Jack recalled a crossroad they'd gone by about a five-minute drive from where they were parked and realized that someone had been waiting there and watching to see if they were being followed.

Is it the same person who parked on the cross street watching when Ferg was murdered? Bet it is. Sure can't wait to meet you.

For a moment Jack felt elated, but the grim reality of the situation told him he shouldn't feel too celebratory yet.

No cover team, unarmed, don't know where they're taking me. He glanced at Zach and Luke. *I'm with a couple of rednecks who are wanted for murder and may have also murdered Ferg. Not only that, these guys are more paranoid than a couple of turkeys before Thanksgiving.* He looked again at the desolate surroundings.

Yeah, this is great. What could possibly go wrong? On with the show.

Soon a black SUV went past and Zach pulled out to follow.

"So that's the boss man," Jack said, hoping to glean more information.

"Yup," Luke said. "Reverend Bob and his son."

"Reverend Bob?" Jack snickered, presuming the moniker was a joke. Sort of like calling big guys Tiny.

"Yes, he is," Zach said seriously while casting Jack a perturbed look in the rear-view mirror. "He retired a couple months past, but he's still a reverend. That don't change nothin'."

"Gotcha." *Guess this isn't the time to tell you I'm an atheist. You morons are liable to shoot me in the name of some god.*

They continued driving for another ten minutes, then headed south for another thirty minutes before going east again.

Jack studied the landscape to memorize where he was being taken. It was fairly desolate and they only passed the occasional farmhouse, each surrounded by acres of flat pastureland.

Thirty minutes later the landscape became a little more rolling as they neared the foothills of the Cascade mountain range. It was then that they turned off onto a muddy side road and stopped in front of a steel gate secured with a padlock.

Beyond the gate rose a wooded, rocky mountain that stood out from the fields like a giant wart on the face of Mother Nature.

Reverend Bob's son, who was clean-cut and about thirty years old, leaped from the SUV and unlocked the gate. They then followed the SUV inside. The son relocked the gate and got back in the SUV to continue on.

Soon the road became steep and twisted as it wove through clumps of forest and rocky outcrops. Zach put the truck into four-wheel drive to navigate the occasional deep muddy rut and several times their progress slowed to a crawl.

Fifteen minutes later, the trees dwindled to scrub brush and they reached the top where powerful spotlights mounted on a telephone pole lit up the yard.

Holy shit!

Jack's first impression was of a military outpost in a war zone. A large cement bunker, complete with narrow slits for windows, had been built deep into the rock. The bunker's roof was flat and covered with large solar panels. Behind the house loomed a metal lookout tower perched on top a steel pole. Across a gravelled yard from the bunker was a steel hangar.

The SUV stopped in front of the hangar and Zach pulled up alongside it while the son got out to slide the hangar door open.

Jack listened to the sound of the rain peppering the roof of the truck as he stared out at the distorted, elongated shadows formed by the spotlights. It left him with an eerie feeling and he wondered, *Is that a cement bunker ... or a crypt?*

"So what y'all think back there?" Luke asked.

"Are we still in the States?" Jack asked, in an attempt at humour as he gestured to the bunker and lookout tower.

"Yup ... and we plan to keep it the good ol' U.S. of A." Luke replied.

"Amen to that, brother," Zach added.

Okay ...

Reverend Bob's son finished pushing the door open and stood to one side. In the headlights Jack noticed a workbench at the far end of the hangar. His pulse quickened. There was a windshield leaning against the left side wall near the workbench.

Jack leaned forward for a better look, but the SUV drove in and blocked his view. Zach pulled in beside it and they all got out.

He wanted to hurry to the other side of the SUV on the pretense of meeting Reverend Bob so he could get a better look at the windshield. Overhead sensor lights had come on when they'd driven in and the hangar was well illuminated, but when he climbed out of the back seat he was too late.

Before him stood a tall, thin man with protruding cheek bones. Jack guessed his age at sixty and noted that he was balding. *He looks familiar ... but from where?*

"Welcome to Eden, my friend," the man said, sticking out his hand. "They call me Reverend Bob."

Jack slung his backpack over his shoulder and shook

his hand. *Okay, your grip is strong. Too strong to be polite. Telling me you have control issues, do you?*

"Pleased to meet you, Reverend Bob," he said, matching the pressure in his grip while returning Reverend Bob's unflinching stare.

Reverend Bob's jawline hardened as he applied more pressure, then he released his grip. "And this here's my son, Jeremiah," he said, gesturing to the young man beside him.

"Call me Jerry," he said, grasping Jack's outstretched hand by the fingers and giving a solitary shake.

Reverend Bob glared at his son, then spoke sternly. "There's nothing wrong with the name you were given. Your mother wanted you to have that name, and even though she is with God, you dishonour her every time you reject it."

Jeremiah grimaced, then hung his head and mumbled, "Yeah, I know. Sorry."

Jack eyed Reverend Bob. *I remember where I've seen your face! That photo where everyone was giving closed-fist Nazi-style salutes — you were the speaker up front!*

"Okay, let's get into the house where it's warm," Reverend Bob said.

A side door to the hangar was on the same wall where the windshield was leaning. Jack hoped he'd have another opportunity to view it on the way out, but it was not to be.

The sliding door was still open and Reverend Bob gestured for them to leave through the front. "Come, this way. I'll pour us a drink and we can relax and get to know each other," he said.

Once outside the hangar, Jack used the pretext of helping Jeremiah tug the sliding door closed so he could take another look, but with the SUV parked beside it he didn't have a large enough angle to see it properly. Then a hand grabbed him by his shoulder and spun him around.

Reverend Bob released his grip and gave him a hard look. "Leave it." He gestured toward the door. "Jeremiah can handle it."

Jack heard the door slide shut behind him. "Oh, okay," he replied, then gave a friendly smile.

Reverend Bob looked at him oddly, then glanced at the hangar door as if pondering something before turning back to stare at him.

Damn it, I've heated him up. Is it the rain and the shadows across his face affecting my brain? No ... I can see it in his eyes. He's evil.

Jack gestured toward the bunker. "Quite the place you've built. I'm anxious to see it."

Reverend Bob stared a moment longer, then turned and headed for the bunker while Jack and the rest silently followed.

Chapter Forty-Two

Entrance to the bunker was gained through a heavy steel door. Inside was a mud room and off to one side was a laundry room. An open door at the end of the laundry room led to a washroom.

As Jack took off his jacket to hang on a row of hooks along with his backpack, he saw Reverend Bob go into the laundry room and punch in a code to disarm an alarm system. Unfortunately, the angle and distance was too great for him to glimpse what the code was.

Everyone entered the main living area. Despite the cold exterior, the interior felt warm and cozy. The living room consisted of a sofa and two reclining chairs placed in a horseshoe pattern around a black bearskin rug. The bear's head, with open mouth to show its fangs, faced a wood fireplace.

Opposite the living room was a kitchen with a picnic-style table. Stairs off the kitchen led to a lower level. Jack eyed the narrow windows strategically located to view all sides of the bunker. They were fitted with steel shutters, but a few were rolled up, which made them look not so obtrusive.

Reverend Bob glanced at Jack. "Bulletproof glass along with one-way glass on the inside," he said proudly. "The shutters are also bulletproof, although with the glass, they probably don't have to be."

"I'll feel safe tonight," Jack said.

"There's more," Reverend Bob said. "I don't know if you noticed the small decorative wood squares alongside the windows, but they cover steel hatches that open to the outside."

"Gun ports," Jack guessed.

"You got it."

"This place is fantastic." Jack gazed around. "Gives me an idea of how our clubhouses should be built."

"It's still a work in progress, but it's coming along fine." Reverend Bob gestured toward the sofa. "You'll sleep there tonight. It folds out into a bed and we'll get you a sleeping bag and pillow to go with it."

"Great, thanks," Jack said. "I hope that bear is dead, though."

The Coggins brothers chuckled and Jack glanced at Reverend Bob. *Will you lighten up or are you still brooding about me peering into the hangar?*

"He won't be botherin' you," Reverend Bob stated. "Shot him myself." He stared at Jack.

Okay ... if you're trying to make me uncomfortable, you've succeeded.

"The bear had two cubs, Dad," Jeremiah interjected. "You should mention that you shot them, too."

"Little bears grow into big bears," Zach said, seemingly offended. "You wouldn't feel bad about it if some day one of 'em —"

"It's all right," Reverend Bob said. He patted Jeremiah on the back and smiled at him. "You've got a big heart, boy. Nothing wrong with that. Your mother did, too. Perhaps that's why I love you as much as I do."

Jeremiah looked embarrassed, but managed to give an appreciative smile.

"Speaking of shooting things," Jack said. "When do I see what I came for?"

"Tomorrow morning," Reverend Bob replied. "Tonight let's get to know each other a little better." He gestured with a sweep of his hand toward the living room. "Y'all make yourselves comfortable while I round us up some Wild Turkey."

Jack took a seat in a recliner and moments later Reverend Bob provided everyone with a glass of bourbon on ice before taking a seat in the other recliner.

Jack took a sip.

I hate bourbon. To me it tastes and smells like dirty socks would.

"That warm your belly?" Luke asked, raising his glass toward Jack.

"Tastes mighty fine!" Jack exclaimed. "Perfect drink on a night like this."

"So," Reverend Bob said, whirling his recliner around to face him. "Tell me … how bad is it up there in Canada?"

"How bad?" Jack asked.

"With all those immigrant sand niggers you let in?"

"Uh, well —"

"Yeah, we heard you let everyone in up there," Zach added. "Must be a lot of terrorists." He glanced at Luke and added, "You can bet that they'll be itchin' to come down here and do somethin'."

"Well, so far there haven't been any big massacres, but —"

"You got many of them jihadists?" Luke asked. "I heard they're the worst."

"No, ISIS is the worst," Zach claimed.

"You wouldn't believe it if I told you," Jack said, shaking his head for effect. "It's like our government is blind."

"You're lucky if it's only your government," Reverend Bob stated bitterly. "I think half of America is blind, too." He put his drink down on a side table and leaned closer, shaking his finger for emphasis. "Our whole country is rotten and it started at the core — our own government." He then picked up his glass and took a large gulp.

"That's fer shore," Zach stated. "As Reverend Bob often says, what we need is a real good cultural cleansin' to clean the mess up."

"Yeah, they should all be sent back to where they came from," Jack replied.

Reverend Bob slammed his drink down on the table and his face became a mottled red. "They shouldn't have been let in to start with!" he yelled. "First ones sneaking in should have been shot! They'd have gotten the message pretty quick!"

Wow, it didn't take much to light your fuse.

"I guess that sums up why I'm here," Jack said. "As I told Vath, we've got a real problem up our way."

"Yeah, we hear you got chinks, A-rabs, rag-tops, and apes from all over up there," Luke chimed in.

"You name 'em, we got 'em," Jack replied.

"It's the same everywhere," Reverend Bob seethed. "It won't be long."

"It won't be long?" Jack questioned.

Reverend Bob looked at him like he was daft. "Until the race wars start!"

"Oh yeah … right," Jack responded, trying to sound like he knew that.

Reverend Bob shook his head, perhaps imagining the horror he imagined. "It'll be utter chaos. We won't be able to depend on our soldiers because there's too many of those monkeys in the military."

"Fuckin' alligator bait is what they should be used for," Zach suggested.

"Nobody will know who they can trust," Reverend Bob continued. "It'll be every man for himself."

"My father wants to organize," Jeremiah said. "He said we need to form our own militia."

"I see," Jack replied. "It makes sense."

Reverend Bob's face came back to its normal colour as his rage subsided. "You've got that already," he noted. "How many chapters of Satans Wrath do you have in Canada?"

"Nineteen," Jack replied. "We're looking at adding two more before the year is out."

"How many in the States?"

"We have about the same number in the States, but mostly out west. We've had some issues with other clubs back east, but we'll get there eventually. Worldwide, we have chapters in over forty countries."

"Over forty countries," Reverend Bob repeated. "And your club is all white. No coloureds allowed, right?"

"Right," Jack replied. "That's written in our club's constitution."

Reverend Bob turned to the others. "You see how they've organized themselves and have like-minded people all around the world?"

Zach, Luke, and Jeremiah all gave grunts and murmurs of understanding.

"That's exactly what I was talking about the other day," Reverend Bob reminded them. "If we are truly going to survive, we're going to have to organize and form allegiances right across the whole country." He eyed Jack, then added, "Or better yet, the whole world." He paused. "Wouldn't you agree?"

Jack tried to look reflective, then said. "Something needs to be done, that's for sure."

"Exactly." Reverend Bob pointed his finger at Jack. "God brought you and me together for a reason. We need to fulfill that reason."

Good, you keep thinking that.

"Don't you agree?" Reverend Bob asked.

"I hadn't thought of it that way," Jack replied. He nodded thoughtfully. "You could be right."

"I know I'm right!" Reverend Bob said angrily.

Yes, how dare I question anything you say?

"How riled are the people up your way over what's happening?" Luke asked.

"Some more than others," Jack replied.

"If a bunch of white folk got murdered and it looked like one of them ethnic groups y'all spoke about were to get blamed for it, do you think folks would rise up an' go after 'em?"

"You mean would it be possible to start a race war up in Canada by killing some people and then framing a certain group?"

"Yeah, that's exactly what I mean," Luke said.

"I don't think so," Jack replied. "We don't have that many guns up there to start with. Personally, I think my club is in the best position to deal with the problem." He looked at Reverend Bob. "With your help ... and God's help, of course."

"Amen," Reverend Bob replied.

The next few hours dragged on, with racial slurs and violent ideology bubbling to the surface with each glass of bourbon consumed.

At 2:00 a.m. Reverend Bob announced that it was time for bed, and Zach, Luke, and Jeremiah headed downstairs.

Reverend Bob unfolded the sofa bed and Jeremiah returned momentarily to toss Jack a sleeping bag and a pillow.

"There, I think that about does it," Reverend Bob said. "You can use the washroom off the laundry room."

Good, go downstairs to bed so I can sneak out for a look at that windshield. He then saw Reverend Bob rearm the alarm system. *Scrub that idea ... for now.*

Later, as he lay on his back on the sofa bed staring up at the ceiling, he thought about Ferg's final moments. *Who drove over him and whose face did he see looking down at him when the trigger was pulled?*

His thoughts drifted to Betty. *The funeral is less than two days away. She has a right to know what happened — but how do I find out who did what?*

Sleep eluded him for the next couple of hours, but eventually he made a decision. *I'll confront Reverend Bob about what happened after I'm shown the weapons. He won't be happy, but I'll say I'm worried about possible loose ends and the fear that it might have garnered police attention.*

Having made that decision, his brain then fought the negative thoughts about whether or not his plan would get him killed.

I'm an operator … it's what I do. It'll work. It has to. My life depends upon it.

Chapter Forty-Three

Although Jack eventually managed to drift off to sleep, Dawson and his team, along with Corporal Frisby and Constable Willisko, stayed awake the entire night.

Earlier the team had tracked Jack's phone through GPS as it moved into a remote wooded area in the mountains. Then the signal said it had become stationary.

Nearby, the team discovered a swath cut through the forest. It was intended for use to fight forest fires, but now it served to hide their vehicles out of sight of the road.

Frisby and Willisko were unarmed, so Dawson made the decision to leave them, along with two of his agents, with the vehicles while he and Special Agent Ray Schneider along with the other two agents crept through the bush to scout the area where the phone had become stationary.

Soon they came to a clearing and realized they were looking down at a logging camp that contained several modular trailers. Lights were on in a couple of trailers and movement of men back and forth from one particular trailer suggested to Wayne that it was the cookhouse.

Dawson and Schneider took up a position in the woods on one side of the camp while the other two agents took up a position on the opposite side in the hope of being able to hear or see something in the event Jack needed urgent help.

When two hours passed, Dawson set up a schedule to have one of the two teams in the bush relieved by the two agents in the cars every two hours. At 2:00 a.m. he nudged Schneider, who sat beside him on a log. "I think the rain is coming to an end."

"It's about time," Schneider replied. "My teeth are chattering so loud I'm afraid it'll give us away."

"Yeah, I noticed. Mine, too. It's good. No chance we'll fall asleep."

"Too wet and cold to do that even if I wanted." Schneider gestured at two of the modular trailers that were side by side and had their lights on. "What the hell do you think they're doing in there? Looking at guns?"

"Tomorrow's Sunday and I notice there aren't that many vehicles around. Bet most of the guys in the camp get the day off. For whoever's left to look after the place, I'd lay odds that they're in there drinking whiskey, maybe playin' cards, getting hammered, and tellin' jokes."

"Son of a bitch," Schneider muttered.

"Yeah, what you said, but I don't care how long we have to sit out here if it means we catch whoever murdered Ferg."

"You got that right," Schneider replied.

* * *

Jack got up at 6:30 a.m., and after using the washroom, he stood in the kitchen and peered out the window at the lookout tower. It was perched on top of a rocky knoll about a half-minute walk from the bunker.

The top of the tower was comprised of a small metal platform with waist-high metal sides and a tin roof, all of which was atop a steel pole with rungs leading to the platform. Support cables strung out from each corner of the platform offered stability.

"I call it the crow's nest," Reverend Bob said.

Jack was startled and turned around and saw Reverend Bob standing in his bathrobe. "Good morning. Hope I didn't wake you."

"No, I'm an early riser," Reverend Bob replied. "I heard you so I came up to turn the coffee pot on, then I'm going to grab a shower." He eyed the lookout tower. "You can go up and take a look if you like."

"Thanks. Being at the top of the hill like that, I bet it offers quite a view," Jack replied.

"You bet it does. From there, you can see most of my property and far beyond." He paused, then added, "This also isn't a hill. We're over a thousand feet high. That qualifies as a mountain."

"Sorry, no disrespect intended," Jack replied. "I was meaning more the knoll it is on."

"Oh." He paused. "That's okay. Sometimes I let the pride I feel about this place get the better of me. Go up and take a look. See for yourself."

"I will. Is anyone else up yet?"

"No, I imagine they're all still asleep."

Jack gestured to the tower. "Okay then, seeing as it stopped raining, while you're grabbing a shower, I'm going to take a peek. I'll hold off on the coffee and have it with you once you're dressed."

"That'd be good. Let me turn the alarm off before you open the door."

Reverend Bob then shut the alarm off, flicked on the coffee pot, and headed downstairs.

One minute later Jack checked the side door to the hangar. It wasn't locked so he opted to enter through it rather than risk sliding the larger door open.

The windshield looked how he suspected it would. The cobwebbed pattern from being struck by Ferg's head was obvious. Specks of dried blood and a couple of grey hairs were still visible in the cracks.

His first thought was to get a hair sample. If the windshield disappeared and he was later required in court, the DNA sample would provide crucial evidence.

Then again, could I still do that and protect Lance? Maybe if the district attorney treated me like an informant and allowed me to testify without my face being seen I could. Or would that be allowed? He eyed the blood and hair in the windshield. *Cross that bridge when I come to it. Get the damned sample.*

A box of garbage bags on the workbench served his purpose for something to wrap the sample in. He tore off a small piece of plastic and returned to the windshield and squatted down to pluck a hair from the glass.

Reverend Bob's voice boomed out behind him. "Find what you're looking for?"

Oh, fuck! Jack scrunched the piece of plastic in his hand and looked over his shoulder. Reverend Bob was still in his bathrobe and his face revealed his anger.

Zach, who was shirtless and wearing work boots with the laces dragging on the ground, stood beside him. The butt of a pistol protruding from the top of his jeans.

Now what do I do?

He heard Luke and Jerimiah running across the yard toward them and subconsciously swallowed, then tucked the piece of plastic in his waistband and stood up before turning to face them.

Reverend Bob gave him a look of utter contempt, then said, "Guess I didn't mention that when I shut the alarm off to the house, I didn't turn it off out here."

Luke and Jerimiah then stepped into the hangar. Like Zach, they were only dressed in jeans, but hadn't bothered to take the time to put anything on their feet.

Reverend Bob gave a sharp nod to Zach, who then reached for his pistol.

Time to start talking … fast.

Chapter Forty-Four

Back at the logging camp, the lights in the trailers had remained on until 4:00 a.m. If the surveillance teams thought they would then be able to get any rest themselves, they were wrong. Not long after the lights went out, hordes of insects descended upon them. By daybreak, their faces had turned into blotchy lumpy masses flecked with bloody red dots from a combined attack by mosquitoes and black flies.

At 7:00 a.m. Dawson got up from the log he'd been sitting on and took a few steps to stretch his legs. He then looked at Schneider, who was stretched out on his back with his legs hanging over the sides of the log. "Remind me for next time to throw some bug spray in the glovebox."

"Let's hope there's not a next — son of a bitch!" Schneider exclaimed and jumped to his feet while shoving one hand down the crotch of his jeans.

"Keep the noise down," Dawson ordered. "What the hell are you doing? Playing with yourself?"

Schneider brought out his hand and carefully examined whatever he'd plucked from his crotch.

"A bloody ant!" Schneider announced, then rolled it between his thumb and forefinger before flicking it away. "Oh, Jesus, I think I got another one," he said, this time shoving his hand down the back of his jeans.

"At least all the hoppin' around you're doing ought to warm you up," Dawson observed.

Schneider didn't appear to be amused and gestured toward the camp. "How long you figure they'll sleep for?"

"Your guess is as good as mine, but the lights only went off three hours ago. I'm bettin' our Mountie stays curled up in his nice warm bed 'til at least noon."

"That bastard. Hope he catches bedbugs."

* * *

The hangar echoed Jack's voice. "You're damned right I found what I was looking for!" he yelled in apparent fury. "Don't even bother showing me the guns I came to buy!"

Zach looked confused. He'd gripped his pistol but had only pulled it halfway out when he hesitated and looked at Reverend Bob.

"We don't deal with amateurs," Jack stated. He then pointed his finger at Reverend Bob and exclaimed, "And you guys are fuckin' amateurs! I can't believe you're still out walking around and not dead or in jail."

Reverend Bob appeared taken aback, then placed one hand on Zach's arm to stop him from pulling out the pistol completely. "What do you mean?" he asked.

"What do I mean?" Jack shook his head as if in disgust. "When I first met Vath he told me Graves damn near got arrested and a cop ended up getting killed. I told him then that I wouldn't deal with you guys because there'd be heat, but he swore that the only link the cops had was Graves. From how he spoke about you guys, he made it pretty clear to me that you took care of Graves. He said that with him dead, we had nothing to worry about."

"That's true," Reverend Bob replied.

"Bullshit! I put my trust in you guys because I thought you knew what you were doing. When I spotted this leaning against the wall last night I didn't know what to think. I'd heard something on the news about a Canadian and a cop getting killed and that one of them was run over."

"You mean Graves and a cop," Reverend Bob said.

"Yes, but at the time I didn't realize it was Graves and only clued in later when I spoke with Vath." He gestured with his thumb toward the windshield. "At first I was hoping to hell it was a coincidence. Thought maybe you'd hit a deer or something, but this morning I decided I better look." He then turned and plucked a hair from the windshield and held it up for them to see. "This ain't no hair from any deer." He glared at Reverend Bob. "What the hell? Why are you leaving around evidence? Do you want us all to be busted?"

Reverend Bob cleared his throat. "No, of course not. We —"

"Fuck you guys," Jack said. "Take me back. We don't deal with people who're this careless."

"Now you hold on a second," Reverend Bob said. "No need to get your britches in a knot." He paused to take a deep breath and after slowly exhaling, said, "I know you boys in that club of yours have had your share of experience when it comes to killing."

Jack stared stone-faced in response.

"That being said, we're not exactly new to it either, and we're certainly not careless," Reverend Bob added. "That's why we changed the windshield ourselves. We only had the opportunity to do that yesterday because it took a few days for us to find one we could get without anyone knowing. By the time we were finished installing it, we had to go get you, so I told Zach and Luke to take it out today and bury it."

Jack looked at Zach and Luke. "Is that true?"

"For darn shore it's true," Zach replied.

Jack looked at Reverend Bob. "So you hadn't forgotten about it and weren't going to leave it lying around?"

"Of course not."

Jack waited a beat. "Then I guess I owe you an apology. I'm sorry."

Reverend Bob gave a conciliatory smile. "That's all right. Glad we got it straightened out between us."

"Perhaps I should've said something last night instead of lying awake all night worrying about it."

"For sure," Reverend Bob agreed. "If something is troubling you, it's best to get it off your chest."

"You're absolutely right." Jack then gave a puzzled expression and glanced at the windshield. "I remember on the news it said the cop had been shot, so why'd you run Graves down with your truck? Why didn't you shoot him, too?"

"It wasn't Graves I ran over," Reverend Bob stated. "An ATF agent showed up and tried to arrest him, Zach, and

Jeremiah. It was the agent who I ran down. I was too far away to try and shoot him." He gestured to Luke and said, "He was hiding behind a car farther down the street and would have tried to shoot him when he was busy hand-cuffing them, but I decided not to risk a shootout with Jeremiah and Zach so close to him. I also figured if he did manage to jump out of the way, Luke could've tried to shoot him then."

"He was a tough son of a bitch, too," Zach drawled. "Gittin' run over didn't kill 'im. Reverend Bob still had to shoot 'im after."

Jack looked at Reverend Bob, who gestured with his hands as if the shooting aspect of the murder was trivial.

You bastard. You're going to pay for what you did.

"We were lucky the guy was by himself," Jeremiah noted.

"Real lucky," Jack stated, with more emphasis than he intended. He stared at Reverend Bob. "So, I've got your word that you don't have any heat? Because I tell ya, our club would be more than a little pissed off to do a deal and have the cops show up and relieve us of our hard-earned dollars."

"I'll swear on the Bible if you want me to," Reverend Bob said solemnly. "The police have no idea who we are."

"Good enough." Jack waited a beat. "Do you think that coffee's ready yet?"

Reverend Bob's face brightened. "I'll cook breakfast, too. You like flapjacks, eggs, and ham?"

"Sure do."

Jack kept the hair plucked from the windshield between his thumb and forefinger. Once back inside the bunker he went to the washroom and wrapped it in the piece of plastic and put it in his pocket.

I've got you! Now show me the guns.

* * *

After breakfast, as Jeremiah rose to clear dishes from the table, Reverend Bob looked at Zach and Luke and said, "Go look after that windshield. Make sure you bury it deep." He then glanced at Jack and added, "When they get back, we'll get down to business and I'll show you what we've got to offer."

Can't be soon enough to suit me.

"Sounds good," Jack replied, then rose and offered to dry the dishes as Jeremiah washed.

"You're a guest," Reverend Bob stated. "Go relax. Jeremiah and I can handle it."

Jack looked out the window toward the tower. "Then maybe I'll go up and check out the view."

"Go ahead. From up there you can see for miles around. I'm sittin' on the best spot God ever made."

"How did you ever find this place?" Jack asked.

"Two brothers who are buddies of mine own the only two farms around. The property used to belong to them, but they looked at it as a worthless chunk of rock. Me, I looked at it like Noah looked at the top of Mount Ararat when he landed his ark."

"A safe haven."

"You got that right," Reverend Bob said emphatically.

"So you built yourself a bunker, and by the looks of

all the solar panels, you have your own electricity," Jack noted.

"Yes and we have our own well. As far as water and electricity go, we're completely off the grid. This year we'll start growing our own food, too."

"Very impressive. Like I told you last night when I first saw the bunker, I thought it'd be really rough inside, like a military outpost or something. I was wrong. It looks great."

Reverend Bob smiled. "Thanks. My two buddies call me Bunker Bob, but I don't mind."

How about I call you Bonkers Bob?

"They'll be wishing they had a place like this when the day comes." Reverend Bob paused to look out at the tower. "Yes siree, it's salvation, my son, salvation." He then turned to Jack. "Go up and take a look. I bet you'll agree. Sometimes I spend the whole day up there, reading my Bible and taking in the view." He smiled, perhaps to himself. "Somehow sitting up there makes you feel closer to God."

If only there was a god ... because I'd love to introduce you to him.

Jack walked up the rocky knoll and then climbed the rungs on the metal pole. He saw that the platform at the top was comprised of a thick sheet of plywood that had been covered in tin. Entry was gained by pushing up on a trapdoor. Once inside, he let the trapdoor fall shut as a safety precaution to prevent accidentally falling through the hole.

A plastic chair was available and he sat down. He could easily see over the top of the tin panels surrounding the railing.

Reverend Bob had not exaggerated how far you could see or the solitude you felt. All of Reverend Bob's outer property was easily seen. In the far distance he could see two farm houses, each on opposite sides of where he sat, but they were barely visible across acres of pasture and harrowed fields.

He then spied what he was hoping to see. Zach and Luke were driving along a road that encircled the perimeter of Reverend Bob's property. Soon they came to a stop and he watched as they retrieved a shovel, pickaxe, and the broken windshield from out of the canopy on the back of the truck. He made a mental note of where they started to dig, then climbed down from the tower and returned to the bunker.

"Spectacular!" Jack announced as he entered the kitchen. "Don't know if I'd want to be up there if there was lightning, though."

Reverend Bob smiled as he hung up the dish towel. "I've got a lightning rod out there that should take care of that, but you're right. I don't know if I'd want to trust it completely. Not that it really matters. The crow's nest provides the most scenic view, but when it comes right down to it, my best eyes are inside the bunker."

"Oh?" Jack asked.

"Come. Let me show you the command centre," Reverend Bob said proudly. "If you still harbour any thoughts that you're dealing with amateurs, you won't when you see this."

Jack followed Reverend Bob and Jeremiah down a half-level of stairs and entered a small room where a desk faced a wall of closed circuit television monitors.

Jack's jaw dropped when he saw how much was visible with the cameras. The entire outside property was monitored. He looked at two monitors that showed where Zach and Luke had parked the truck. One camera clearly displayed the front of the truck while the other was positioned from behind. Other cameras were trained on different parts of the property, including several on the road leading up to the bunker.

A surprise raid is going to be next to impossible.

He then concentrated in an effort to memorize which parts of the property were monitored and which weren't. If a tactical unit were to come in, his information could be extremely valuable.

Then there's the bloody tower … I'm going to need another look from up there and compare it with what can be seen from this room.

"What d'ya think?" Jeremiah asked.

"Truly amazing," Jack replied. "I doubt a rabbit could come onto this property without you knowing."

Reverend Bob stood with his hands on his hips and appeared to admire the display of monitors. "The perimeter is covered 100 percent, but I could still use a few more alarm sensors and night-vision cameras to fill in the gaps. Some of the money from what you purchase will see to that."

"These cameras all night-vision?" Jack asked.

"For sure. They work as good at night as in the day. No use only being half safe. Security is what it's all about."

Soon you'll be getting all the security you can imagine. It's called prison.

"Besides cameras," Reverend Bob continued, "I've got the perimeter completely monitored with sensors, as well as a few sensors inside my property."

"Cameras and sensors," Jack noted. "This place really is impenetrable."

"It's getting there. The sensors have been a bit of a pain. They sound like smoke detectors going off and usually it's been the wind or a couple of times it was deer or racoons. I adjusted some of them to avoid the racoons, but a few still need to be moved or readjusted."

"I think it's impressive the way it is."

Reverend Bob pointed to a monitor. "Looks like the boys are done."

Jack glanced at the screen and saw the truck returning. He then looked at Reverend Bob. "This place must've cost a fortune."

"There's money to be made selling religion if you do it right," Jeremiah said dryly.

"It put clothes on your back and food in your mouth," Reverend Bob stated gruffly. He then turned to Jack and rolled his eyes. "It wasn't all from the church. A lot of the money came from an inheritance I received when my father-in-law passed."

"Yes siree. Good ol' Moonshine Bill … he ran quite an operation," Jeremiah said sullenly. "Mind you, there was that time when four people went blind after —"

Reverend Bob jammed the end of his finger into Jeremiah's chest, forcing him to take a step back. "He raised your mother and she was a fine person!"

Jeremiah's mouth gaped momentarily and he hung his head. "I, uh, know that." He cleared his throat. "I'm going to the can."

Reverend Bob stared after him as he left, then he looked at Jack and gestured with his hands as if to say he didn't know what to do. "I love that boy with all my heart," he said, "but he does have a mind of his own sometimes."

Being able to think for yourself isn't a bad quality, but a domineering bastard like you wouldn't understand that.

"He's young," Jack stated. "Many men don't really appreciate their fathers until they get older."

"Maybe, but this is my house. He should show more respect."

You're the king and absolute ruler of your own castle all right. Nobody better dare challenge you on that.

The sound of Zach and Luke entering upstairs ended the discussion. "Down here," Reverend Bob yelled. "It's time to show Jack what real firepower is all about."

A moment later, Jack followed everyone deep into the bowels of the bunker. They descended to the next level, which had three bedrooms and a washroom, before continuing down to the final level, which housed the master bedroom, complete with an attached washroom and a king-sized bed.

Reverend Bob turned to Jack. His words were solemn. "What I'm about to show you is something few people know about. I'm placing trust in you by letting you see it, but you don't have my complete trust, understand?"

"Not really," Jack replied.

"Let me put it another way," Reverend Bob stated. "The ammo for the weapons you're about to see is available, but I'm not going to allow you to ever be in a position to turn our own guns against us."

Jack chuckled. "That I understand. It's simple business. We'll feel the same need to be cautious when it comes to the money." He glanced at Reverend Bob. "No worries, we'll come up with a way to ensure everything is done in a way that everyone feels safe."

"We figured you'd have experience at doin' that," Luke said.

Reverend Bob disappeared into a walk-in closet and Jack heard a rumbling sound. He was then waved in.

The rear of the closet contained a hidden entrance leading to another room. One side of the room contained floor to ceiling shelves laden with canned food and sacks of rice, but it was the other side that really caught his attention. Wooden crates were stacked in piles, while others were strewn about on the floor. Many of the lids were open to reveal that they contained everything from handguns to military-grade automatic rifles.

This is it. I've done it. Now all I need to do is get the hell out....

Chapter Forty-Five

"You have to bless America," Reverend Bob said as he gestured to the crates. "We have our Second Amendment."

Yes, it was written in 1791 to assist the militia in the event of an armed invasion from another country. Do you really think your military needs a bunch of civilians coming to their rescue these days?

Jack decided not to respond to the comment and opted instead to examine an M16 assault rifle leaning against a crate.

"You don't have any laws like that in Canada, do you?" Zach said.

"No," Jack replied.

A law written when they used flintlock pistols and muskets. He gazed at the assault rifle he was holding. *With a weapon like this, any deranged person could easily turn a mall or theatre into a slaughterhouse. The carnage would be devastating.*

"I can tell by the look on your face that you wish you did," Zach noted.

"You read my mind," Jack replied. "Particularly if it allowed us to get all your military assault rifles. If we could get them in the hands of the average citizen in Canada, things would be far better." He saw the nod of agreement from Zach and Luke.

What a couple of assholes....

"Well, these ought to help you some," Reverend Bob said. "Go ahead. Check 'em out. Look in any crate you want ... except for the ammo boxes."

Jack took a few minutes to rummage through a few of the crates, including one case containing silencers. He looked at Reverend Bob and said, "Your collection is impressive. They're all new?"

"Top quality for sure," Reverend Bob stated. "So go ahead, take your time. Spend the rest of the morning deciding what you'd like to buy. After lunch we'll go down to the range and you can try them out. That way if you change your mind or want something different, we'll be able to sort it out before talking price."

"You have an actual shooting range?" Jack asked.

"Shore do," Luke said.

Why am I surprised?

"The range isn't finished yet," Reverend Bob said, "but it'll do for the moment."

Jack then turned his attention to the crates, where he spent the rest of the morning examining the weapons and pretending to make decisions while listening to Reverend Bob extoll the features of the various weapons. He also did a silent tally of the number of the crates and the weapons they contained. In the end, he estimated there were approximately nine hundred firearms in total.

When he'd finished setting aside what he was pretending to buy, he'd selected twenty-one Benelli M4 semi-automatic 12-gauge combat shotguns, sixty-three M16A2 assault rifles, twenty-one silencer-equipped sniper rifles with night-vision scopes, a hundred Uzi pistols, a hundred Glock 19 pistols, plus another two hundred pistols that included a mixture of Taurus, Kel-Tec, and Ruger brand names. Other things, like laser-grip sights, silencers, and ammunition were still to be decided upon when they went upstairs for lunch.

Following a lunch of chili con carne, Reverend Bob arranged for Zach, Luke, and Jeremiah to take one of each weapon Jack had selected and put them in the Ram, along with a few weapons he hadn't picked in the event he wanted to change his mind. Zach lingered around the truck while Jeremiah and Luke made more trips to bring up and load the ammunition.

Really boys, I'm not going to rob you. I'd like to arrest you, but I can't even do that without burning Lance.

When they'd finished loading the pickup, Zach and Luke left in the truck while Reverend Bob, with Jack beside him and Jeremiah in the back, followed in the SUV. As they bounced along and skidded through a few muddy ruts, Jack tried to make small talk, but Reverend Bob seemed tense and uncommunicative. *Is he concentrating on the road … or have I done or said something to set him off again?*

"Anything wrong?" Jack finally asked.

Reverend Bob gave him a sideways look as he gripped the wheel. "What you've selected is worth a lot of money."

"Yes, but I thought we were going to negotiate the final price once my selection was confirmed?" Jack replied.

"Which I figure will be about 1.25 million."

"That's what we agreed to, more or less, depending upon what extras you're throwing in."

"And you boys happen to have that much money lying around? In U.S. dollars to boot?" He cast Jack a suspicious glance.

"For sure. We do a lot of business stateside. In fact, our B.C. bud is world-renowned. Usually our problem is try-ing to launder U.S. dollars into Canadian currency along with smuggling it back into Canada."

Reverend Bob still seemed troubled.

"That's not really what you're worried about, is it?" Jack questioned. "You're worried about whether or not we intend to rip you off."

"The thought has occurred to me."

"I mentioned one idea with Vath earlier. Didn't he tell you?"

"No, he doesn't even know me."

"My one suggestion was to do several transactions in smaller lots, but personally I think that adds to the risk of getting caught. What I'd prefer is that once you and I have settled on price and I get my bosses to go along with the weapons I've chosen, I'll come back to the States. At that time you hold me hostage wherever you like while someone from here goes to Canada and is held on our side of the border — either Zach, Luke, or Jeremiah. It doesn't matter to me which one. Then do the deal all at once. After that, each hostage is set free and everyone goes on their merry way."

"I guess that'd guarantee nobody is out to rob anyone," Reverend Bob replied.

"I'd be the one who goes to Canada, right Dad?" Jeremiah quipped from the back seat.

"Uh, sure, you could do that," Reverend Bob replied.

I know. Otherwise Zach and Luke would likely be arrested. "Oh? Your own son?" Jack turned and smiled at Jeremiah, then looked at Reverend Bob. "That makes me feel better. Definitely shows you wouldn't try to rip us off."

"Certainly not. I'm a man of my word." He glanced at Jack. "And with you volunteering to put yourself as hostage, obviously you're not planning to rob us either."

"Hell, no. I value my hide too much to try that."

"That's how we'll do it, then," Reverend Bob said. He cast another look at Jack. "Hope you don't feel offended, but until the moment arrives when I have the money, I'm still not taking any chances with you."

Jack brushed off Reverend Bob's concern with a wave of his hand. "No offence taken. I wouldn't trust me if I was in your shoes either."

"Glad that problem is out of the way, so I guess the big question is when? You still have decisions to make on things like ammo, silencers … laser grips, no doubt. Also have a bunch of night-vision binoculars and such. You might even decide to change what you've selected after you try them out."

"I think I'll be happy with what I've already selected," Jack replied.

"Either way, I expect you to be able to decide exactly what you want before the day is over."

"I will. That's definite," Jack replied.

"Good. So if we get you back to Canada tomorrow, how long will it take you to get back to me with a firm commitment and a date for the exchange?"

"There's a possibility that my bosses may want to make some small changes to the models I've selected."

"Uh-huh."

Jack gave the appearance that he was reflecting on the matter. "Even if they do, that would be minor. If anything, I expect they'll want to purchase more than what I've told you."

"More? How many more?" Reverend Bob asked anxiously.

Jack paused, pretending to think. "Maybe another two hundred and fifty. If we did, I'd expect to get more of a discount from the price we're paying for each one as it stands now."

Reverend Bob's mouth momentarily flopped open, then he put on a poker face and said, "I think you're already getting a good deal, but if you buy that many more, I could maybe move on price a little."

"So, with that in mind … let me think … rounding up the cash in U.S. dollars … making the final decision as to how many of what types …" *Yeah, your face is already lighting up with greed.* "I'd say we'd be ready to do the deal within forty-eight hours of me returning to Canada."

"Forty-eight hours!" Reverend Bob exclaimed. "I thought it'd take longer for you to talk to all your chapters?"

Hell no, the sooner you get me back to Canada the better.

He eyed Reverend Bob. "I won't get into the intricacies of it, but basically my bosses on the West Coast have the power to make the decision."

Reverend Bob smiled broadly. "God bless you."

It would be nice if she did. Mind you, I usually refer to her as Assistant Commissioner.

Jack saw the Ram ahead of them slow, then turn onto what was little more than a path and disappear through a clump of trees. He noticed a birdhouse in a tree where the truck had turned. It was the third one he'd seen since they left the bunker and knew that they contained hidden cameras because they matched some of the views he'd seen from the command centre.

Reverend Bob followed, and seconds later they entered a rock-strewn clearing. He parked the SUV and they got out.

The clearing had obviously been formed when a landslide had slipped from the mountain years before. A sheer rock cliff left in the aftermath had created a perfect backdrop to stop bullets.

Near the base of the cliff, a piece of cable like the ones used to anchor the lookout tower was strung across the clearing and wrapped around trees on each side. A few torn and shot up pieces of target paper dangled from strips of masking tape attached in increments along the cable. A couple of the targets fluttering in the breeze displayed remnants of human silhouettes.

Off to one side of a rock-cleared lane through the middle of the range, wooden stakes had been marked with red paint to number distances, starting at three hundred yards near where they stood and dwindling down in number as they neared the targets.

"Like I said, it's a work in progress," Reverend Bob stated as he gazed around. "Someday I'll have a separate range for small arms that'll be equipped with motorized pulleys to retrieve the targets, but for now this'll have to do."

"Looks more than adequate to me," Jack replied. He briefly studied what was before him. Judging by the length of the cable spanning the clearing and the remnants of strips of masking tape, he guessed the range could easily accommodate as many as thirty people in a line to shoot at the same time.

Reverend Bob appeared to have read his thoughts. "Yeah, sometimes a few of the boys come over to practise. I usually invite a couple dozen or so, then we have a few drinks. Gives us time to talk and prepare for what the world will be like in the future."

You mean with everyone living in bunkers and pointing weapons at each other?

"Sounds like a smart thing to do," Jack replied. He then watched as Zach and Luke drove to the back of the range, where they hung a dozen of the silhouette targets along the cable. On the way back they laid weapons down at various intervals, starting with the pistols and eventually putting rifles down as they drew near.

"You're set to go," Reverend Bob said when Zach parked beside them. "Jeremiah will walk along with you. Any questions or changes you want made, let him know. Same if you need more ammo. He's got a bunch in his backpack, but if you need more, tell him, and he'll run back and get it for you."

You don't want me walking back on my own. You're afraid I'll hide a gun on me.

He glanced at Jeremiah. "That's nice of you. Thanks."

Jeremiah smirked, but Jack couldn't tell if it was because he'd figured Jack knew the real reason or not.

"We'll start at the ten, then work our way back," Jeremiah said, slinging the backpack over his shoulder.

They then walked up to the ten-yard indicator, where Jack picked up a Glock that lay beside four other makes, including an Uzi pistol. He ejected the magazine and saw that it was loaded.

"They're all loaded," Jeremiah assured him.

Jack gestured back toward the vehicles, where Reverend Bob, Zach, and Luke waited. "Aren't they afraid I'll take you hostage?" he chided.

Jeremiah grinned. "My dad actually worried about that, but I insisted."

To prove to your dad that you're a man and are finally starting to make your own decisions?

"I told him I didn't think you'd be that stupid," Jeremiah continued.

"Don't worry, I'm not."

"Good thing, because both Zach and Luke have sniper rifles and each of them can shoot the eye out of a bullfrog at three hundred yards."

Jack glanced back and saw Zach and Luke looking through the scopes of sniper rifles they'd rested across the hood of their truck. "Sure glad I'm not a bullfrog. I'd hate to croak."

Jeremiah looked briefly amused, but then became serious. "It wasn't my idea to have them do that. I'm not scared of you." He paused, then scowled. "If my dad had his way, I'd never be allowed out of the bunker."

"He wants to protect you. Besides, sniper rifles at

that distance are the only practical weapon for them to have."

"Yeah, I know." He picked up a stone and threw it, seemingly at no place in particular, then looked back at his dad. "My mom died of cancer when I was six years old. Since then he's barely let me out of his sight. He treats me like I'm still six years old." He then scooped up another stone and threw it at the remnants of an old target. He missed.

"At least he loves you," Jack noted.

Jeremiah turned to face him. "Yeah, I know, it's just … well, I bet you think it, too."

"Think what?"

"That my dad's a little looney. So are his friends when it comes right down to it."

Yes, but I don't want to tell you that.

"You disagree with all of this?" Jack asked, gesturing with a sweep of his hand at the gun range, then toward the top of the mountain.

Jeremiah let out a snort. "I think it's all bullshit. I don't see us being attacked. Nobody wants to die. Why can't we all just be friends and get along?"

"It doesn't work that way."

"Why not?" His eyes searched out Jack's. "I'd rather make friends with people. Not get guns and kill them."

"Sometimes life doesn't leave you much choice when it comes to killing people," Jack replied. He then aimed at a target and fired several shots, more out of a desire to change the conversation than to see how the gun performed.

After he fired a few rounds from each of the pistols, they moved back to the fifteen-yard indicator and repeated the process until they were at the twenty-five-yard indicator.

Jack's lack of prowess in shooting handguns became more obvious the farther he retreated.

"I take it that guns aren't really your thing," Jeremiah stated, with some amusement when a couple of Jack's shots missed the target completely.

"Handguns aren't really my thing," Jack replied truthfully. "Let's move back to the hundred-yard marker and I'll try the others."

"Sure thing."

"Shall we pack the weapons back with us?"

"No, leave them. Zach and Luke have them all counted. They're supposed to retrieve them when you're done."

"Gotcha."

Upon reaching the hundred-yard marker, Jeremiah handed Jack a couple of loaded magazines for an M16 assault rifle. "So, tell me, what do you think?"

"Of what?"

"What my dad says ... that the end of the world is near type of shit."

"I don't know." Jack waited a beat. "Maybe we will end up killing each other. End up in a world where only the strong survive."

Jeremiah shook his head in apparent frustration. "You kinda sound like my dad, but I don't get it. We're supposed to be the land of the free. Seems like we're all just paranoid — I don't think anyone knows anymore what being free and civilized really means."

Good thinking kid. Now use your brain and go someplace else and leave this all behind.

Jack eyed him for a moment. "What do you plan on doing for the rest of your life?"

"I don't know. I used to be a computer tech, but quit when we moved here. It's all so depressing, wondering if what my dad says is true."

"What about Zach and Luke? What do they do around here?"

"Uh, actually they're my cousins and are just sort of vacationing here. Not sure where they'll go after. Maybe Alaska."

After they get their cut of the money, you mean.

Jack's voice became serious. "Maybe you should get out and experience the world yourself. Check out the planet and meet people from different cultures. Sometimes it changes your view about things and could make you better-informed."

Jeremiah gave him an odd look.

Yeah, that was a dumb thing to say. I'm supposed to be a racist.

"That way," Jack added, "it might not make you feel so bad when you do have to pop some low-breed son of a bitch because you'll know what they're really like."

Jack sensed that Jeremiah was staring at him as he fired a burst of three shots from an M16 — all landing in the central mass of the target.

I feel like a piece of garbage. Hopefully someday I'll have an honest talk with you.

The next hour passed by, then Jack turned to Jeremiah and said, "I've had enough. All these are fine weapons."

"Glad you think so," he replied.

"Should we tear down the targets?"

"Naw, leave 'em. Zach an' Luke'll look after everything."

They trudged back to where the vehicles were parked.

"Good timing," Reverend Bob said, looking up at the darkening sky. He eyed Jack and said, "So? What do you think?"

"I think I'll go with what I picked to start with."

"Fine by me. We'll go back to the bunker, figure out what extras you want, then do the math."

"Sounds good.

"Then first thing in the morning we'll have you on your way," he added.

That sounds even better.

"Y'all shore you want them pistols?" Zach questioned, ignoring an elbow he received in the ribs from Luke. "Because, man, I ain't never seen someone that bad with a pistol before."

"It was pretty bad," Jack admitted.

"Y'all no good with a pistol," Luke said in an apparent attempt to make him feel better, "but damn, y'all sure good with the long barrels."

Zach nodded respectfully. "Yup, there's no doubt about that. No siree."

"You're right about the pistols, though," Jack said. "I'd be better off to throw the damn thing at someone than try to shoot them."

Reverend Bob chuckled. "Aw, heck, look at me. I'm not that good with a pistol either, but my driving makes up for it!"

Jack resisted the urge to punch him in the face and instead guffawed with everyone else.

Chapter Forty-Six

The rest of the afternoon was spent negotiating the overall cost of the weapons along with the accessories and the potential cost for other weapons that Reverend Bob hoped Jack's people might be interested in.

"You maybe want to code these figures into your phone so you don't forget?" Reverend Bob suggested as they discussed the different figures.

What phone?

Jack glanced at Reverend Bob. "I don't like to have a paper trail on something like this. I've got a good memory when it comes to numbers."

Speaking of which, I'd like to see the view from the tower again....

Reverend Bob pursed his lips. "You're smart. I can see why you were picked."

It was 5:30 p.m. when Reverend Bob opened a new bottle of Wild Turkey. After pouring everyone drinks, they toasted their new business relationship.

"About tomorrow morning," Jack said, after settling back in the recliner. "I'd planned to meet a friend at Bellis Fair at noon tomorrow, but if possible I'd like to get there an hour or two before so I can do a little shopping."

"No problem," Reverend Bob replied. "I'll have someone drive you." He then locked eyes with Jack. "Until the deal is completed, I'll be staying home."

Being robbed is going to be the least of your problems, pal.

Jack faked a yawn. "I also don't want another late night like last night. I need to keep my brain sharp if I'm going to remember all those numbers, let alone the different makes and models."

Reverend Bob glanced at his watch, then took the hint and rose from his chair. "I'll heat up some stew and then we'll have an early night. In the morning I'll see to it that you're on the road right after breakfast."

"That sounds great."

While Reverend Bob busied himself in the kitchen, Jack made small talk with Zach, Luke, and Jeremiah. After a few minutes he'd finished his bourbon and put the glass down.

"I'll get you a refill," Jeremiah offered.

"Naw, thanks. Maybe later," Jack replied. "I need to clear my head and go over everything in my mind. I'm going out for a walk and take in some fresh air."

"It's raining and the wind has picked up," Reverend Bob said from the kitchen.

"That's okay," Jack replied.

"Are you sure?" Reverend Bob questioned as he peered out the kitchen window. "It's starting to look a little nasty out there."

"I like it like that," Jack replied. "My jacket's waterproof. Besides, there's something about walking in this weather that makes me feel good ... more alive."

Reverend Bob shrugged. "Dinner will be ready in about twenty minutes."

"I'm going to help my dad and set the table," Jeremiah said as he rose to his feet. "We'll call you when it's ready." He then paused and gestured to the black bearskin rug and said, "Oh, and Jack, you look like a bear in that jacket. Be careful my dad doesn't shoot you."

Jack grinned and gave a wave of his hand in response. A moment later he did his best to appear nonchalant as he wandered into the yard and studied the layout of the land while trying to recall which areas were monitored by cameras and which weren't.

Billowing black clouds darkened the already approaching night sky and the wind and rain had intensified. When the motion sensors turned on the overhead spotlights, he knew he didn't have much time to see what he wanted, so he hustled up the knoll to the tower and quickly climbed the steel rungs to the top.

* * *

"That about does it," Reverend Bob said, turning the heat down on the burner as he continued to stir the stew. He looked toward the living room. "Zach! Stick your head out the door and call Jack. Tell him it's ready."

"I saw him climb up to the crow's nest," Jeremiah said. "The wind is gusting pretty good. He might not hear you."

"In this weather?" Reverend Bob exclaimed. He peered outside.

"No worries," Zach said. "I got his number yesterday when he and Vath were at the restaurant. I'll phone him."

A moment later it became apparent that Zach had made the call, but it wasn't Jack that he was talking to.

"What's going on?" Reverend Bob demanded. "Who're you talking with?"

Zach gestured with his hand. "It looks like Jack lost his phone. Got some guy says he found it in his coat pocket."

"His coat pocket?" Reverend Bob reiterated. "Let me talk to him."

After taking the phone, Reverend Bob's conversation with the stranger was brief. "Did you happen to be in the Jack in the Box restaurant last night?"

"Yes," the stranger replied. "I don't understand. How did it get into —"

Reverend Bob cursed vehemently and terminated the call.

"Dad? What is it?" Jerimiah asked.

"We've been had!" Reverend Bob screamed in rage. "Jack ditched his phone at the restaurant last night! He figured out we knew they were being followed!"

"Oh, shit," Zach said. "He's a fucking cop!"

"How dare he come here!" Reverend Bob spluttered. "This is my home! Nobody tells me what I can or can't do! Not here!"

"What're we going to do?" Luke asked.

Reverend Bob didn't reply. He was already running toward the master bedroom.

* * *

As Jack gazed out from the tower, he spotted the arc of light when the bunker door opened. Reverend Bob stepped out first, followed by the others. They then crowded around and looked up at him.

What are they doing?

He leaned over the railing and waved. He received an immediate answer to his question when Reverend Bob raised an M16 and let loose.

Jack gasped and pitched himself backward onto the floor as bullets ripped through the roof, tin railing, and then the floor. In a panic, he shoved himself as far back as he could while frantically fumbling to yank his belt free from his jeans.

Chapter Forty-Seven

Reverend Bob ran up the rocky knoll toward the tower with the others behind him, then paused to fire another burst.

"Dad!" Jeremiah screamed out. "Look!" he yelled.

Jack had wrapped the ends of his belt around his wrists and hung on to it as he slid down a cable that was anchored in the ground on the far side of the knoll. He knew the angle was steep, but planned to control his speed by crossing his wrists to tighten his belt around the cable to slow his descent.

In theory his plan might have worked, but adrenalin, panic, and another burst of bullets made speed his top priority. He hit the ground feet first, but the momentum literally carried him head over heels down the rocky slope.

He'd managed to put his arms and hands up to protect his face and head as he crashed and rolled, but tendons snapped and tore around one knee.

After coming to a stop, he guessed that he only had a few seconds as the men charged up the other side of the knoll. The closest patch of bushes and trees was slightly farther down the hill and he scrambled to his feet.

If he hadn't been injured, he may have been able to run the short distance in time, but instead he took one step and fell to the ground and grabbed his knee in pain.

The sound of the men spurred his desperate attempt to escape. He tried to hop down the hill on one foot, but the ground was wet and slippery and he lost his footing when he jumped over a small ledge of rock and fell again.

He was only a car length away from the foliage, but before he could move, a burst of gunfire sent bullets whizzing above him. It was as if the bushes and trees in front of him were being hit with an invisible lawnmower. The sound of leaves and branches being shredded could be heard in combination with the thunk of bullets and splinters of wood flying off the trunks of trees.

He instinctively flattened himself on the ground along the side of the ledge. It was only shoulder-width high, so he raised his head slightly and was able to see over. Light cresting the hill from the spotlights in the yard revealed the silhouettes of the four men running down the slope toward him.

Oh shit, my face will be like a beacon. He ducked back into the shadow and shoved his face into the wet dirt while tucking his hands under his chest to hide their white skin.

The sound of their feet came closer ... then stopped along the ledge above him.

Do they see me? Is the next bullet going to be in the back of my head?

His senses had become acute. The wind and rain had subsided, as did the noise it produced. What he heard now was the sound of his own heavy breathing. He forced himself to take slow, even breaths. Then he heard another noise that he couldn't seem to control.

I've never heard my heart pounding so loud! How is that possible? They're bound to hear it!

He heard the men panting heavily as they, too, felt the exertion they'd undergone. *Their hearts have to be pounding, too … but how long before they look down and see me?*

The smell of rotten leaves and earth flooded his brain.

Will this be my last memory?

Another burst of gunfire caused his body to twitch.

"Come on," Reverend Bob said, "he can't be that far ahead."

"Maybe y'all got 'im already," Luke said.

Jack heard the thud and felt the vibration of a boot landing near his head as someone leaped over the ledge. Then more footsteps pounded the ground as the men charged past him.

They didn't see me!

He smeared muddy soil onto his face, then turned his head slightly so he could glimpse with one eye. The men were searching along the fringes of the bush. *Come on, keep going. Give me a chance to go the other way....*

"He's not here, and we'll never find him like this," Reverend Bob shouted to the others. "Everyone get back to the bunker and grab a weapon. We'll do this proper."

Shit, they're coming back! This time walking. I'm lying right in front of them! They have to see me! He crammed his body into the shadow of the ledge as tight as he could and watched.

Reverend Bob, Jeremiah, and Luke passed by him and stepped back onto the ledge, but Zach stopped an arm's length away from his head and turned to look back at the bushes.

"You should've waited until he came down from the crow's nest, then shot him," he heard Jeremiah say.

Reverend Bob didn't respond to the comment. Instead he shouted, "You can't hide for long, Jack! This is my place! I make the laws here! Come out now and we'll talk!"

"Dad, you're all out of breath. You need to calm down."

"Don't you tell me to calm down! I'll calm down when he's dead!" Reverend Bob swore under his breath. "Zach! Get a move on. Standing there won't help."

Jack peered up at Zach's face as he turned around.

Don't look down. Don't look down. Oh, Christ, don't step on me, either....

Zach took a quick leap onto the ledge to join the others.

Okay, everyone keep going. Keep going.

"Luke, grab a rifle with a night-vision scope and man the tower," he heard Reverend Bob order. "I'll man the cameras in the command centre. Zach ... Jeremiah, you two stand by ready to go when he's spotted. That's if Luke doesn't nail him first." He paused. "Boys, we're going to get this Judas son of a bitch!"

As if the damned night-vision cameras aren't enough, you're putting a guy up the tower with a night scope, as well? He took a moment to think about his predicament. *I've got to move, but where?*

As the men headed back up the knoll, he mapped a route out in his head that he hoped, with a great deal of luck, was one he could traverse without being seen. If it worked, it would take him to the edge of the property.

Then what? The perimeter is completely monitored and there are only open fields beyond. Maybe hide near the gate and hope I can jump whoever decides to leave when they get out to unlock it? He gave a snort. *Don't like the chances of that, but then again, I don't like my chances lying here either.*

He waited until the men disappeared over the top of the knoll, then followed after them in the hope that they'd expect him to either be going in the opposite direction or be hiding in the bush.

When he neared the crest, he dropped to a crawl to peek over. He watched as the men approached the bunker, then he eyed the hangar. Making it to that hangar was his next step.

The front of the hangar and one side was visible from both the tower, as well as a closed circuit television monitor, but he knew the far corner was not visible by either, provided he kept close to the building.

If he did make it to the hangar, then tried to leave the far corner and head for the bush, there was a stretch of yard to cross that would make him visible from the tower. His hope was that when Luke was in the tower he'd be looking in the opposite direction.

Then self-doubt entered his mind. *Is there a camera monitoring the ground between the far back corner and the bush?* He tried to remember the monitors he'd looked at in the command centre but for a moment he drew a blank.

Don't second-guess. Go with your first instinct.

As the men entered the bunker, he thought, *How much time do I have? Five minutes maybe?* A glance at the rocky outcrops told him that the quickest way to the hangar was to take the path leading to the bunker, then proceed from there.

Pain in his knee reminded him of his vulnerability. *Can I get down there before they come back outside or Reverend Bob starts watching the monitors? If they all go down to get weapons and more ammunition … damn it, quick talking to yourself and do it.*

He rushed forward, but his knee gave out and he ended up scrambling and rolling down the rocky knoll like a wounded three-legged animal, clenching his teeth as he went to keep from crying out in pain.

When he reached the bottom, he had to pass close to the door of the bunker. It also faced the hangar. The two structures were only a stone's throw apart, but the yard was well lit so anyone opening the door as he was crossing the yard would see him. There was also another problem. The yard and area surrounding the hangar was gravelled — which meant it could not be crossed in complete silence.

You can do it. You can do it, he said to himself as he hobbled and lurched his way across the yard. He was rounding the back of the hangar when he heard the bunker door open, followed by voices. *Close. Too close.*

He knelt to make his head less visible and peeked around the corner. Zach, Luke, and Jeremiah had come out of the bunker. All were carrying weapons. The distinctive barrels of Zach's and Jeremiah's weapons identified them as M16s, capable of firing forty-five to sixty rounds a minute when on semi-automatic. They were also deemed 100 percent accurate at a distance of three hundred metres.

Luke's weapon was different and was of a type Jack had fired earlier in the day. It was an M110 semi-automatic sniper rifle equipped with a night-vision scope — considered effective at eight hundred metres. To top it off, Luke had a set of binoculars dangling from his neck. *Oh yeah, they'll be night-vision as well.*

Luke slung the rifle over his shoulder and trotted up the knoll toward the tower, but Zach and Jeremiah took another direction and walked toward the hangar.

Jack ducked out of sight. By their voices, he knew they'd stopped close by. He glanced behind him. His plan to make a run for the treeline would have to wait. The gravel at the back of the hangar wasn't as compacted and he knew the crunch of his steps would give him away.

Okay, so I'll wait until they go back inside. Luke won't hear me once he's up the tower — and will hopefully be looking away from here.

"So, you don't think anyone else knows about us?" he heard Zach say.

"We really put him through the ropes before we met him," Jeremiah replied. "Once he ditched his phone, I don't see how anyone would know. It was after that when we met up with him."

"Yeah, and I didn't find one when I searched his backpack. I figured Luke would've noticed he didn't have it on him when he searched 'im, but I guess he figured it was in the backpack. Either way, he didn't have a second phone."

"And if he was wearin' a wire or somethin', Luke would have found that when he searched him."

"For shore," Zach replied.

"I'm pretty sure nobody knows he's here. Still, I told Luke to keep an eye in all directions in case someone was coming to try and rescue him."

Goddamn it.

"But the more I think about it," Jeremiah continued, "I don't think anyone will."

"Yup, I agree. Once we find him, we can pretty much do anything we want. Ain't nobody gonna know. If we take 'im alive, we can skin 'im like a possum and find out what he knows."

That's a pleasant thought....

"It's cold. Let's go back inside," Jeremiah suggested.

As the sound of their footsteps retreated, Jack peeked around the corner. Luke had reached the top of the tower and was using the binoculars to scan in all directions.

Okay, maybe he'll tire of doing that after a while. He then eyed Zach and Jeremiah. They remained standing inside the open door to the bunker. *Come on, guys. Go back inside where it's warm and close the door.*

Neither did, and over the next half-hour there were a few shouts back and forth to indicate that neither Reverend Bob or Luke had seen anything.

At 8:00 p.m. Luke complained that he was cold and a moment later Jeremiah relayed that Zach would relieve him as soon as he went to the washroom and then they'd take turns manning the tower in one-hour shifts.

A few minutes later Jack saw Zach climb up the tower and Luke then descended and joined Jeremiah at the entrance to the bunker.

Are they going to stand there all night? Jack felt his frustration growing, then decided that he'd chance making his next move at 9:00 p.m., when Jeremiah was climbing up the tower to take his turn in the hope that Zach would be distracted at that point.

At 8:30 p.m., Jeremiah and Luke, both with their weapons slung over their shoulders, left the bunker and started strolling toward the hangar. *Really, guys? Couldn't you go for a walk someplace else?* He ducked back and listened at the sound of their footsteps crunching on the gravel, coming closer with each step. *Come on, you assholes! Turn around and go back to the bunker!*

Seconds later he knew they'd passed by the front of the hangar and were approaching along the side toward the end where he was hiding.

Shit!

He tried to ignore the pain in his knee and hobbled along close to the hangar where rain had washed away and compacted some of the gravel. He then rounded the corner to the far side and stopped.

The footsteps followed, and when he heard them approaching along the back of the hangar he knew he was in serious trouble. He couldn't continue around to the front because he'd then be visible from both the tower and the camera monitor.

He looked at the treeline. *No way. They'd hear me and I'd be cut in half long before I could reach it.*

Desperation sunk in. *Can I jump these guys when they round the corner? Even with my bad knee, surprise will be on my side. If I grab the strap to an M16 and tear it off whoever's shoulder and use it before the other guy shoots me or I'm knocked to the ground, maybe* — Jack paused.

Shit, I'm going to die.

As hopeless as he felt it was, he crouched near the corner of the hangar with his hands readied in front of him as he prepared to leap up on one leg in a surprise attack.

Reverend Bob's voice erupted from near the door of the bunker. "Still nothing?" he yelled.

"Not a thing," Zach yelled back from the tower.

"Where's Jeremiah and Zach?" Reverend Bob yelled.

"We're here," Jeremiah yelled out from around the corner where Jack was crouched.

The crunch of gravel retreated and he breathed a deep sigh of relief. He stared at his trembling hands, then made fists to try and stop it.

I'm getting far too old for this shit.

"He's had to have holed up behind a rock or something," Reverend Bob yelled. "We'll get him sooner or later. Either if he tries to move or after daybreak."

"Could be a long night for him," Zach shouted down. "It's starting to rain again."

"Yes, a little help from the Almighty doesn't hurt," Reverend Bob replied.

Jeremiah's voice then sounded from the opposite side of the hangar. "How did he get the bikers to help him? That's what I'd like to know."

"Maybe they didn't," Reverend Bob replied. "Vath might have set us up."

Their voices then became murmurs, so Jack crept back along the end of the hangar and peeked around the corner. He saw Reverend Bob go back into the bunker while Jeremiah and Luke stood in the open doorway.

In ten minutes it would be Jeremiah's turn to go the tower to replace Zach. *That's when I'll head for the treeline. But then what? What chance do I have of one person leaving on his own and me jumping them at the gate? Or even trying to hide and hope someone shows up to rescue me?*

The rain had started again, heavier than before. He stood close to the hangar for protection, but the wind was gusting and his jeans were soaked within minutes.

Maybe it's good, he told himself as the rain ran down his face. *It'll help cover the noise from the gravel.* He glanced at his watch. *Five minutes to go. But then what? Think!*

As he stood there shivering he put his hands in his pockets and felt the piece of plastic that he'd used to wrap Ferg's hair sample.

What were his last few moments like? Thinking you survived being run down, only to be shot in the face....

He fidgeted with the piece of plastic between his thumb and forefinger as his mind replayed what Ferg went through. It gave him an idea.

An idea that might work if I can make it to the shooting range without being riddled with bullets.

Chapter Forty-Eight

At 9:00 p.m. Jack saw Jeremiah head toward the tower. Zack was also watching and started to descend the tower to meet him.

Perfect! Should give me time!

He hurried back to the far side of the hangar and then cut out across open ground toward the treeline. He moved slow as he tried to be stealthy, wincing each time the gravel crunched out of fear that Luke would hear him. When he was three-quarters of the way across, he looked back and saw Jeremiah's silhouette entering the top of the tower. *Forget stealth — go!*

Moments later he crawled behind a bush and waited. There was no yelling from the tower that he'd been seen; better yet, there was no barrel of a sniper rifle aimed in his direction. Luke also hadn't appeared from around the side of the hangar. *So far, so good.*

His next goal was easy to achieve. It took only a couple of minutes to make his way through the bushes to connect

with the road leading out. When he arrived at the edge of
the bushes, he paused.

*Okay ... focus. I don't think this section of the road is
monitored ... but he also mentioned sensors. Where the hell
would they be? If the perimeter is covered 100 percent, what
percentage is the inside covered?*

He crawled on his belly through the mud and clay on
the road, pausing to roll in it to camouflage himself, before
continuing on. Although the rain added to his discomfort,
it also aided him in being able to slide downward with
less effort. In places where the design of the road offered
a small embankment or ditch, he used it to his advantage.
In other areas, he kept to the ruts.

For the parts of the road that he knew were monitored,
he cut a wide swath around them through the forest, but
out of fear of tripping a sensor, even in those areas he
decided to crawl as much as he could.

It was 10:30 p.m. when he reached the turnoff to the
range. In the darkness he could make out the birdhouse
containing a camera that had strategically been placed on
a tree to monitor the main road.

He lay in the mud and stared at it. *If I wasn't injured,
I could probably run down there and be at the gate in ten
minutes ... if help was arriving ... which it isn't. Then again,
there are at least two cameras monitoring the road between
here and the gate. I wouldn't have ten minutes before they'd
be on me.*

He crawled off the road onto the lane leading to the
range and didn't rise until he got to the clearing. Here he
was completely out of sight of the tower and he hoped in
an area where there were no sensors or cameras.

* * *

It was approaching midnight when Reverend Bob pointed to a camera monitor and yelled, "I see him! I see him!"

Jeremiah and Luke raced down the flight of stairs to the command centre.

"There, there!" Reverend Bob exclaimed, stabbing at a monitor with his finger.

Both Jerimiah and Luke huddled in for a look. One of the monitors showed Jack heading down the road. He was limping, then stumbled and fell before getting to his feet again.

"He came out of the bush here," Reverend Bob indicated, touching the screen. "If he'd come out a little farther down, I wouldn't have seen him.

"I think you may have winged him," Luke suggested.

"Luke, hang on to your M16!" Reverend Bob ordered. "Jeremiah, you keep monitoring."

"Dad! Bullshit!" Jeremiah said. "I'm not your little boy anymore. I'm coming with you!"

Reverend Bob was taken back. "Uh —"

"He'll be out of camera range in a couple of minutes," Luke noted.

Reverend Bob turned to Luke. "Okay, you stay. With luck he'll be dead in a couple of minutes. Otherwise, you may see him when he enters the next zone before the gate. Zach won't be able to see him from where he is, but phone him and let 'im know what's going on."

Reverend Bob piled into his SUV as Jeremiah, clutching an M16, hurried to get into the passenger seat.

Seconds later they careened down the road to where Jack had been seen.

The tension, coupled with the excitement they felt, reduced both of them to silence. The only noise was that of the windshield wipers and the sound of the engine as both men stared out the window, trying to see past the outer reaches of the headlights.

It was when they rounded a sharp curve that Jeremiah broke the silence. "There he is!"

Jack was visible in the headlights, limping and scrambling wildly down a straight section of the road ahead.

"Get ready!" Reverend Bob yelled as he jabbed at the power button to lower the driver and passenger windows. "If he bolts left, pass the gun to me! If he goes right, then you shoot 'im."

The headlights revealed the panic on Jack's face when he glanced back and saw the SUV racing toward him. He spun to the left, but only took one step before slipping in the mud and landing face-first on the road. He started to rise and then slipped again.

At this point Reverend Bob knew Jack didn't have time to get to safety — and believed he knew it, too, when he raised his muddy fist and gave him the finger.

"That fucker! We got 'im!" Reverend Bob screamed while ramming the gas pedal tight to the floor.

Chapter Forty-Nine

It happened in an instant. A loud zing followed by a thunderous crash of twisting metal and broken glass. The cable, smeared with mud and tied diagonally across the road from one tree to another, was virtually invisible until the last second. It took less than that for the SUV to hurtle along the cable and into the tree it was tied to.

Jack scrambled to his feet, grabbing a jagged fist-sized rock he'd placed in his pocket as he lurched toward the SUV. He'd expected the airbags to go off, but was hoping that he'd be able to bash one of them on the head and grab a weapon before they recovered. His intended target was the passenger, thinking there was more chance of that person being armed.

He didn't know who the passenger would be because the headlights had blinded him and he'd only caught a quick glimpse of Reverend Bob's face when he gave him the finger.

As he drew closer and viewed what was before him, his

jaw slackened at the unexpected carnage. The airbags had not deployed.

Jeremiah lay with his upper body sprawled on the hood after being propelled through the windshield. His head was twisted back at an odd angle and part of his skull was bare with the scalp hanging to one side.

You're dead....

The windshield on the driver's side had held, but a large circular mass on the glass blurred what was happening inside. Movement said that Reverend Bob was still alive.

Jack hustled around to the driver's side as Reverend Bob pushed himself off the dash where he'd been wedged above the steering wheel. He then slumped sideways against Jeremiah's legs and started coughing up blood.

Jack yanked on the driver's door, but it only opened a crack. Briefly they locked eyes, then Reverend Bob looked toward the passenger seat. Jack saw the barrel of the M16 protruding above the seat on the far side.

Reverend Bob winced as he struggled to move Jeremiah's legs aside in a bid to reach the weapon.

No you don't, you bastard!

He yanked on the door again, but it still didn't open, so he opted to smash the driver's side window with the rock. It prodded Reverend Bob to try harder and blood spluttered from his mouth as he reached over his son's legs and grappled for the barrel.

He was too late. Jack reached through the window and grabbed him by his shirt collar and hauled him back.

Reverend Bob then made a feeble attempt to twist and break free, but the effort caused him to gurgle and cough up more blood.

Got a broken rib or two through your lungs, asshole?

Jack then gripped him with both hands and started to drag him out through the side window. It was then that he saw Reverend Bob fumbling with the airbag cover. *What are you doing? Trying to hang on to the steering wheel?*

The cover popped off and Reverend Bob then reached inside the cavity.

Oh, shit! Jack grabbed his wrist, smashing it back against the steering wheel while shoving his own hand in. He felt the butt of a pistol and pulled it out. As he did, Reverend Bob broke free and made another reach for the M16. He stopped when Jack fired the pistol into the air.

"That's the only warning you're getting," Jack yelled.

Reverend Bob paused, then slowly pushed himself into an upright position. He looked at Jack and nodded.

Jack grabbed him by the collar with one hand and started to haul him out through the window.

"My boy," Reverend Bob gasped as he tried to twist his body and peer onto the hood as he was being dragged out the window.

Your boy? Now you worry? You stupid bastard! Your boy is dead because of you.

"Is he …?"

"Gee, I don't know. Why don't you ask him," Jack replied sarcastically. He then shoved the upper portion of Reverend Bob's body onto the hood so he could see his son's head.

"Jeremiah! Jeremiah!" Reverend Bob let out an anguished cry. "Oh, Lord, no! Please have mercy —"

"Yup, I'd say he's dead." Jack waited a moment as Reverend Bob stared at his son's body. "Too bad you decided that guns outweigh the value of a seatbelt or an airbag. Or is that part of your constitutional —"

Reverend Bob's phone rang and their eyes met as Reverend Bob fumbled for his pocket.

"Not a chance!" Jack yelled, yanking him off the hood and slamming him onto the ground on his back.

Reverend Bob's body convulsed and he spewed more blood while Jack took the phone from his pocket.

"Yeah," Jack said, by way of greeting as he stood up.

"Rev! You okay?" Luke asked excitedly. "Zach came in. He heard a crash and then a shot!"

"I got 'im," Jack gasped, disguising his voice by making it sound croaky. "But he strung a cable across the road and I wrecked my truck. My boy's hurt bad. Both of you get —"

"No!" Reverend Bob managed to splutter. "Don't —"

Jack's first instinct was to kick Reverend Bob in the groin, but his leg was in too much pain so he opted to fall with his elbow across his chest instead. A bloody mist sprayed out of Reverend Bob's mouth, covering Jack's face, but it ended any further words that Reverend Bob might have uttered.

"What was that?" Luke asked.

"Jeremiah's hurt bad," Jack said as he lay across Reverend Bob's chest with his hand clamped over his mouth as an extra precaution. "I don't want him moving until you're both here to help. Hurry!"

When Jack shoved the phone in his pocket, he realized that Reverend Bob appeared to have lost consciousness. He rolled off his chest and sat on the ground staring at him. Pink bubbles escaped from Reverend Bob's mouth and turned to foam as it oozed down the side of his chin.

I wonder if I lay you on your side if it would help keep one lung clear so you could breathe?

He got to one knee.

Then again, I wonder if you hadn't shot Ferg in the face if he'd still be alive? Either way, I guess we'll never know.

He stood up and retrieved the M16 from the SUV.

Five minutes passed before Zach and Luke arrived and slid to a stop in front of the cable before bursting out of the truck and running across the road toward the wreck. It was then that Jack stood up from the far side of the SUV and aimed the M16 over top of Jeremiah's lifeless body.

"Please, give me an excuse to shoot you," he pleaded.

Neither did.

Chapter Fifty

By late Sunday night, Dawson and those with him were more than a little worried.

Dawson brooded about what to do as he sat on a log beside Schneider. The last contact with Jack had been the night before when he'd called them from the washroom of the Jack in the Box restaurant.

The only good thing was that Sunday appeared to have been a relaxing day at the camp. There were no indications from anyone they saw moving back and forth between the trailers to indicate anything was amiss.

"Even if he couldn't get a chance to call, you'd a least think the asshole would have done us the courtesy of taking a walk outside so we'd know he was okay," Schneider grumbled. "He should know that we'd be sitting in the bush watching."

"I know. It worries me. Then again, he's a Mountie. God knows if he's even had any training or experience when it comes to working undercover. He might be sleeping."

"More likely passed out from drinking all night," Schneider replied in a tone that revealed his displeasure. He pushed a button on his watch to illuminate it. "It's one a.m. We've only got twelve hours before Ferg's funeral starts."

Dawson was distracted when he heard their replacements approaching. He gestured toward them and said, "Good, they're here. They can feed the bugs for a while. Let's get back to our car."

Schneider eyed the logging camp as he stood up. "You know somethin'? If they haven't killed him, I think I will."

They returned to their vehicle and Dawson cranked up the heat. At 1:15 a.m. his phone vibrated and he quickly fished it out of his pocket.

"Is it Jack?" Schneider asked excitedly.

Dawson looked at the call display. A combination of disappointment and frustration came over him. "Nope. Washington area code," he replied.

* * *

Jack felt smugly satisfied when he used Reverend Bob's phone to call Dawson. He knew they'd be upset — but also knew the news he had to share would make up for it.

He paused after his call was answered. "Hi, Wayne. It's Jack. How're you doing?"

"How the fuck am I doing?" Dawson yelled.

Oh, you're really pissed.

"Jesus Christ, it's about time you called!" he roared.

"Sorry, I've been a little busy. This is the first chance I've had. Where are you?"

"Outside the bloody camp. We've been taking turns watching from the bush and have been worried sick. You should've given us a sign to let us know you were still alive."

"Sorry about that."

"Ferg's funeral is in twelve hours, by the way."

"I know." The thought of the funeral caused Jack to feel depressed as he stared out the open window of the Ram at the Coggins brothers. They were both sprawled face down on the road beside him. Each facing in opposite directions with their hands tied behind their backs with their own belts.

"So, what's happening?" Dawson asked.

"What camp are you at?"

"The logging camp. What'd you think? All of us will need fucking blood transfusions for all the mosquitoes and God knows what other things have been chewing on us."

"I'm sorry."

"You could have at least gone outside for a walk or somethin' and then called us."

"I wasn't able to."

"Why not?"

"I thought you might have placed a wrong number call to me?"

"I tried! Three times! Check your messages."

"I see." Jack waited a beat. "Zach said it didn't go to voice messaging when he called."

"Zach? Zach who?"

"Zach Coggins. He and his brother Luke are with me right now."

Dawson's voice dropped a level. "I'll be damned." He then said to Schneider, "He's with the Coggins brothers."

"That's great," Schneider said in the background. "So, it was them who killed Ferg?"

"No," Jack stated to Dawson. "It was another guy by the name of Reverend Bob."

"Reverend Bob?" He paused. "How close are Zach and Luke to you? Do you have much time to talk?"

"I'm sitting in a truck and they're outside. Talking isn't a problem."

"Okay … good," Wayne replied. "This Reverend Bob, is he there, too?"

"Yes, but he's dead."

"He's dead?"

"Yes, him and his son. A kid by the name of Jeremiah. I killed them both by arranging to have them smash their truck into a tree."

Dawson paused. "Goddamn it! This isn't the time to be playing jokes! Maybe you think it's funny, but —"

"I'm not joking."

"Bullshit you're not! We'd have heard something!"

"Listen to this," Jack said, placing the phone in his lap before firing a burst of three bullets from the M16 over the heads of the Coggins' brothers. He then yelled, "I told you to lay still and no talking!"

"We weren't talking," Zach whined while squirming deeper into the mud.

Jack picked up his phone. "You hear that?"

"Jesus Christ! Where are you? We didn't hear any shots here."

"I'm not sure. About a two-hour drive southeast of Ferndale."

"What the hell?"

"Let me bring you up-to-date, starting when Vath and I were at the Jack in the Box restaurant Saturday night."

"Hang on; I'm gonna put my phone on speaker so Schneider can hear."

Jack then outlined what had taken place and was only interrupted by the occasional expletive.

"Holy God, mother of Jesus," Dawson exclaimed when Jack finished.

"Give me a sec," Jack said, then he reached in the glovebox and retrieved the truck's ownership papers. It gave the owner's name as Robert Finnius along with a rural address.

Wayne listened as Jack gave him the address. "Schneider tapped it into his phone. According to Google, you're about a three-hour drive from where we're at."

Jack sighed. "I'm sorry, Wayne. Tell Ralph and anyone else with you that I'm sorry. Apologize to Betty, too."

"For what?" Wayne replied. "As far as I'm concerned, you should get a medal."

"The funeral. You won't be able to make it out here, clean up the mess I made, then make it back in time."

"You'd be surprised," Wayne replied. "Unlike you Mounties, we don't ride horses," he added jokingly. "Any place to land a chopper where you're at?"

"I'm close to a rifle range they made. A few rocks for the pilot to watch for, but still lots of room to land."

"Good. We're on our way. I'll call you once we're in the air. When we get close, flash the headlights and we'll be able to use the chopper's spotlight to find it."

"Will do."

"And Jack … hang on to the phone you're using, okay? At least until we get there."

Chapter Fifty-One

It was 2:45 a.m. when Dawson, Schneider, and four other ATF special agents arrived by helicopter. Corporal Frisby and Constable Willisko had been sent back to Canada, as their function to assist the cover team was no longer needed.

Jack watched as the Coggins brothers were taken into custody. He then turned to Dawson. "Mind if I borrow your phone to call my wife? She'll be worried, and I don't want to use Reverend Bob's phone in case the number falls into the hands of the bad guys later."

"I almost forgot," Dawson said, reaching into his pocket. "I had my guys retrieve your phone from the camp. I won't tell you what the guy said when we roused him out of bed, but he wasn't happy."

Moments later Jack limped down the road out of earshot and called Natasha. "Hi, hon. Everything is okay and we can talk."

"Did something bad happen?"

"Why do you say that?"

"It's the middle of the night, and I know you like to reach out to me if you've been through some sort of ordeal."

"Actually, something good happened. The investigation is completely wrapped up and I'm watching a bunch of ATF agents take some bad guys into custody."

"You found out who murdered Ferg?"

"Yes."

"That's great to hear." Natasha paused. "I hope it gives Betty some comfort."

"I hope so, too. She doesn't know yet, but soon will."

"Where are you?"

"In a backwoods area somewhere in Washington. I'm not exactly sure."

"Your voice sounds awful. Are you really okay?"

"Really tired, but I'm okay. I need you to — ouch! Son of a — sorry, I need you to do something for me."

"It doesn't sound like you're okay. You're hurt, aren't you?" Natasha said accusingly.

"I sprained my knee doing some zip-lining. Really … I'm okay."

"Zip-lining? Sounds like you were having fun." She paused. "Too bad you hurt yourself. I'd have thought that was safe."

"I thought so, too, but it wasn't as much fun as you'd think. The cable was at too steep of an angle and I crash landed."

"That's crazy!"

"Yes, it was."

"Sounds like the owner is vulnerable for a lawsuit," Natasha noted.

"I'm not really into suing people," Jack replied. "I killed him instead," he added flippantly.

Natasha was silent for a moment. When she spoke, her voice was sombre. "Was this the same person who killed Ferg?"

Jack's reply was lighthearted and factitious. "Yes, how did you know?"

"It's not funny, Jack. I'm scared enough for the work you do. You laughing about killing someone doesn't help."

Jack took a moment. "You're right. I'm sorry. I'm still coming down from what happened. I feel tense and jittery. I think I was trying to convince myself that what happened didn't freak me out."

"Are you, uh, concerned with how he died?"

"No, not at all. He tried to drive over me and then hit a tree and died from his injuries minutes later. Everything's okay in that department." When Natasha didn't respond, he continued. "Honest. I'm safe. Lots of ATF agents are with me and the only remaining bad guys are in custody."

Natasha sounded irritated. "You said there was something you needed me to do."

"Yes, I need you to phone an informant and first tell him he no longer owes me anything because the guy who killed the ATF agent is dead."

"By the ATF agent, you mean Ferg?"

"Yes, but my informant only knows him as the ATF agent."

"And you're not calling your informant because …?"

"I was about to get to that. I'm not calling in the event someone down the road decides to check who I called. I don't want them to know I spoke with the informant at this time."

"A grey area," Natasha stated, matter-of-factly. "What if they check this phone?"

"I've got a disposable phone in the top drawer of my bedside table that I keep in case I need it for a UC scenario. Use it, but go for a drive, then call him when you're at least ten minutes away from the house. Make sure you stick to residential areas so our car isn't observed by any street cameras. After that, turn the phone off before returning home."

"This needs to be done when?"

"As soon as we hang up."

"So I should probably take the boys with me."

"You'll be less than thirty minutes. It's up to you. I'm sure they'll be okay."

"You're going to be cooking a lot of dinners," Natasha muttered.

Jack pretended to chuckle, but in reality he was feeling apprehensive over what he was asking Natasha to do.

"After I tell your guy that he doesn't owe you anything, then what?"

"Tell him that the car salesman is back in Canada and doesn't know anything about what happened, but may find out soon."

"Okay, anything else?"

"Yes. Tell him I'm sorry, but my identity as a police officer has been exposed. He's going to have to handle that element of risk that he and I spoke of. He'll know what it means."

"And that's it?" Natasha asked. "Only those three things?"

"Yes, that's it. No, wait. Also tell him I feel like I owe him one get-out-of-jail-free card."

"Okay … you feel like you owe him one. Got it. So when will you be home?"

"Hopefully later tonight. I've got a lengthy statement to write, which I'll get started on right away. I also expect that I'll be taken back to Seattle to be interviewed."

"Ferg's funeral is this afternoon. Are you going to make it?"

"Maybe not to the funeral, but I want to pay my respects to Betty."

"Tell her I'm sorry, as well. I feel so bad that I can't go."

"I explained to her earlier why you couldn't. Don't feel bad. You're a cop's wife. She'll know how you feel."

"I know, but tell her anyway."

"Okay."

"After I pay my respects to Betty, I'll need to get a ride to the border. I'll call you when I know more."

"Good. I better get going if you want this done."

"I love you, Natasha Lynne Taggart."

"I love you, too, Jack Bruce Taggart."

Chapter Fifty-Two

Jack's next call was to Rose.

"Are you okay?" she asked, after he explained what had happened.

"I'm fine. I sprained my knee coming down off the tower, but other than that I feel good. Great to be alive."

"And you're telling me that the person who is dead is definitely the one responsible?"

"Yes, it was Reverend Bob. He told me himself how he drove over him and then shot him after. He and his son are both dead."

"And you killed them," Rose murmured, perhaps to herself.

"It was either them or me."

Rose's tone became cynical. "So, what a surprise. The person who murdered your friend is dead."

"It's not like I had a choice," Jack said. "I'm told that about two dozen law enforcement officers will be here within the next hour or two. This will be investigated thoroughly. I'll be writing my statement as soon as I hang up and there'll be lots of evidence to support what I say happened. The Coggins brothers may even tell the truth because they weren't the ones who shot at me."

Rose was silent for a moment, "Okay, I believe you. It's just ..." She then stopped talking.

"Just what?"

"These situations that you keep getting yourself into ..."

"Like I said, it was either them or me. You've got to believe that."

Rose's sigh was audible. "I do believe you. Let's hope Lexton does, too. Keep me posted."

* * *

By 7:00 a.m. there were numerous agents from the FBI, ATF, and Washington State Police at the scene. Dawson, Schneider, and Jack were shuttled back in the helicopter to Seattle.

Shortly after arriving at the ATF office, Jack finished writing his statement. It was 9:00 a.m. when he went to a coffee room with Schneider. In the meantime, Dawson copied his statement to hand out to his superiors for a hastily scheduled meeting.

As they waited in the coffee room, Jack saw Schneider looking at him. He seemed both nervous and embarrassed.

"Something wrong?" Jack asked.

"Yeah ... there is." He cleared his throat. "I want to apologize for how I behaved the night Ferg was killed. I know it wasn't your fault. What I said and how I acted when I called you was way out of line."

"It's okay," Jack replied. "You weren't the only one who was angry with me. I was angry at myself for not crossing the border that night. I still am."

"I'd say you more than made up for it."

Jack grimaced. "What I did might help, but nothing can make up for what happened."

Schneider swallowed. After a few minutes of uncomfortable silence, he said, "Hey, how about you wait while I go find you a crutch to use? You look like you're in a bit of pain."

"Thanks. That'd really be appreciated."

Jack didn't mind Schneider's excuse to leave. He felt exhausted and preferred to be alone with his thoughts. Thoughts that when you're exhausted turn into questions. Questions that make life seem impossible to handle as your mind plays with the "what ifs." *What if I'd crossed the border that night, would Ferg still be alive? What if I was shot and killed last night? What if the cable broke and I was run over? What if …*

He closed his eyes in a bid to fall asleep, but the thoughts prevailed. When he did start to drift off, his body would twitch and he'd wake up.

At 10:15 a.m., Dawson and Schneider walked into the coffee room together.

"Here you go," Schneider said as he handed Jack a crutch. "I was going to have the guys sign it for you, but most of them are still out at the scene."

"That's okay. Thank you," Jack replied, then stood and adjusted the crutch to fit his height. He looked at Dawson. "I'm ready. I imagine your Internal Affairs or whoever oversees this sort of thing will want to interview me."

"Not today," Wayne replied. "Your statement was so detailed that nobody had any questions. It also matches the evidence at the scene, right down to the bullet holes through the tower and shell casings found along the top of that rocky ridge where you hid. If anyone does have any questions, they can contact you later."

"Good," Jack replied.

"What we're going to do is go back to my place, shower, change, and get ready for Ferg's funeral." He glanced at his watch. "We might even be able to squeeze in a nap."

"Uh, about the funeral, I —"

"If you're worried about what to wear, I've got some clothes that I think will fit you. If they don't, don't worry about it. I've already spoken with Betty and she wants you to have a seat beside her. She won't care about what you're wearing."

"No, it's not that. I'm an undercover operator and would prefer not to have my picture on the news. Being close to her would ensure that."

"Oh," Wayne replied, looking somewhat taken back. "I hadn't thought of that."

"Would you tell her that I really appreciate the gesture, but I'm sure the media will be everywhere."

"That'll be for certain," Schneider agreed.

"What I'd like to do is meet her privately for a few minutes," Jack added. "Perhaps before the funeral?"

"Okay … I understand. I'll arrange it," Dawson said.

"Then I'd like a ride to the border, or considering that all of you'll want to be at the funeral, I could take a bus. I really don't mind."

"Not on your life," Schneider replied. "If Betty heard that, she'd chew our asses off."

"Or more likely skip the funeral and drive you herself," Dawson said.

"We'll get you a ride," Schneider promised. "Leave it to me."

* * *

It was 12:40 p.m. when Wayne ushered Jack through the rear door of a church and into a small room. There he saw Betty standing beside two ATF agents who he recognized from the scene.

Betty was wearing a navy blue skirt and matching jacket with a white blouse. It struck Jack that the clothing didn't look sombre enough for a funeral.

She appeared to read his thoughts. "Of all my outfits, Ferg liked this one the best," she said as she approached.

Jack nodded, then swallowed. "Natasha sends her love and is sorry she can't be here."

"I understand. It's okay."

The silence that followed seemed awkward. Betty wasn't the first officer's wife he'd met whose husband had been murdered, but it didn't make it any easier.

What can I possibly say that would comfort you?

She hugged him while he held the crutch with one hand and hugged her back with the other. They held each other tight for a moment before she stepped back.

"Thank you," they each said in unison, then smiled when they realized each other's reasons for being grateful.

No other words were needed.

Chapter Fifty-Three

It was late afternoon when Jack finally arrived at Canada Customs after being shuttled to the border by Washington State Police patrol cars. He'd called Rose when he left the church and she was there to meet him when he cleared Customs.

"You've had quite a time, Sergeant Taggart," she said as he got in the car.

Jack was taken by surprise. "Really? I got it?"

"Staffing called this morning," Rose replied mundanely. "The new position in our office is official. You need to confirm that you'll accept it, but yes, then you'll have your third stripe."

"Super. And Laura?"

"She's being offered her corporal's stripes and can move into your spot, providing you move out of it, that is."

"I'll accept it. That's a given."

"Okay then." Rose paused, then, as if it was an afterthought, said, "Congratulations."

You don't seem particularly happy ... or were you so certain that we'd be promoted that you aren't surprised?

He cleared his throat. "Have you called Laura to let her know? I'm certain she'll have another piña colada on the beach to celebrate."

"I thought you should be the one to break the news to her."

"Thank you."

"How was the funeral?" Rose asked, then glanced at her watch.

Her tone sounds obligatory, as if it is something she should ask. It's like she doesn't care.

Jack frowned, then thought, *I guess when it comes down to it, most police funerals are the same. Solemn ... depressing ... bagpipes ... containing your grief to appear strong for the public. Followed by the release of raw emotion at the wake.*

"You did make an appearance, didn't you?" she asked.

"I spoke to his wife before the funeral. I wanted to avoid the media." He paused. "I also don't believe in going to funerals. It seems so phony to have someone preaching over someone they probably didn't know."

"I agree."

Any joy Jack felt at being promoted had vanished as he thought about the funerals he'd attended in the past. "I don't want one if I die, but in this case I thought I owed it to Betty to show my respect."

Rose appeared to pick up on how he felt. "Tired?" she asked.

"Exhausted. Have only had about three or four hours sleep in the last two days."

Rose bit her lower lip as if thinking about something.

"What's going on?" Jack asked. "Is everything okay?"

Rose cast him a sideways glance. "You tell me. This afternoon I received a call from Lexton after she'd gotten off the phone with Inspector Dyck."

"I see." Jack looked out the passenger window. "Cold for May, don't you think?"

"You're not going to ask what it was about?"

Jack looked at her. "If I was talking to Lexton, I'd play innocent, but with you I decided not to pretend."

"Oh," Rose replied. After a pause she said, "Thanks for the vote of confidence … I think."

"You think?"

"I know for you that trust is not an easy issue and I appreciate you being open. At the same time, I have to admit that the secrets you hold scare me."

Jack was quiet for a moment. "It's not the ones I hold that scare you. It's the ones I tell you about that keep you awake at night."

"Those I can deal with. It's the unknown that worries me more."

"I see."

I'm so bloody tired I can't think straight.

"So … anything you'd like to tell me?"

He looked at her. *Guess she's not going to let this drop.*

"Forget 'like' to tell me," Rose prodded. "I know you don't, but do anyway."

Jack gazed out through the windshield and allowed himself to take a deep breath before turning back. "I take it that Erich Vath was murdered today?"

Rose glanced at him. "I figured you knew."

"Do you know the details? How did it happen? Was whoever responsible caught?"

Rose looked at him in surprise. "You don't know?"

"No, otherwise I wouldn't have asked. I only guessed that it was him." He saw her face brighten. *Good, maybe you don't think I had a hand in it. Sorry, Rose. I trust you, but there's no reason for you to know.*

"When he walked out to his vehicle to go to work this morning someone shot him. Once in the chest and once in the head. A witness who heard the shots looked out their window and saw one person running away and said the person was wearing a hoodie and a ball cap."

"That's what Kondrat and Pratt wore when they killed Irving."

"I know. A gun was also located at the scene."

"Okay, tell Lexton, or I-HIT for that matter, that a Glock with laser grips might indicate the Death Heads. Kel-Tec 9mm pistols could indicate the United Front." He yawned. "Then again, they should know that."

"It was neither. They found a Walther PPK."

"A Walter PPK?" Jack smiled. "Hey, it sounds like the culprit is James Bond."

"I don't think Lexton would find that amusing," Rose replied.

"Does she want to see me?"

Rose shook her head. "She knows what you've been through in the last couple of days. I'm to take you home, but relay anything you may have to say about the matter."

"If it had nothing to do with the Death Heads or the United Front, then I'd suspect revenge as a motive," Jack stated.

"That came up in my conversation with her, but as she pointed out, there's been nothing on the news yet about what took place last night."

"A news announcement wouldn't have been necessary. Tell her that Reverend Bob had many friends and followers. If you check my file at work, you'll see lots of photographs, including one where he was giving a speech in a room full of men. At least one of whom was a county sheriff."

"I see." Rose appeared to think about it, then said, "I imagine there were also lots of officers involved once you called the ATF to let them know where you were."

"Dozens from multiple agencies showed up. It might not be on the news yet, but word of Ferg's killer being caught is likely known to every cop in Washington."

"You want me to suggest to Lexton that a cop came up from the States first thing this morning and did the murder?"

"There'd have been a lot of talk about what happened last night. We have white supremacists up here, too. A call could have been made. It wouldn't be a leap of faith to think someone killed him because they thought he was an informant."

"A leap of faith," Rose mused. "Do you think Lexton will buy it?"

Oh, shit. She sees through me.

Jack sighed. "I suspect she's smarter than that. You are."

Rose looked at him curiously. "I suspect she may be smarter than me, but she doesn't know you as well as I do. Perhaps she'll believe it."

"Hope so. I'd like her to trust me," Jack replied.

Rose shrugged. "It doesn't matter if she places her trust in you or not. As long as there isn't evidence to the contrary, she's forced to accept the evidence before her."

"Exactly." Jack brooded as he stared out the window.

As long as there isn't evidence to the contrary.

Author's Note

From 1968 to 2011 over 1,516,000 Americans have been killed with firearms within their own country. Far more than that have been wounded, and many of those have been left with permanent disabilities.

In 2013, according to the American Centers for Disease Control, slightly less than two-thirds of the gun-related deaths were from suicides, while one-third were from homicides. Approximately 1 percent was from other causes, such as accidents.

Of interest is the fact that in 1996, Australia severely tightened their gun laws. According to the *Journal of Public Health Policy*, over the next seven years, both the suicide and homicide rates dropped by half.

In 2010, it was reported that 358 homicides in the United States involved a rifle and 6,009 involved a handgun. A further 1,939 homicides involving firearms did not note the type of firearm used.

In 2013, there were 33,636 firearms-related deaths in the United States, which was categorized as 11,208 homicides, 21,175 suicides, 505 deaths classified as accidental, and 281 classified as "undetermined intent."

In 2015, firearms in the United States were used to kill 13,286 people, excluding suicides.

The World Health Organization, in a study of developed countries such as Australia, New Zealand, and Japan, as well as those in Europe, discovered that the homicide rate in the United States is seven times higher than elsewhere.

Attempts by American politicians to curb the slaughter of people due to firearms has been unsuccessful because of the culture of fear, strong support from pro-gun groups, and the protection afforded by the Second Amendment in the U.S. Constitution, which ensures the right of the people to collect and bear arms.

The consequence of the gun laws in the United States may be best illustrated by a recent statistic from Global News, which reported that you're more likely to be shot to death in the United States than you are to die in a car accident in Canada.

BOOK CREDITS

Acquiring Editor: Sheila Douglas
Developmental Editor: Allison Hirst
Project Editor: Jenny McWha
Copy Editor: Dominic Farrell
Proofreader: Jennifer Dinsmore

Cover Designer: Laura Boyle
Interior Designer: Lorena Gonzalez Guillen

Publicist: Michelle Melski

DUNDURN

Publisher: J. Kirk Howard
Vice-President: Carl A. Brand
Editorial Director: Kathryn Lane
Artistic Director: Laura Boyle
Director of Sales and Marketing: Synora Van Drine
Publicity Manager: Michelle Melski

Editorial: Allison Hirst, Dominic Farrell, Jenny McWha, Rachel Spence, Elena Radic
Marketing and Publicity: Kendra Martin, Kathryn Bassett, Elham Ali

FRA

SWEET VALLEY TWINS

Summer Diaries
Collection

including

ELIZABETH,
NEXT STOP JR. HIGH
JESSICA,
NEXT STOP JR. HIGH

BANTAM BOOKS
TORONTO · NEW YORK · LONDON · SYDNEY · AUCKLAND

Visit the official Sweet Valley Web Site on the Internet at:
http://www.sweetvalley.com

SWEET VALLEY TWINS SUMMER
DIARIES COLLECTION
A BANTAM BOOK : 0 553 50728 1

Individual titles originally published in USA by Bantam Books
First published in Great Britain in this Collection

PRINTING HISTORY
Bantam Collection edition published 1999

Copyright © 1999 by Francine Pascal

including

ELIZABETH, NEXT STOP JR. HIGH
First published in USA, 1998
Copyright © 1998 by Francine Pascal

JESSICA, NEXT STOP JR. HIGH
First published in USA, 1998
Copyright © 1998 by Francine Pascal

The trademarks "Sweet Valley" and "Sweet Valley Twins" are
owned by Francine Pascal and are used under license by
Bantam Books and Transworld Publishers Ltd.

Conceived by Francine Pascal

Produced by Daniel Weiss Associates, Inc,
33 West 17th Street, New York, NY 10011

All rights reserved.

Cover photo by Oliver Hunter
Cover photo of twins © 1994, 1995, 1996 Saban – All Rights Reserved.

Bantam Books are published by Transworld Publishers Ltd,
61–63 Uxbridge Road, Ealing, London W5 5SA,
in Australia by Transworld Publishers, c/o Random House
Australia Pty Ltd, 20 Alfred Street, Milsons Point, NSW 2061, Australia,
and in New Zealand by Transworld Publishers, c/o Random House
New Zealand, 18 Poland Road, Glenfield, Auckland, New Zealand.

Printed and bound in Great Britain by
Cox & Wyman Ltd, Reading, Berkshire.

SWEET VALLEY TWINS

Elizabeth: Next Stop, Jr. High

SWEET VALLEY TWINS

Elizabeth: Next Stop, Jr. High

Written by
Jamie Suzanne

Created by
FRANCINE PASCAL

BANTAM BOOKS
NEW YORK · TORONTO · LONDON · SYDNEY · AUCKLAND

To Mia Sanitsky

One

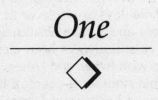

Dear Diary,

Well, here I am on my way to the airport. I can hardly believe the big day is finally here! I'm excited but kind of nervous too. This isn't the sort of thing I expected to be doing the summer before eighth grade. Of course, eighth grade may not be anything like what I was expecting either, so I guess it all kind of makes sense.

Jessica is sleeping next to me in the backseat. Actually, to be completely accurate, she's sleeping *on* me and drooling on my shoulder. I'm a little surprised she decided to come along and see me off—we all know how she feels about her beauty sleep, and it *is* pretty early.

I'm glad she came, though. It's going to be

incredibly strange being apart from her for such a huge chunk of the summer. Five weeks is a long time. Especially since Jessica and I have never really been separated before, not for more than a few days. Even though there are moments—OK, sometimes whole days or weeks or months—when I think that Jess and I have absolutely nothing in common, we've still always been close. They say that's how it is with twins, and I guess it's true.

In a way, this summer is proof of how different we are. Because if Jessica and I were exactly alike (like some people think when they see our identical long blond hair and blue-green eyes), we would both be spending the month of August in the same place. Instead I'm off to Costa Rica while Jessica is staying behind in Sweet Valley to hang with her friends in the Unicorn Club.

Jessica isn't the only one I'm going to miss. There's Mom and Dad, of course, and Steven (even though he'd never admit it, I know he'll miss me too). I'll definitely miss my friends, especially Maria Slater—she's the one who gave me this travel diary as a going-away present. She said she picked it out because it's small enough to take with me everywhere. She's smart that way.

"See? It's smaller than those paperback mystery novels you're always carrying around," she told me when I unwrapped it.

"Thanks, Maria," I exclaimed, running my fingers over the cloth-covered diary. "It's perfect!"

"You'll probably be too busy to read much on this trip. But you ought to write down everything that happens so you'll always remember it." She smiled. "Of course, the way you write, it will probably turn out sounding like a novel anyway."

"Thanks," I said again, reaching over to give her a hug. Leave it to a good friend like Maria to know me so well—and to choose the perfect gift! She really understands how important this trip is to me. In fact, I liked the diary idea so much, I bought one for Jess and left it on her pillow. She'll have a little surprise waiting for her when she gets back from leaving me at the airport!

I still remember how excited I was when I first found out about the Rain Forest Friends and their work. It was a few weeks after school let out for the summer. I was browsing the Internet for information I could use in an article I was writing for the school newspaper. The article was about student volunteering, and I was finding tons of interesting stuff I could use.

After a while I came across a link that mentioned California teen volunteers. That's when I found it—a Web site about an organization called Rain Forest Friends that sponsors teenagers to go all over Central America to help with lots of different projects. They had an urgent notice on the site, asking for volunteers ages twelve and up from southern California to join a trip to an area of Costa Rica that recently suffered heavy flood damage.

The villagers in the area had lost a lot of buildings—houses, community centers, schools—that they needed help rebuilding.

"Wow," I whispered, staring at the computer screen. It was almost *too* perfect—I mean, I'm thirteen years old, I live in Sweet Valley, California, and I've even done some volunteer work with Houses for Humans, so I have a little bit of experience with building. Plus I've always believed that volunteering is really important. I've spent a lot of time working at the local homeless shelter and other places, and it always makes me feel great to help someone else. The Costa Rica project sounded like an incredible way to spend part of the summer. I quickly scanned the rest of the Web site, then took down the phone number and went to talk to my parents.

I found them in the living room, reading the newspaper. They listened carefully as I told them all about the Web site and the Costa Rica project.

"Costa Rica?" my dad said when I finished, wrinkling his brow like he always does when he's thinking hard about something. Mom looked thoughtful too. "That sounds like a very interesting and worthwhile trip, Elizabeth," she said. "But Costa Rica is awfully far away. And you've never traveled that far on your own before."

I could tell what they were thinking—that I was kind of young to be heading off to the rain forests of Central America all alone. I didn't blame them for being nervous. That's their job as parents. But I had to make them understand that I could handle it.

"I know," I said. "But I wouldn't be by myself, not really. I'd be with a whole group of kids from nearby towns plus some adult supervisors."

Dad was nodding. "True," he said. He exchanged a glance with my mother. "Give us a little time to think it over, Elizabeth. Oh, and let me have that phone number so I can call the Rain Forest Friends and check them out."

I gave him the piece of paper. "Thanks," I said. "Whatever you two decide, I want you to know I appreciate that you're considering it."

Mom smiled and patted me on the arm. "You're welcome. Now could you set the table for dinner, please?"

"Sure, Mom." I headed toward the kitchen, humming under my breath. From the way my parents looked and sounded, I was feeling optimistic that they would say yes. *Costa Rica, here I come!* I thought happily.

Jessica thought I was nuts, of course.

I guess she overheard my parents talking about it because the first thing I knew, she was storming into the kitchen with her hands on her hips. "Are you crazy, Elizabeth?" she cried. "Why would you want to go to some lame rain forest where there isn't even any decent shopping?"

"Come on, Jess." I opened a cabinet and took

out five plates. "It'll be interesting. Besides, I'll be helping people who need it. It's not like I'll be bored."

She rolled her eyes, opened the refrigerator, and grabbed a diet soda. "Yeah, right," she said. "Chopping your way through some snake-infested rain forest for the excitement of doing manual labor? Living in native huts where there probably isn't indoor plumbing or even a place to plug in your hair dryer? That sounds a little *too* interesting to me." She slumped down into her chair and popped the top on her soda.

"It's not going to be like that," I protested. "The villages we'll be helping are really more like towns. There's plumbing and electricity and everything."

"But I thought we were going to spend the whole summer relaxing and getting ready for our big eighth-grade year," Jessica said, pouting. This is probably a good time to mention that our school district is getting rezoned for next year—and nobody knows where they'll be going to school or with whom. I think Jessica has been feeling a little nostalgic and wanting to spend as much time as possible with her friends. She's probably worried that things will never be the same again if the Unicorns get split up. But at least she and I can be certain that *we* won't get split up.

I shoved her soda can aside so I could set down her plate. "There will still be time for that," I reminded her. "The trip to Costa Rica isn't until

August." I sighed. "Besides, I'm not sure I'll want to spend too much time sitting around and thinking about our big eighth-grade year. Not until we know more about what's happening."

Jessica just shrugged and waved her hand at that, as if she wasn't worried at all. But I know she really is, and I am too. That's another good thing about going to Costa Rica—I won't have to spend my summer worrying about whether I'll get sent to a new school or not!

So I was thrilled—even if Jessica wasn't—when my parents decided that I could go to Costa Rica if I really wanted to. They said it was because I've always been so responsible and mature. That made me feel good, even though I think Jessica was sort of annoyed. She always tells me that being responsible and mature are way overrated, but I guess this time she was wrong.

Once I knew I was going, the days seemed to fly by. Maria helped me do more research on the Internet and at the library so I'd be prepared for life in Costa Rica. She even found an old Spanish phrase book in her attic.

Maria and I also found some information on the Net about constructing simple buildings. The most interesting Web site was called "Coco's Cost-Cutting Construction Concepts." I printed out that one since I thought it might come in handy. I know the Rain Forest Friends work with pretty tight budgets, so any cost-cutting tips should be useful.

After all her help, I was hoping that Maria might decide she wanted to come to Costa Rica with me. But she's been accepting more acting jobs lately, and she got hired to star in a made-for-TV movie that would be shooting during July and August. I was sort of disappointed when I realized that I wouldn't know anyone on the trip. Oh, well, I'd just have to make friends.

Still, part of me was glad to be leaving Sweet Valley for a little while. I said something about that to Maria when we got together the other day. "I liked things at Sweet Valley Middle School the way they were," I told her, playing with the ruffle on my pillowcase. "I don't know if I'm ready to have them change."

Maria nodded. "You mean all this talk about the new districting and stuff? We still don't know for sure that it's going to happen."

"But we know that it *probably* will," I reminded her. "I heard some of us may be reassigned to a new junior high school and that we might get mixed in with the kids from Secca Lake. If that's true, eighth grade may not be anything like we were expecting."

"It may be better," Maria said hopefully. "We might get to meet lots of cool new people and get out of our rut."

I shrugged. "I liked our rut. And what if we can't stand the new people?"

Maria looked at me in surprise. "That doesn't sound like you, Elizabeth," she said. "I thought you liked trying new things. Like this trip to Costa Rica, for instance."

I shrugged again. "This is different," I said quietly.

I don't think she understood what I was so worried about. But I was definitely worried. Was I ready to handle all these changes? At SVMS the teachers and classes and activities were familiar. All the other students knew what to expect from me. I knew what to expect from them. And this fall Jess and I and our friends were finally supposed to get to be in charge. I would edit the school paper and maybe the yearbook. Maria would be president of the drama club. Jess and Lila seemed to think they were shoo-ins to be cocaptains of the Boosters, Sweet Valley Middle School's cheerleading squad.

Now we might have to start over. Nothing will be the way we thought it was going to be. We're all going to have to prove ourselves all over again.

Oh, well. I guess whatever is going to happen will happen, and we'll just have to get used to it— somehow. All I can say is that I'm going to concentrate on having a great experience in Costa Rica—so that no matter what happens when eighth grade starts, at least I'll have a wonderful summer adventure to look back on.

Well, Diary, I'm on my way! Our plane took off a little while ago, and we're settled in for the long flight to Costa Rica. It's all starting to feel more real, and that makes me more nervous and excited than ever.

Jessica actually woke up long enough to come inside the airport with the rest of us (even though she totally denied she'd been drooling, even after I showed her the huge wet slobber spot on my T-shirt!). I noticed she'd brought a white plastic shopping bag with her, but when I asked her about it, she stuck it behind her back.

"Not until we get inside," she said, with one of those mysterious eye twinkles that means she's up to something. I figured I'd find out what it was soon enough. Jessica can never keep a secret for long.

I was starting to get choked up as we went through security and walked toward my gate. Mom was holding my hand, and all I could think about was how I wouldn't see her—or any of them—for five whole weeks. It was such a bizarre feeling, I couldn't talk much while we were walking. I didn't really know what to say, and I was afraid if I said any of the stuff I was thinking, I would burst into tears.

Finally we got to the gate and sat down near the front. Almost nobody else was there yet—we were kind of early, which was my fault, I guess. I like to be on time, and I definitely didn't want to miss my plane, so I made sure we left the house way before we needed to. The only other person sitting in our section was a pretty girl with dark hair who had spread her stuff out on the last row of seats, near the candy and soda machines. I later found out that her name is Tanya—she's part of the Rain Forest Friends group too. But I didn't think about her too much at the time because I was too busy trying not to cry.

Mom seemed kind of choked up too because she didn't say much. She just kept telling me to "be careful" and "make sure you take your vitamins." Dad pretty much said the same stuff, though he also added "send us lots of postcards so we know you're doing OK." Steven kept telling them to get a grip.

I guess Jessica finally had enough of their weepy looks because she stood up and grabbed my arm in one hand and that white plastic bag in the other.

"We'll be right back, OK?" she told our parents. "I think Lizzie and I need a moment alone."

I was kind of surprised. Jessica usually isn't the sentimental type. I let her drag me over behind a soda machine where Mom and Dad couldn't see us. The only people around were that dark-haired girl and a small gaggle of girls a little younger than us who were pumping change into the soda machine and talking loudly about how much they'd loved their trip to southern California.

Jessica didn't notice the other kids at all. She was digging around in that plastic bag of hers.

"OK, Lizzie," she said briskly. "I know you, so I'm sure you probably didn't think about how long five weeks really is."

"I'm just starting to realize it," I began, assuming she was feeling the same way I was. "I don't know how I'm going to—"

She interrupted me before I could go on. "That's why I decided it was up to me to make sure you had the necessities for a trip of this kind."

(Actually, looking back over what I just wrote, I'm not sure I got that last quote quite right. Jess doesn't usually use words like *necessities*. She probably said something more like "all the majorly important stuff you'll totally die without.")

Anyway, she went on to pull a bunch of rock CDs and movie magazines out of her bag. She showed them to me, looking very proud of herself.

"See?" she said. "This way you'll have something to do at night after a boring day of hammering and sawing or whatever." She kind of shuddered when she said that, probably imagining how awful my fingernails were going to look by the end of the trip.

"Thanks, Jess." I didn't know what else to say. The materials the Rain Forest Friends sent me after I signed up specifically asked us to leave American pop culture—in other words, stuff like CDs and movie magazines—at home so we'd be able to give the local culture a chance. I planned to follow that advice. I didn't even pack any American books except one mystery novel to read on the plane. I figured I'd be too busy to read once I got to Costa Rica anyway, just like Maria said. And if I did have any spare time, I planned to spend it writing down my daily experiences in this diary.

But I knew Jessica would never understand any of that. And I didn't want to hurt her feelings, especially after she had gone to so much trouble.

"I love them," I told her, taking the bag. "These are great!"

"I used up all my allowance buying this stuff," she said proudly. "But I figured you needed it more than I did. After all, there's always plenty of cool music and cute guys right here in Sweet Valley. And if I need anything, I can always just beg Lila to buy it for me."

"Well, thanks, Jess. It was really sweet of you."

She beamed. "You're welcome." Suddenly she grabbed me in a big hug. "I'll miss you, Lizzie," she whispered in my ear.

I hugged her back hard, trying to keep my eyes from welling up. "I'll miss you too. A lot."

She pulled away after a few seconds, looking slightly embarrassed—she doesn't like mushy scenes much—and we headed back to Mom and Dad. After about a million more hugs and kisses and reminders, they noticed their time in the parking lot was running out. By then more people were showing up at the gate, including the adult chaperons from Rain Forest Friends who would be flying to Costa Rica with us. I told my family it was OK for them to head home, even though I could tell they didn't want to. (OK, except maybe for Jessica. She was yawning every two seconds and looking sleepy again.) So after another two million hugs and kisses—Steven even gave me a quick hug— they left.

I waved until I couldn't see them anymore. That was when I really felt like crying, but I reminded myself that I was about to set off on an adventure I would remember all my life and that I'd be helping a lot of people too. That cheered me up a little.

Then I saw the white plastic bag poking out of my carry-on. I really didn't want to bring along the stuff Jess had given me, but I didn't want to just throw it away either.

While I was trying to figure out what to do, a voice interrupted my thoughts.

"Hi! My name's Andy. Are you a Rain Forest Friend by any chance?"

I turned and saw a tall, skinny boy with glasses and reddish brown hair standing beside my chair. I smiled at him. "Hi, Andy. I'm Elizabeth. And yes, I'm part of the group."

"Me too." He sat down on the seat next to mine, dumping his duffel bag on the floor at his feet. He pushed his glasses farther up his nose. "I feel kind of dumb. I just spent ten minutes talking to a group of girls over by the soda machine before I realized they weren't part of our trip at all. They were just here on vacation from Canada." He shrugged and grinned sheepishly. "I went over and introduced myself, and I guess I was so excited, I just started talking. So I didn't figure out the truth until the girls started counting their change and talking about scraping together enough money to buy some magazines to read during the flight to Toronto."

"I think I saw those girls too." Then I smiled—Andy had just given me a great idea. If those Canadian girls wanted magazines, I knew where they could get some. . . .

"Hey, Andy," I said. "Would you do me a favor?"

"Sure," Andy replied. "Anything!"

"Can you keep an eye on my stuff for a minute? I—uh—need to go to the ladies' room."

"No problemo," he said, giving me a double-handed thumbs-up. "That's Spanish for 'no problem.' You can count on me, Elizabeth."

"Thanks." I took Jessica's gift and went back over to the spot behind the candy and soda machines. But the Canadian girls were nowhere in sight. For a second I just stood there, feeling disappointed.

Maybe they went to the gift shop, I thought. *Or maybe—*

I heard loud giggling coming from the ladies' room nearby.

Aha! I thought. *That must be them.* I was about to go into the ladies' room, but then I started to worry that they might think that a stranger giving them a gift in the bathroom was a little weird. So I leaned the bag against one of the candy machines, where the girls would be sure to see it as soon as they came out. Quickly I scribbled a note on the front of the bag: *To our Canadian visitors—have a great trip home!* Then I scooted back to my seat, grinning from ear to ear with the thought that I'd managed to do a good deed even before my trip got started.

When I got back to my seat, Andy was waiting for me. He smiled as I sat down. "Nobody came near your bags, Elizabeth," he said. "I watched them the whole time."

"Thanks, Andy." I smiled back. Andy was kind of goofy, but he seemed sweet. "So, how did you find out about this trip?"

Andy's face lit up. "Actually, it's a really interesting story. You see, my parents signed me up for an after-school Spanish class because I've always been really interested in foreign languages, and . . ."

I listened for a few minutes as Andy chattered on and on. But then suddenly I caught a flash of bright red out of the corner of my eye. I turned to see what it was.

It was a backpack, and it was being carried by a

boy who had just ambled into our section. He was about my age, kind of tall, with curly brown hair, hazel eyes, broad shoulders, and a sort of Jessica-like twinkle in his eye.

Even though I knew I was being rude to Andy (who luckily didn't seem to notice since he was caught up in a highly detailed description of his dog), I couldn't seem to stop looking at the new guy.

I'm not sure why. I mean, he was pretty cute. But I always thought that was one more thing that Jessica and I *don't* have in common—she gets totally distracted whenever she sees a guy who's even the slightest bit good-looking. I, on the other hand, happen to think there are lots of things that are more important than checking out guys, cute or not. In fact, just about the only guy I've ever thought was interesting in that more-than-a-friend way is Todd Wilkins. And lately I haven't even been thinking about him all that much, I guess because we've both been so busy—me with the end of the school year and then with planning this trip, and him with basketball and the swim team and other stuff.

But I definitely wasn't thinking about Todd Wilkins at that particular moment. Especially when the curly-haired guy dropped his red backpack on the first row of seats and glanced at one of the adult chaperons. "Yo," he called. "Is this where the Rain Forest amigos are hangin'?"

That got Andy's attention. He glanced over at the new guy. "He must be with us."

I nodded. I couldn't seem to tear my eyes away from the guy with the red backpack. I guess I must have been staring a little, because he noticed me. And then—he *smiled*. Needless to say, I was totally embarrassed. I couldn't believe he'd caught me gawking at him. I was about to turn away.

But then for some reason Jessica's voice popped into my head with one of her all-time favorite phrases: *"Go for it, Lizzie!"*

And suddenly I knew what she would do if she were in my place right now. If Jess had been staring at a cute guy and he'd caught her, she wouldn't just blush and turn away. No, she'd do something bold and daring, like wink at him or blow him a kiss. That made me wonder if maybe I hadn't been too shy around guys in the past. Maybe now that I was almost in eighth grade I needed to start being more daring, like Jessica. What harm could it do to try it out and see what happened?

All these thoughts raced through my head in about half a second. So the curly-haired guy was still smiling at me when I decided to follow my twin's advice and go for it. I'm not as bold as Jessica is, so I couldn't quite bring myself to wink or blow kisses. I decided to start simple: I smiled back.

*   *   *

SUNDAY, 9:30 P.M. (COSTA RICA TIME, THAT IS)

I'm here! I'm really here!

I would have trouble believing it except that the sights and sounds and smells keep reminding me that it's true. We all felt it as soon as we got off the plane in San José, the capital of Costa Rica. It's always pretty warm in southern California, especially in the summer, so the hot, humid weather here wasn't too much of a shock. But just about everything else seems very different. Even the furniture in my hotel room looks exotic!

It's really beautiful here, even though we haven't left the city yet. Everything is green, flowers seem to be blooming absolutely everywhere, and I've already seen several kinds of birds and bugs I can't identify. Plus I spotted a cute little lizard on the wall of the airport as we were getting off the plane.

This has been one of the longest and most interesting days of my whole life. And it's only the first day of my trip!

One of the most interesting things about today was meeting J.P. That's his name—the curly-haired guy with the red backpack. After I smiled at him back at the airport, he came over to where Andy and I were sitting. "Hi there," he said. "Are you two Rain Forest Amigos too?"

Andy nodded and answered for both of us since

my throat had suddenly gone strangely dry. "My name's Andy, and this is Elizabeth."

"I'm J.P." He plopped down across the aisle from us, leaning back and spreading both arms out across the backs of the seats. "Nice to meet you."

"Where do you go to school?" Andy asked him.

"Greengrass Junior High," he replied. I had heard of the school—it's about fifteen miles from Sweet Valley. "I'll be in eighth grade next year," he added.

"Us too," Andy put in. "Right, Elizabeth?"

"Um, yeah," I said, glancing at J.P. out of the corner of my eye. For some reason I didn't want him to get the impression that Andy and I were—together. I mean, it was already obvious that J.P. was nothing like thoughtful, kind, serious Todd Wilkins. In other words, he wasn't what Jessica would have called my "type." He was more like Jessica's type—playful and fun loving. And cute, of course.

J.P. and Andy started chatting about how much fun this trip was going to be and stuff like that. I mostly just nodded and listened and let the two guys do the talking. I was feeling a little tongue-tied. Maybe I was just tired from getting up early.

Still, hadn't I just made a decision to try acting more like Jessica for a while? This was the perfect opportunity. Even if I had no real interest in J.P., that didn't mean I couldn't—well—*flirt* with him a little. It would be good practice.

As I was trying to remember some of the millions of flirtatious comments I'd heard Jessica make to guys in the past, we all heard a voice calling Andy's name. Andy turned and squinted across the seating area.

Suddenly his eyes lit up behind his glasses. "Hey," he said. "It's my friend Duane. I didn't know he was coming on this trip!" He gave J.P. and me a quick, apologetic smile. "We're in the science club together at school. I should go say hello."

I glanced across the room and saw a chubby boy wearing a *Star Trek* T-shirt waving eagerly in our direction.

"No problem," J.P. said.

Andy quickly gathered up his things, pausing just long enough to smile shyly at me. "Bye, Elizabeth," he said. "I hope I'll see you later." Without waiting for an answer, he rushed away toward his friend.

Then J.P. and I were alone. There was a moment of awkward silence while I desperately tried to come up with something witty and interesting to say. What on earth does Jessica find to talk to boys about anyway?

J.P. saved me. He started right in again where he'd left off, talking about the trip. I did my best to keep up. It went something like this—

J.P.: So what made you decide to join the Amigo crusade, Elizabeth?
Me: Uh, um, well, uh, it sounded like fun.

J.P.: Yeah, that's what I thought. I heard you can go white-water rafting and surfing in Costa Rica and all kinds of other cool stuff. Also, the wildlife is supposed to be amazing. There are 136 types of snakes.

[OK, he didn't actually know the number—I remembered it from my reading. Here's what he really said:]

J.P.: I heard they have, like, about a million kinds of snakes.

Me: Snakes are interesting. [Duh!]

J.P.: Uh, sure. So anyway, do you know anyone else on the trip?

Me: No. Do you?

J.P.: Yeah, there are two or three other kids from Greengrass here. [I think it was about this time when he gave me this really amazing smile that made him look cuter than ever.] But you're probably way too cool for them, Elizabeth.

Me: [blushing like a lobster] Um, uh, uh . . .

Lucky for me, our boarding announcement came right at that moment. J.P. and I pulled out our boarding passes, and it turned out that we were in different rows.

To tell the truth, I was kind of relieved. I wasn't sure I was ready for a whole flight sitting next to him and trying to make conversation. So far, my experiment with acting more like Jessica wasn't going too well. As I waited in line to board the plane I suddenly thought of all sorts of clever, fascinating things I could have said to him.

But instead I'd just sat there like a dork and said almost nothing.

I tried not to think about that as I joined the line of students waiting to board.

I got on the plane and made my way down the narrow aisle. There were about twenty-five of us from the program on the plane, and we were all seated in the same section. I recognized the pretty dark-haired girl from the airport sitting by the window in my row. I sat down next to her and introduced myself.

"Hello," she said, looking me up and down as if she were trying to figure out whether I was worth talking to or not. "I'm Tanya. Where do you go to school?"

"Sweet Valley. I'm going into eighth grade." It felt kind of weird not to say "Sweet Valley Middle School," but she didn't seem to notice.

"I go to Greengrass Junior High. I'll be in eighth grade too."

"Greengrass? Really?" I said, thinking of J.P. "I heard that's a good school."

"One of the best in the state." She gave me a rather smug smile, then glanced down to check her seat belt. "It's not really bragging for me to say that, because I'm one of the people who helped make it so great."

"What do you mean?"

"I was the president of the seventh grade last year, so I got to help make a lot of the decisions that affected the whole school," she said. "I'll probably be president of the whole student council this year even though that office usually goes to a ninth-grader." She brushed a strand of dark hair off her cheek. "The principal already named me yearbook editor because I had the highest grades in the school last year."

I had to stop myself from rolling my eyes. For someone who didn't think she was bragging, Tanya sounded awfully conceited. Still, I couldn't totally blame her. It sounded like she had a lot to be conceited about.

I decided to change the subject. "What made you decide to come on this trip?" To be honest, I was pretty interested in hearing the answer. So far, Tanya didn't exactly seem like the sensitive, giving, do-gooder type.

"I won a state essay contest on Costa Rica," she said. "This trip was the grand prize. My parents don't have to pay a cent for it."

So that explained it.

"It's kind of silly, though," Tanya went on as the Fasten Seat Belts sign came on and the plane started to taxi toward the runway. "I mean, this trip would normally be a good learning experience for someone, but I already know just about everything there is to know about Costa Rica because of my research for the essay!" She shrugged and gave me that smug little smile again. "Still, I guess it will look good on my permanent record."

"Well, I'm sure that's true," I told her. "But I hadn't really thought about it that much. I was too excited about getting to help rebuild those flooded villages. Especially since the work I did with Houses for Humans was so fun and rewarding."

For the first time she looked slightly impressed. "You worked with Houses for Humans?"

I nodded. "I volunteered on a project with them last year."

"That's nice." Tanya settled back in her seat as the plane began to gather speed for takeoff. "I'm glad I'm not the only one with some building experience. I've worked on four Houses for Humans myself."

I felt my jaw drop. *Four* Houses for Humans? Was there anything Tanya hadn't accomplished? I couldn't help thinking that she should forget about eighth grade and just head straight for college right now. Or maybe the White House.

Still, even though I was impressed by the things Tanya had done, I didn't find myself liking her very much. In fact, the more I talked to her, the more I found myself getting annoyed with her. There was one thing she said that bugged me a lot. I guess I had mentioned something about the interesting plants and animals we were going to see in the rain forest.

"That should be interesting, of course," she said, even though she didn't sound like she really thought it was interesting at all. "But I'm not going to waste a lot of time looking for animals I can just go see in the zoo."

"But seeing them in the zoo isn't the same," I protested. "The exciting part will be finding them in their natural habitat. And spotting them will probably be a challenge, since I read that a lot of species are pretty shy, and others only come out at night, and—"

"Whatever." She rolled her eyes. "You can do all the animal spotting you want as long as you're not on my work team. Because I intend to make sure that I win the Outstanding Volunteer award when this trip is over, and that means my team is going to have to work hard."

"What award?" I asked.

"They present an award at the end of the trip," she explained. "To the person who did the most to help the project." She tossed her head so that her dark, thick hair bounced around her face. "But don't get your hopes up. I intend to win. If there's one thing I've learned, it's that being a winner is important. Very important. Even if *some* people don't seem to get that."

As she said that, she looked sort of ahead and across the aisle. I'm not positive, but it looked like she was staring right at J.P.!

It was weird. And there was more. A little while later I saw J.P. walk past on his way to the bathrooms at the back of the plane. On his way back he paused by my seat just long enough to smile at me. And I wouldn't swear to it, but I think he winked too! It was over so fast, I wasn't sure whether I had imagined the whole thing.

But that wasn't even the most interesting part. After he looked at me, he looked over at Tanya, who was taking a nap. His smile faded into a scowl, and he hurried back to his seat even though for a second I thought he was going to stop and talk to me.

I guess I shouldn't be surprised that they know each other. After all, they both go to Greengrass. But there seems to be something going on between them. Something even more mysterious than the puzzle in the mystery novel I read on the plane. What does it mean? I have no idea.

But I guess I have the next five weeks to find out.

Two

$\Diamond$

We were supposed to sleep in this morning to make up for our long, tiring day yesterday, but I was much too excited to sleep. I was wide awake by eight A.M. I couldn't wait to get started on our building—I almost wished we weren't stuck in the city for two more days of orientation and sightseeing, even though I was sure that would be interesting too.

I was tying my shoelaces when there was a knock on the door. I jumped up, a little startled.

"Who is it?" I called, glad that I had already gotten dressed and straightened my room. For a split second I was sure that it was J.P. at the door. I have no idea why. I hadn't seen much of J.P. since our talk at the airport—we had all been so exhausted after the long flight from the United States that most of us had headed straight for bed when we got here. I hadn't even thought about him very much. Still, his grinning face was the first thing that flashed into my mind right then.

It flashed out again quickly when I heard the response from the other side of the hotel door. "It's me, Elizabeth—Andy. Duane and I are heading down to breakfast. Do you want to sit with us?"

I sighed. "Sure, Andy," I called back, hurrying toward the door. "I'm ready."

Our program leaders, Marion and Robert, gave us a little "Rain Forest Friends" presentation at breakfast in the hotel dining room. They seem pretty cool. Marion is a graduate student; she's petite and pretty with auburn hair and a wide smile. Robert looks a few years older than Marion. He's one of the tallest and thinnest people I've ever met. His light brown hair sticks straight up in front, like Steven's sometimes does when he first wakes up. Somehow, though, I don't think Robert is the kind of person who cares much about how his hair looks (unlike Steven the Stud, ha-ha). He seems very nice but also very serious and thoughtful.

As we ate, the leaders stood and asked for our attention so they could tell us a little more about what we would be doing. Andy and Duane even stopped talking about the latest goings-on of the science club long enough to listen.

"Welcome, volunteers," Robert began. His voice was just as serious as the expression on his face. "You are about to embark on an adventure that will make a big difference in the lives of needy people."

"That's right," Marion went on. "Plus it will be a lot of fun if you approach it with the right attitude. I know you're all eager to help; otherwise you wouldn't have signed up for this trip. But it won't be all work and no play. You'll have plenty of opportunities to learn about Costa Rican culture and explore the rain forest you'll be working in. You'll probably see plants, birds, insects, and reptiles that you've never seen before, especially if you ask your host families for help in spotting them. By the way, Costa Ricans are known as *Ticos*, and I think you'll find the villagers you meet to be very friendly and helpful. All the host families you'll be staying with speak English, so you won't have any problems communicating with them or asking them for help. They can also translate between you and the other villagers."

Even though I was interested in what Marion was saying, I suddenly found my attention elsewhere. J.P. had just wandered into the room, yawning and scratching his head. He had obviously just rolled out of bed—his curls were wilder than ever and there was a big pillow crease on his cheek—but he still looked really cute.

Robert noticed him come in and frowned. But he didn't say anything as J.P. scooted into the nearest empty seat with a sheepish grin.

I frowned a little too. Everybody else had managed to get here on time. What was J.P.'s problem? His lateness irritated me—maybe a little more than it should have.

Besides, if J.P. had shown up on time, I could have been sitting with *him* instead of Andy and Duane.

Robert and Marion were still talking, and I did my best to pay attention as they explained that we would be divided into two construction crews that would be working in two neighboring villages. Actually, they're almost like two parts of one big village since they're only about a quarter of a mile apart, separated by a strip of rain forest. So we'll all be able to visit each other easily if our friends end up on the opposite team.

Then they talked about the Outstanding Volunteer award that Tanya had mentioned on the plane. The plaque will be presented on the last day of the trip to the student who has done the most for the project. I had to admit that it would be awfully cool to win an award like that. It would make a nice souvenir, and every time I looked at it, I would remember that I had done something important with my summer vacation instead of just sitting around the pool.

As I was trying to figure out if the award would look better on my desk or hanging above my bed, I was distracted by a sudden motion near the door. I looked over and saw that it was J.P.— again. He had just loaded his spoon with pineapple chunks and was pretending he was going to shoot the boy across the table with it. Or maybe he really was planning to shoot it. I never found out because a sharp voice from the front of the room interrupted him.

"Young man," Robert snapped. "Are you paying attention?"

Ha! I thought. *Busted.*

J.P. dropped the spoon and sat up straight. "Uh, sorry about that," he said. "I was listening. Really. I'll test the airborne velocity of this pineapple— uh—later."

Robert glared at him for a second, giving J.P. the same look my father gives Steven when he's doing something really irritating. "I hope so," Robert said. "There won't be any time for goofing off on this trip. The villagers are counting on us to finish their new buildings before our five weeks are up. That's all the funding we have for this project. So if it doesn't get done now, it may not get done for a long time—especially since it's the rainy season and a lot of groups don't work now at all."

At last J.P. had the decency to look sheepish. "Sorry," he said.

Robert glared again and looked like he wanted to say something else, but Marion interrupted him. "Don't let Robert scare you too much," she said with a kind smile. "As I said before, there will be time for fun as well as work. But it *is* important to remember that our main goal is to complete our building projects before we leave. People are counting on us." She looked around at the whole group as she said it.

"And anyone who can't remember that," Robert added, "doesn't need to be here at all. I would hate to have to send any of you home." He looked as though he meant it too—the part about hating it as well as the part about sending us home. Robert was very serious, but I could tell he was a caring person. He glanced at J.P. once more before starting to describe the ecologically sound building materials we would be using.

I snuck a peek at J.P. too. He was sitting quietly, listening to Robert speak. I was glad that Robert had yelled at J.P. He deserved it. He had been goofing off and acting stupid when he should have been paying attention. But I couldn't help noticing one more time how cute he was, even with that pillow crease on his face.

I bit my lip and forced my gaze back to my breakfast, still confused. What did I think of J.P.? I didn't know. Even when I was annoyed with him, I couldn't help wanting to look at him and talk to him and get to know him better. Weird.

I snuck another look at J.P., who had loaded his spoon up with pineapple again. I rolled my eyes. Clearly Robert's little speech hadn't impressed him much. But I decided that Robert was right. The work was the reason we were all here. I didn't want to waste time on some guy who wasn't serious about the project and could only distract me. No matter how cute he was.

TUESDAY, 9:40 P.M.

I will never understand boys.

I know I already decided not to waste any more time thinking about J.P. But that's not so easy when he always seems to be popping up in front of me wherever I turn.

I hardly saw him yesterday. Instead I spent the day with the geek twins. Sorry, I know that isn't very nice. But Andy and Duane really are pretty nerdy. They're not just charter members of their school's science club. No, they're also really into the chess club and marching band and the Science Fiction Fan Society and the Young Birdwatchers' club too. Not that there's anything wrong with those things. But Andy and Duane sometimes seem to forget that not everybody is as fascinated with all that stuff as they are. Duane is much worse than Andy—actually,

Andy is really smart and has a good sense of humor. But when the two of them get together, *run for your life!*

So after breakfast this morning, when Marion told us to break into groups for a day of sight-seeing, I was actually glad when Tanya grabbed my arm.

"You should be in our group, Elizabeth," she said. "You seem to be the only person I've met on this trip who knows anything at all about anything."

I shrugged, hiding a smile. I guessed some of the things I'd told her about myself on the plane must have sunk in after all. "OK," I said.

I smiled tentatively at the two girls standing behind Tanya. One of the girls smiled back. She was a little shorter than me, with hair almost the same shade of blond as mine, although hers was shorter and fluffier and kind of encircled her head like a halo. Her eyes were big and round and a really pure baby blue. Her face was kind of round too, and she had a button nose and a really big, open, friendly smile

"Hi," the blond girl said. "I'm Kate. This is Loren." She gestured at the third girl, who was very pale and thin. She didn't smile or nod or say "nice to meet you" or anything.

"Hi, I'm Elizabeth," I said, liking Kate immediately. I wondered how she had gotten roped into being in Tanya's group. "It's nice to meet you. Both of you," I added, glancing at Loren, who just shrugged.

Tanya tossed her head impatiently. "Come on, let's go," she commanded. "Marion is taking people to the museum, and I don't want to get lousy seats on the van."

I sighed. Spending the day with Queen Tanya wasn't looking like it would be any more fun than hanging out with the science nerds.

Still, I survived somehow. I even managed to have some fun, mostly thanks to Kate. She turned out to be just as friendly as she looked— and funny too. We spent half the day giggling over the way the guard at the museum kept saying *"pura vida, pura vida"* (which means "good" or something like that) every time we walked past him. Once we caught on, we started walking past his station every few minutes to see what he would do. He just kept saying *"pura vida, pura vida."* But I guess he realized we were joking around with him. Because when we were getting ready to leave the museum for good, he said, *"Hasta luego, mi hijitas. Pura vida!"* and winked at us.

Tanya wasn't the least bit amused by our little game with the guard. Jessica sometimes accuses me of being too serious, but I don't think Tanya has any sense of humor at all. And I have no idea what Loren thought about any of it. She didn't say more than three words the entire day.

After some more sightseeing we all headed back to the hotel dining room for dinner and some last minute instructions on life in the rain forest. The four of us found a table near the front of the room. Marion was sitting nearby, but Robert was nowhere in sight. Neither was J.P. Not that I cared.

Kate and I kept chatting as we ate, with Tanya throwing in a snotty comment once in a while. Loren just concentrated on her food. By now I knew that Kate went to the same school as J.P. and Tanya. I also knew that Kate had come on this trip mostly because she's crazy about animals and birds, and she's hoping to see lots of interesting species while she's here. But she's also looking forward to helping build homes for needy people. In fact, she's so serious about it that her big blue eyes fill up with tears every time she talks about it.

After we all had our food, Marion clapped for attention. She started off by explaining that tomorrow morning we would be taking a bus to a large town near our villages. Then she told us some of the things we would need to know to have a fun and safe time in the rain forest.

As she was describing several types of poisonous snakes we might encounter, J.P. came in—late again, I couldn't help noticing—with a group of three other boys. They were all laughing and talking loudly. It took them a second to realize that Marion was speaking. One by one the other three boys fell silent. But J.P. had his back to Marion, and I guess he was in the middle of telling a joke or something because he kept going.

". . . and so then the dog asked why they didn't make cowboy boots in his size. And . . ." J.P. looked confused as one of the boys gestured to him frantically. "And . . ." He looked around and spotted Marion frowning. "Oh." Suddenly J.P. realized that everyone in the room was staring at him. He grinned. "Ha-ha. Uh—oops."

Marion nodded sternly, although it looked to me as though she was struggling not to laugh. I rolled my eyes. J.P. was just lucky Robert wasn't around.

"Take your seats, boys," Marion said, and the four of them looked around for empty chairs. The other three boys found seats quickly, but J.P. was left standing.

I glanced at the empty seat between me and Loren, but I didn't say anything. *Let him find a seat at another table*, I told myself. *We don't need him throwing food at us.*

But Marion had just spotted the empty seat. "Here you go, J.P.," she called. "There's a free seat right there by Elizabeth Wakefield."

J.P. grinned. "Elizabeth Wakefield?" he exclaimed, loudly enough for the entire room to hear. "Great! I must be the luckiest boy in the whole wide world!" He clasped his hands to his chest and fluttered his eyelashes dramatically.

I blushed up to my scalp as Loren shot me a surprised glance and Kate giggled. Tanya was scowling. I didn't meet any of their eyes. I couldn't believe J.P. had said that—what would everyone think?

Most of the other kids were snickering as J.P. loped across the room toward our table. He was grinning broadly, as if he were very pleased with himself. But he stopped short when he reached the table and saw who else was there.

"Oh. Hi, Tanya," he said, his tone suddenly subdued.

"Hello, J.P.," she replied icily. "It's nice to see you've matured so much over the summer."

The sarcasm in her voice was so clear that no one at the table could have missed it. But J.P. didn't respond. Instead he sat down and turned to me with a big smile. "So, Elizabeth," he said. "What did you girls do today?"

I gulped. Having him sitting so close, looking so cute, made me feel a bit light-headed. *You're not Jessica*, I told myself firmly. *Get a grip!*

"Um, I think we'd better listen," I whispered, gesturing to Marion, who had started speaking again.

J.P. shrugged. "Whatever," he said. All of a sudden he didn't seem very interested in talking to me—not even to tease me or embarrass me. He was too busy shooting dirty looks at Tanya, who was pointedly ignoring him. Things stayed pretty much the same way until the meal ended, when J.P. slunk off with hardly a word to any of us.

It's like I said.

I will never understand boys!

Three

We checked out of the hotel this morning and got ready to head out into the rain forest. The villages where we would be working were a pretty long way from the city, so we needed to get an early start. Marion and Robert explained that we would be staying overnight in San Sebastián, which is the largest town in that area, before heading on to our two villages, Valle Dulce and Gemelo, the next morning.

I was one of the first people on board the bus. I sat down near the front so I would have a good view out the windows. Tanya sort of smiled at me when she got on, and she took a step forward, obviously planning to sit with me. I guessed she'd gotten over that whole scene with J.P.—she'd seemed kind of angry about it all evening, even after J.P. left.

I smiled back weakly, feeling trapped. I had been hoping to sit with Kate, but I didn't want to make Tanya mad. I began preparing myself for a long, dull ride spent listening to her talk about herself.

"Heads up!" someone shouted.

It was J.P. He hopped up the bus steps and pushed past Tanya. Actually, he hardly touched her at all as he went by, although by the way she jumped back, you would have thought he'd poked her with a red-hot branding iron or something.

"Hi, Elizabeth," he said, stopping by my seat. He gave me a huge grin and made a sort of little half bow. "Is this seat taken?"

"Um, no," I said, feeling flattered and kind of bashful at the same time in spite of myself. "I guess not. Go ahead."

He sat down, and then he turned and sort of smirked at Tanya. She just stalked past and sat down a few seats behind us.

That made me feel kind of weird. I don't like making enemies, especially with someone I might have to work with for the next five weeks. And whatever was going on between J.P. and Tanya, I didn't want to end up in the middle of it.

But I also felt strange because I still didn't know quite what to think about J.P. I kept flip-flopping back and forth in my mind. One second I was determined to avoid him since he was so distracting and goofy. The next I would find myself thinking that I should get to know him better. I was realizing that there was something really cool about J.P., and I'm not just talking about how cute he was. It was something about his personality—the way he wasn't afraid to say and do whatever he wanted. Maybe some of the stuff he did annoyed me—like being late. But I could imagine what Jessica would say about that if she were here: *Give him a break, Lizzie. He's just having fun!*

Maybe that was true. After all, even if we were here to work, we were also here to have fun. J.P. really knew how to do that. Did I? Or was I more like Tanya, who was so busy worrying about her junior-high transcript and being mature that she forgot to enjoy herself?

Next to me J.P. was craning his neck around, looking behind us. "No offense, Elizabeth," he said. "But this is a really lame seat. Come on, let's move to the back."

I hesitated. Like I said, I had chosen that seat so I would have a good view. We wouldn't be able to see out nearly as well from the back, and besides, I had read that a lot of the roads in Costa Rica aren't even paved, so I was afraid it would be really bumpy back there.

I opened my mouth to explain all of that to J.P. But he was already halfway down the aisle. "Wait!" I called.

He turned around for a second. "Come on!" he called to me. "Backseat is where it's at!"

For a second I almost stayed where I was. Kate would be here soon; she could sit with me. Who needed J.P.? But I felt my legs moving on their own, standing up and stepping out of the seat. *I just don't want to be rude*, I thought. I scooted out of the seat and hurried down the aisle, trying not to notice the dirty look that Tanya flashed me as I walked past her seat. When I reached the back, J.P. hopped up and offered me the window seat, which I gladly accepted.

Then we got started. I was a little nervous about finding things to say to J.P., but as it turned out, I didn't have to worry. He kept me laughing with all sorts of jokes and stories. I actually found myself having fun listening to him. True, he was kind of silly and loud. But he was smart too. And he seemed to be pretty nice—like none of his goofing around was really meant to be mean.

Still, my opinion of him kept doing that flip-flopping thing.

He told me about an art project he'd done last year. *He's artistic!* I thought.

Then he started describing some of the practical jokes he'd played on his older sisters. *What a jerk*, I thought.

He asked me a lot of questions about my work for the school newspaper and acted really interested in what I told him. *Hmmm. Maybe he's OK.*

Then I told him about Jessica, and after he found out I was a twin, he decided to start calling me Bob, as in Bobbsey twin. *Aargh!* I thought.

Flip. Flop. I just couldn't make up my mind one way or the other.

Between laughing at J.P.'s silly stories, getting annoyed at his immature comments, and watching the interesting scenery, the first hour or two of our bus trip flew by. But after a while I noticed that the ride was getting bumpier and the road was getting narrower as we made our way through some mountains. We came to an area that went up and down steeply every few minutes and around a lot of hairpin turns, and I found myself getting kind of nervous, especially since the bus driver didn't slow down much for most of the turns. In fact—and I might have been wrong about this—he seemed to be *speeding up* for the turns.

I said something about it to J.P. He didn't seem scared at all, though.

"Don't worry," he said, making his voice as deep as he could and flexing the muscles in one arm. "I'm a manly man, and I won't let anything bad happen to a pretty lady like you."

I rolled my eyes. I wasn't exactly counting on J.P. to come to my rescue if the bus crashed. But then I realized belatedly that he had called me pretty. I started blushing madly. I didn't want him to see, so I turned my face toward the window.

That was when I saw it. We were careening straight toward a steep drop-off, going way too fast to stop!

My heart froze. I was too scared to scream. Instead I dug my fingernails into the back of the seat in front of me and sort of whimpered. This was it. We were all going to end up horribly mangled in some Costa Rican hospital! I tried to squeeze my eyes closed, but they were glued to the cliff we were about to go over.

Meanwhile J.P. noticed my look of terror and leaned over to see what I had seen. But when he saw the drop-off, he just grinned and shouted "Yee-ha!" at the top of his lungs. He grabbed me, wrapped both arms around me, and squeezed. "I'm protecting you!" he yelled right in my left ear.

For a second I thought he was crazy. Then, as the driver spun the steering wheel and I realized it was just another hairpin curve, I started to feel embarrassed for panicking like that. Then I forgot all about that feeling when I remembered J.P.'s arms were still around me. That made me feel flustered, and confused, and . . . well, I wasn't sure what else.

He loosened his grip a little so he could pull back and look at me.

"This is great, isn't it, Bob?" he said. "Sort of like a ride at Disneyland."

I frowned and opened my mouth to disagree. I had really been scared, and I didn't think it was fun at all. Then the bus swooped around another curve, throwing me toward J.P. His arms tightened again, and he laughed.

I did too. I couldn't help it—his laugh was catching.

Go for it, Lizzie! Jessica's words floated through my mind again. I didn't have to think too hard to figure out what she would do if she were me.

Suddenly I found myself thinking that maybe being scared had its advantages. Maybe J.P. was a goofball, but he was really cute—and his arms *were* awfully strong. . . . "Oh, no!" I cried, glancing out the window. "Here comes a sharp one!"

It was stupid, I know. Those roads probably were really dangerous. But I truly had forgotten that for a minute. Suddenly I felt as though I'd gotten a little bit of insight into why Jessica and her friends do all the harebrained things they do.

I guess that sometimes it's easy to get caught up in the moment.

THURSDAY, 11:15 P.M.

So much happened today, Diary! I'll write about everything in a second, but first I have to get one thing off my chest:

Tanya is a total jerk!

I feel much better now. OK, so let me start from the beginning.

We got to San Sebastián right on schedule. It was a colorful, bustling town, much smaller than the city, but still full of interesting people and things to see. We had just enough time to eat dinner and take a look around before collapsing in exhaustion.

I woke up early again this morning. But when I looked at the second bed in the room, I noticed that Loren was already up and gone. I wasn't sorry about that. I'd been disappointed when Marion had assigned us a room together. And Loren had hardly said two words to me as we were getting ready for bed. Still, I knew it could have been worse. I could have been stuck with Tanya. I'd much rather room with someone who doesn't talk at all than someone who only talks about herself.

I was pulling on my shorts when the door to the room flew open. I glanced up, expecting it to be Loren.

"Oops!" Kate cried, blushing. She quickly closed the door again. "Sorry, I guess I forgot to knock! I was too excited," she said from the hall.

I hurriedly fastened my shorts and called out, "That's OK, come on in!" I smiled as she opened the door again. *At last, someone to talk to who might actually talk back,* I thought wryly. "I'm almost ready. What's up?"

"Good news." Kate perched on the edge of Loren's bed while she waited for me to tie my shoelaces. "Marion and Robert just posted our assignments in the lobby, and you and I are in the same village—Valle Dulce. Not only that, we'll both be staying with the same host family, the Herreras!"

"That's great!" I exclaimed. "Do you know who else is in our village? What about Loren and Tanya?"

Kate wrinkled her nose. "Loren's with us. But Tanya got the other village, thank goodness." She giggled. "Sorry, that's kind of mean."

"It's OK," I said quickly as I finished tying my shoes and stood up. "I understand, believe me." I was relieved that Tanya and I were in different villages. Maybe now I wouldn't have to hear any more about her perfect grades and prize-winning essays.

I couldn't help wondering which village J.P. was in. But I didn't want to ask Kate and let her know that I cared. Not that I did—not much anyway. I was just curious. "Why don't we head down to breakfast?" I suggested. "Maybe on the way we can stop by the lobby so I can check out the good news for myself." *And see exactly who else is on the list for Valle Dulce,* I added silently.

Kate nodded agreeably. "Let's go!"

When we reached the lobby, there was a small group of kids clustered in front of the list. I stood on tiptoe, trying to see past the girl in front of me. I scanned the names on the Valle Dulce side quickly, taking note of mine and Kate's. A little farther down I spotted another familiar name, and my heart soared.

"Yo, Bob," a voice called behind me at that moment. It was J.P. "Which village did you get?"

"Valle Dulce," I said. "And stop calling me Bob." I turned to face him and saw that Andy and Duane were standing with him.

J.P. grinned. "Me too! Andy and I are bunking together. Right, dude?" He punched Andy lightly on the arm.

Andy nodded, but he looked kind of sad. Duane looked even sadder, and I guessed that meant he was in the other village—Tanya's village. *Poor guy*, I thought.

I glanced back at J.P. He was bouncing up and down on the balls of his feet. "This is it," he crowed. "We're almost there. Time to get down to business."

I gulped, realizing that he was exactly right, although maybe not in the way he meant. Here I was, all aflutter because I was on the same team with a cute guy—a cute guy who insisted on calling me *Bob*, no less. But was that really what I ought to be feeling? Shouldn't I be more concerned with being on a team where all the members were serious and dedicated to our project? We had a real job to do, and nothing should stand in the way of that. Maybe I would have been better off if J.P. had ended up with Tanya. Welcome to my flip-flop world.

Kate, for one, didn't seem to share my concerns. "This is going to be so much fun!" she cried, clapping.

J.P. grinned at her. "You said it," he declared. "And I'm ready for it. Fun's my middle name!"

Just then Marion strode into the lobby. "I'm glad to see you found our list," she said. "But you'd better go grab some breakfast—the bus will be here to pick you up in half an hour. We'll stop at Valle Dulce first, then continue on to Gemelo. Got it? Good. Then let's eat. You'll need to keep up your strength for all that building!" She grinned at us, then led the way into the dining room.

Half an hour later we were in line, waiting to board the bus. I was standing between Kate and Andy, and J.P. and Duane were in front of us. Loren and Tanya were standing with a couple of other girls nearby. Marion and Robert were outside the bus door, checking off our names on a clipboard.

"Here we are, Cap'n," J.P. announced as we passed the adults. "Right on time."

"That's kind of a miracle, actually," Marion said with a chuckle, glancing at her watch. "Things in

Costa Rica hardly ever run on schedule."

"I guess that's why *you* like it here so much, J.P.," I joked. "After all, you're always late."

The others laughed, but J.P. turned and cocked one eyebrow at me quizzically. "Oh, really?" he said with a slight smirk. "I didn't realize you were paying such close attention to my schedule, Bob."

I blushed, wanting to sink into the ground. I should have known better than to try to tease J.P. He always had a perfect comeback.

I smiled weakly and moved forward to climb onto the bus. I sat down next to Kate, and J.P. slid into the seat behind us.

"Hey, Bob," he said, speaking more quietly than usual. "I was just kidding back there. I hope I didn't embarrass you or anything."

I shrugged quickly. The last thing I wanted was for him to think I was some kind of hypersensitive jerk. "No big deal," I said. "Hey, J.P., did you know that Kate is a really great horseback rider?"

After that the half-hour ride to Valle Dulce passed quickly. Kate and I watched the fascinating Costa Rican scenery slide past the bus windows. J.P. sat behind us, cracking jokes the whole time. Andy and Duane were across the aisle, still trying to come to terms with the fact that they weren't going to get to spend the entire trip together. I think they were trying to cram a whole five weeks' worth of *Star Trek* discussions into that half-hour ride. Meanwhile Tanya and Loren were sitting a couple of seats ahead. Every time there was a burst of laughter from our group, Tanya shot us a dirty look over her shoulder.

When our bus pulled up in front of Valle Dulce's town hall, it seemed as though the entire population of the village was there, waiting to greet us.

"Those of you continuing on to Gemelo, feel free to get off and look around, stretch your legs," Robert called as the driver pulled over. "It will take us a while to get all the luggage sorted out anyway."

The Herreras were the first ones to rush forward to greet us as we climbed off the bus. Robert pointed to Kate and me, and before I knew it, we were totally mobbed. At first I wasn't even sure how many of them there were because they talked so quickly and jumped around so much. But I soon figured out that there were six people in the family, two parents and four kids. (There's also a grandmother who lives with them, but I didn't meet her until later, when I got to their house.) Veronica and Jorge are the oldest Herrera kids—they're around my age. Eugenia is six and Ricardo is four, and they're both adorable, with big brown eyes and dark hair.

Mr. and Mrs. Herrera (actually, I guess that should be Señor and Señora Herrera) smiled at us, then stepped away to talk to Marion and Robert. Meanwhile Veronica was grinning at us, looking excited.

"Awesome to meet you, Elizabeth and Kate," she said. "We are going to have a majorly cool time in Costa Rica. You will like our house too— my parents are kind of clueless, but they are not bad for old fogies. Anyway, I am totally psyched that you have come here to rebuild our community center; I loved watching American TV, movies, and music videos there. It even had a VCR—I was so very bummed when it got destroyed by the floods."

Veronica talked really fast, and for a while I thought we weren't going to be able to get a word in edgewise, but she finally had to pause to take a breath. I opened my mouth to say something about how happy I was to be there. I was also going to compliment her on how well she spoke English—she hardly had an accent at all. And no wonder—from all the American slang she'd packed into a few sentences, I guessed she had watched a *lot* of American TV! I thought it was cute how she had picked up all those words and expressions.

But before I could say a word, Tanya spoke up. She had gotten off the bus and was standing nearby, listening to the whole thing.

"Give me a break," she said scornfully, looking down her nose at Veronica. "We're here to rebuild your village, not to talk about American TV. And we definitely don't need to practice our *awesome* American slang from the 1980s."

Veronica looked mortified, and I was *furious!* What was Tanya's problem? Veronica was being nice and friendly, and Tanya had just made her feel like a total idiot.

J.P. was listening too, and I guess he was thinking the same thing I was because he jumped right in.

"Yo, Veronica, your English is awesome," he said, totally ignoring Tanya. "Where did you learn to speak it so well?"

I struggled to suppress a laugh. Awesome? Since when did J.P. use a word like that? Ever since Tanya had used it to make Veronica feel stupid, I guessed. J.P. is so cool sometimes—of course he would find a way to use Tanya's rude comments against her.

Veronica gave him a shy and kind of grateful look. "I have learned some in school. But mostly I learn by watching TV and movies at the community center. I mean, I used to before the flood."

"Well, you must be *majorly* brainy to pick it up that way," J.P. said sincerely. "When it comes to Spanish, I'm totally clueless. I can't even count to ten—no matter how many times I watched them do it on *Sesame Street* when I was a kid! How does it go—*uno, dos,* trees, quarter, sink. . . ."

Veronica giggled. "I have often seen *Sesame*

Street at the community center," she said. "My little sister and brother love Elmo, but personally, I think Cookie Monster is awesome. He is my favorite character."

"Mine too," I said. "Cookie is *totally* awesome." I smiled at J.P. Hey, I know just as much slang as anybody.

Tanya may be a jerk, but she's no fool. She caught on pretty quick. She shook her head and muttered something under her breath about how immature we all were. Then she stomped away and climbed back on the bus.

I didn't shed a single tear when she left.

After the bus headed off toward Gemelo, the Herreras took Kate and me to their house for lunch, which was great—and very filling! It turns out that in Costa Rica, lunch is the most important meal of the day. We had all kinds of typical Tico dishes, including *chorreados*, which are sort of like corn cakes, *arroz con pollo*, which is a chicken dish, and lots of other things.

Delicious!

After we finished eating, Veronica and Jorge pointed the way toward the construction site. Marion had asked the whole group to meet there for one last set of instructions and information. Meanwhile Robert would be talking to Tanya and Duane and the others over at the other village.

About half the others were already there when Kate and I arrived. There were about a dozen kids in our group, including Kate, me, J.P., Andy, and Loren. The two boys weren't there yet, but I spotted Loren sitting in the front row next to a girl named Tiffany. "This is so exciting," Kate whispered, her eyes sparkling as we sat down on the ground behind a couple of guys named Ricky and Will.

I nodded and started to answer. But at that moment Andy plopped down right next to me. "Hi, Elizabeth," he said. "Hi, Kate."

Before we could answer, another voice broke in. "Yo, Bob!" J.P. exclaimed breathlessly, hurrying over and taking a seat behind me. "Here I am—on time for once. Right?"

I rolled my eyes. "Right. And don't call me Bob."

J.P. just grinned and then said hi to Kate.

"That was really nice, J.P.," Kate told him sincerely. "What you did back there for Veronica, I mean."

J.P. waved his hand. "No big deal," he said. "Tanya's evil. I didn't want her to ruin things."

Andy turned to me and said quietly, "I'm glad we're on the same team, Elizabeth. I'm looking forward to working with you."

"Thanks, Andy. I'm looking forward to it too." His steady gaze was making me a little uncomfortable. Why was he looking at me like that? And did he have to sit so close—practically in my lap? Didn't he know he was being kind of rude? Either he had no social skills whatsoever, or—suddenly a terrible thought occurred to me. *Uh-oh,* I thought. *Does Andy have a—a crush on me?*

I didn't have much time to think about it since Marion had just arrived and called for our attention. I sighed and settled back to listen. I could worry about this latest case of weird boy behavior later.

Marion told us that we would be rebuilding the community center that was destroyed in the floods. She wanted us to elect a leader to act as our foreman and oversee the construction (the kids in the other village will be doing the same thing) since she and Robert won't be staying in the villages with us all the time. We'll be under the supervision of our host families and a local builder who will stop by occasionally to help us.

The first thought that popped into my mind was that J.P. would make a fantastic foreman. I mean, he has a way of making everything—even riding over dangerous roads in a creaky old bus—seem like tons of fun. Plus he's obviously smart and talented. And if he had such an important job to do, maybe he would even calm down a little and stop goofing around so much. Perfect.

I guess Kate must have thought so too because as soon as Marion asked for nominations, she stuck up her hand and suggested J.P.

I looked over at him, expecting him to be psyched, but he was frowning.

"Sorry," he said, sitting up straight. "The whole leader thing isn't really my scene."

"But J.P.!" Kate's big blue eyes were wider than ever. I could tell she was as surprised at his reaction as I was. "You're perfect for the job. You did that scale model city in art class last year." She turned to look at the rest of us. "It won first prize in our school's fine arts fair."

"Sorry," J.P. said again. "I'm just not into being the boss." He shrugged. "Besides, an art project is one thing. A real building is another. I don't have that kind of experience."

Marion was nodding. "All right," she said. "We're not going to draft you for the job if you don't want it. And actually, your comments gave me a good idea about who might make an appropriate foreman." She turned and smiled straight at me. "I understand from her application that Elizabeth Wakefield has done some work with Houses for Humans. Is that right, Elizabeth?"

"Yes," I replied. I was about to go into more detail about the project I worked on (mostly to explain that I had just done whatever the foreman told me to do, since Marion kind of made it sound like I practically built the whole house myself), but Marion wasn't finished.

"In addition to her hands-on construction experience, Elizabeth appears to be a natural-born leader. She gets straight A's in school, she was editor of her sixth grade paper, she . . ."

Marion went on listing my achievements. But I wasn't listening too closely because by now I realized that Marion wanted *me* to be the foreman. And I wasn't sure how I felt about that.

I like being in charge—sometimes. But I'm not like Jessica, who always wants to be the center of attention. When I pictured myself building homes in Costa Rica, I had imagined working as part of a team, side by side with the other kids. Not bossing them around and being responsible for the whole project. It was sort of scary to think about having a whole village counting on me to build them a new community center. Granted, it was just a one-room structure, but it was still a real building.

But I didn't know how to say that without sounding like a big baby. And somehow I didn't think copying J.P.'s little speech was going to work for me—especially not after all the things Marion had just said about me. I smiled weakly.

"Um, OK," I said. "If you really think I can do it. And if nobody else wants the job."

"You'll do great," Marion assured me. She dug in the pocket of her khaki shorts and brought out a key. "This is the key to the office shack. It's right over there." She pointed to a shed on the other side of the clearing, then turned back to address the group. "The rest of you are dismissed. Enjoy your first evening in Valle Dulce, but try not to have *too* much fun." She grinned. "You've got to be up bright and early tomorrow to get down to work."

The other kids scattered as Marion brought me the key to the shed. She said it was where I would find the tools, materials, instruction manuals, and all the other stuff I'd need for *my* community center building.

Yikes! What had I gotten myself into? It was just lucky I had all those helpful hints from the Coco's Construction Concepts Web page. And I reassured myself with the thought that Robert and Marion would be dropping by, not to mention the local builder.

As Marion hurried off I turned the key in the lock and stepped into the office shack. I looked around. There was a desk in one corner with a little battery-operated fan, a lamp, some pens and papers and stuff, and even a portable CD boom box. Nearby was a wall rack containing a bunch of tools, and half of the shack was filled with large piles of lumber, scraps of metal, old tires, and other junk.

I locked up again and wandered back toward the Herreras' house. I figured I should offer to help prepare dinner and see if I could be useful in any other ways. It seemed the least I could do since the family was letting me live in their home for more than a month.

On my way down the little path leading through the strip of forest between the site and the main part of the village, I ran into J.P. He grinned at me, and before I knew it, I was in the middle of another weird boy conversation that made me question my whole opinion of him once again. It went something like this:

J.P.: Hey, Bob. How's it going?

Me: Don't call me Bob.

J.P.: [with a goofy grin] Sorry. I guess I'd better start calling you Foreman Bob now, huh? So where are you off to, Foreman Bob?

Me: I was just going back to the Herreras' to see if I can help with dinner.

J.P.: Cool! Maybe you can get extra credit with your home ec teacher for it.

Me: You're so funny.

J.P.: Hey, are you sure you should be talking to me, Foreman Bob? I mean, I'm just a regular guy, not a superachiever like you.

Me: What?

J.P.: Maybe you should talk to Andy instead. You guys can discuss the latest world chess championships.

I was starting to get really annoyed by that point. Maybe he was just kidding around as usual, but it didn't seem that funny this time. He was acting as if he thought I considered myself better than him, kind of like Tanya. I guess it was because of all that stuff Marion had said about me.

But if J.P. was waiting around for me to apologize for being a good student, he had a long wait ahead of him. I happen to like learning. Besides, being smart doesn't mean you can't have a sense of humor or that you don't know how to have fun. It doesn't mean I'm anything like Tanya. I'm starting to think I was right when I decided to stay away from him. In fact, I'm not going to write about him or even think about him anymore.

I know, I'm flip-flopping again.

But I mean it this time. I'm going to start right now. After all, there are lots of better things to think about. Like the local wildlife, for instance. Kate's already spotted about twenty kinds of birds and ten kinds of reptiles. She even caught a glimpse of something she thought was a coati, which is sort of like the Costa Rican version of a raccoon.

Sometimes it's hard to believe that I'm really in Costa Rica, but every time I look around, the interesting new sights convince me. I wish I had a tape recorder to catch the sounds that start to come out of the rain forest when the sun goes down. It's as if there are a million kinds of bugs, frogs, and who knows what else (monkeys? I heard there are some here, though I haven't seen any yet) all joining in a big chorus, chirping and croaking and screeching away. Over dinner tonight Mrs. Herrera said the sound gets almost deafening sometimes, but they're all so used to it, they hardly notice.

*   *   *

Despite my vow to forget about J.P., I woke up this morning thinking about him. I just couldn't get that conversation—if you could call it a conversation—out of my mind. It really bugged me that J.P. seemed to be judging me, even in a joking way, because of what Marion had said.

Kate and I got dressed in the spare bedroom in the Herreras' house, which is where we're staying while we're here. It's a small room, not much bigger than the bathroom Jess and I share at home. But it's cozy and welcoming, thanks to the colorful curtains and bedspreads, several carved wooden knickknacks, an embroidered wall hanging of a rain forest scene, and other homey touches.

Kate yawned and glanced at her watch as she reached for her shoes. "It's almost time for breakfast at the construction site. Are you psyched for our first day?" she asked cheerfully.

I sighed. "Well, the breakfast part doesn't sound too bad," I muttered. I wasn't looking forward to seeing J.P.—or starting my job as foreman, thanks to his teasing.

Kate's big blue eyes clouded over with concern. "What do you mean, Elizabeth?"

"I don't know." I finished buckling the belt on my shorts. "I think I would be more excited if someone else was foreman and I was just a worker like everyone else."

Kate gazed at me. "You mean you don't want to be foreman?"

"It's not that," I told her. Then I remembered that she goes to the same school as J.P. and Tanya. "How well do you know J.P.?" I asked.

She shrugged and sat down on the edge of her bed. "Not that well," she said. "We go to the same school, but we hardly have any classes together. He's in all the advanced classes because he's supposed to be some kind of genius."

"Really?" That didn't make much sense to me. If J.P. was so smart in school, why had he been so down on my grades and everything?

Kate nodded. "That's what they say. I guess that's why they keep him in those classes even though he's practically flunking out of most of them." She shrugged again. "If you ask me, he's kind of a slacker. Or maybe I should say partyer. He loves to have fun, and he hates to be serious or work at anything he doesn't think is interesting. And he doesn't think much about school is interesting except maybe art class. He's really good at that."

"Oh." Now it all made much more sense. And suddenly I had another thought. "Is that why Tanya doesn't seem to like him? Because he goofs off too much?"

Kate giggled. "Not exactly. She and J.P. used to be a couple. They went out through half of seventh grade. But they broke up at the end of the year."

"Oh." That explained a lot. A *lot*. Although I had a hard time picturing how a mismatched pair like J.P. and Tanya could get together in the first place.

The Herrera kids were still sleeping when we left our room, and Mr. and Mrs. Herrera were getting ready to leave for San Sebastián, where they both have office jobs. Kate and I said good-bye to them and headed over to the construction site, where Marion had laid out a picnic for us. She told us that most of the food had been prepared for us by the villagers. I could believe it. It was all just as delicious as yesterday's lunch had been. My favorite dish was made with rice and beans and called *gallo pinto*, which Marion explained was the Tico national breakfast.

Robert came by in a four-wheel-drive vehicle to pick up Marion at around nine o'clock. Before they left, they called us all into the clearing in front of the construction site for a few last-minute announcements. They said they'll be stopping by our two villages (oh, and by the way—Robert happened to mention that Tanya was elected team leader at her village. Big fat hairy surprise!) as often as they can to see how we're doing.

It turns out there are at least half a dozen groups of kids working in different parts of this area, not just our two. Marion and Robert have to help them all. That's why they're not staying full-time in Valle Dulce or Gemelo. They'll be in San Sebastián and on the road for most of the next five weeks.

Anyway, they told us the main shipment of construction materials for the buildings is on the way. It was supposed to arrive before we did, but I guess it's hard to keep roads clear in the rain forest, and the truck was delayed. Since the trucking company is donating their services, they aren't exactly sure when they can get the stuff here now. It could be tomorrow, it could be next week.

Robert said it shouldn't affect us much. We'll need to spend the first couple of days preparing the ground and building the foundation, and after that we have enough wood stacked behind the office shack to get most of the framing done. The local builder would come help us when the materials arrived. Until then, I was in control.

Before they left, the adults also mentioned something interesting about Tanya's village, Gemelo. A lot more homes there were affected by the floods than here, so the Rain Forest Friends didn't want to ask the villagers to put up the teen workers in their houses. Instead they set up a bunch of tents for them to sleep in. It sounds like the tents are pretty snazzy—each person gets his or her own private one, they have canvas floors and screened zip-up windows to keep the mosquitoes and other bugs out, stuff like that—but the point is, they're still tents. So I guess those of us in Valle Dulce really lucked out!

The rest of the day went well. I was nervous about getting started, but the rest of the crew was a lot of help. A boy named Ty had helped his father with the foundation of their new garage. A girl named Sumi had some good ideas about organizing the materials. And Andy was great at translating the directions that are in Spanish.

Otherwise not much happened. The good news was that J.P. stopped calling me Bob. The bad news was that he called me Madame Foreman all day instead, and at lunch he kept offering to pour me more juice and serve me more food in this ridiculous French waiter voice. He even offered to chew my food for me, which cracked up everyone except me (and Loren, who smiles about as often as she talks). Ugh! I really don't know what I should do about him. I wish Jessica were here to help me come up with a plan.

Four

◇

Boy, Diary—has this been a long, confusing, exciting, weird, interesting, and sometimes even fun day!

Our second day of work went pretty well. I managed to ignore most of J.P.'s teasing and goofing around, and the rest of the team worked really hard. We got a ton of work done on the foundation, and I was sure we'd be ready to start framing soon. By the time Kate and I headed back to the Herreras' for dinner, we were dirty, hot, hungry, and exhausted.

We gobbled down the food Mrs. Herrera had prepared for us, then headed off to shower and change clothes. Veronica and Jorge had promised to show us around the rain forest when we were ready.

When I got back to the kitchen, I was surprised to find a small crowd gathered there. Mr. and Mrs. Herrera were bustling around near the stove. Sitting at the big wooden table where we'd eaten dinner were Veronica, Jorge, their grandmother, and a clean-scrubbed Kate. But they weren't the only ones. J.P. and Andy were there too, along with the Costa Rican family they were staying with.

"Oh," I said when I came in. "Hi, everyone."

As soon as she saw me, Veronica jumped up.

"Cool!" she cried. "Here is Elizabeth. Kate and the guys and I were just about to come search for you. These dudes are dying to check out the forest." She waved a hand in the direction of J.P. and Andy. "So they're coming with us, okeydokey?"

I hesitated. I had been looking forward to exploring the rain forest with Kate and the Herrera kids. But it didn't sound quite as appealing when I knew I'd have to put up with J.P.'s jokes and Andy's lovesick stares. "Maybe we should do it tomorrow," I suggested. "Kate and I should probably stick around and help clean up from dinner."

Jorge, Veronica's brother, rolled his eyes. "Not necessary, Elizabeth," he said. He has a stronger Spanish accent than his sister, but his English is really good too. "It is finished already."

Mrs. Herrera turned away from the sink, where she was filling a teakettle with water while her husband set some pastry-type things on a platter nearby. "Don't worry, Elizabeth," she said. "Go along and have fun."

"But—," I started to protest.

J.P. interrupted. "Hey, maybe dragging Bo—uh, I mean Elizabeth out to the rain forest isn't such a good idea. I mean, there are lots of bugs and things out there." He grinned at me. "Snakes too. A lot of girls are scared of that stuff."

I scowled at him. Bugs aren't my favorite thing in the world, but they don't bother me the way they do some people—like Jessica's friend Ellen Riteman, for instance. Ellen is so scared of spiders that if she sees one, even a teeny-tiny one twenty feet away, she screams at the top of her lungs and jumps up on the nearest piece of furniture as fast as she can. I know because once she tried to get away from a daddy longlegs by jumping onto the picnic table behind our house, but then she saw that there were *two* daddy longlegs on the table right next to her! She jumped off so fast that she ended up spraining her ankle.

I'm not like that. Bugs don't bother me. And I'm certainly not afraid of snakes unless they're poisonous. I was actually looking forward to seeing some of the interesting varieties I'd read about.

Somehow, though, I didn't think J.P. would be impressed if I put it that way. So I just said, "I'm not afraid of a few bugs and snakes. Are you?"

"No way." He threw me a challenging look. "But I don't think I believe you. If you're not afraid, then prove it. Come to the rain forest with us right now."

"I don't have to prove anything." I was starting to feel really annoyed at his attitude. I turned to Mrs. Herrera again. "Are you sure I can't help with anything?" I offered. "I can finish making tea or coffee if you like, so you can sit down and relax."

"Me too," Andy spoke up earnestly. "I don't mind staying here with Elizabeth and helping out." I rolled my eyes. I guess it was sweet of him to offer, but I wasn't really looking for an excuse to spend quality time with Andy.

Mrs. Herrera just laughed and patted me on the shoulder. "I told you, *macha*, everything is under control here. Run along with the others and have some fun. You too, Andy." (By the way, I asked Veronica later about what her mother had called me. Veronica explained that Ticos love to give people nicknames, especially descriptive ones. Mrs. Herrera had called me *macha*, which means "blond-haired girl." Earlier, during dinner, I had noticed that Mr. Herrera referred to Kate as *gata*, which Veronica said means "blue-eyed girl.")

"You heard her," J.P. put in. "Come have some fun. If you dare." He waggled his eyebrows at me.

I sighed. "Well, all right. Let's go."

I followed as Veronica and Jorge led the way through the back door. The moon was out, so it was pretty bright even though the sun had set. I hadn't been out that way yet, and I was surprised to see a big grove of palmlike trees stretching off behind the house. Veronica and Jorge explained that their family raised bananas on this piece of land, even though both her parents have office jobs. When I looked up at the tree I was passing, I recognized a clump of small greenish bananas growing way up at the top of the tall, skinny trunk just beneath the palmy leaves.

I didn't have much time to think about bananas, though. J.P. caught up to me and gave me a taunting smile as we all turned to follow Veronica and Jorge into the rain forest that stretched along the side of the banana trees. "Are you sure you're not scared, Bob?" So we were back to Bob again.

I rolled my eyes. Before I could say anything, there was a shriek from ahead. It was Jorge.

"Aaah! *Aaaahh-yiiiiiiiii!*" he yelled loudly.

"What?" we all cried. "Jorge, what's wrong?" We rushed to see.

He was on the path leading into the rain forest, his eyes wide and his trembling finger pointing to something just off the path. "Eeeee!" he cried. "Look—a snake! I think it may be poisonous!"

I saw the snake right away. It was small and greenish brown, and it was starting to slither off into the underbrush. In the strong moonlight I recognized it right away from my research. It was a small tree boa, less than a foot long. That's a pretty common type of snake in Costa Rica, and it's perfectly harmless at that size since boas kill their prey by squeezing rather than by venom. I guessed that Jorge knew that too and was just trying to play a trick on us. I was sure of it when I glanced quickly at Veronica and saw that she was holding a hand over her mouth to hide a grin.

I looked around to see if anyone else was in on the joke, but Kate and Andy were backing away, looking worried. J.P. was standing his ground, but his smile had faded a little, so I guessed that he was scared too—though I was sure he would never admit it. Guys can be really ridiculous about stuff like that.

Then I had an idea. I decided I would handle this Jessica style.

I jumped forward. "I'll save you, Jorge!" I cried, pretending to be terrified but brave. I shoved my way past him and quickly reached down toward the snake. "Get away, you monster! Leave us alone!"

Behind me I could hear a loud gasp from Kate. "Elizabeth, be careful!" she shrieked. I felt kind of bad about tricking her, but I couldn't stop now.

I leaped up suddenly and sort of fell back toward the group. (By now the snake had disappeared into the thick underbrush that surrounded the path. Poor thing, I'm sure it was terrified by all the noise.)

"Aaaah!" I screamed loudly. "Help! I've been bitten! I feel woozy. I think I—" With that I slumped down onto the ground and pretended to pass out.

"Oh, no!" Kate squealed. "What should we do?"

"Don't panic!" J.P. said worriedly. "We have to—"

"Psych!" I cried suddenly, opening my eyes and jumping to my feet. "Gotcha!"

Veronica and Jorge started laughing hysterically. "Good one, Elizabeth!" Jorge said.

Veronica was almost doubled over, she was laughing so hard. "You are funny, Elizabeth!" she cried. "That was majorly cool!"

By now the others were laughing too. "You really had me going," Andy told me, still looking a bit nervous as he glanced at the spot where the snake had been.

"Me too," Kate exclaimed breathlessly.

J.P. hadn't said anything yet. When I glanced at him, he was giving me an admiring look. "What do you know," he said, shaking his head. "A practical joker."

I smiled, feeling as though I had scored a point or two in his eyes.

Then I had to go and ruin it. "For future reference," I said, looking at the other Americans, "you should know that that was a small, common type of tree boa. They're not poisonous, and they're probably more scared of you than you are of them."

"Wow!" Kate's eyes were wide and admiring. "How did you know that, Elizabeth?"

I shrugged. "I did my homework before I came,"

I said. "I checked out all the poisonous kinds of snakes so I'd be sure to recognize them if I ran into one."

"I did that too," Andy admitted. I noticed that he was blushing a little. "But I sort of panicked and forgot when I actually saw the snake."

I smiled at him reassuringly. "That could happen to anyone."

"Almost anyone," J.P. put in. His voice sounded odd, so I turned to look at him. He wasn't laughing anymore. "You would never make a mistake like that, would you, Elizabeth? You're always prepared."

What? I glanced at the others, who all looked as surprised as I felt.

"Yeah, I'm prepared," I said defensively. "Do you have a problem with that?"

There was a tense second. Then J.P. laughed. "No problem," he said lightly. "I'm just jealous because you're queen of the snakes and I'm not." He bowed low, scraping his hands on the ground in front of me. "All hail Queen Bob!"

The others laughed. I guessed they were relieved because he had avoided starting a real argument. I forced myself to laugh a little too. But I didn't feel very amused. Right then and there, I decided that enough was enough. For the rest of the time Jorge and Veronica were showing us around—pointing out more wildlife, explaining which plants and things were poisonous, even taking us to peek at Gemelo, which was only about a ten-minute walk through the forest—I stuck close to Kate and Andy and avoided talking to J.P. at all.

I've decided I'm going to do that as much as possible from now on. I may have to work with J.P., but that doesn't mean we have to be friends, especially if he's so determined to make fun of me every chance he gets.

SUNDAY, 10:10 P.M.

I still can't believe what happened at lunchtime today. For most of this morning I thought things were going really smoothly. But it was just the calm before the storm.

As we started to work, a few of the kids complained about the heat, which was worse than usual today, but most of them worked really hard. J.P. was cracking jokes the whole time, of course, including quite a few at my expense. He had gotten tired of calling me Madame Foreman and had shortened it to Madame Bob.

I did my best to ignore him.

By the time we broke for lunch, I was feeling pretty good. We had gotten even more done than I'd hoped, and I estimated we would be finished with the framing by Thursday afternoon at the latest. I remember hoping that the supply truck would arrive soon, maybe even today, so we wouldn't lose any time.

The villagers had set up a long table in a shady

area behind the construction site, where we eat lunch each day as a group. A few of the villagers brought out our food and drinks and then left us to our meal. The food was delicious as always, and it was pleasant sitting there beneath the trees, listening to the monkeys chattering and the birds calling in the forest. I was sitting with Kate and Andy and Sumi and Will, talking about what we had to do that afternoon.

We had been eating for a while when Veronica wandered out of her house with her little sister, Eugenia. The two of them came over to say hi and see how we were doing. I told her how much we'd gotten done already, feeling proud of our hard work.

"Cool," Veronica said. "Why don't you reward yourselves and come hang out in the forest with us? There's lots more to see in the daytime."

"Sorry," I said, smiling at her eagerness. "We got a lot done, but there's a lot more to do. We have to keep working."

J.P. was sitting a few seats down, but I guess he'd been listening, because he leaned over. "Come on, Madame Bob," he called. "Don't be such a slave driver. Let's have some fun. After all, we're finished with the foundation."

I shot him an annoyed look. "Not quite," I reminded him.

He shrugged and looked around the table. The other kids on the crew were listening by now, and some of them were whispering to each other.

"Please, 'Lizabeta?" Eugenia pleaded. "We want have fun!" (She doesn't speak English quite as well as the older kids.)

"Please, 'Lizabeta?" J.P. grinned and imitated the little girl. He clasped his hands in front of him. "We worked hard all morning. Don't we deserve a break?"

"But if we keep working, we have a chance to get ahead of schedule," I pointed out.

"Is that supposed to convince us?" J.P. rolled his eyes. "And hey, don't the words *summer vacation* mean anything to you?" A few other kids mumbled agreement.

Andy jumped to my defense. "Come on, guys," he said. "Elizabeth's right. We should keep working. Maybe we can be finished with the framing by the time that supply truck gets here."

"But here in Costa Rica schedules are often late," Veronica spoke up. "The truck might not arrive for a week yet or even more. And why should you all waste an awesome day like today when it could start pouring dogs and cats tomorrow?"

J.P. pushed back his empty plate and stared at me with that challenging look in his eye. "Come on, boss lady," he taunted. "You heard Veronica, and she should know. She lives here. Now are you going to let us go? Or do we all have detention?"

I bit my lip, feeling trapped. Once I thought about it, I could see why they wanted to go explore.

Still, it was only our third day of work. We had a responsibility to do our job—that was why we had signed up for this trip. I had to forbid J.P. and the others to go. It was the right thing to do.

But I was scared. What would happen if I said no and they went anyway?

Sometimes being a leader stinks.

Before I could decide what to do, little Eugenia let out an excited squeal. "*Mira!*" she cried. "Big bird!" She was pointing to a huge, brightly colored parrot perched on the roof of a nearby building. I recognized it from my research as a scarlet macaw.

As we all turned to see, the bird let out a raucous caw and flew off, heading for the thick rain forest on the far side of the construction site. Eugenia was already running after it, with Veronica right behind her. Before I realized what was happening, most of the other kids had hopped up and were racing after them, shouting and laughing as they tried to catch up to the beautiful parrot. Even Kate got caught up in the excitement. Within seconds almost everyone had disappeared into the rain forest. Only Andy and I were left sitting at the table.

Andy stared after the others, looking shocked. "I can't believe they just ran off like that," he exclaimed. "They'd better come back so we can get back to work."

"I don't think we should hold our breath," I told him. I could already guess what was going to happen.

Once the other kids were out there in the rain forest having fun, they weren't going to want to return, especially if they believed they had earned some free time. And unless I missed my guess, J.P. would talk them all into believing exactly that. Hadn't he almost convinced me just now?

Andy was shaking his head. "Now I can see why Marion wanted you to be foreman," he said. "You're the only one here with a sense of responsibility."

For some reason Andy's words made me feel even worse. In fact, I felt like I might start crying. Not only had the other kids totally ignored me, but now they were all off having fun while I was stuck here—left out. Had I made a mistake by not letting them go in the first place?

The rest of the afternoon was miserable. Andy followed me around like a puppy dog, hanging on my every word and staring at me constantly. After a couple of hours I was ready to strangle him.

Not that he's not a really nice guy, of course. He's smart and well read, and he wouldn't be bad looking if he'd fix his hair and maybe get more attractive frames for his glasses. Actually, he'd be kind of cute. But there's no way I would ever be interested in him. Anyway, today I really wished he would leave me alone so I could feel sorry for myself in private. This had been my chance to be a cool foreman, and I had blown it.

The others got back right before it was time to head back to the main village for dinner. They came running into the clearing with J.P. in the lead just as Andy and I were putting away our tools. They all seemed breathless and happy. Even Loren was actually smiling.

"Yo! Bob!" J.P. cried when he spotted me. "We're back. Did you miss us?"

I scowled at him and didn't answer.

Andy stepped forward. "It wasn't very nice of you guys to run off like that," he said. "Elizabeth was being a responsible foreman, and it was really rude to ignore her."

Kate bit her lip guiltily. "Oh, no," she said. "I didn't think about that, Elizabeth. I'm sorry."

"I'm sorry, too, *macha*," Veronica said quickly, hurrying over and putting her arm around my shoulders. "We weren't trying to dis you. But you should have come with us. We had so much awesome fun!"

"Yeah," put in a girl named Anne. "Veronica showed us all sorts of cool stuff in the rain forest. We saw a river and waterfall . . ."

". . . and a lot of interesting birds and animals," Sumi said.

Kate nodded, her eyes shining. "I saw more parrots and some monkeys, and I even spotted a sloth hanging upside down way up high in a tree."

"It was cool," Loren added. Now I knew they'd had a great time. I'd never heard her say so many words at once.

They continued to describe their day, not seeming to notice that it was making me feel horrible. Obviously I had missed an amazing time. And for what? It wasn't as though Andy and I had gotten a ton of work done by ourselves. In fact, we hadn't been able to do much work at all without the others' help. That had given me plenty of time to feel sorry for myself and Andy plenty of time to stare at me. But it hadn't done much in the way of getting the community center built.

Oh, well. Who needs fun on their summer vacation anyway?

MONDAY, 9:35 P.M.

When I got to the site this morning, I prepared myself for more taunting remarks from J.P. about what happened yesterday. Kate and Veronica had spent all evening apologizing (whenever Veronica's parents and grandmother weren't listening, that is). But I was sure that J.P. wasn't feeling sorry about the adventure at all. He'd probably spent all night concocting more new and humiliating jokes at my expense.

But nobody even looked up as Kate and I arrived. Kate wandered off as I went to unlock the office shack, and soon she and Andy were arguing over some obscure species of plant they had spotted by the side of the house yesterday. Tiffany was giggling as Will and Ricky tried to speak Spanish.

Loren was listening as Ty talked about baseball. Sumi, Anne, and Bridget were chatting about school.

Only J.P. was being quiet. That was pretty unusual for him. And I quickly noticed that whenever he looked my way, a new expression came over his face. Not amusement, not mischievousness, not unfriendliness . . . I couldn't figure it out at first. It took me a while to recognize it.

It was pity.

As soon as it dawned on me I felt more horrible than ever. J.P. wasn't bothering to tease me anymore because he actually felt sorry for me. After all, I had proved I was a dork in front of everyone.

It was humiliating. And I wasn't sure how to react.

I kept trying to figure out a way to show J.P. that I wasn't the totally lame, boring person he thought I was. Then I kept trying to figure out why I cared what he thought. My thoughts went around and around, circling between those two points. And finally the truth dawned on me.

I didn't want J.P. to stop teasing me.

I definitely didn't want him to think I was a dork.

I . . . liked him.

As in *crushville*.

I tried to come up with another explanation, but there was none. How could I actually *like* him when he drives me *nuts*?

For the first time I understood how Jessica feels when she's trying to impress some jerk like Bruce Patman. Well, maybe not Bruce. He's way more obnoxious than J.P. could ever hope to be. Meaner and snobbier too. But you know what I mean.

Thinking of Jessica made me feel homesick. I guess maybe that sounds kind of babyish. But Jessica is always a really good person to talk to—especially about guy problems. She would probably know exactly what I should do about J.P.

So basically it's hopeless. I've finally discovered that I like J.P.—at the exact same moment he's decided I'm a loser. And we're stuck together for the next four weeks!

Five

I just read over what I wrote on Monday, and I guess I was feeling pretty down. But a lot can change in a day or two!

The thing with J.P. was bugging me all day yesterday. I didn't want his pity. I didn't want him to think I was a total loser.

It was all I could think about all day, and by evening it was driving me berserk!

I decided I had to talk to him. So after dinner I went next door to find him. He wasn't there, but Andy was. He told me J.P. had gone off to try to spot bats in the rain forest. Andy looked kind of disappointed that I had come over looking for J.P. and not for him, but I didn't have time to deal with that just then.

I went out into the forest. It didn't take me long to find J.P. because he was singing the theme song from that old TV show *Batman* at the top of his lungs. I could have told him that wasn't a very good way to spot wildlife, but I figured I'd better avoid saying anything that made me sound like an even bigger dork.

He looked surprised to see me. "Oh, hello, Elizabeth," he said. "Out here looking for your library card?"

I bit my lip. I couldn't believe it, but I actually missed hearing him call me Bob. "Ha-ha," I said weakly. "Actually, I was looking for you."

"What's up?" That pitying look was back.

"I think—," I began, but I didn't get any further because I heard someone calling my name. It was Andy. I pressed my lips together to keep from screaming with frustration as he raced over to us, breathless and red faced. He was running so fast, he tripped over a big tree root and almost went flying flat on his face. J.P. jumped forward just in time and caught him.

"Thanks," Andy gasped once he was upright again.

"No problem, man," J.P. replied. "Were you looking for our fearless leader? Here she is." He waved a hand in my direction.

I was annoyed at Andy. He knew I had come out here looking for J.P. So why was he butting in?

Andy didn't notice me glaring at him, though.

He was really worked up about something. "Listen, I just heard some big news," he exclaimed. "I—I—it—"

He was so overwrought that he was sort of sputtering, having trouble getting the words out. J.P. reached over and thumped him on the back.

"Spit it out, Andy!" he cried. "Before you choke."

Andy nodded, took a deep breath, and started speaking again more slowly. "One of the local kids just told me," he said. "He said the supply truck got to Gemelo this afternoon right after lunch."

I frowned, not understanding. What Andy was saying didn't make sense. "But that can't be true. Gemelo is only a quarter of a mile away," I said. "If the truck had been there then, it should have been to our village just a short while after that."

Andy was already waving his hands around. "I know," he said. "But listen, that's what I'm trying to tell you! The truck was going to come here next. But while it was in Gemelo, Tanya stole the gas cap and hid it!"

"What?" I gasped. "Why would she do that?"

But even as I said it, I already knew the answer. Tanya wanted to win that Outstanding Volunteer award at the end of the trip. She wanted it a *lot*. So she decided to deliberately delay the supply truck. If it was stuck in her village, our village wouldn't get our supplies on time. That would give her crew a big head start on their building and make her look like a great leader.

As I was thinking all that, Andy was saying approximately the same thing. He's pretty smart. He had figured it out right away too, even though he said none of the adults had any idea what had happened to the gas cap.

J.P. caught on quickly. His grin faded and was replaced with a grim expression. "Yeah," he said. "That sounds like Tanya."

"It's not fair." I was furious. We were supposed to be here to help these people, not to get into some big competition over winning the Outstanding Volunteer plaque.

My first instinct was to get in touch with Robert and Marion and tell them. But the thought of that made me uncomfortable for a couple of reasons. For one, some people (J.P. for instance) might think I'm kind of a goody-goody, but I've never been the kind of person who tells on others. Besides that, we really didn't have any proof about what Tanya had done. I had no trouble believing it, but an adult would probably want to give her the benefit of the doubt.

No, we had to take care of this ourselves. At first I considered going over to Gemelo and confronting Tanya. If I reminded her why we were really here, maybe she would see how selfish she was being and return the gas cap. I don't know, appealing to Tanya's softer side didn't seem *too* likely to work, but maybe it was worth a shot.

I was getting ready to tell the two guys that idea.

But suddenly out of nowhere another idea popped into my head. A daring idea. A sneaky idea.

Another very Jessica-like idea!

"Listen," I said casually. "I think we can handle this on our own."

"But shouldn't we tell someone?" Andy said anxiously. "If we don't get our supplies soon—"

"Don't worry about it," I interrupted. The idea was turning itself over and over in my mind. It would be risky, yes. But I could do it. The details were already coming into focus. "Have you told anyone else what you heard?"

Andy shook his head. "I came straight out to find you."

"Good." I glanced at J.P., who was staring at me curiously. "You'll keep quiet too, right?"

He shrugged. "Sure, no problem."

He didn't say anything more, but I could see that he was wondering what I was up to. I'm sure he figured I was planning to run straight to Robert and Marion. Boy, was he ever wrong.

I spent the next few hours planning my scheme. The only detail that worried me was finding another snake, especially in the dark. I borrowed a flashlight from Jorge, then hid out in my room, pretending to sleep, until the house fell silent.

I decided I might as well start looking in the same spot where Jorge had found the young tree boa. I snuck out of the house, tiptoed through the banana grove, and headed into the rain forest.

After a few minutes of shining the flashlight around in the underbrush, I spotted a small boa similar to the one we'd seen before. I got as close as I could before making my move—I didn't want to make a mistake and grab a poisonous viper! I managed to grab it, picking it up by the neck just behind the head as I'd seen people do on TV, though it did its best to wriggle out of my grasp and slither away.

"Sorry, little snake," I whispered. "I need your help." I tucked it into the pocket of the Windbreaker I was wearing and zipped the pocket shut. The snake wiggled around a bit, then seemed to accept its fate and settled down.

I grinned as I headed for the path to Gemelo, trying to imagine what Jessica would say if she could see me now. She hates snakes. She thinks they're gross and slimy, no matter how many times I tell her that their skin is actually smooth and sort of rubbery. She wouldn't touch a snake if someone paid her a million dollars. At least that's what she claims. Personally, I think if it came right down to it, she'd *kiss* a snake if someone paid her a million dollars to do it.

Not that I intended to kiss this particular snake. But I did have big plans for it.

I hurried along the path to Gemelo, listening to the night sounds all around me. I had read about how a lot of creatures in the rain forest are more active after dark, and that seemed to be true. It was amazing how many different calls, whistles, shrieks, croaks, and so on I heard during that ten-minute walk. It was kind of scary, actually, even though there was a bright full moon and I had my flashlight.

Still, I knew I wasn't in any real danger as long as I stayed on the trail, which was wide and easy to follow. The only big meat-eating animals in the Costa Rican forests are jaguars, and I'd read that they're afraid of humans and hardly ever seen near villages. And I knew how to recognize the most common poisonous snakes—ten-foot bushmasters, six-foot yellow beard vipers, and smaller, but still deadly eyelash vipers—so I could steer well clear of them. Not that they were likely to bite me through my jeans and heavy boots.

Soon I was at the outskirts of Gemelo. The tents where the student volunteers were sleeping were off to the right. I stuck my flashlight in the pocket that didn't have the snake in it and crept along just inside the screen of trees until I reached the camp. Now all I had to do was find Tanya's tent.

I got very lucky. All the tents had little name tags stuck to the front of them, and Tanya's tent was at the edge of the group, close to where I was standing. I spotted it right away.

I spent a few more minutes getting the lay of the land and figuring out my exact moves. The tent was about six feet long and four feet wide, with zippered entrances at the front and back. There were also a couple of windows, but they were zipped shut as well, so I couldn't see in. That meant I couldn't check to make sure Tanya was sleeping. But I figured that by this time of night, it was a pretty safe bet.

When I was sure I had figured out the best way to carry out my plan, I took a deep breath. My heart was beating fast. Was this really me, Elizabeth Wakefield, the responsible, smart, serious girl everyone knew? Was I really going to do something so sneaky, and risky, and crazy—without any prompting or pleading from Jessica at all? Usually she's the only one who can talk me into doing daring things.

But now, here I had gone and talked myself into it!

I decided not to put it off any longer or I would lose my nerve. I unzipped my jacket pocket and grabbed the snake. It seemed kind of annoyed—I think it must have gone to sleep in my nice, warm pocket while I was walking.

"Here goes nothing," I whispered to it. Then I crept forward as quietly as I could to the back of Tanya's tent.

Holding my breath, I unzipped the rear door a few inches. Then I crouched down and peered in.

It was dark in the tent, and it took my eyes a few seconds to adjust. I could hear the sound of deep breathing, but it took a moment before I was able to pick out the shadowy blob lying just a foot in front of me. It was Tanya, and she was obviously fast asleep. It was warm in the tent, and she had pushed the top part of her sleeping bag halfway down her body. *Perfect!* I thought.

Now that the moment was here, I wasn't nervous at all. I reached forward silently, the wriggling snake in my hand. Nudging the sleeping bag back a little farther to create an opening, I sort of tossed the boa as best I could into the warm, dark depths of the sleeping bag. I quickly scooted back and rezipped the tent door. Then I moved aside and held my breath, waiting.

I didn't have to wait long. After a few seconds I heard some shuffling sounds from the other side of the tent wall. That was quickly followed by an ear-shattering scream.

"Bingo," I whispered to myself, grinning.

A second later I heard Tanya scrabbling at the front of the tent, then quickly unzipping the door. At the same time, even over her continuing screams, came the sounds of people stirring in the surrounding tents.

"What's going on out there?" a male voice shouted from a nearby tent.

"Qué ruido!" someone cried from over toward the houses.

"Help! Help!" Tanya wailed at the top of her lungs.

I knew I had to act fast. Soon Tanya's piercing shrieks would have the entire village wide awake.

I unzipped the back of the tent just enough to scoot through. Whipping out my flashlight and covering it with my hand so it wouldn't show through the tent wall, I began my search. I figured I had five minutes at the most before Tanya returned with a snake-hunting posse.

There wasn't much in the tent. Just the sleeping bag, one large suitcase, and a small leather backpack. I decided to check the backpack first. I opened the main compartment and searched through the contents. The gas cap wasn't there, but something else was—a very familiar-looking white plastic bag.

I gasped and yanked it out to look inside. Sure enough, it was full of rock CDs and movie magazines. It was the going-away present from Jessica! I didn't stop to think much about it at that moment—just shoved it under my jacket and kept searching—but obviously Tanya must have overheard Jess and me at the airport, then later saw me sneaking back to leave the bag for the Canadian girls. And she decided to pick it up and keep it for herself.

But as I said, I didn't have much time to think about it then. I could still hear Tanya's screams somewhere in the distance, along with a growing number of other voices. I continued my search and soon found what I was looking for in one of the backpack's outside pockets. The gas cap was wrapped in some paper towels and shoved way down to the bottom. I stuck it in my jacket pocket and zipped it in safely.

Then I paused. I couldn't leave that poor, innocent little snake in the tent. Crawling toward the back entrance, I paused at the sleeping bag. I unzipped its whole length, but the small boa was nowhere to be seen.

I glanced around worriedly. Where had it gone? I started to search the corners of the tent, but just then the chorus of loud voices seemed to get louder—as if they were heading in my direction.

Uh-oh. Tanya's coming back with reinforcements, I thought. *Sorry, snake,* I added reluctantly. *You're on your own.* I hoped it had escaped through the open front or back flaps while I was searching. I quickly escaped out the back flap myself, zipping it behind me. Seconds later I was back in the rain forest, safely hidden from the people who were now streaming toward Tanya's tent. Tanya herself was in the lead, a grim expression on her face and her prissy lace-trimmed nightgown waving in the breeze.

I grinned. I'd done it! But I didn't stick around to gloat. I didn't want to risk being spotted. I hurried through the trees to the place where the main road entered the village. The supply truck was parked there, dark and silent. The gas tank was on the side closest to the forest, so I was able to quickly dart out and screw the gas cap back on without being seen. Once that was done, I hurried back to the trail and raced toward home, laughing to myself all the way.

About halfway here I realized something. I had known that my plan was necessary because it was the best way to ruin Tanya's evil plan. But now I saw that it had been more than that.

It had been fun! In fact, it was by far the most fun I'd had since the trip began. Maybe the most fun I'd had all year!

Hmmm. Did that mean Jessica had been right all these years? Something to think about. . . .

Anyway, it turned out that the snake hadn't escaped after all. Because Robert and Marion stopped by our village the next morning to talk to us.

They gathered us all in the main clearing again. "Something happened in Gemelo last night," Robert began abruptly, staring around at all of us. "Someone played a prank on Tanya, the team leader over there, and we want to know if anyone here had anything to do with it."

"What kind of prank?" J.P. called out.

Robert shot him a suspicious look and said nothing. But Marion spoke up. "Well, we're actually not completely sure it was a prank. But somehow a snake got into Tanya's tent even though she claims it was zipped closed. It found its way into her sleeping bag."

There was some laughter at that, as well as some horrified gasps. I guess people's reactions depended on how they felt about snakes—and about Tanya.

"It's not funny," Robert said sternly. "This could have been a very serious incident if she had been bitten."

"Luckily the snake wasn't poisonous," Marion added quickly and soothingly. "One of the village boys was among the people who helped her search for the snake, and he recognized it. It was just a small, common type of tree boa, quite shy and harmless. They released it back into the forest."

I was busy pretending to be as shocked about this whole story as everyone else. But out of the corner of my eye I noticed J.P. turn to look at me when Marion mentioned the kind of snake. He was giving me an odd look.

I grinned briefly in return, then turned away. I wondered if he had guessed my secret. He knew I had some kind of plan to get back at Tanya. And he knew I could tell the difference between a poisonous snake and an ordinary one.

I hadn't thought about it when I came up with my plan, but now I wondered. Would this help convince him I wasn't so dull after all?

Marion and Robert said a few more words about how we shouldn't think of this as a competition, how pranks can sometimes be mean or dangerous, etc. They also said that as soon as the gas cap was found, the supply truck would be on its way, so we should work hard so we would be ready.

I could hardly stop myself from smiling when they said that. I had a strong feeling the gas cap would be discovered very soon. And I could only imagine what everyone would say when they saw that it was right back on the truck where it belonged.

Elizabeth Wakefield, you are a genius!

Six

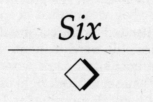

Earlier today I had a great idea about what to do with the bag of stuff I'd taken back from Tanya. When I grabbed it, I just sort of thought that she shouldn't have it because it wasn't hers. But I still didn't want it either.

Then I realized who would really appreciate it. Veronica! I knew it wasn't easy for her to get the kind of stuff that was in that bag, and I was sure she would love it.

I didn't want anyone else to see me give it to her, though. For one thing, I didn't want anyone to think I had ignored instructions and brought the stuff with me. More important, if Tanya had shown it to anyone (which I seriously doubted, but you never know), I would be busted.

So I waited for a chance to talk to Veronica alone. Everyone was around at breakfast, and it was Veronica's turn to help her parents clean up afterward, so I couldn't say anything then. I made sure the plastic bag was stuffed deep down in my suitcase, then headed for the construction site.

The supplies still weren't there, of course, but we still had almost a full day's work to do on the framing. So we all set to work right after breakfast.

We worked hard all morning, and I was feeling pretty good about it. Somehow my sneaky trick on Tanya had made me feel more confident about being foreman, even though nobody else knew about it. Well, except maybe J.P. He still didn't say much to me, but that pitying look was gone, and he kept glancing at me curiously when he thought I wasn't looking.

We broke for lunch and then got back to work. Veronica wandered by a little while later to say hi. Seeing my chance, I pulled her aside and quickly whispered that I had a surprise for her after work.

"You must spill your guts immediately, Elizabeth," she squealed. "Otherwise I will die! I will totally die!"

"Ssh!" I hushed her, looking around nervously. If she kept this up, someone would hear. "I can't tell you in front of everyone. It's a secret."

That only made things worse. "Ooh! I love secrets!" Veronica exclaimed. "Please, please, please tell me now, OK? We can sneak into the forest where nobody will hear."

I should have known she'd react that way. After all, she reminds me so much of Jessica—and since when could Jess ever wait even two seconds to hear a juicy secret? I was about to insist that we wait until my crew finished for the day. That would only be a few hours from now, and I didn't think it would be right to leave even for a few minutes. There were more than enough people to finish the framing, but the supply truck might arrive at any time.

Then I stopped to think about that. Who knew how long it would take someone to notice that the gas cap had been returned? Besides, after all the rains and flooding, a lot of the roads around here were in pretty bad shape. It might still take a long time for the truck to get here, and then I would have stayed for nothing.

I didn't want to miss any more chances for fun. Not after what had happened the other day. After all, why should I feel guilty about leaving my crew for a few minutes? Hadn't they all run off without a second thought for me just a few days earlier? I deserved some time off too. They owed it to me. Didn't they?

I was a little bit uncomfortable with that line of thought. It sounded kind of selfish. But hadn't it been selfish of them to ignore me and run off chasing a parrot all afternoon?

I had to stop worrying about it. *Go for it, Lizzie!* I told myself, just like Jessica would do. Then I grinned at Veronica. "Go distract everyone for a second," I whispered. "I'll sneak away and meet you in the banana grove in ten minutes."

Veronica giggled with delight. Then she winked and strolled away.

I continued to work. A moment later I heard Veronica shriek loudly from the other side of the site. "Ow!" she cried. "Somebody help me. I think I stepped on a nail!"

For a second I nearly threw down my tools and rushed to help her. Then I realized that this was her distraction. So while everyone else hurried toward Veronica, I hurried in the opposite direction— toward the Herreras' house.

I knew Mr. and Mrs. Herrera were working today, and the little kids and their grandmother were spending the day with some friends in Gemelo. So I didn't have to be quiet as I rushed inside and grabbed the white plastic bag out of my suitcase.

I hurried to the meeting spot and waited for Veronica to show up. When she arrived, laughing breathlessly, we raced away into the forest.

"Follow me, *macha*," Veronica said. "I know the most awesome place to go."

Ten minutes later we emerged in a beautiful little clearing. "Oh, Veronica!" I exclaimed. "It really *is* awesome!" I looked around at the mossy, shaded ground, the rapidly tumbling stream that cut the clearing in half, and the tropical birds flitting around the edges of the clearing in the tall trees of the rain forest canopy. It was positively gorgeous.

She grinned. "Jorge and I come here often with our friends," she explained, sitting down cross-legged on the bank of the stream. She pointed at the water. "We call this stream Río Risa, which means 'river of laughter,' because the water sounds like it's always giggling. It joins up with a large river just a short distance away."

"It's wonderful," I told her. "I'm so glad you brought me here. And now . . ." I reached for the bag.

Needless to say, Veronica loved my gift. She was practically in heaven as she pulled out each CD and magazine. Her family doesn't have a CD player, but her neighbors (the ones J.P. and Andy are staying with) have one, and there's also that portable one in the office shack, which she's sure Marion will let her borrow sometime. I made her promise not to show her new things to anyone— not even Jorge—until after the five weeks were up. I didn't want anyone to find out I stole them from Tanya, even if they had been mine to begin with.

Anyway, I guess after that I kind of forgot about going back to work. Veronica and I were having so much fun, talking and laughing and getting to know each other better.

I was telling Veronica all about one of Jessica's crazy ideas when a loud voice interrupted me: "So this is where you've been hiding out all day!"

I whirled around with a gasp, fearing that Robert and Marion had somehow discovered I was missing and tracked me down. But it wasn't them. It was J.P. And he was grinning.

Suddenly feeling nervous, I stared back at him. He looked incredibly cute in his cargo shorts and pocket T-shirt. For about the millionth time I wondered what he really thought of me.

I gulped. "Uh, we were just heading back to the village," I said quickly.

But Veronica and Jessica turned out to have even more in common than I thought. Not only did Veronica somehow sense what was going on, but she decided to do something about it. "Don't worry about walking me back, *macha*," she said. "I must go now anyway to help Mamá prepare dinner. You might as well stay here with J.P."

Before I could respond, Veronica tossed me a quick wink, then took off at top speed. A second later she had disappeared into the forest.

I grinned weakly at J.P., shifting my weight from foot to foot and feeling more nervous than ever now that we were alone. But I was also feeling something else. I guess you'd call it anticipation. This was it—it was my chance to find out how things stood between us. If there was anything between us at all.

J.P. spoke first. "So, Bob," he said casually. "I was just thinking about that snake they found in

Tanya's tent night before last. I wonder who could have put it there?"

I couldn't help it—my heart gave a little involuntary leap when he called me Bob. And it was obvious that he'd figured out I'd been responsible for Tanya's snake. I gave what I hoped was a casual shrug. "Who knows?" I said, trying to imitate the coy tone of voice Jess uses when she's teasing a guy she likes. I wasn't about to give him the satisfaction of being right too quickly. "I have no idea how it could have gotten there."

"Hmmm." J.P. stroked his chin thoughtfully. "Are you sure you don't know anything about it?" He took a step or two closer until he was standing just a couple of feet away. He raised one eyebrow and wriggled it quizzically.

He looked so silly that I couldn't help giggling. "Nope," I replied. I had to tilt my head back a little to look him in the face since he was a few inches taller than me. "I have no idea. Maybe it just slithered in there by itself." I giggled again. "It could have used its tail to unzip the door."

J.P. laughed. "Maybe," he agreed. "Or maybe somebody here is keeping secrets."

"Maybe," I said mysteriously. "So what are we going to do about it?" I don't mind saying I was feeling pretty pleased with myself. *So this is what flirting is all about!* I thought. Whenever I'd tried to flirt with a guy I liked in the past, like Todd, I'd usually ended up feeling pretty stupid and awkward. But this was different. This was fun!

"Well, I could ask my witness," J.P. said.

For a split second I started to panic. Had someone seen me that night?

Then I saw that he was pointing to the front pocket of his T-shirt. Now that I looked closer, I saw a bulge there. "I found the accomplice behind the banana grove this morning," he said. "Now are you going to tell me what happened, or do I have to ask the little guy here?" He patted the bulge gently.

"You can't trick me that easily," I retorted. "I know you don't speak Snake."

"Curses. Foiled again." J.P. pretended to think hard for a second, putting a finger to his chin and frowning. "Well, then," he said at last. "As I see it, there's just one solution. We'll have to play truth or dare." He gave me one of his challenging grins. "If you dare, that is."

"I dare," I said quickly. "You can even go first if you want."

"Good." He put his hands on his hips. "Elizabeth Bob Wakefield, truth or dare?"

For a second I was tempted to say dare, just to see what he would come up with for me to do. But I changed my mind. I was feeling bolder but not quite that brave. "Truth," I said firmly.

"OK." He grinned. "Here's your question. Did you put that snake in Tanya's tent night before last?"

Rules are rules, right? I knew I had to answer truthfully. "Yes," I said. "I did."

"Aha!" he crowed. "I knew it. So why did you do it? Simple revenge?"

I was trying to figure out how to answer. But just then I noticed movement in J.P.'s shirt pocket. A second later the snake inside stuck its head out into the air, flicked its tongue once or twice, and started to slither up toward his shoulder.

My heart stopped. I swear it did. Because it wasn't another tree boa—it was an eyelash viper. And it was poisonous!

Later, once I thought about it, I saw how he could have made that mistake, especially if he'd found the snake near the same spot where we'd seen the other one. It was about the same size as the young boa, and the coloring was sort of similar, though the viper had a faint diamond pattern on its back. But it also had one very important distinguishing feature that helped me recognize it so fast—a sort of visor-shaped thing over its eyes, which is what gave it its name.

I was horrified when I saw that snake crawling out of J.P.'s pocket. I knew from my research that several people die each year in Costa Rica from being bitten by eyelash vipers. He was incredibly lucky that it hadn't bitten him when he picked it up! But now it was winding its way straight toward J.P.'s face. . . .

"Hold still!" I shouted. At the same time I

leaped forward and knocked the snake off to the side, sending it flying onto the ground a few feet away. It lay there stunned for a second before slithering off into the underbrush.

J.P. looked a bit stunned too. "Hey, what did you do that for, Bob?" he demanded, sounding indignant. "I was going to keep him as a pet while we're here."

Now that it was over, I felt a bit woozy. I collapsed onto a nearby fallen log (after checking to make sure there were no snakes on it). I knew we had both been lucky. That snake could have bitten J.P. through his shirt before I ever saw it, and it could have bitten me on the hand when I knocked it off. I didn't like to think about what might have happened next.

J.P. was still staring at me, waiting for an explanation.

"That—that wasn't the same kind of snake," I explained shakily. "It wasn't a boa at all. It was a viper—a poisonous one. Really poisonous."

J.P.'s face turned pale. "You're not kidding me, are you?" he asked softly.

I shook my head. And I guess he could tell from my face that I meant it because he plopped down on the log next to me.

"Wow," he said flatly. "Wow." I could tell he was realizing just how close he had come to getting bitten.

He turned and gave me a serious look. I was still

feeling shaky, but I also couldn't help noticing how close together we were sitting. When he faced me, I was looking straight into his hazel eyes.

"Thanks, Elizabeth," he said. "That was a close one. From now on I'm not going to touch anything else in this place without checking with you first."

I smiled weakly. "Good."

He smiled back. "In fact, I'm going to stick to you like glue from now on. You don't mind, do you?"

"No."

That was all I could say. Because my heart had stopped again. This time it was because his face was moving closer. Then closer still. His eyes were locked on mine. I felt myself leaning forward a little bit in response to the look he was giving me. Was he going to kiss me? His gaze was pulling me toward him like a magnet. Closer . . . closer . . .

I closed my eyes, anticipating fireworks, but instead I got—shouts. Faint shouts coming from the direction of the village.

We pulled apart at the same time. "What was that?" I asked, but I was thinking, *Drat, drat, drat!* Just like that—our romantic moment was ruined. The Kiss That Never Was.

He shook his head. "Sounds like something big," he commented with a little frown.

But now that we had pulled apart, my senses were coming back to me. Maybe someone had noticed we were missing. Maybe they were heading this way, searching for us. I didn't want anyone to catch us like this.

"Come on," I said reluctantly. "I guess we should see what's going on."

He nodded and climbed to his feet, reaching down a hand to help me up. He stepped aside to let me go down the path first, putting one hand on my back to guide me along. Then he dropped his hand again, and we walked along almost as if nothing had happened. Which it hadn't, not really.

But I knew something *had* happened. Something special. I wasn't sure I understood it, but maybe that didn't matter. I did my best not to let my grin of pure happiness break out into laughter as we walked toward the village. Now I was really glad I had gone off with Veronica earlier. I was even glad J.P. had grabbed the wrong snake. Otherwise this wonderful moment might never have happened!

We got our first glimpse of the construction site through a thick screen of tree branches and hibiscus bushes. Even so, we saw right away what was going on. The supply truck had arrived. When I saw it, I felt like kicking myself. If only I'd let Tanya keep the stupid gas cap, J.P. and I could have hung out in that clearing all afternoon!

That gave me an idea. Another very wicked, Jessica-like idea. Once upon a time I would have ignored it. But since starting this trip, I've realized that those wicked, Jessica-like ideas can sometimes be the very best ideas of all.

"Come on." I grabbed J.P.'s hand and dragged him back farther into the trees before anyone spotted us.

He looked surprised. I noticed he didn't drop my hand, though. "What is it?"

I grinned. "Nobody knows where we are, right? And there are plenty of people around to unload the supplies from the truck."

"Yeah." J.P.'s eyes were already starting to sparkle. "So?"

I shrugged. "It's going to be dinnertime soon. We won't be able to start doing any serious building today. So what's our hurry to get back?"

"I'm in no hurry," he said smiling down at me. "Besides, I still have a few things to ask you about your trip to Tanya's tent. We'd better go discuss it back in that clearing."

I quickly turned and headed back. I knew he was just joking around, but I didn't want him to ask me again about why I had planted the snake. I wasn't sure how I should answer that question.

Somehow I didn't think J.P. would approve of the main reason, which was to get the gas cap back so we could get started on our building. He might think I was being competitive, like Tanya herself, instead of fun loving and daring. And I liked having him think I was fun loving and daring. Actually, I was feeling pretty fun loving and daring just then. Anyway, I didn't want to actually lie to J.P., but I figured that if we never got around to discussing my little trip to Tanya's village again, there would never be any reason to share the whole truth.

"I'm right behind you, Elizabeth," he said.

I smiled. *What a bonus*, I thought. *Not only is this turning out to be the most wonderful afternoon of my life—but J.P. has finally stopped calling me Bob!*

Seven

When we got to the site this morning, we found that the local builder had shown up. His name is José and he can't be much more than sixteen or seventeen years old. And he's absolutely gorgeous. At least that's what Veronica says. As soon as she laid eyes on him, she was head over heels in love. She's been hanging around the site all morning, helping with the work. Especially any work that José happens to be involved in.

Actually, Veronica kept trying to get me to come help her flirt with José. But I wasn't much help. José is so serious that he didn't seem to notice us at all except as part of his group of workers. He just kept ordering us to do different tasks, hardly giving us a second to take a breath let alone try to flirt with him or even talk to each other.

While I was busy counting nails and sawing two-by-fours, I kept thinking that there had to be a way to make this more fun. I knew I had started out wanting to work as hard as I could, but that just didn't seem to be enough anymore. Whenever I glanced over at J.P., I saw him working away diligently. I guess it was because he'd had so much fun hanging yesterday (he never did kiss me, by the way, but we still had a great time), so now he could throw himself into his tasks with extra energy. It was sort of like the way the others had settled down to work after taking that day off last Sunday.

But that enthusiasm would be sure to fade quickly if we didn't get to have more fun than José was letting us have at the moment. I was the foreman. It was up to me to do something about the situation. But what?

I couldn't help thinking about Jessica. She always managed to find time for fun. How did she do it?

Suddenly I knew the answer. Jessica didn't just find time for fun—she *made* time. And that gave me a great idea.

I pulled Veronica aside and told her I had a plan. Her eyes lit up when I told her what it was, and she promised to help.

"What an awesome idea, Elizabeth," she said. "You're brilliant!"

I was feeling pretty brilliant too. And I was sure Jessica would be totally proud of me if she were here.

SATURDAY, 12:30 A.M.

Well, Diary, my plan is in action. Veronica, Kate, and I stayed in all evening and were awake half the night making our flyers, but it will all be worth it Monday night!

The flyers look really cool. They say Rain Forest Rave: Be There or Be Square! in English and Spanish. Then they have the time and place to meet. We're having the rave at a larger clearing just past the one with the little stream. Veronica suggested the place; she said it would be perfect. It's right off the main path, and she says that everyone knows where it is.

It was thinking about Jessica that inspired the idea for the rave. She loves to dance more than anything, and then of course there were those CDs she gave me. . . . It was sort of a natural, really. I figured, what could be more fun than a big, cool dance in the rain forest? OK, I know it's kind of bringing American culture here, which we weren't supposed to do. But after seeing how much Veronica loves American music, I figured the local kids would be into it. (And I'll admit it—the thought of possibly slow dancing with J.P. in a moonlit clearing made the idea seem even better!)

I was a little doubtful when Veronica said she wanted to invite José. He seemed kind of serious, and I was afraid he might give away our secret to the adults. But I just couldn't say no when she has such a huge crush on him. He didn't say much after we gave him the flyer, just sort of read it and nodded. I'm keeping my fingers crossed, and so is Veronica (for a different reason!).

MONDAY, 11:59 P.M.

Veronica, Jorge, Kate, and I slipped out of the house right after dinner and raced to the clearing. A few other helpers were already waiting for us there, including J.P. and Andy. We got things set up with the portable CD boom box we borrowed from the office shack and some tall torches Veronica found somewhere. I was a little nervous about the fire, but then Jorge pointed out that the vegetation is so wet right now that it's not a big danger. Plus we stuck them in the ground well away from any trees.

I was glad they talked me into it because the torches looked amazing. The firelight really made the clearing look cool. Plus it would have been hard to dance in the dark.

Finally everything was perfect. A folding table at the edge of the clearing groaned under the weight of sodas and snacks. The boom box sat on a smaller table with a stack of CDs beside it. The torches flickered and danced around the edges of the "dance floor," which was really just a wide, flat, grassy area of the clearing.

"It looks fantastic," J.P. declared. He let out a whoop. "Let's party!"

I laughed excitedly. His spirit was catching. "Hey, Veronica, why don't you do the honors?" I pointed at the boom box.

Veronica grinned. "Definitely." She stepped over to the table and popped in a disc. Within seconds loud music replaced the sounds of the rain forest. The pounding beat seemed to bounce off the trees and echo back from the canopy.

"Yeeee-ha!" J.P. crowed. He started dancing all by himself, and that was all it took. Soon the rest of us were dancing too.

I hardly noticed when the other kids started to show up. As the circle of sky visible above the clearing grew darker and darker, until the twinkling stars shone almost as brightly as the glowing torches, the clearing magically became more and more crowded. By the time I sat down on a fallen log to catch my breath and look around, there must have been twenty or thirty people packed into the clearing.

J.P. sat down next to me, breathing hard from his enthusiastic dancing. "Whew!" he exclaimed. "This is great. Looks like your idea was a huge success!"

"Thanks. I'm glad everyone is having fun." I scanned the crowds of happy kids, both Americans and Ticos. Suddenly my jaw dropped. "Call me crazy—," I began.

"You're crazy," J.P. said promptly.

I rolled my eyes and continued. "—but isn't that Andy dancing with Kate over there?"

J.P. looked where I was pointing. He grinned. "What do you know."

I could hardly believe my eyes. There was a fast song playing, but Kate and Andy had their hands locked together and were swaying gently to a slow beat that only they seemed to hear. They were gazing into each other's eyes and smiling. Come to think of it, Andy hadn't been staring at me all the time lately, and now I knew why!

"I never would have guessed that they liked each other," I commented. "I mean, Kate is so pretty and bubbly and sort of lighthearted, and Andy is so serious and shy."

J.P. shrugged. "You know what they say," he said, scooting a little closer to me on the log. "Opposites attract."

I smiled up at him shyly, wondering if he was going to kiss me. But at that moment Veronica rushed over to where we were sitting. She looked cuter than ever in the light from the torches, which picked up highlights in her dark hair and made her deep brown eyes sparkle. "Elizabeth!" she cried excitedly. "Guess who just got here?"

I turned to look at the path leading back toward the village. José was standing there, looking awkward and serious compared to the giddy dancers just a few yards away.

I winked at Veronica. "It looks like he needs someone to talk to," I commented.

"Definitely," J.P. put in. "You can't let your guest be a wallflower, Veronica."

Veronica giggled. "I'm on my way." She dashed off in José's direction, and seconds later she had him by the arm and was dragging him toward the dance floor, chattering nonstop the whole time.

"Come on," J.P. said, hopping to his feet and stretching down one hand to help me up. "I love this song. Let's boogie!"

I laughed and let him pull me toward the dance floor. We found a spot near the edge of the crowd, under the branches of a large, low-growing palm tree. For the next three or four songs we danced nonstop.

Then a slow, romantic song came on. I suspected Veronica had something to do with it; it was a ballad from one of her CDs that I knew was one of her favorites.

J.P. grabbed both my hands and pulled me close so he could wrap his arms around me. I put my arms around his waist and rested my head on his shoulder. It was wonderful. But about halfway through the song, it got even better. He tugged gently on my hair. I looked up, wondering if something was wrong. But as soon as we were face-to-face, he kissed me! It took me by surprise, but in the best possible way. As I kissed him back I could hardly believe it was happening—the incredible kiss, a dreamy ballad blasting from the CD player, the flickering torches, the lush rain forest surrounding us. . . . I couldn't imagine anything more romantic if I tried.

J.P. and I were so busy kissing that I didn't notice Tanya come up to us.

I saw her arrive a little earlier. She came along with some of the other kids from Gemelo, but she seemed determined not to have fun. She kept making snide little comments about how wrong it was to import American culture. What a hypocrite!

Now she came up beside J.P. and me and cleared her throat really loudly. "Glad to see you two are having fun," she said sarcastically.

J.P. pulled away from me and gave her an annoyed look. "Oh, hi, Tanya," he said. "I'm surprised you recognize fun when you see it. You must have learned something on this trip after all."

I was wishing she would go away and leave us alone so J.P. and I could get back to what we were doing. But she seemed to have no intention of leaving anytime soon. She was standing with her arms folded and one foot tapping impatiently.

"What do you want, Tanya?" I asked, feeling pretty impatient myself.

"I want to talk to you, Elizabeth," she replied

evenly. "I have something important to say."

Somehow as soon as she said that I knew exactly what she wanted to talk about: She had figured out my little prank from the other night. I gulped. I should have known she would recognize the CDs we were playing and figure it out.

I realized that I couldn't let J.P. know the truth. Everyone thought Tanya had returned the gas cap on her own. If he found out I took it, he might guess that was the whole reason I snuck over there. Then he would go back to thinking all I care about is working hard and winning the contest. And he might stop liking me, which I definitely didn't want to happen.

I gave J.P. what I hoped was a flirtatious look. "Hey, J.P.," I said. "Uh—all that dancing made me really thirsty. Would you mind getting me a soda while I talk to Tanya for a second?"

He tried to argue, talking about the romantic moment and the great song and some other stuff. I don't really remember his exact words because the whole time I had the uncomfortable feeling that he was saying it all to make Tanya jealous.

Eventually he left, though, and Tanya and I were alone under the palm fronds.

Tanya was furious. She'd hidden it when J.P. was there, but now she really let it out. At first her words were so jumbled and angry that I had trouble following them. But I soon realized that she had guessed the truth.

"I know you put that snake in my tent," she spat out finally. "And I know you stole the gas cap and those CDs."

My heart was pounding nervously. For the first time I realized how bad it sounded when you said it straight out like that.

Then I remembered that the situation wasn't that simple. Tanya had stolen that gas cap herself; I was just returning it to where it belonged. And the CDs and magazines had been mine to begin with.

I reminded her of those things, managing to sound a lot calmer than I felt.

"I know all that," Tanya snapped, her eyes still flashing fire. "I'm not an idiot. I know I can't squeal even if I wanted to." Tanya glanced around to make sure no one was listening. Then she leaned a little closer. "I just want you to know that I know," she said in a low, nasty voice. "And I want you to know that I'm going to get back at you for what you've done. Somehow."

Before I could say another word, she stalked away and disappeared into the crowd. I bit my lip and stared after her, wondering what she had in mind. What could she do to me? She wouldn't dare risk getting in trouble and losing that Outstanding Volunteer award.

She's probably just trying to scare me, I told myself, hoping it was true. A second later J.P. reappeared and reported that the sodas were gone, and I had to pretend that everything was fine while we figured out what to do about getting more refreshments.

I managed to forget about Tanya's threat—mostly anyway—and have fun for the rest of the evening. We would probably still be out there dancing if Mr. Herrera and a few of the other adults from the village hadn't come to break it up. I guess we hadn't kept the secret as well as we'd thought. They were very cool about it, though—Mr. Herrera even asked Kate and me to dance with him for the last song. It was a fast one, and the three of us joined hands and skipped around in a circle. It was silly but fun. Halfway through, Veronica and Jorge came running over and pushed their way into the circle, and then J.P. and Andy and a few other kids from our village joined us too. Before long half the people in the clearing were holding hands and dancing around together. It was a perfect way to end the night.

Well, almost end it, that is.

After the last dance the adults shooed most of the kids home. Soon only Veronica, Jorge, Andy, Kate, J.P., and I were left. With the help of Mr. Herrera and the other adults, we set about cleaning up the clearing. Veronica had already spirited the CDs into a bag she had brought with her and was now packing away the leftover food. Andy and Kate were working together to extinguish and gather the torches. Jorge and his father were folding up the refreshments table.

I looked around for something to do. Noticing the

boom box, I walked over and grabbed it. "I'm going to return this to the office shack," I said. "I can take the table back there too, if someone will help me."

I had someone in particular in mind, and luckily he's pretty quick to take a hint. "I've got it," J.P. said. He grabbed the table and folded down the legs. "Let's go."

"I think everything's under control here," Mr. Herrera called to us as we left the clearing. "So we'll just meet you two back at the village."

"Right," Veronica called out in a singsong voice. "Don't be long, you two!"

I blushed, but I didn't really mind her teasing. J.P. grinned at me and winked.

The two of us didn't talk much as we headed through the forest toward the village. But it still felt really romantic as we strolled along after such an incredible evening.

When we got to the office shack, I unlocked the door and we both went inside. J.P. set the CD player on the desk, then turned to face me.

I felt my heart start to beat faster as he looked at me, then took a step closer. I thought he was going to kiss me, but instead he spoke. "You're really something special, Elizabeth," he said softly.

"You are too," I replied.

"I can't believe I didn't even know you two weeks ago." J.P. shook his head.

"J.P.," I said hesitantly. "There's something I want to ask you. It's about Tanya."

"Tanya?" he repeated. "What about her?"

I felt like kicking myself for bringing it up, but it was too late. Besides, if Tanya was going to hold a grudge against me, I had to know why. And it would have been obvious that there was some history between her and J.P. even if Kate hadn't told me.

"Kate told me that the two of you used to go out. But it seems like there's still some angry feelings between the two of you. Do you think she's mad at me because of you?"

J.P. nodded thoughtfully. "It's possible," he admitted. He didn't look angry or annoyed that I had brought up Tanya's name. Just sort of sad. "When I first got to know her, I thought Tanya was really cool," he said. "But she started to change. She was always talking about school and grades and boring stuff like that. She never wanted to just kick back and have fun anymore."

"Oh." I felt a little weird, hearing that. I couldn't help remembering how J.P. had acted when he thought I was just a serious, boring goody-goody.

"That wasn't really why we broke up, though," he went on. Now he did look kind of angry. "It was something she did. Last year in art class I built a scale model of a city—I worked on it for two months. It was no bigger than a chessboard. My art teacher talked me into entering it in our school's fine arts fair."

I remembered that Kate had mentioned something

about J.P.'s award-winning project. "You won, didn't you?"

"Yes—no thanks to Tanya." J.P. shook his head grimly. "The night before the contest she came to my house to hang out. We had been sitting on the porch, and Tanya excused herself to go to the bathroom. I decided that I wanted to show the city to her—she had seen me working on it but hadn't seen it finished yet. When I went to get the city, which was locked away in my dad's study so nobody would touch it—I got there just in time to see her holding my cat above it." He paused and glanced at me. "She was going to drop the cat on the city. The project would have been ruined, and I never would have known she'd done it. Boots would have taken all the blame."

I gasped. I had already guessed that Tanya was competitive. But now I realized it went beyond that—she was downright ruthless. "Why would she do that?" I cried.

"Isn't it obvious? She wanted to win that fair herself." He shrugged. "But never mind Tanya." He moved closer and took my hands in his own. "I don't want to think about her. Not when I'm standing here with you."

He kissed me softly. But just then we heard voices coming and realized we'd better go before we got caught.

It was just as well. My mind was swirling with what he'd told me. If Tanya would do something so sneaky to her own boyfriend, what would she do to me?

But that wasn't all I was worried about. I kept thinking about J.P. and me. Why did he like me anyway? Was I really the fun-loving girl he thought I was—the kind of girl who organizes a rave in the rain forest? Or was I the kind of person he thought I was after Marion's little speech about me—a dull overachiever who only cares about grades and being the best? I thought the second description was closer to the truth—at least it had been until recently.

But maybe I'm changing now. Maybe this trip is helping me to become a different kind of person. And maybe that's a good thing. I'm starting to think I was so serious before that I never really let myself open up to a guy, not even Todd Wilkins. Now that I've met J.P., I finally know what I was missing.

After all, what good are brains and good grades and achievements without heart and soul and *fun*?

Eight

◇

It was kind of anticlimactic slogging along on our construction job after the excitement of the Rain Forest Rave. Robert and Marion stopped by late in the morning. They'd heard about the rave from some kids in Gemelo. I wouldn't be surprised if Tanya had something to do with that. Robert gave us a long, disapproving lecture. He said we're supposed to be here working, not partying.

At the end he turned to look at me. For a second I was afraid he was going to punish me for being the one who planned the rave. But I guess he didn't know it was me. He just told me I need to keep a closer eye on things so this doesn't happen again. That struck me as incredibly funny, and I had a hard time holding back my giggles until after he and Marion drove off. I wasn't the only one. As soon as the two adults were gone all the kids started laughing.

Then we got back to work. Everyone was kind of sleepy after our late night, but we did our best. A little while after Robert and Marion left, José turned up to see how we were doing. He told us the support beams and exterior walls should all be up by the day after tomorrow. Then he said he'd be back in a couple of days to check on us. Veronica had just showed up to help (she slept in this morning—lucky her!) and looked really disappointed that he was leaving.

Nothing much happened for the next couple of hours. We stopped for lunch, then got back to work on the support beams as José had instructed.

I realized I needed to bring out a bunch of tools from the office shack, so I asked J.P. to help me get them. We went inside and started grabbing the stuff we needed.

That was when I saw them. Along with the boards and sheets of metal and other junk piled on one side of the office shack, there was a huge pile of old tires—the kind that float—inner tubes. Suddenly a little lightbulb went on in my mind.

"Hey, J.P.," I said casually. "I just had a truly fabulous idea."

He turned, saw me staring at the inner tubes, and immediately guessed what I had in mind.

"You're not thinking about blowing off work this afternoon to go tubing, are you?" he said.

"Why not?" I was a little surprised that he sounded so hesitant. "We're all so tired from the rave that we probably won't get much done anyway. And this way we'll be happy and well rested so we can get back to work fresh and eager tomorrow."

The reasons just popped out, as if someone else had thought of them for me. It all seemed to make such perfect sense that I was amazed J.P. couldn't see it too.

He still looked a little bit worried. "Yeah, but José said . . ."

I did my best to copy that little pout Jessica always uses when a guy isn't doing what she wants him to do. "Hey, if you want to hang out with José, be my guest," I teased. "But if you want to hang out with me . . ."

"OK, OK," he said with a laugh. "You're the boss, right?"

He still didn't seem totally enthusiastic. But that wore off pretty quickly once we gathered the rest of the gang and headed for the river. Veronica and Jorge showed us a fantastic stretch of river for tubing. We spent the entire afternoon floating along, having splash fights, dunking each other, and generally having a great time.

Between all that exercise and our lack of sleep, we were all pretty worn out by dinnertime. I almost fell asleep in my soup. But it was worth it. The adults didn't suspect a thing—they think we spent the day at the building site.

And we still have all day tomorrow to make up the work we missed. It shouldn't be a problem—it will be sort of like the way Jessica always leaves all her weekend homework until nine o'clock Sunday night. She has to rush to get it done, but she always manages to pull it off somehow. All we have to do is work a little longer tomorrow to make up for today.

WEDNESDAY, 9:10 P.M.

I found out the most exciting thing this morning! Today was market day in San Sebastián. It happens once a month—people from Valle Dulce, Gemelo, and about half a dozen other nearby villages gather in San Sebastián's main square for a full day of eating, shopping, and socializing.

"It is awesome, *macha*," Veronica told me over breakfast. "Everyone goes and has a blast. There are tons of food booths, crafts, musicians, boat rides, performing monkeys and parrots, and all sorts of other cool stuff to do and see."

By the time she finished describing it, I had made up my mind. "We have to find a way to go!" I told Veronica and Jorge when their parents were out of earshot. "How can we get there? San Sebastián must be at least ten miles away—we'd need a ride."

Veronica grinned and exchanged a glance with Jorge. "I'll see what I can do."

As soon as I got to the construction site I told everyone about the market. "Veronica is going to try to find us a ride," I added. "Who's in?"

Most of the kids seemed pretty psyched about the whole idea. Tiffany, Kate, and Anne immediately started discussing all the shopping they wanted to do. Ty started asking questions about the boat rides I'd mentioned. Andy wondered aloud if he would be able to find a book on local birds and plants.

I glanced at J.P., expecting him to be as excited as everyone else. But he was frowning. "We're supposed to have the support beams and walls up by the end of the day," he said.

I had been expecting someone to bring that up. But I was surprised that it was J.P. Luckily I had an answer ready for him. "No problemo," I said with a grin. "We've got Coco on our side!"

You see, that morning I had remembered the Web page I'd printed out. It had all sorts of useful tips for saving time and money.

I passed it around the group, explaining exactly what we needed to do. "If we follow the tips and work as fast as we can," I finished, "I figure we can have the walls and beams up in less than two hours."

"Then what are we waiting for?" Ty called out. "Let's go!"

We got to work. A few of the others were a little worried at first because we weren't following José's instructions. But they relaxed once they saw how well Coco's methods were working. And how *quickly* they were working.

While the rest of us were busy at the site, Veronica managed to track down a high-school-age friend who agreed to drive us all into San Sebastián. By the time a battered, rust-blotched green van pulled up to the construction site, we were putting the finishing touches on the walls.

"All right!" J.P. shouted as he hammered in one last nail. "That should do it. Is everyone ready for fun?"

While the others cheered and dropped their tools, I grinned. "Last one in the van is a rotten guava!"

When we got to San Sebastián, there were mobs of people in the town square, talking, laughing, eating, buying things. Veronica and Jorge spotted some friends from school and rushed over to say hello. Kate and Andy wandered toward a nearby food stall. The others scattered every which way.

"Where do you want to start?" J.P. asked, grabbing my hand.

I squeezed back. "I want to see it all!" I declared.

He grinned. "Let's go!"

We plunged into the crowd, trying to take in everything at once. First we stopped for a quick snack at a stand that sold something called *cajeta de coco*. It tasted sort of like fudge, and it had coconut in it and I don't know what else. Then we moved on to a section of the square devoted to local crafts and other gift items. I found lots of great souvenirs for people back home. I bought a woven shirt for Jess (purple, her favorite color), some local crafts for Mom and Dad, a hat for Steven, cute little tree frog pins for Maria and a few other friends, and a hand-carved flute for myself. J.P. liked Steven's hat so much that he got one just like it for himself. At one booth we saw a cool movie poster that we were sure Veronica would like, so we both chipped in to get it for her. By that time we were carrying so much stuff, we couldn't hold hands anymore. But we were having a fantastic time.

After a while we went looking for Veronica. It wasn't easy to track her down in the crowd, but somehow we found her. She was thrilled by the movie poster.

"It is so awesome!" she exclaimed. "I must figure out a really cool place to hang it up."

J.P. wanted to go watch some boat races that were just starting, so I decided to walk around with Veronica for a while. We tossed the stuff we'd bought into her friend's van, which was parked on a narrow side street nearby, then headed back toward the square.

That was when we had our first bit of bad luck all day. Veronica and I were turning the corner to reenter the square when we saw José walking toward us, a frown on his face. It was too late to run. He'd spotted us.

"What are you two doing here?" he demanded.

I gulped. I knew José would never approve of using Coco's shortcuts, even if it made perfect sense. We had to come up with an excuse he would believe.

I glanced at Veronica, but she was no help. She was gazing at José with a goofy, adoring smile on her face. I was on my own.

"No problemo, José," I said, thinking quickly. "Um, the work is progressing steadily back at the village."

Veronica looked at me, seeming surprised. Before she could say anything to give us away, I went on.

"So," I said to José. "What are you doing here?"

I was hoping to distract José from his own question by changing the subject. Jessica does that all the time. Mom and Dad are usually too smart to fall for it, but it always works on Steven.

"I came to bargain for some copper wire," José replied. "But you have not answered my question. Why are you two here?"

"It's OK, José," I said smoothly. "The work is going so well that we figured we had time to come over and pick up some . . . uh . . . gravel. We were going to surprise Marion and Robert by building a path from the road to the front door."

"Oh." José thought about that for a second while

I held my breath. "Then the beams and walls will be finished by the end of the day?"

I let out the breath I was holding. "Oh, yes. I can practically guarantee it," I assured him. "The rest of the crew is back at the village hard at work."

I heard Veronica let out a little gasp, and out of the corner of my eye I saw what she had just seen. Andy and Kate were strolling past just a few yards away at the edge of the market square, hand in hand. They were so wrapped up in each other that they didn't even notice us—or José.

I froze. José was facing away from them right now, but he could turn his head at any moment. As soon as he saw Kate and Andy he would realize I'd been lying.

Veronica saved the day. She grabbed José by the hand.

"Listen, I never got a chance to tell you what a radical time I had with you at the rave," she said, fluttering her dark eyelashes at him. "Thanks a million. It was totally awesome and . . . *romantic*."

It was obvious that José had no idea what to say. He stared at Veronica blankly for a second, his face slowly turning pink. "I too enjoyed—er, that is— you are quite—um . . ." He paused, clearly completely tongue-tied. "I must get my wire," he finished at last, his face bright red by now.

I quickly checked the spot where Kate and Andy had been, but they were gone. Whew! It had worked!

"We will come along and keep you company," Veronica told José, following as he hurried toward the square. "Right, Elizabeth?"

I guessed what she was thinking. We might need to distract him again if we ran into anyone else from the crew. I was tempted to leave the job to Veronica alone. She obviously knew exactly how to distract José. Still, I was afraid she might get distracted herself and forget to keep a lookout for the others. So I tagged along, feeling like a third wheel but not really minding too much.

It wasn't easy, but we did it. For a while it seemed that every time we turned around, someone else from the crew popped into sight. First it was J.P., who was still watching the boat races. He spotted us at the same time I spotted him. I nudged Veronica. She took José by the arm, which distracted him more than long enough for J.P. to back away into the crowd, out of sight.

We encountered Kate and Andy again too. They were sitting on a bench at the edge of the square, eating what looked like tortillas. Andy's eyes widened when he saw us, and I was afraid he was going to choke on his tortilla. But Kate grabbed his arm and dragged him out of sight behind a craft stand while Veronica stood on tiptoes to whisper something into a blushing and completely distracted José's ear.

When I noticed Jorge heading in our direction, I wasn't sure what to do since he wasn't officially a part of the crew. Still, I decided it would be better if José had no reason to be suspicious at all. So I poked Veronica on the shoulder, and she gave José a big, impulsive hug as Jorge quickly changed directions and melted into the crowd.

I can't remember how many times we had to repeat our little game. But finally I guess José got so overwhelmed by Veronica's attention that he had to leave. He quickly bought his copper wire and mumbled something about getting back to work. I'm not sure if he was talking about himself or us. We walked him back to his car. And just before he got in, he blushed deep red, then leaned over and gave Veronica a lightning-fast kiss on the forehead before leaping into the front seat and driving off at top speed.

Maybe with most guys that wouldn't seem like much, but coming from José it was practically a wedding proposal. Veronica was so happy, she just drifted around the market for the rest of the day in her own dream world. Every time J.P. and I saw her, she blew us kisses and grinned her head off.

There's no doubt about it—romance is in the air!

Nine

Tanya never gives up.

Lucky me, I hadn't seen her since the rave. But tonight she came over to Valle Dulce after dinner. I had just left the house to look for J.P. when I ran into her.

She had just been to the construction site, and she clearly wasn't pleased with what she saw there. She was totally nasty to me and also to Kate and Andy, who happened to be standing nearby, examining the large orchid plant growing on the side of the Herreras' house.

"You guys think you're so great," Tanya spat out, crossing her arms. "But I heard you've been goofing off every day." She glared at me. "I can't figure out how you can give your crew so much time off and still get your work done. There's something going on, and I plan to find out what it is."

"Maybe Elizabeth's just a better leader than you are," Andy said loyally.

"That's right," Kate added. "Maybe you should take lessons from her, Tanya."

Tanya tossed her head and stalked away without answering, heading back toward Gemelo. A minute or two later J.P. came by, and I forgot all about Tanya.

But later, when I thought about her visit again, I felt pretty annoyed. It was obvious that she only came over to see how our work compares to hers. Maybe she *should* take some lessons from me and my crew—lessons on how to lighten up and have some fun. After all, we're proving that we can finish everything we need to do and still take time to enjoy ourselves. It's too bad she can't learn the same thing.

SUNDAY, 9:20 P.M.

Coco is the greatest!

Sorry I haven't had much time to write in the past couple of days, Diary. I've been too busy. After the success of market day I realized just how useful Coco's Cost-Cutting Construction Concepts could be. On Friday, Coco's tips saved us so much time that we finished all our tasks by lunchtime, so we spent the whole afternoon in the rain forest. I'm not sure what the others did, but J.P. and I hung out in "our" clearing for most of the day. Yesterday afternoon we finished in time to go hear a local band Veronica knew about at a village a couple of miles away.

And the best part is, our building is going great! Robert and Marion stopped by today and seemed impressed. They said that everything looked perfect.

Who knew being superefficient would be so easy? Not to mention so much fun!

WEDNESDAY, 9:58 P.M.

Sorry, Diary—I know I should be writing every day, but I just can't seem to keep up. But I have really good excuses. The other day, after Marion and Robert left, we all knocked off work early for a lizard-catching contest. It was Veronica's idea. J.P. and I worked as a team, but we didn't do very well. We only caught three lizards. The "prize"—a crown Veronica made out of leaves and vines—went to Andy, who caught seven. Kate gave him a big kiss to congratulate him, which I guess was an even better prize than the crown, judging by the look on his face.

We've done a bunch of other fun stuff in the past few days too. One afternoon we found a coconut grove and Jorge tried to teach us how to climb the tall, skinny trunks. J.P. got about eight feet up and then slid down. He scraped his elbow pretty badly, but as soon as I kissed it he claimed it felt totally better. We also snuck out the CD player again and had a sing-along and dance contest. Yesterday Veronica took us to the beach to look for nesting turtles.

Whoever first said that all work and no play makes you dull must have been a genius. We're all having tons of fun, and the work is going great. José stopped by yesterday, and he seemed really pleased with our progress. He even singled out Veronica, praising her for pitching in to help with the work. He said he used to think she was "flighty" but that I was obviously a good influence on her. Believe me, Veronica and I had a good laugh over that one after he left! If anyone has been influenced lately, it's me. Veronica and J.P. have helped show me that having fun is just as important as being serious and responsible. I just hope I remember that in a few weeks when I start eighth grade!

FRIDAY, 10:10 P.M.

It's hard to believe my Costa Rican adventure is almost over. We're flying home in just over a week, next Saturday to be exact. Part of me feels like I just got here, while the other part feels like I've been here forever. I have to admit, I am really starting to miss home—the people, the food, even the TV. I wonder how Jessica is doing? I can't believe I haven't spoken to her in almost four weeks!

But I'll see her and everybody else before too much longer. What I'm thinking about more right now is how much I'll miss these incredible times in the rain forest with J.P. and the rest of my new friends.

Yesterday afternoon J.P. and I stole away to celebrate the two-week anniversary of the day we got together—that day that everything changed between us. It was really romantic. J.P. surprised me with a bunch of tropical flowers he'd gathered from the rain forest. Then we relived our first kiss. It was so wonderful—something I'm sure I'll remember for the rest of my life. Just like I'll remember everything else about this wonderful trip.

The community center is almost finished, mostly thanks to Coco's Construction Concepts. When José stopped by yesterday, he could hardly believe how much we had done. He promised to bring Marion and Robert back with him tomorrow to see it. Meanwhile Jorge went over to the other village this morning and found out that Tanya's house isn't anywhere near finished.

Could life possibly get any better than this?

Ten

I should have known it was all too good to last.

Here's what happened. We got started extra early at the construction site this morning since we knew that Robert, Marion, and José would be stopping by. And our hard work paid off. By the time they pulled up at the site, the new community center was pretty much finished.

It still needed some paint and a few other finishing touches, of course. But the building part was done, and that was the important thing—the part we were brought to do. Robert and Marion were incredibly impressed.

"You kids have been one of the best work crews we've ever seen," Robert declared, stepping back and looking over the building as we all watched. "I can't believe you did so much so fast."

"Me either," Marion agreed. "You guys have done a fantastic job." Her eyes twinkled as she glanced at us. "That's why we've already decided to have a big party to celebrate the completion of the community center."

I gasped in surprise along with the rest of my crew.

"A party?" J.P. cried. "Cool!"

Marion grinned. "Robert and José and I already told the kids from Gemelo that they should quit work early today and come over. Your host families have offered to make some refreshments." She paused to wait for the excited whoops and shouts to die down before continuing. "So by the time you all finish cleaning up the site and putting the tools away, it will be time to celebrate!"

I noticed that even Robert didn't look as serious as usual. In fact, he looked thrilled. "I'm so proud of you all," he said. He paused and traded a glance with Marion. "By the way, we've been considering having our award presentation this afternoon. I think it's pretty obvious who the outstanding volunteer should be."

Veronica elbowed me in the ribs. I blushed and smiled as Robert winked at me.

"OK, everyone," I said in my best foreman's voice. "Let's get those tools put away!" We all scattered to do our part as José and the adults hurried down the path toward the village.

I was helping Kate gather up a pile of leftover two-by-fours when J.P. found me. "Well, well," he said. "I wonder who Robert could have meant just now? Do you two have any idea?"

"I don't know," I joked. "But if you ask me, we should give the award to Coco."

Kate giggled. "True. We *could* have done it without those concepts . . ."

". . . but we couldn't have had this much fun while we did it," I finished, raising my hand for a high five.

By late afternoon the party was in full swing. All the American kids and a lot of Ticos from both Valle Dulce and Gemelo came, bringing food and drinks and even some more CDs. Everyone gathered in the clearing in front of the new community center and started eating, dancing, and having a great time. I stuffed myself with delicious Costa Rican food, then headed for the area near the boom box to work it off.

I started dancing with J.P., but before long the other boys from my crew started cutting in. I ended up dancing with all of them at least twice. I even danced with Duane, who had come over with the other kids from Gemelo. He only stepped on my foot once, and he hardly talked about *Star Trek* at all.

I was having a great time. The only dark spot was Tanya. Anytime I went within ten yards of her, she glared at me like she thought she could turn me to stone or something. I wasn't surprised, but it was still kind of unnerving. I wasn't exactly comfortable with the thought that she obviously hated me so much. *Who cares?* I told myself at one point. *Let her stare all she wants. She's just jealous because she knows she'll never win that award now.*

The sun was beginning to set when Robert hopped onto the front steps of the new community center and clapped. "May I have your attention, please?" he said. Then he repeated his words in Spanish.

Someone turned off the CD player, and we all started gathering around him. I felt my heart start to pound nervously as I guessed what was coming. J.P. must have guessed too—he squeezed my hand and winked at me.

When everyone was listening, Robert went on, still repeating his words in both English and Spanish. "As you can see, your beautiful new community center is finished—and well ahead of schedule." He smiled at all of us from the work crew before continuing. "Our student volunteers have done a wonderful job, and we congratulate them. And now, on behalf of the Rain Forest Friends organization, Marion and I would like to present this award to the volunteer who has done the most to make this day possible." He held up a shiny wooden plaque. "I am very pleased to present this honor to our Valle Dulce team foreman—Miss Elizabeth Wakefield!"

My crew erupted into loud whoops and cheers.

All the Ticos and most of the volunteers from Gemelo joined in.

As I walked toward Robert to accept my award I glanced around for Tanya, wondering how she was taking this. But she was nowhere in sight, and I soon forgot about her as Robert handed me the polished wooden plaque. It had the Rain Forest Friends logo carved onto it along with the name of the village and the date and the words *Outstanding Volunteer*.

"Thank you—*muchas gracias*," I said as I accepted it. "This is a great honor. But I want everyone to know that I never could have done it without my wonderful crew—J.P., Kate, Andy, Ty, Tiffany, Loren, Will, Sumi, Ricky, Anne, and Bridget, and of course our honorary crew members Veronica and Jorge Herrera. You're the best, guys! Let's give them a big hand."

The crowd cheered loudly as my crew grinned and waved. Since everyone still seemed to be expecting a speech, I said a few more words, thanking Marion, Robert, and José and wishing the villagers many years of pleasure from their new community center. Then I stepped down to the sounds of more cheering, feeling a little embarrassed at all the attention but happy at the same time.

The music started up again, and J.P. and I got right back to dancing.

That's when I noticed Tanya. I happened to be

facing the office shack when she suddenly emerged from behind it. *What was she doing back there?* I wondered idly. I smiled as I answered my own question. *Probably hiding out so she didn't have to watch me accept that award.*

Feeling a tiny bit guilty about my mean thought, I glanced at her again. This time I noticed that she wasn't scowling like she had been all afternoon. In fact, she had a strange sort of half smile on her face.

What's that all about? I wondered. For some reason her expression suddenly made me kind of nervous. She looked like a cat who had just swallowed the world's most delicious canary.

I craned my neck to get a better look, but just then Ricky and Sumi danced by, blocking my view. I took a step to the side, trying to see where Tanya was going.

"What are you doing?" J.P. asked, moving aside to match my steps.

I jumped. I had almost forgotten where I was. "Oh, nothing," I lied. For some reason I didn't want to tell him the truth.

At that moment Ty danced past and punched J.P. on the arm, and J.P. turned to chat with him. That gave me the chance to look for Tanya again. I spotted her over by the boom box, whispering something to José.

I watched as the two of them headed toward the office shack, with Tanya leading the way. José was frowning, and Tanya looked happier than ever. But just then Marion shouted for everyone's attention. I saw that Veronica was standing beside her, grinning from ear to ear.

"Sorry to interrupt," Marion said cheerfully once someone had turned off the music once again. "But I thought it would be fun to do something to christen your new community center. And Veronica Herrera has just generously volunteered to donate a brand-new poster, which will be hung to decorate the main room." She held up the movie poster that J.P. and I had bought Veronica at the market.

How sweet of her! I thought. When Veronica glanced over at me, I gave her a thumbs-up.

"What a cool idea," J.P. whispered to me, his warm breath tickling my ear a little. "It's perfect— Veronica will probably spend a ton of time at the community center anyway, so she'll still get to enjoy the poster."

"And what could be more appropriate," Marion went on, "than for our award-winning team foreman to have the honor of hanging the poster. Elizabeth? How about it?"

"Sure," I called out with a smile. "But only if Veronica will help me!"

Someone handed me a small hammer and the poster, and someone else gave Veronica a couple of tacks. Then the two of us went into our new building. There wasn't enough room inside for everyone, so the rest of the party goers crowded around outside the wide windows to watch.

I held the poster against one wall. "How does this look?"

"Majorly awesome!" Veronica exclaimed. She stepped forward and poked one tack through the corner of the poster into the wall. I raised the hammer.

"Here goes!" I cried gleefully. I swung the hammer and hit the tack square on the head—once, twice, three times. "OK," I said. "Next tack, please, Veron—"

That was all I had time for. Because just then, with a creaking, cracking, groaning, splintering sound, the wall with the poster on it tipped forward—and started to fall right toward us!

Veronica and I both screamed and jumped back, trying our best to cover our heads. I don't think I've ever been so scared in my life. It seemed as though the whole building was collapsing right on top of us! Everyone watching must have been pretty worried too because I could hear gasps and shrieks and cries from all around.

A second later, with a loud *crash*, the top part of the wall smashed to the ground—right in front of the door. Veronica and I were trapped.

Luckily no more of the building seemed ready to collapse. So we just stood there, in the middle of a community center that suddenly had only three and a half walls instead of four, with the entire population of two villages and all the student volunteers looking in at us.

Their faces were still worried at first. But we must have looked pretty silly standing there with hammer in hand and broken pieces of wall at our feet. Because after a few seconds of stunned silence there was a nervous titter from somewhere in the crowd. That was all it took. Everyone burst out laughing.

My face was so red, it felt like it was going to burn off. Veronica looked really embarrassed too. But I knew she couldn't possibly be feeling the same amount of humiliation and shame I was feeling. She wasn't the team foreman. She hadn't been responsible. She wasn't the—gasp!—"outstanding volunteer" who had led the way in building this defective community center.

"What in the world is going on here?" I heard Marion cry from somewhere outside. "What happened?"

"Maybe Elizabeth huffed and puffed and blew the house down!" shouted some joker whose voice I didn't recognize.

"This is no laughing matter," Robert's stern voice broke in through the laughter. A moment later I saw his face poking in through the window. "Girls, are you hurt?"

Veronica and I shook our heads. Then we went to the window, and Robert helped us climb through it.

Once I was outside, I noticed that not everyone was laughing. The other members of my crew looked just as embarrassed as Veronica and I did. Andy's face was flaming, and Kate's big blue eyes were watery. J.P. was frowning, and most of the others looked either ashamed or confused.

I also noticed something else. Tanya had returned and was pushing her way to the front of the crowd. José was behind her, looking grim.

Andy saw Tanya too. He spun around and pointed at her. "She did it!" he shouted. "Tanya sabotaged our building. She'll do anything to win!"

There were murmurs of surprise from the crowd. Even Tanya looked startled at Andy's words.

Robert frowned. "That's a serious accusation, Andy," he said severely. "Do you have any proof of what you're saying?"

Kate was tugging on Andy's arm, obviously trying to calm him down. But he wasn't paying any attention to her.

"Elizabeth didn't want me to tell anyone," he said. "But Tanya was the one who stole that gas cap the very first week. She wanted to make the truck late so her team would get a head start."

Tanya gasped. "You . . . you . . . ," she sputtered angrily, glaring at me.

But Andy wasn't finished. "She wants to win, no matter what. But there's no way I'm going to let her make Elizabeth look bad like this!" He waved his hand at the half-collapsed building. "Not after she worked so hard and was such a great foreman!"

My cheeks were still flaming, though now it was as much from shame as from embarrassment. I knew the truth, even if poor Andy was too clueless to see it. Tanya hadn't had anything to do with the wall collapsing. It was my fault—because I wasn't a great foreman at all. I wasn't even an adequate foreman. I was a horrible one. I had cared more about having fun and sneaking off to hang with J.P. than I had about doing a good job. Why hadn't I seen it sooner?

I glanced over at J.P. to see what he was thinking. He was staring back at me, his eyes narrowed and his face thoughtful.

I gulped, knowing that he was finally figuring out what had happened. All this time he'd thought I put that snake in Tanya's tent as a funny way of getting revenge. That's what I had let him think. But Andy's words had reminded him about that stupid gas cap. You wouldn't have to be as smart as J.P. to put two and two together and realize that I took back the gas cap to get the project moving.

I wanted a chance to talk to him, to explain. But just then José spoke up. His face was like a stone. "I have something to show you," he told Robert and Marion. "Come with me."

Robert and Marion followed him, and the rest of us drifted along behind them. Veronica fell into step beside me, looking nervous. "What happened?" she whispered.

I didn't know what to tell her. I just shook my head and shrugged helplessly, hating the nervous look on her normally happy face. *Could this day possibly get any worse?* I wondered.

Naturally the answer to that question was yes.

José brought Robert and Marion to the supply pile at the back of the office shack. As soon as the adults saw it their faces darkened.

The day had definitely just gotten a *lot* worse. There was way too much stuff left over—too many extra nails, struts, supports, and everything else. Now the adults knew that we'd cut corners. *Why didn't we hide the extra supplies?* I thought desperately. But even as I thought it, I knew that wouldn't have done any good. They would have figured it out soon enough anyway.

Why did I ever believe that someone named Coco would know anything about construction?

There was a tense moment of silence. Then Robert, Marion, and José all started yelling at once, mostly at me. What could I have been thinking? Why hadn't I followed their instructions? How could I be so irresponsible? Etc., etc., etc.

"I know what she was thinking," J.P. broke in after a moment, pushing his way to the front of the crowd. "Actually, I just figured it out." He stared at me, his face white and his expression cold. "Elizabeth wanted to get our building up first. That's all she cared about all this time."

His angry words stung so much that I felt tears

spring to my eyes. "No, that's not true," I protested weakly.

"This was all about beating Tanya." J.P. had turned away from me by now, as if he couldn't stand to look at me anymore. He spoke to the adults. "About winning. I can't believe she's so competitive and selfish she would actually build an unsafe community center. But I guess it's true. We were idiots to trust her—all of us."

With that he shook his head in disgust and hurried away without another glance in my direction. I wanted to run after him, but I didn't dare. I had to handle the construction situation first. Still, it was breaking my heart to know that J.P. thought I'd betrayed him—just like Tanya had.

Robert and Marion took over then, ordering the rest of the kids to keep quiet. "We'll need some time to figure out what to do," Marion announced.

"I don't need any time," Robert declared angrily, turning to glare at me. "I know exactly what we should do."

I felt my whole body start to shake. *This is it*, I thought. *He's going to send me home. And he's going to do it in front of the whole village.*

I knew it was only what I deserved. But that didn't make it any easier to face.

Marion grabbed Robert by the arm. "Wait," she said. "Let's not be hasty. We should talk about this." She glanced at me. "Elizabeth, you'd better return to the Herreras' house now."

Robert didn't look particularly happy about that, but he didn't argue. And I didn't give Marion a chance to change her mind. I turned and raced for home, grateful to escape all those accusing, disappointed, and confused faces.

Halfway there I heard footsteps running after me. *J.P.?* I wondered, my heart jumping nervously. Maybe he had realized he had been unfair. Maybe he was following me to apologize and offer his support.

But when I turned, I discovered that it was Veronica who had followed me. "Elizabeth!" she gasped. "Wait! I want to come with you."

I was so happy to see her that I forgot all about J.P. I held out my arms, and she grabbed me in a big hug. She didn't say another word, but she didn't have to. I could tell that I had at least one friend left in this village.

We continued to her house and huddled in the guest room, wondering what would happen next.

"They can't send you home," Veronica kept repeating. "They just can't."

"Of course they can," I told her sadly. "Robert was practically frothing at the mouth to do it. And I don't blame him one bit. I really messed up."

"But you did your best," Veronica argued loyally.

I just shook my head, feeling too sick at heart to answer. She was being a good friend, but I knew the truth. I hadn't done my best. Not even close. I had let having a good time get in the way of doing a good job, and now everyone knew it. Why hadn't I recognized that until it was too late?

A little while later there was a knock on the door and Jorge stuck his head in. "There you are," he said.

Veronica jumped up and ran to her brother. "What's happening?" she demanded anxiously.

Jorge shook his head. "It is not good news." He sat down on the bed next to me and gave me a sympathetic look. "I stuck around after you left to see what would happen. As soon as you two were out of the way the truth came out, bit by bit."

I wasn't sure I wanted to hear the rest, but I nodded at Jorge. "Go on."

He shrugged. "At first nobody wanted to talk. But Robert—well, he kind of insisted. So finally the other kids admitted that they spent almost half the time they were supposed to be working doing, um, other things."

"You can say it," I said dully. "They admitted they spent their time goofing off. And that I let them."

Jorge nodded. "Someone even told Robert and Marion about Coco's Construction Concepts." He sighed. "They did not like hearing about that at all. . . ."

The rest of the evening was like more of the same bad dream. Mr. and Mrs. Herrera came home and dragged Veronica off to her own room. They said they were very ashamed of her; they seem to think she was a bad influence on me and the other American visitors. I tried to tell them it was all my fault, but they wouldn't believe me, even after I told them the whole truth about everything that had happened.

I stayed in my room after that, hiding my head under the covers when I heard Kate come in. I didn't want to talk to her. I wasn't sure I would want to talk to anybody ever again. Maybe instead of sending me home, Robert would agree to fly me to Siberia, where I could live out my days all alone, where I couldn't mess up other people's lives or make a big fool of myself.

I couldn't help thinking about how disappointed my parents would be in me. They sent me on this trip because they thought I was a responsible person. I'd really let them down. I'd let down my crew, the Herreras, and all the other nice people of Valle Dulce. I'd let down Robert and Marion and José and the rest of the Rain Forest Friends. And maybe worst of all, I'd let myself down. I'd ignored everything I ever thought was important.

And for what?

Eleven

◇

When I woke up this morning, the first thing I remembered was that we had finished building the recreation center. For a second I felt pretty happy—until I remembered everything that happened after that, and my heart sank like a stone.

When I poked my head out from under the sheet, I saw that Kate was already gone. I didn't blame her. I wouldn't have wanted to stick around and talk to me either.

Somehow I managed to drag myself out of bed and get dressed. I wasn't looking forward to facing the Herreras and the rest of the village. But what choice did I have?

I snuck past the kitchen and headed outside,

hoping to find J.P. before dealing with everybody else. I wanted a chance to explain myself to him—to see if we could make things right again between us. He wasn't at his host family's house, but Andy and Kate were. They told me J.P. had gone into the rain forest right after breakfast to be alone.

Neither of them looked me in the eye while we were talking. They both seemed pretty upset.

"Are you guys mad at me?" I asked, fearing the worst.

They hesitated, looking at each other. Then Kate smiled tentatively.

"Sort of," she admitted in her soft, kind voice. "But we were responsible too. We knew that we weren't following José's instructions. I guess we all just got sort of—swept up in the moment."

I swallowed hard and nodded, grateful that they were being so nice about the whole situation. I liked both of them a lot, and I hated the thought that my carelessness had hurt and embarrassed them.

"Thanks," I said, my voice sounding funny because of the lump in my throat. "I just want you to know I'm—sorry." I choked out the last word and fled.

I headed into the rain forest, listening carefully. J.P. was never very quiet, and I tracked him down soon enough. He was sitting on a log in a small clearing, tossing twigs at a hole in a tree trunk. He looked up quickly when he heard me approaching.

"Oh. It's you." He frowned, then looked away and tossed another twig at the hole. "Shouldn't you be off challenging Tanya to a spelling bee or something?"

"Look, J.P., I know you think I did everything just to win that stupid contest," I said, looking at the ground to avoid his angry gaze. "I wanted you to know that you're wrong. Yes, I did sneak over to get the gas cap so we could start working. But only because I wanted to make sure the villagers got their community center. I'm not ashamed of that. And the reason I cut all those corners after that *wasn't* to beat Tanya."

I paused and took a deep, shaky breath, feeling the tears gathering somewhere just behind my eyes. I knew I had to hurry up and get out what I had to say because I was going to start crying any second.

I gulped and looked him straight in the eye for the first time. "It had nothing to do with Tanya at all. The only reason I did it was to have time to be with you. To have time to play and have fun. I never cared about winning."

He looked a little confused. "Really?" he said. "You did all that for me?"

I nodded and wiped my eyes. "I didn't think you'd like me if I wanted us to work all the time." Then I realized that wasn't quite fair. "Actually," I corrected quickly, "*I* didn't want to work all the time when you were around. I wanted to hang out with you instead."

J.P. dropped the twigs he was holding and leaned back, looking uncertain. There was a moment of silence.

"Anyway," I said at last, "I'll probably be sent home today."

I felt a pang, thinking about that. I couldn't imagine what Mom and Dad would say when they found out. At least I knew that Jessica wouldn't judge me too harshly. Actually, she would probably be proud of me. She'd probably think we were becoming more alike as we got older, and for a while there I would have thought she was right. Now I wasn't so sure. I don't think Jessica has ever felt as guilty about anything in her entire life as I did about the mistakes I'd made on this trip.

Meanwhile J.P. was looking upset at my words. "They can't send you home now." He stood up and hurried over to me. "If they do, I'll go home too!"

"No, you can't, J.P." I grabbed his hands. "Please stay. You have to make sure that Veronica doesn't get in too much trouble. It's all my fault, but her parents don't understand that. You have to help her."

J.P. bit his lip, then he nodded and squeezed my hands. "OK," he said, his face more serious than I had ever seen it. "I guess we owe Veronica something. Both of us."

We didn't talk much after that. He hugged me awkwardly, and then we sat on the log for a while, each of us busy with our own thoughts. Finally I realized that I couldn't stay out here any longer. I had to go back and find out whether I was staying or being sent home in disgrace.

"I've got to go," I said, trying to sound braver than I felt.

J.P. just nodded. "Good luck," he said softly.

I reluctantly went back to the Herreras' house, planning to try one more time to convince Veronica's parents not to punish her for what I had done. When I walked into the kitchen, I found Robert and Marion sitting at the table, waiting for me.

"Hello, Elizabeth," Marion said when I came in. Her normally happy face looked somber. "Sit down, please. We need to talk."

I gulped. So this was it. "Go ahead," I said in a tiny voice, sinking into a chair. My hands were shaking, and my stomach was winding itself in knots. "I'm listening."

Marion and Robert exchanged a glance, then Marion spoke again. "I won't lie to you, Elizabeth. After what happened yesterday, Robert and I discussed sending you home to California today."

"That's right." Robert tapped his long, skinny fingers on the table. "But then we realized that by the time we arranged for a bus to take you back to the city and booked a flight, it would be almost time for you to leave anyway. Besides, one of us would have to escort you to the capital, and we can't really afford that."

Marion smiled for the first time since entering. "True," she said. "But we also realized that you're still pretty young and that you're usually a responsible girl."

What were they saying? I started to hope in spite of myself.

"That's why we've decided to give you a second chance," she said. "An opportunity to help fix your mistakes. We suspected you would welcome that opportunity."

"Although all we really care about is getting the community center built. Built *right*," Robert put in.

Marion ignored him and went on. "This time we're asking José to stay on full-time to supervise. He'll be in charge. But you and your crew will have a chance to repair and rebuild the community center building—if you think you're up to it."

I could hardly believe my ears. They were giving me a second chance? It was more than I deserved. But I wasn't going to tell *them* that. "Definitely!" I exclaimed. "We'll do a fantastic job this time. You'll see!"

Marion smiled at my excitement. "Good," she said, reaching out and patting me on the arm. "I hope you will."

They left to spread the word to the other volunteers, and I just sat there for a few minutes, thinking about how lucky I was. Kate came in a few minutes later, all smiles. She had just heard the news and was just as happy as I was about it. She even hugged me and said she wasn't mad at all anymore.

"Honestly, Elizabeth, this trip has been one of the greatest experiences of my life," she explained. "Andy and I realized that—in a way—we should be thanking you for all the fun we've had. Even if we do have to make up for it now in order to get the community center built."

I was so grateful for her nice words that I couldn't speak for a moment. So I just hugged her again.

We started our repair job right away. At first José frowned every time he glanced at me, but once he saw I was serious about working hard, he eased up a little.

Veronica spent the whole day working steadily along with the rest of us. So did Jorge. They didn't even go home for lunch. They said they wanted to eat with us so they didn't miss a minute of work. In Veronica's case, I suspected she was also avoiding her angry parents.

I didn't blame her. And I didn't forget for one moment that it was all my fault.

MONDAY, 9:05 P.M.

Kate and I are so totally wiped out from work today that we came in to bed right after dinner. Kate is already asleep. But even though my body is tired, my mind is still wide awake.

We're making progress on the community center. José looked over all our work at the end of the day—and actually smiled! I'm starting to think we might really get it finished in time. I'm keeping my fingers crossed!

Veronica is still working like a dog. I think her parents are finally starting to believe she isn't responsible for what happened. Mr. Herrera talked to me about it after breakfast this morning. He said Veronica had always been kind of excitable and flaky, so at first he and her mother were ready to blame her for this mess. But when they thought about it, they realized she had actually been acting more responsible and mature lately than usual. Mr. Herrera even said he still thought I was a good influence on her! Can you believe that? It made me feel kind of good on the one hand but kind of sad on the other because I know I haven't been nearly as good a role model for her as I could have been. But I'm doing my best to make up for that now.

TUESDAY, 10:00 P.M.

Even after a really hard day of work, there still seems to be so much more to do before the community center is finished. And no wonder— we were supposed to have five weeks to build this place, and now we're trying to rebuild it in less than a week. I guess all we can do is try our best. At least the foundation is solid.

J.P. and I haven't had much time to be together except at lunch. I miss having fun and hanging, but not as much as I thought I would. It's kind of a relief in a way to be throwing myself into all this hard work. It's a different kind of fun—it's rewarding.

José stood up while we were eating lunch today and told us he was really pleased with our progress. He thinks if we push ourselves as hard as we can for the next day and a half, we can finish the repairs by the end of the day on Friday.

I sure hope he's right. We have to leave the village early Saturday morning to get back to the airport in time for our flight home.

Things at the Herrera house are almost back to normal now. Veronica's parents decided not to punish her when they saw how hard she was working to help make things right. They're proud of her, and I am too. She's a "majorly awesome" friend, and I'll miss her when I go home.

I'll miss this place too. I've really gotten used to falling asleep at night to the sounds of the birds and other creatures of the rain forest. Sweet Valley will seem awfully quiet in comparison!

Twelve

◇

Up until the final hour I was sure we were going to have to leave the community center unfinished. J.P. and Kate were up on the roof nailing on the last few shingles just as the sun dipped down behind the horizon. The rest of us had just finished our final jobs too. José was so happy, he actually hugged Veronica before he realized what he was doing.

But he realized it soon enough and started blushing furiously. "I'd better go call Marion and Robert," he muttered, hurrying off.

The rest of us just stood there for a minute after he left, staring at the rebuilt community center. "I can't believe it's done," I said after a moment. It still hadn't quite sunk in.

"I know," J.P. agreed. "It seems like there should be a thunderclap or something. You know, so we know we really did it."

"No, that's OK," I said quickly, shuddering as I pictured a sudden flash of lightning setting the building on fire. "Just having it finished is enough for me."

Kate smiled. "Still, maybe J.P. is right. Maybe we should have some kind of, you know, house-warming."

"Don't you mean community-center-warming?" J.P. quipped.

But Sumi was nodding. "We *should* do something to celebrate."

"Like what?" Ricky said. "I don't have the energy for another party!" He pretended to collapse on the building's front steps.

I knew what he meant. I was exhausted. But it still seemed as though we should mark the occasion somehow.

"I know!" Veronica said. "Wait here." She raced away before we could question her. She was back five minutes later, holding something. She held it up and winked at me. "Should we try again, *macha*?"

I recognized the ill-fated movie poster. "But how—"

Jorge grinned proudly. "I rescued it from the rubble," he explained. "It wasn't even wrinkled! Well, not much anyway."

This time we all went inside to hang the poster. And this time the walls held as Veronica and I tacked it up.

When we were finished, Veronica and I stepped back to stand with our friends. "It looks *perfecto*," I said.

"*Sí*," Veronica agreed. "Totally awesome!"

"A toast," Mr. Herrera said a little later, holding up his glass. "To our American friends, Elizabeth and Kate!"

Everyone cheered as Kate and I blushed. We were crowded around the dining table with the entire Herrera family, enjoying our last dinner in Costa Rica.

"Thanks," Kate said. "And thanks for letting us stay here."

"There is no need for thanks, *gata*," Mrs. Herrera told her with a smile. "You and Elizabeth are part of our family now. You are always welcome."

"Really?" I blurted it out without thinking. I couldn't help it. I was surprised that Mrs. Herrera would say such a thing—about me, that is, not Kate—after all the trouble I'd caused.

Mrs. Herrera chuckled. "Of course, *macha*," she chided me gently. "We will always consider you part of our family. You have brought our home so much laughter, happiness, and love."

"Totally!" Veronica put in, which made everyone laugh.

"*Sí*, Elizabeth," Jorge said, helping himself to another piece of bread. "And even though Robert and Marion took back that plaque, I think you are an 'outstanding volunteer.'"

"I agree," Mr. Herrera said. "And more important, you're an outstanding person. Both of you," he added, including Kate in his smile.

I was so touched that I was afraid I might start to cry. But at that moment little Eugenia jumped up from her seat. "'Lizabeta! Kate!" she cried. "No go home! You stay!"

"Stay! Stay!" little Ricardo added, pounding on the table with his soupspoon.

That made everyone laugh again, including me. I glanced around at the happy faces of my host family, and for a second I wished that I really could stay. But I knew that even when I was back home in Sweet Valley, I would always remember their kindness.

We sat around the table for a long time, talking and laughing. But finally I excused myself. I had arranged to meet J.P. in the banana grove after dinner. It was time for us to say good-bye. I knew we would see each other tomorrow—after all, we would be on the same plane. But tomorrow was sure to be busy, and rushed, and full of other people. Tonight it would just be us.

He was already waiting for me when I reached the meeting spot. We started walking toward our usual path into the rain forest. We didn't say much at first, just held hands and walked.

Once we were out of sight of the houses, we stopped. He turned to look at me. "You're really great, Elizabeth," he said softly. "I've never met anyone like you."

"You're great too," I replied. I wasn't sure what else to say. Suddenly I had no idea what to say to this guy I'd shared so much with this summer.

So instead of talking, I decided to act. I leaned over and kissed him.

He kissed me back. The kiss was really nice, but this time it had a different sort of mood to it. Does that sound weird? Can a kiss have a mood? Anyway, what I mean is, I think we could both sort of tell that this was some kind of ending.

A week or two ago that would have made me really sad. I hadn't thought I would want my time with J.P. to end. But now I wasn't so sure. Maybe being with him had been the kind of thing that wasn't meant to last too long. I don't know. But I noticed he hadn't said anything about getting together after we got back home, even though we only lived a few miles apart. And I didn't quite feel like saying it either.

Eventually the kiss just sort of drifted off, and we moved apart. J.P. looked down at his feet. "So I guess this is it, huh, Bob?"

"Something like that," I agreed, smiling at the goofy nickname in spite of myself. "School will be starting pretty soon."

That reminded me of the gossip back home in Sweet Valley. I wondered if everybody knew what was happening with the schools yet. Maybe I would find out tomorrow. Maybe not.

Either way, I realized as J.P. and I wandered back toward the village, I would deal with it. My trip to Costa Rica had been really educational, though not in the ways I had expected. I found out a lot about myself—maybe more than I really wanted to know. But I guess I'm glad I did. Because even if my attitude didn't change completely, even if I'm not ready to blow off all my responsibilities and concentrate on fun (like a certain twin of mine), I think I have changed at least a little.

I hope I won't ever totally toss my responsibilities out the window again like I did for a few weeks there. That was way too extreme. Then again, maybe the way I always was before this trip was another kind of extreme. Maybe I've been *too* serious and responsible up until now.

Is it possible to find a way to live in between those two extremes? I don't know, but I'm going to try. I'm still going to take school and other things seriously, but I also want to make some real time for fun, maybe even for romance. Who knows? In any case, I expect that will make eighth grade a whole lot more interesting—no matter what happens.

I just hope the people back home can handle my cool new attitude!

SWEET VALLEY TWINS

Jessica: Next Stop, Jr. High

SWEET VALLEY TWINS

Jessica: Next Stop, Jr. High

Written by
Jamie Suzanne

Created by
FRANCINE PASCAL

BANTAM BOOKS
NEW YORK · TORONTO · LONDON · SYDNEY · AUCKLAND

To Jenna Sanitsky

One

Dear Jess,

Surprise!!!

By the time you read this, I'll be well on my way to Costa Rica. I ran back upstairs and put this on your pillow just before we all left to go to the airport this morning. I wanted to surprise you, but it's too bad I won't see your smile when you find this purple-fabric-covered notebook when you get home.

It's a diary.

I'm writing this note in the first few pages of *your* diary because I know how hard it is to face a blank page. I figured I'd sort of break it in for you. I guess you're wondering why I'm giving you a present when it's not your birthday. It's a "going-away present" even though *I'm* the one who's gone away.

Now don't start crying (again). I'm sure you've

already depleted your tear ducts on the ride home from the airport.

Was Steven nice, or did he torture you by telling you how many people die of snakebites in the rain forest? I'm guessing he opted for torture. I'm also guessing that Mom and Dad spent the entire ride home from the airport telling him to stop teasing you. But since they were trying (unsuccessfully) not to laugh, it just encouraged him. (Do I have ESP or what?)

Don't listen to anything he says. I'm going to be just fine. And I'm going to have a great time. Building houses in the Costa Rican rain forest is right up my alley.

Still, I'll miss you. Try not to forget what I look like. (Hee, hee!) Of course, if you do forget, you could just look in the mirror. See that girl with blue-green eyes, long blond hair, and the dimple? That's you.

I look exactly the same.

Seriously, Jess, the only thing that's worrying me about going to Costa Rica is leaving you here in Sweet Valley. I know that you and Lila haven't been so tight lately and your summer's not working out the way you had hoped. I've been getting the feeling you're a little lonely. (See! I *do* have ESP.)

All I know is that when *I'm* feeling lonely, writing in my diary helps. So if you start to feel lonely or worried—remember the Elizabeth Wakefield motto: Scribble! It works.

I'll see you in a month, and I'll think about you every single day.

Love,
Elizabeth

P.S. Please try not to murder Steven while I'm gone.
P.P.S. Or Lila Fowler.

SUNDAY, 6:30 P.M..

Dear Diary,

I don't know if having an identical twin with ESP is good or bad. I *did* cry all the way home from the airport. Steven *did* tell me that the snakes in Costa Rica were a thousand feet long and could swallow an average-sized thirteen-year-old girl whole. Mom and Dad *did* tell him to keep quiet. They *did* laugh hysterically when he did his imitation of Elizabeth being swallowed by a giant snake. And yes, I *did* want to murder him.

"No, no," Steven screamed in this really high voice that was supposed to be Elizabeth's. "I haven't finished my homewoooooooooork!" He trailed off and finished with a great big gulp and belch that was supposed to be the snake.

Even I had to laugh at that last part. Does that make me a horrible person?

I guess not. In fact, I know I'm a wonderful person. Because I love Elizabeth even though she is a straight-A student, five thousand times more responsible than I am, and always doing something to help other people or save the world. Only a very mature and incredibly fabulous sister could love a sister like *that*. (Ha-ha!)

I'm glad I had a little surprise present of my own for Elizabeth, which I gave her at the airport. It was a bag of CDs and movie magazines. I know Elizabeth is looking forward to going deep into the rain forest and leaving civilization behind. But who could spend a whole month with no rock and roll and no celebrity gossip?

Anyway, when I got home and found this diary, I thought it was a nice idea—a very Elizabeth idea. But I really couldn't see myself writing in it.

Elizabeth's been gone for twelve hours, though, and I've just got to talk to someone. These days there's no point at all in trying to talk to my so-called best friend, Lila Fowler.

If I talk to Lila, I'll have to hear all about what Wiley said. And what Wiley did. And what Wiley thinks. Blah, blah, blah. Wiley, Wiley, Wiley. Brag, brag, brag.

If I hear one more word about Wiley Upjohn, I'm going to *upchuck.*

I can't believe how Lila is letting this I-have-a-boyfriend-and-you-don't thing go to her head. It's not even like he's that cute. He's definitely not that tall. Maybe half an inch taller than Lila. *Maybe!*

The only thing Wiley Upjohn has going for him is the fact that he's in high school—or he will be in September. This is something that Lila manages to work into our conversations about every two seconds.

Wiley Upjohn is ruining my whole summer.

And it was supposed to be the best summer of my life. The summer I would always remember. The summer before eighth grade.

The last summer of the Unicorns.

See, this might be the Unicorns' last summer together as a club. It's hard to believe, but I might not be going to Sweet Valley Middle School next year. Our school district has been rezoned. Nobody knows yet which school they will be going to in September.

Before we heard about the rezoning plan, all the Unicorns were psyched about going into the eighth grade. Being in eighth grade isn't like being in high school, but it's still a pretty big deal because you're finally at the top of the middle-school heap.

And let me tell you, I'd waited a long time for this.

When I joined the Unicorn Club two years ago, I was a sixth-grader. Janet Howell (she was president of the club then) was an eighth-grader. During that first year Janet and the seventh-graders really made me and the other sixth-graders jump through hoops. And boy, did we jump!

Why? Because the Unicorn Club was made up of the prettiest and most popular girls at Sweet Valley Middle School. Everyone wanted to be a Unicorn, and I was no different. I mean, no matter how bossy Janet Howell got and no matter how mean the other Unicorns acted, I hung in there because I wanted to be part of the club.

Then last year Janet Howell went on to high school (thank goodness—I mean, she was my friend and all, but let's face it—the girl could be a total nightmare sometimes) and some other members dropped out. The only people left were me, Ellen Riteman, Lila Fowler, Mandy Miller, Rachel Grant, and Kimberly Haver.

We elected Ellen Riteman president. Ellen was a way cooler leader than Janet. Ellen's nice even if she is a little ditzy. OK, make that a *lot* ditzy. But she did a good job of holding the club together and didn't let the power go to her head.

So all in all, everybody was happy last year. And everybody was the same age. Everybody except Kimberly, that is.

She's a year older than the rest of us, so she was an eighth-grader while we were seventh-graders. Even though she wasn't the president, Kimberly couldn't resist pulling rank on us now and then.

Don't get me wrong. I love Kimberly. She's one of my best friends, and I'm going to miss her next year when she's at high school. But before I heard about the rezoning thing, I had decided that I wasn't completely heartbroken that she was leaving Sweet Valley Middle School. Because once Kimberly was gone, that meant that all the remaining Unicorns would be eighth-graders. We'd all be equals. Nobody could make me do things I didn't want to do anymore.

But now if we split up and go to different schools, there won't even *be* a Unicorn Club next year. That's why this is the last summer of the Unicorns.

We all made a solemn vow to make the most of

it and to spend as much time together as we could. I was psyched to have the best summer ever.

I was, like, *so* naive.

Everything started off great. But somewhere in the first week of July, Lila showed up at Casey's Ice Cream Parlor with Wiley Upjohn. That's when everything changed.

Janet Howell, our former president who is now a sophomore in high school, is Lila Fowler's cousin. Turns out it was Janet who set Lila up with Wiley.

Janet said that since Wiley was going to be in the ninth grade and Lila was going to be in the eighth grade, it was a perfect match. Lila would get to go to all the high-school dances, etc. *Plus*—she would have a cool date for all the eighth-grade parties no matter which school she ended up at.

That was the end of the "equality" dream. Let's face it, having a boyfriend gives you a lot of clout in a club like ours. Getting a high-school boyfriend was like taking a quantum prestige leap.

Within a week of dating Wiley, Lila was "unavailable to hang." Whenever I called her, she was on her way to meet Wiley somewhere.

When she *is* available to do stuff—with me and the rest of the Unicorns—she acts like a Janet Howell clone. Laying down "the rules according to Lila." Telling us how to act if we want high-school guys to like us. Telling us how to dress. Who the cool bands are and what songs we should memorize. Stuff like that.

Now everybody's worrying about what Lila thinks and whether they're acting cool enough.

And Lila's version of acting cool can be a drag. None of the Unicorns acts interested or excited about anything or anybody anymore.

I wish Lila and Wiley had never gotten together. It's ruining everything.

SUNDAY, 8:00 P.M.

Dear Diary,

I'm back. Lila just called me, and guess who she yakked, yakked, yakked my ear off about?

Wiley, of course.

It sounds horrible, but I almost hope Lila and I *do* wind up going to different schools next year. I just don't think I can stand having to hang out with Lila and listen to her gloat.

MONDAY, 12:00 P.M.

Dear Diary,

I just read over what I wrote yesterday. I realized that I sounded totally jealous. Gee, what a surprise. Because I *am* totally jealous.

This last week has been a major bummer. Kimberly and her folks are at Waterworks, this fabulous new theme park. Mandy's grandmother is here, so she doesn't have time to do anything. Rachel and her dad went to his company golf tournament in Arizona. And Ellen's dad took her and her little brother on a camping trip.

I'm totally bored. I've got nobody to hang with— I've been forced to do stuff *all by myself!* And every single time I leave the house, I wind up running into Lila and Wiley. I went to the mall and there they were. I went to a movie, and they sat down *right behind me.* I took a walk, and they were sitting on a park bench holding hands. I pretended not to see them and got out of there *fast.*

According to Lila, Wiley's going on some boat trip with his family next week and she just doesn't know how she's going to "survive the separation." (I wanted to—but did not—puke when she told me that.)

Maybe it's a good thing everybody has been out of town. If anybody had been around to listen, I probably would have said something really nasty about Lila and I would have looked as jealous as I feel.

Only you know how rotten I feel, Diary.

I probably couldn't even talk to Elizabeth about this. She thinks the Unicorns are, like, the most superficial bunch of airheads in Sweet Valley. She would think I was totally dumb for letting myself get all upset.

She would also tell me that I should have planned something for myself this summer besides hanging with the Unicorns because they're not the kind of girls you can count on.

But I didn't *want* to do anything else this summer. I wanted to spend time with my friends. I wanted it to be like old times. I especially wanted to spend time with Lila. My "best friend." How could I know she would hook up with Wiley Upjohn and have no time for me?

It probably wouldn't bother me so much if it were any other Unicorn. But Lila and I have been competing our whole lives, and Lila always wins. Always. It's so *frustrating*.

Lila Fowler's dad is Mr. Fowler. That's Fowler as in Fowler Enterprises.

Mr. Fowler is a multigabillionaire, and Lila is an only child. Her folks are divorced, and her mom lives in Europe somewhere. The "no mom" deal makes Lila's dad feel so guilty, he spoils Lila to death.

Get this—*Lila has her own car!!!*

She can't even drive—*but she has a car!!!* The chauffeur drives her around in it. She has her own charge cards. She has *everything*.

It's not fair.

And now she's got a boyfriend in high school and *I hate her guts!*

I don't think I'm going to write in this diary anymore. It's not making me feel better. It's making me feel worse.

I'm outta here, and there goes the phone.

MONDAY, 12:35 P.M.

Dear Diary,

Good news! I can stop feeling sorry for myself now.

When the phone rang, it was Rachel.

Rachel Grant is as rich as Lila is. She and her dad live in a big mansion right next door to the Fowlers.

Anyway, Rachel and her dad are back from the golf tournament, and she's having a slumber party tonight. Everybody is coming back today, so the whole club will be there—even Lila.

It's about time!

I don't know if I'm the only one who's feeling sentimental about this last-summer-of-the-Unicorns thing, but somehow it's just really important to me that we all spend some time together. Honestly, I'm a little scared about next year. What if I'm the only one who has to go to a new school? What if nobody likes me there?

Oh, ugh. I can't start thinking about that now—I need to start figuring out what to wear to the slumber party!

Two

Dear Diary,

Things change!!!

Big news!!!

Great news!!!

I'm not a writer, so it's hard to know where to start. So much stuff has happened since I last wrote anything.

I guess I'll start at the beginning of Rachel's slumber party.

When I got to Rachel's, Ellen and Mandy were already in the living room, listening to the latest addition to Rachel's incredible CD collection. Mandy was dancing. Her eyes were closed, and she bounced her head back and forth, letting her hair flop. When she opened her eyes and saw me, she broke into a big sunny smile and blew me a kiss.

Mandy's one Unicorn who'll never be "too cool to care." She's a very friendly, sweet, sincere person. These days she's majorly emotional too. She'll cry over anything. Everything is, like, a "major moment."

Mandy started wearing beaded braids over the summer. She's also got some green and pink extensions. It's a great look for her. Very Mandy. Only hipper. Mandy's always had a lot of fashion flair. She's got long thick brown hair, big green eyes, and a powerful imagination. She could probably walk into a hardware store and come out with a great outfit.

Ellen has done some major appearance improving too. She still has her straight brunette bob, but she's cut her bangs supershort. She was wearing really good makeup and way wide jeans with a ribbed top. Ellen's tall and kind of lanky, so it was a good look on her. She twirled across the living room like a model and gave me a hug—which made me feel good. "What do you think? There was an outlet mall in the town near the campgrounds. Dad sprang for a shopping spree. I wish you had been with me, though. It just doesn't feel like a shopping spree without you."

"I think you look great," I told her.

All my worries were slipping away. Nobody was acting *hipper than thou*.

Rachel hugged me too and then plopped a cap on my head. The Grant Open was printed across the top. "A present from the tournament," she told me. "I brought one for everybody. I really missed you guys."

Rachel looked great. Her dark brown skin was practically glowing. The only makeup she was wearing was red-tinted lip gloss. And she wore her hair in lots of dreads that hung almost to her shoulders.

I was really starting to feel better about everything. We were all together again. Tight. Friends.

"I love your outfit," Rachel told me.

"Really?" I hadn't felt completely sure about my tie-dyed slip dress and platform mules. It was a little over the top for me. During one of my long and lonely afternoons I went to the mall and drowned my sorrows in a cheeseburger and sale shopping.

"It's great," Rachel said. "You look like a highschooler. *Hey!* Turn down the music," Rachel yelled at Mandy. "I think the pizza guy is here."

Mandy turned off the music, and Rachel ran into the front hall. She threw open the door and let out this loud guffaw.

Mandy and Ellen came into the front hall to see what Rachel was laughing about. I went too. When I saw, I started to laugh so hard, I almost fell off my platforms.

It wasn't the pizza guy. It was Kimberly.

I swear she looked two inches taller than she was the last time I saw her. They must put something in the water at Waterworks. Miracle-Tall or something.

Kimberly is very athletic—and she had obviously spent a lot of time swimming. Her light sunburn made her blue eyes look even bluer. And her pink face went well with her exotic getup.

She had on an extra-large Hawaiian shirt, long baggies, and some dopey grass skirt over them.

Kimberly started swaying back and forth while singing a song that was probably supposed to sound like a Hawaiian guitar but came out sounding like a cat with a really bad cold.

"This isn't a theme party," Rachel told her. "But I like your costume anyway."

Kimberly grinned, reached into her tote, and produced a necklace of flowers. She placed it over Rachel's neck. "Yes, it's true," she said in a game-show-announcer voice. "You, Rachel Grant, and all of the Unicorns have won a fabulous, all-expenses-paid trip to Hawaii!"

"What?" we asked, and everybody sort of stared at everybody else.

Kimberly grinned, whipped off the grass skirt, and pulled a letter out of her bag. "You guys have heard me talk about Aunt Pippa, right?"

"Yes," Ellen said.

"No," Rachel said.

"I can't remember," I said.

Kimberly pushed her wavy dark hair back off her face.

"Aunt Pippa is my dad's sister. She's never gotten married, and she was a surf bum for years. Actually she wasn't a surf *bum*, she was a surfing *champion*. But it drove my dad crazy anyway. He thinks everybody should get a job and live like he does. Anyway, two years ago she won the lottery."

"That is so cool!" Ellen said, and gave a low whistle.

"It was," Kimberly agreed. "Because she bought this chain of surfing shops in Hawaii and got really successful, and now she lives in this big luxury condo on the island of Oahu. Anyway, her present to me for graduating eighth grade is a house party. She's going to treat me to tickets for the whole club to fly out to Hawaii and spend the month of August at her condo. Basically the rest of the summer. She even bought the tickets already!"

There was this stunned silence. Like nobody could believe it. Then we just went nuts.

Ellen screamed like a game-show contestant. I jumped up and down until I realized that I could break my neck in those platforms I was wearing. Rachel hooked her arm through Kimberly's, and they started twirling each other around. And Mandy just started to cry.

That's when Lila walked in.

We all tried to tell her what was going on, but we weren't making any sense, so we quieted down and Kimberly delivered the thrilling news all over again complete with hula dance.

And did Lila have the common courtesy to look thrilled? Scream? Jump up and down?

No.

First thing out of her mouth: "I've been to Hawaii so many times, I'm not sure I really want to go again. Besides, I don't want to be away from Wiley that long."

I felt like somebody had just kicked me in the stomach. Hurt, yeah. But also too surprised to react.

"But he left *you* to go out of town," Rachel pointed out. (Two points, Rachel.)

Lila looked irritated that anybody mentioned it. Then she glanced at her watch. "Oh! He should be calling me about now." She gave Rachel and me this sickening smile. "He calls every day that we're apart."

"He only left this morning," I pointed out.

Of course, Lila didn't appreciate that remark, but I didn't say anything else because really and truly, I didn't want to make her so mad that she wouldn't come to Hawaii.

She might be making me sick to my stomach these days, but she's still my best friend. It just wouldn't feel like a Unicorn trip without her.

Sure enough, the little mobile phone in her purse started to ring, and Lila answered it in this silly, breathy falsetto. "Hello-o-o-o?"

It was Wiley. She took the phone into the living room and stayed in there for about an hour.

The rest of us wandered into the den off the living room so that Lila could have some privacy. Everybody was totally excited about going to Hawaii. We couldn't stop talking and giggling. Mandy was boo-hoo-hooing because she was "so touched" that Kimberly's aunt was giving her such a great present. And she was "so touched" that Kimberly had thought about all her friends. And she was "so touched" that Rachel was having this slumber party. And—

"Knock it off!" Kimberly begged. "If you don't stop, we'll all start bawling."

Everybody laughed at that—especially Mandy. Even *she* sees the humor in the fact that she's turned into the sentiment queen of Sweet Valley.

Then again, look who's talking. I've been feeling very sentimental myself. In fact, I was feeling so sentimental that I knew that the trip just wouldn't be fun for me at all if Lila didn't go.

Besides, I had a feeling that once we got to Hawaii, things would be different. Without Wiley around she'd be the old Lila again. A snot, sure. But a snot who had time for me and the rest of the club.

Finally Lila appeared in the doorway. My heart started pounding. I held my breath. *Please say you're going!* I thought. *Please! Please! Please!*

She took a ten-second dramatic pause before she announced—"Wiley says he wouldn't want me to give up a trip with my friends. He's very unselfish," she added. "So I'm going."

Then the old Lila came out. She grabbed my hands, and we started jumping up and down together. "Look out, Hawaii—here come the Unicorns!"

So now there's only one teeny-weeny hurdle left.

The old parental permission slip.

TUESDAY, 5:00 P.M.

Dear Diary,

Here's how it went down.

I laid it out for Mom and Dad. I told them that Kimberly's aunt was treating us all to plane tickets and a month at her condo in Hawaii. I told them that the entire Unicorn Club was invited. And I told them that if they didn't let me go, it would ruin my whole life, destroy my emotional health, and make it impossible for me to ever finish my education and get a job. Dad said he was willing to take that chance.

I pointed out that not finishing school and getting a job would mean that I would have to live with *them* for the rest of my life.

Mom turned pale and called Kimberly's mom from our phone in the kitchen.

I went into the living room, grabbed the cordless, and hid in the hall closet so I could listen in on their conversation.

Kimberly's mom told Mom that the offer was for real. But Mrs. Haver also said that Pippa was "unconventional."

"Nuts!" I could hear Kimberly's dad yelling in the background. "She's not *unconventional*. She's *nuts!*"

Of course, that just made me more determined to go. But Mom got all concerned and told Mrs. Haver that she and my dad would have to talk it over.

I was less than thrilled. *We'll have to talk it over* is right up there with *We'll see.*

It means *no*.

I immediately called Kimberly on her line—the one that rings in her room. I told her that my parents were grumbling and that she should do something quick! Like put a gag on her dad and get her mother to call again.

A few minutes later the phone rang.

I listened in again. It was Mrs. Haver. She seemed pretty amused and told my folks that they shouldn't pay too much attention to anything Mr. Haver said because he was totally traditional and had a hard time relating to Pippa's lifestyle—which was more "relaxed" than most people's.

"Nuts!" I could hear him yelling. "Her approach to life is nuts!" (I guess Kimberly didn't get any cooperation with the gag request.)

Kimberly's mom shushed Mr. Haver, and then she told my folks that she had complete confidence in Pippa's ability to supervise and chaperon us during the trip.

"Then you're nuts too!" I heard Mr. Haver yell in the background. "She'll have them on the first plane back to Sweet Valley. Trust me."

Fortunately my parents think that Mrs. Haver is a very smart lady—and that Mr. Haver is wound a little too tightly.

So after making me sweat it out for a couple of hours while they "talked it over," Mom and Dad gave the project two thumbs-up. (Or would that be *four* thumbs-up?)

Oh—who cares? All that matters is that the answer is *"yes!"*

TUESDAY, 8 P.M.

Dear Diary,

Here's the update on permissions secured regarding Operation Hawaii:

                    Jessica—Go

Rachel—Go
Lila—Go
Mandy—Go
Ellen—Go
It's a go, Houston.
Ready for liftoff!

Three

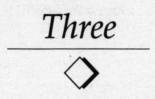

Dear Diary,

We've been on the plane now for about four hours. Lila started out sitting next to me, and we got along great for about the first thirty minutes. Then she zapped me.

"Jessica," she said. "I don't want to hurt your feelings. But there's something I've been wanting to tell you."

"What?" I asked. She sounded so serious, I thought she was going to tell me I smelled bad or something.

"It's about that tie-dyed dress."

"What about it?"

"Lose it," she said.

I stopped worrying about how I smelled. Suddenly a big wad of irritation balled up in my chest. "Why?" I asked, trying not to sound as peeved as I felt.

"Wiley and I saw you in Music Mania in that outfit, and he didn't like it."

I opened my magazine and stared at it hard. "Tough," I said, not looking at Lila.

"Don't get mad. I'm telling you this for your own good. Wiley says clothes like that make girls look like they're trying too hard to be noticed."

(I couldn't believe this was coming from somebody who rides around town in a chauffeur-driven car with vanity plates that say Lila Rules.)

But I didn't make any sarcastic remarks about the car since I enjoy riding around in it myself. So I just said, "Oh, yeah? Since when is Wiley Upjohn a girls' fashion expert?"

She groaned. "I knew you were going to be this way."

"What way?" I demanded.

"You're going to make things so hard on yourself." Lila sighed as if she felt sorry for me. "Next year is going to be a key year."

"What are you talking about?"

"Jessica! It's the year before we go to high school. Whatever rep we get in the eighth grade is going to follow us. You've got to get your image right this year. The last two years were all about experimenting. Now it's time to get serious."

As much as I wanted to tell her to go jump off the wing, I couldn't help thinking she might have a point. I'd been looking forward to eighth grade because I thought we could finally be who we wanted. Wear what we wanted. Hang out with who we wanted.

But the way Lila was putting it, it was going to

be worse than when we were sixth-graders. Because if you make mistakes in the sixth grade, nobody holds it against you. You're a sixth-grader; what do you know? But it sounded like eighth-grade mistakes wound up on your permanent record.

On top of everything else—I might be, like, *a new kid!*

"Just think about it," Lila urged, patting me on the arm. Then she got up and went over to sit with Kimberly for a while.

I looked out the window at the clouds. They looked like cotton candy.

In spite of feeling irritated with Lila and worried that I might ruin my whole life by wearing a tie-dyed dress that Wiley Upjohn didn't like, my heart just kind of soared. How could I be unhappy miles up in the sky on my way to Hawaii?

Lila's just going through a phase. She's dating a guy in high school, so she thinks she knows everything. She'll get over it once we get to Hawaii and start having fun. (Or once Wiley dumps her for some girl in high school.)

Once we get to Hawaii, it's going to be just like the old days. All for one and one for all.

WEDNESDAY, 8:30 P.M.
(HAWAIIAN TIME—IT'S 10:30 IN SWEET VALLEY!)
Dear Diary,

Things change. I know I said that already, but I just can't get over how *fast* things change. One minute you're soaring through the clouds, and the next minute you're hitting the ground with a hard thump.

I guess that was a metaphor. (Unless it's a simile. I'll have to look it up.) Whatever it is, it's pretty good. Maybe I can use it in a book report sometime. But I'm not going to think about book reports now. I've got enough to worry about.

Anyway, there I was flying through cotton candy, thinking everything was just great—and it *was* for a while.

The view as we were coming in for the landing was incredible. Hawaii is made up of lots of islands. There are eight main ones: Hawaii, Maui, Kahoolawe, Molokai, Lanai, Oahu, Kauai, and Niihau. From the air the islands looked like green jewels sprinkled across blue velvet.

We landed in Honolulu on the island of Oahu. We got our bags and felt really grown-up because we were going to get ourselves to the condo. Nobody met us or anything. Pippa had sent Kimberly a letter with instructions on how to get ground transportation.

Mandy read to us from Pippa's letter. Kimberly found the bus stop at the airport. Ellen figured out which bus was ours. Rachel bought the tickets. I made sure everybody's bags were stowed. And Lila got the driver to take a picture of us all standing in front of the bus.

We were a real team.

Pippa lives outside the city on the coast. As I looked out the window at the surf I didn't think it was possible to be any happier. I always thought California was beautiful, but Hawaii is like paradise.

Everywhere I looked, I saw trees, color, and ocean. It's gorgeous. It even smells good. Like tropical flowers, fruit salad, and salt water.

"This is going to be the best vacation ever," I said happily. "Sun, sand, and nothing but Unicorns."

Mandy pushed her extensions back off her shoulders and adjusted her Grant Open billed cap. "We're going to have such a good time. No parents."

"No obnoxious brothers and sisters!" Ellen added.

"No obnoxious sixth- and seventh-graders!" Rachel said with a laugh. "We'd better enjoy it now. Because in September we're going to be surrounded by them."

Everybody laughed. But I noticed that Kimberly turned red and looked out the window. I figured she was embarrassed. We tend to forget she's a year older. Maybe she thought we were making fun of her because *she* had been hanging with seventh-graders when she was an eighth-grader.

Before I could say anything, we hit a part of the beach that had tall buildings along it. Very fancy-looking buildings. Kimberly stood up. "This is our stop," she announced.

I noticed her voice sounded kind of flat. I hoped we hadn't hurt her feelings.

We all shouldered our bags, got off the bus, and crossed the street. It felt really strange to get off a bus and walk up to a luxury building on the beach. The doorman wore white pants and a Hawaiian shirt.

It was obvious he was expecting us because as soon

as he saw us he grinned and went inside for a big dolly. "Aloha!" he said as we piled our bags on top of it.

"*Aloha?*" Ellen giggled. "I thought that meant good-bye. We just got here."

"*Aloha* means hello *and* good-bye," he told us with a grin. "Welcome to Hawaii. I'm Mickey. Ms. Haver said I should take you right up."

We walked into the lobby of this gorgeous building and almost fell over, we were so dazzled. The building had a big atrium in the middle with a huge fish tank. The fish in it were so exotic, they didn't even look real.

Then we all got in this big glass elevator and went up, up, up. It was *très* plush. Even Lila and Rachel looked impressed.

Finally we were at the top.

"She has the penthouse?" Ellen asked Kimberly in a whisper.

Kimberly nodded. "I guess. I've never been here before. The last time I visited Pippa, she lived in a little one-room bungalow."

The elevator doors opened. There was only one apartment-door entrance on the whole floor. It was right across from the elevator. As soon as the elevator went *ding* the door to the apartment swung open.

"Hi!" This really young-looking person with braces opened her arms and threw them around Kimberly. "I'm so glad you guys are here. I've been waiting and waiting!"

"Wow," Ellen whispered to me. "Pippa looks even younger than us."

I rolled my eyes. Honestly, sometimes Ellen is so dense, it's hard to believe she finds her way to school. "That's not Pippa," I whispered back.

"Who is it?" Rachel asked.

I shrugged. I had no idea. But whoever it was had reddish brown shoulder-length curly hair, a sprinkle of brown freckles, and bright green eyes with thick lashes. She wore cutoffs and a big T-shirt that said Pippa Surf Shack.

Mickey rolled the bags into the living room, and Kimberly turned to us. "Guys, this is my cousin Marissa." She didn't look anybody in the eye when she said it. "Marissa, this is Jessica, Lila, Rachel, Mandy, and Ellen."

Marissa flashed us this big metallic grin. "Hi. We're going to have so much fun!"

"I thought Pippa didn't have any kids," Lila said. (Not bothering to whisper, of course.)

Marissa giggled. "I'm not Pippa's daughter. My mom is Renatta. She's Pippa's and Kimberly's dad's sister. Get it?" Then without waiting for an answer, she just kept on talking. "I've been here about two weeks already. It's been a blast. Pippa and I get along great. I've helped her do a lot of inventory and stuff at a couple of her stores. She's really busy these days. But now that you guys are here, we are going to party, party, *party!*"

She pretended to do the twist and then threw back her head, laughing like a donkey. Hee-haw!

Rachel was looking at her as if she were a talking monkey or something, but Marissa didn't notice.

She skipped—*(skipped)*—around the sofa and examined the big dolly piled with bags. "I was so glad to find out that most of you are eighth-graders. I was afraid that you guys wouldn't want to hang with me because I'm a seventh-grader," she babbled. "But if Kimberly hung with you when you were in seventh grade, then you guys obviously don't worry too much about the age thing."

She pointed at Rachel and Lila. (Rude!) "Mickey," she says, like she owns the place, "put these two in the room at the end of the hall."

Rachel's eyebrows rose until they practically disappeared into her hairline.

Lila's mouth dropped open—like she couldn't believe this little kid actually had the nerve to refer to her and Rachel as *these two*.

Then she pointed at me. "You and Kimberly can be in with me," Marissa continued. She looked at Ellen and Mandy and put a finger to her chin as if she were thinking. "I guess you two can sleep on the couches and use the bathroom in the hall. Just try to keep your stuff neat so the living room doesn't look like a mess, OK?"

Ellen shrugged, like she didn't care where she slept, but she looked sullen. I didn't blame her. Who would want to be told not to make a mess by a seventh-grader? It was insulting.

I shot a look at Kimberly. She was looking around the apartment, checking out the living room and the big attached kitchen. I waited for her to say or do something. But she didn't. Her face was red, and she wouldn't meet anybody's eyes.

I realized suddenly that Kimberly had known all along that Marissa was going to be here but hadn't told us. That's why she had looked so funny on the bus when Rachel made that comment about not having any seventh-graders around.

Rachel and Lila followed Mickey down the hall after flashing Kimberly a superdirty look.

"Come see our room," Marissa said eagerly. She grabbed Kimberly and me and started shoving us down the hall.

The room was really nice. Big. Two single beds and a roll-away cot over by the window. Marissa pointed to me. "You can have the cot." Then she pointed to one of the beds. "Kimberly, you can sleep here."

"When is Pippa coming back?" Kimberly asked.

Her voice was flat. Not unfriendly. But not warm and cousinly either.

"She'll be home soon," Marissa promised—completely oblivious to the fact that Kimberly seemed less than thrilled to see her. "But she left me money, and I'm supposed to go pick up dinner at the restaurant next door. I'm going now. Want to come with me? The headwaiter there is really nice. Cute, too. I think he likes me. He's probably about eighteen. His name is Luke, and he's from Idaho. He says his father came for a vacation and decided to stay for the rest of his life, so the whole family just up and moved. He has brown hair in a ponytail. Usually I like guys with blond hair, but—"

Yak, yak, yak. Was she ever going to shut up?

"I'll go see how Rachel and Lila are doing," I said, escaping out the door and leaving Kimberly with Marissa, the Amazing Babbler.

The bedroom door at the end of the hall was open, and I saw Rachel and Lila in there. Ellen too. I hurried in, and Ellen shut the door behind me.

"*Who* was that?" Rachel exclaimed.

"Kimberly's first cousin," Ellen answered, blinking. "Didn't you hear? Her mom is—"

"I know that, Ellen," Rachel snapped. "Get a clue or get out, would you?"

Ellen closed her mouth and looked hurt.

"Hey," I said softly. "Chill out." *We just got here and we're already arguing?* I thought. Not a good sign.

Rachel sighed. "I'm sorry, Ellen. It's just that this Marissa person came as kind of a shock. She could ruin our whole vacation. Talk about pushy!"

"That's OK," Ellen mumbled.

There was a soft knock at the door.

Lila popped up and opened it a crack. It was Kimberly.

Lila took her by the hand, pulled her into the room, and shut the door firmly. "*What* is that girl's problem?"

Kimberly rolled her eyes. "I know Marissa is hard to take. What can I say? She's always been that way."

"Did you know she was going to be here?" Rachel asked in her Rachel-for-the-prosecution voice.

Kimberly plopped down on the bed and sighed glumly. "Pippa told me she was visiting and might stay over until the end of the summer. But I didn't know for sure until this afternoon. Marissa's mom wasn't sure she wanted her to stay while we were here because we're older and everything. Marissa's very impressionable."

Lila sucked in her breath and got this real offended look on her face. "So Marissa's mom thinks we might be a bad influence on her little daughter?"

Kimberly shrugged. "Well . . . yeah."

There was a long silence while everybody tried to decide whether they felt insulted or flattered.

"She can't stay," Lila announced.

"You're going to have to do something," Rachel put in.

Kimberly pushed back her hair. "I'll talk to Pippa," she promised. "Maybe she can come up with some tactful way to send Marissa home."

There was another knock at the door.

Everybody froze. Was it Marissa?

Rachel got up and answered the knock with her face all twisted up in a big scowl. "Yes?" she growled, jerking open the door.

It was Mandy.

"Pippa's home," she said. "Come out into the living room and say hi."

It's hard to describe Pippa. I've never really known a grown person like her. She looks about my mom's age or maybe a little younger. But she has long blond hair to her waist and a deep tan, and she seems really cool.

When Pippa saw Kimberly, she grabbed her in a

hug, picked her up, and twirled her around. "You're so tall," she cried. "And I'm so glad to see you!"

Kimberly grinned. "Thanks for letting us come."

Pippa let go of Kimberly, draped her arm over her shoulders, and turned toward us. "Let me see if I can guess who these people are," she said. "My hobby is telepathy." She put her hand over her forehead and made this humming sound. Then she came over to where we stood.

"You're Jessica," she said, putting her hand on my head.

Then one by one she identified every single person. "Ellen, Rachel, Mandy, and Lila."

"That's amazing!" Rachel gasped. "How did you do that?"

Pippa let out this deep laugh, opened a drawer, and pulled out a photo. "From this."

We all gathered around and started to laugh. It was a picture of us taken last year. Obviously Kimberly had sent Pippa a picture of her friends and written who was who on the back.

Mandy sighed unhappily. "Darn. We look like little kids in that picture. If you can recognize us all from that, then we've wasted a lot of time and money this summer trying to look more grown-up."

Pippa smiled and put the picture away. "Trust me. It's better to grow up on the inside than on the outside. Where's Marissa?"

"She went to pick up dinner," Kimberly told her.

Pippa nodded. "Great. I'm starved. I'm sorry I wasn't home when you got here, but I'm adding two new Surf Shops and a hotel gift shop to the chain, and I've had to spend a lot of time checking things out. Marissa's been a big help."

"Listen, Pippa," Kimberly began. "About Marissa ..."

Pippa walked around the counter into the kitchen. She jerked open the refrigerator door and began taking out sodas for everybody. "She looks great, doesn't she?" Pippa put in, cutting Kimberly off before she could say anything nasty. Pippa put the sodas down and gave Kimberly a level stare across the counter. "I'm so glad to have *both* my nieces here," she said, emphasizing the word *both*. "I'm so glad that they *both* feel comfortable and welcome. And I know that you are *all* going to look out for each other so that I don't have to act like a grown-up and make you guys play nice. Right?"

The message was clear. We were going to have to put up with Marissa—or else.

It was a setback. No doubt. Here we were, planning on an all-Unicorn vacation—and now we had to include a nonstop-talking, braces-wearing, donkey-laughing, pushy seventh-grader.

I started to feel a little angry with Kimberly for not warning us.

But like I said before, one minute you're up in the sky and the next minute you're bumping along on some concrete. Things change. And when Marissa came in the door, whatever was in the takeout bag smelled like heaven. My anger disappeared, and I was flying high again.

One way or another, things would work out.

They had to. We were thousands of miles from home. On an island. What choice did we have? We could either work it out or start swimming.

We fell on the food like we were starving.

Right now I'm sitting on a window seat looking out at the ocean with a big moon reflected on it after a dinner that was not to be believed. I don't know what they put in the food here in Hawaii to make it taste so good.

I'm so full, it's hard to imagine that I won't sink to the bottom of the ocean tomorrow.

Pippa had ordered us some kind of fish that was baked with nuts and fruit and rice. I had two helpings, and I don't even like fish.

We had mango ice cream for dessert, and there was enough for everybody to have as much as they wanted.

During dinner Pippa didn't tell anybody to sit up straight or stop talking with their mouth full. She didn't say one word about the music that Mandy put on—which was giving even *me* a headache. Pippa didn't even say anything when Ellen had a fourth helping of ice cream. I can't think of one single adult I have ever met who could watch somebody eat four bowls of ice cream and not have to warn them that they would get sick or that their teeth would fall out.

This trip is definitely going to be the best Unicorn trip ever. The only blot on the landscape is Marissa.

Marissa babbled about surfing and equipment all through dinner. She helped out in some of the Surf Shops, so now she thinks she's a big surfing expert. You'd think *Marissa* was the surfing champion instead of Pippa.

After dinner Kimberly showed us some of Pippa's trophies. She's won, like, every surfing contest in the world. And she doesn't brag at all.

If I had won all that stuff, I'd never shut up about it.

And if *Lila* had won all that stuff, she'd have billboards up all over California announcing what a big deal Lila Fowler was. Too bad the only thing she could brag about at dinner was her "high-school boyfriend."

She was obviously trying to impress Pippa by telling her about Wiley. Pippa asked a lot of questions about him, but I could tell she was only doing it to be polite. Only an egomaniac like Lila would believe that Pippa, a world surfing champion, would actually *care* that Lila Fowler was dating some ninth-grader nobody ever heard of.

Ha!!!

Uh-oh! I hear Rachel and Lila whispering. They're motioning me to come down to their room. I don't like the look on their faces. Something's up.

More later . . .

Four

Dear Diary,

The minute I walked into Rachel and Lila's room, I knew there was going to be trouble.

Everybody was there except Kimberly and Marissa.

"OK, clearly Kimberly has no influence over Pippa at all," Lila said. "I can't believe her. She got us here under false pretenses. She knew there was a possibility that Marissa was going to be here, but she didn't say one word because she knew we wouldn't come. I would never have left Wiley if—"

I groaned and rolled my eyes. I couldn't help it.

"What?" Lila demanded, real defensive. "What's your problem?"

"Would you cut the *Romeo and Juliet* act?" I begged. "You can live without Wiley Upjohn for a few weeks."

"You don't understand," Lila said in this soap-opera voice. "You've never had a serious relationship with a guy in high school and—"

I pretended to play the violin.

Lila reached into her pocket and whipped out a platinum credit card. "That does it. Marissa may be Kimberly's cousin, but she's not mine, and I personally don't intend to let her ruin what's left of my vacation." Lila walked over to the phone. "I'm booking myself on the next plane out. Who's with me?"

Her hand hovered over the receiver.

I felt a huge lump rise in my throat. Did this trip mean so little to Lila that she would walk out on it over something so small? "Guys! Please!" I said. "This may be our last summer together," I reminded them. "Am I the only one who cares?"

Mandy chewed her fingernail. She's the nicest Unicorn of all of us—including me. And like I said, she's very sentimental. I waited for her to say something. Something in defense of Marissa. Or Kimberly. Or the trip. But she didn't. She looked torn. Like she might decide to leave with Lila.

I looked around the room. There were a lot of stony faces. I hadn't realized until then just how much influence Lila was starting to have over the club. It was scary.

Finally it was Ellen who spoke up. "Lila," she said in a small voice. "We just got here. I don't want to go home."

I probably shouldn't have been surprised. As

ditzy as Ellen is, she's not the follower she was in the sixth grade. After a year as president she's become more confident about being her own person.

"I don't want to go home either," Mandy blurted out—like she felt OK about saying it now that Ellen had. Her eyes were on Lila, though.

Lila shot a look at Rachel. "What about you?"

Rachel's eyes flickered. Rachel was the newest member of the Unicorn Club. Belonging to the club meant a lot to her when she first joined. Did it still? "I'm staying," she said after a long pause.

I felt glad about that. But in a way it made me sad because being a Unicorn meant more to Rachel than it did to Lila. And Lila had been a Unicorn much longer than Rachel.

"Please stay, Lila," I said softly. "Please."

I couldn't believe I was begging Lila to stay. Over the years we've had lots of fights. Most of the time I'm thrilled to see her split.

Not this time, though. I had the feeling that if she left now, it would be for good. We'd never put our friendship back together.

Finally Lila's shoulders relaxed. She frowned and stuffed the card back in her pocket. "OK. OK," she said—like she was doing us all some big favor. "I'll stay. But somebody's got to keep that conceited little pit bull called Marissa under control."

I couldn't help thinking that Marissa wasn't any more obnoxious or conceited than Lila.

Still, I went over and sat down next to Lila. "So what if Marissa tags along with us?" I asked in a gentle voice—not ugly or anything. "What differ-ence can it make?"

Lila lifted her chin. "If we were back home, I'd say we were committing social suicide by letting Marissa hang with us. She's a dork. Period."

"But we're in Hawaii," I reminded her. "Nobody will ever know."

"Jessica's right," Mandy said.

Ellen nodded.

"So we're all cool?" I asked.

"What about Kimberly?" Rachel asked. "What do we say to her?"

"Let's try not to make a big deal out of it," Mandy said. "I'm sure Kimberly feels weird enough. And we don't want to get her into trouble with Pippa. Let's try to be nice to Marissa."

So, Dear Diary, the storm seems to be over for now.

After the meeting I came back to the room I'm shar-ing with Kimberly and Marissa. They're in Pippa's room, so I've got a little privacy to get caught up here.

Oops! Just heard Pippa's door open. I can hear Pippa's deep laugh and Marissa's giggle. Kimberly is laughing too. I guess they had a little private family reunion.

Here they come.

Bye.

THURSDAY, 8:30 A.M.

Dear Diary,

By the time we went to bed last night, I was feeling totally good. The cot was really comfortable. When I lay down and turned out the lights, I could see a ton of stars out my window. I fell asleep looking at them.

I must have been asleep a long time, even though it seemed like one minute I was looking at stars and the next minute I was watching the sun come up.

I don't usually wake up early, but I guess I was just so excited to be in Hawaii that I woke up on my own. And there was this incredible bright orange-and-pink ball rising in the sky.

It just made me want to sit up and shout, *Good morning!*

So I did.

You can imagine how happy this made Kimberly. Not very. Kimberly is very grumpy in the morning.

But Marissa sat straight up in bed. Then she got up and jumped from her bed onto Kimberly's and from Kimberly's bed onto my cot. "Incredible!" she crowed, looking out at the sunrise.

Then she practically fell on my stomach. The two of us started laughing so hard, the cot began to jiggle and then . . . *wham!* . . . it collapsed right underneath us.

Both of us thought that was hilarious, but Kimberly just grunted something extremely uncomplimentary about sharing a room with hyenas and pulled the cover up over her head.

Since Marissa and I were the only two people interested in getting up, we decided to go into the kitchen and fix a big breakfast for everybody. But Pippa was already up and dressed and frying bacon in a huge pan.

Bacon is the world's best alarm clock. It wasn't long before the smell had lured everybody out of bed and into the kitchen. Marissa made fresh-squeezed orange juice while I manned the toaster.

It was a great breakfast, and I took mine out on the balcony. It's still a little cool, so that's why I'm working on my diary instead of my tan.

I figure in another hour it'll be time to hit the beach. Inside the condo I can hear everybody talking and laughing. I can hear Marissa giggling. For some reason it's not bothering me today. In fact, I think she's kind of funny.

I have a feeling that everything is going to work out just fine.

SUNDAY, 1:00 P.M.

Dear Diary,

I can't believe it's been three days since I wrote anything. But there's been so much going on, I haven't had time. Today is a rainy day, so I'm finally getting a chance to catch up.

Hold on while I read what I last wrote.

Note to myself: Don't *ever* write the words *everything is going to work out just fine*.

The minute you do that, you're toast.

After breakfast that first day Pippa took us on a drive around the island. She's got this fabulous Suburban, and we all packed in. We drove through Kapiolani Park, which extends from Waikiki Beach to Diamond Head. Then we went (at my request) to the Ulu Mau Village, where there's a model of a Hawaiian chief's village. I thought it was totally interesting. I think Ellen and Mandy did too, but they wouldn't admit it because Lila and Rachel were both acting like it was a big snooze. I don't know if they acted that way because seeing the village was my idea or because they had both been there before—twice.

Nobody snoozed, though, when we went to the Royal Mausoleum, which has the remains of five Hawaiian kings and one queen, Queen Liliuokalani. She was the last monarch in Hawaii and a very great lady. And she wasn't just a queen; she was a composer too. She wrote "Aloha Oe." I've heard that melody all my life, but I never knew where it came from.

We stopped for dinner at a little roadside seafood place. Everybody was so tired and sleepy by the time we got home that we just fell into bed.

The next morning Pippa had stuff to do, so we decided to hit the beach.

We took our towels, sodas, sunscreen, magazines, hats, sunglasses, sandals, wraps, snacks, and floats down to the beach and set up shop.

Marissa spread out her towel next to mine.

That was OK.

Marissa said she really liked me a lot and felt very comfortable talking to me.

That was OK.

Then she told me that because she liked me so much and felt so comfortable talking to me, she was going to give me some advice.

That's when I knew I was in trouble.

"Jessica," Marissa said, "have you ever thought about low lights? It would really bring down that yellow in your hair."

"My hair isn't yellow," I said, trying not to sound insulted. I don't like to brag, but everybody always says that my hair is one of my very best features. And here was this . . . this . . . this . . . *seventh-grader* . . . giving me advice about low lights.

I heard Lila give a little snort of laughter on the other side of me. Like she thought it was funny and I was getting what I deserved for sticking up for Marissa the night we got here.

Marissa sat up a little and stared at me hard. Then she nodded. "You're right. I think it just looks too yellow because of that lipstick. That's not a good pink on you."

Lila rolled over. She was laughing so hard, I could see her shoulders shaking.

"You should trade lipsticks with Lila," Marissa went on. "The apricot she wears is all wrong with her coloring, but she would probably look good in that pink."

Lila quit laughing. She rolled over and scowled at Marissa. Then she stood up with a little huff and dusted the sand off her legs. "I'm going in," she said haughtily.

"By yourself?" Marissa asked in this grown-uppish *reminding* voice.

Lila paused. Even though her tone had been annoying, Marissa was right. All of us knew better than to go in the ocean without a buddy.

Lila looked at me—obviously hoping I would volunteer to go in with her. I pretended to be absorbed in my book. It was windy, and I really wasn't ready to go in.

Nobody else volunteered to go either.

"Guys!" Lila urged. "Come on!"

"I'll go into the ocean with you, Lila," Marissa chirped, like she had no clue that Lila couldn't stand her. She hopped up and dropped her sunglasses on her towel.

"There's a bathing suit shop at the end of the beach," Marissa said, turning toward us. "We could all walk down there in a little while and maybe Ellen could find one with boy-cut legs."

"I don't want one with boy-cut legs," Ellen argued.

Marissa frowned. "But you should. It would take an inch off your thighs. Yours too, Jessica," she said with a smile.

My jaw fell open. Ellen's thighs don't need an inch off them, and neither do mine. Our thighs are just fine. Was Marissa actually telling us we looked . . . *fat*?

I could see Lila's mouth twitching. Like she was trying very hard not to laugh again. "Marissa," she said, egging her on. "We're so lucky you're here. Obviously we need all the help we can get."

Marissa didn't pick up on the sarcasm at all. "Oh, I love to help people," she said seriously. "That's what friends are for. And I'm so happy we're all going to be friends."

Then she punched Lila on the arm. "Race ya," she said—like she was about ten. She tore down to the water.

Of course Lila was too dignified to race. So she

made a big show of not hurrying. She stretched, put her hair in a ponytail, and then turned to me. "You might want to put on a hat," she drawled. "The sun is really going to bring up that yellow in your hair."

I threw my paperback at her just as she turned and ran toward the water, laughing.

Rachel sat up and watched Lila and Marissa diving into the waves. "Kimberly . . . ," she began. "About Marissa . . ."

Kimberly was lying facedown. "There's nothing I can do," she said, her voice muffled. "I don't want to hear it."

Rachel sighed and lay back down. "Well," she said. "At least there's one good thing about Marissa."

"What's that?" Mandy asked.

Rachel started to laugh. "She didn't tell me *my* thighs looked fat."

"Ha-ha," Ellen said.

Everybody settled down to their books and magazines. I couldn't help taking my little mirror out of my tote and checking my face. Was my lipstick really too pink?

Then I told myself to stop worrying. I was an eighth-grader. Why was I worried about what some little seventh-grader with braces thought?

Low lights! She didn't know what she was talking about.

It was while I was looking in the mirror that I saw the *cute guy!*

He and some other guys were coming down to

the beach behind us. Feeling kind of like a spy, I watched him. What a babe!

He was tall and had straight brown hair down to his shoulders. His eyes were bright blue. He was laughing at something one of his friends had said, and he had these superwhite teeth.

My heart started thumping like crazy.

That's when I realized that Mandy was talking to me.

"Jessica!" she was saying. "Hello? Are you there?"

"Yeah . . . I was just . . ."

"Deciding where to put the low lights?" she teased.

"You're hilarious." I put down the mirror. "What did you say?"

She leaned over Rachel and whispered, "I said that there are a lot of cute guys around."

"I noticed."

"Pippa said there's a club down by the pier. It's teens only tomorrow night. Let's go."

"Sounds like a plan," I said, already trying to decide which of my fabulous new sundresses to wear.

I looked back over my shoulder, wondering what the cute guy and his friends were doing. They were only a few yards away, and miracle of miracles, he looked right at me.

His blue eyes met mine, and he smiled.

Then a Frisbee came sailing toward him, and he dove for it. He didn't look back at me. He was too busy running around and laughing.

But we had made eye contact. It was a start.

After a little while the cute guy and his friends

left the beach. But we stayed and spent the rest of the day swimming, bodysurfing, and hanging.

I kept hoping the cute guy would come back, but he never did.

By late afternoon everybody was pretty pooped. We decided to go take showers and then find burgers. I decided to take one last walk along the beach to see if I could spot the cute guy.

Marissa offered to walk with me.

At first I wasn't too thrilled to have her with me. But then as we walked along she leaned over and found a sand dollar. Whole. Unbroken.

I told her I'd never found a whole one. Ever. And that she was lucky.

She told me she *was* lucky. Lucky that the Unicorns had come.

Then she handed me the sand dollar and told me it was a present. She said that she was going to remember this summer forever—because it was the first summer she had had friends.

I didn't know what to say. I felt flattered but also guilty. Because I know the other girls really don't like her. They're only tolerating her. They aren't really her friends, and neither am I.

But I couldn't tell her that. So I just thanked her and said it was really nice of her to give me the sand dollar.

Then I felt even guiltier. Because I knew that if *I* had found the sand dollar, I would have kept it.

I heard somebody calling us and saw Kimberly waving from the balcony. It was time for dinner.

Hold on. The phone is ringing.

It's Wiley. For Lila. She's giving me this dirty look like she wants me to get out of the alcove so she can sit here and have some privacy while she talks to Wiley.

No way.

Let her call him back on her stupid little mobile phone, which she has to have with her every single moment of the day in case Wiley needs to tell her something urgent, like that it's raining back in Sweet Valley.

Now she's whispering.

Now she's giggling.

Now she's whispering and giggling while looking at me so I'll think she's talking to Wiley about me.

I'm not going to give her the satisfaction of watching her put on a big show, so I'll finish this later.

Five

◇

Dear Diary,

Later . . .

(Lila spent about two hours talking to Wiley. Their phone bills are going to be huge.)

Now that she's off the phone, she's sitting in the living room draped over the sofa, looking languid and lovelorn. Watching her is really making me feel ill, so I'm turning the other way while I write.

Back to the story . . .

OK. So the next day (which was yesterday) we were all going to the teen club.

The entire day was devoted to primping, starting the minute we got up. Fingernails. Toenails. Hot oil treatments. Plucking. Steaming. All that stuff is very time consuming, and before we knew it, it was five o'clock and time to start the serious dressing part of the evening.

Marissa went into the bathroom around five and *would not* come out. I thought Kimberly was going to have a total conniption. Finally Kimberly decided to get ready in Pippa's bathroom and I went in and shared Rachel and Lila's bathroom—which annoyed them, but I really didn't have any choice.

When Kimberly and I got back to the room, Marissa was *still* in the bathroom.

"Think something's wrong?" Kimberly asked.

"Maybe we should call the fire department," I suggested. "Maybe she's stuck in the tub."

Finally the door opened and out she came.

"Ta-da!" She twirled out of the bathroom like a ballerina. "How do I look?"

"You look great," I said, and I meant it. I was floored. Her hair was on top of her head in a messy updo, and she had on a short sundress with a flippy skirt in a big, bold, black-and-white check.

"I think I look like I'm in at least the ninth grade," she said proudly.

Kimberly, who was standing in front of the dresser trying to get the clips into her hair, turned around and rolled her eyes at me.

I rolled my eyes back.

"I'm going to show Pippa." Marissa flounced out of the room and down the hall to Pippa's room.

Modesty is not Marissa's best sport. All afternoon, while we had been primping together, she had been getting more and more full of herself.

Everyone was getting pretty sick of her. But when Lila had raised the possibility of leaving Marissa at home while we all went to the club, Kimberly vetoed it. Pippa wouldn't stand for it, she told us.

I wasn't too thrilled about having Marissa come to the teen club with us, but I wasn't as bugged as Lila. I was in too good a mood to be bugged by anything. I hadn't seen the cute guy again, but somehow I had a feeling he would be there.

"Whoooaa!" Rachel said, coming into our room. She looked at me and turned her thumb up.

I had on my new lime green dress with butterfly cutouts on the back. My hair was down and loose, and I had long swinging earrings made out of abalone that picked up the green of my dress. "You look gorgeous," I told Rachel, returning the compliment.

Rachel had on white silk pants with a bright red silk shirt tied at the midriff. It was all very sixties Cher-glam. Rachel pretended to model and then flopped down on the bed. "Hurry up!" she yelled to Lila and the others.

"*I can't,*" Mandy shouted from the bathroom across the hall. "*I'm having a hair emergency!*"

Ellen came in, laughing. "Mandy's pink extension fell out. Has anybody seen it?"

That broke us up, and we all started looking around the apartment for it. Finally Lila found it out in the hall. She came back in holding it between her fingers with her nose wrinkled. "I think it got stepped on, and there seems to be something gummy stuck to it."

"Ewwwww," we all chorused.

Mandy went over and examined the damage, then she dropped it in the wastebasket. "Oh, well," she said with a sigh. "At least I've got the orange and green ones."

"If I were you, I'd get rid of those too," Marissa piped up. "Nobody wears those things anymore," she said in this obnoxious woman-of-the-world tone of voice.

"Marissa!" Kimberly said sharply. "Why don't you keep your opinions to yourself?"

Marissa didn't look fazed. "Hey!" she said. "If you can't trust your friends to tell you the truth, who can you trust?"

"We *are* Mandy's friends," Lila said. "And we happen to like the extensions."

"You're kidding," Marissa said, like she couldn't believe we all had such terrible taste.

"Let's gooooo!" Rachel shouted.

And that was the end of that.

Everybody ran around finding their purses and stuff. I noticed Mandy was looking at herself in the front-hall mirror while we waited for the elevator. "They look great," I whispered. "Don't worry."

Mandy gave me a weak smile. She looked really pretty in a vintage raspberry silk sheath and matching sandals. She pressed her lips together and tweaked her extensions. "That kid is starting to work my nerves," she said.

"That kid is starting to work everybody's nerves," Ellen muttered.

"Can't you *do* something?" Lila asked Kimberly.

"Like what?" Kimberly wanted to know.

Before Lila could answer, Marissa came out of the apartment all smiles and talking a mile a minute as usual.

"The teen club is such a cool place," she said breathlessly. "Everybody goes there—all the kids from this stretch of the beach and all the kids whose parents are staying in the hotel on the other side of the cove. Don't worry if you don't know anybody. I'll introduce you to all the people I know and—"

Good thing the elevator bell rang. I thought Lila might just strangle her.

We walked to the teen club. Marissa managed to totally irritate everybody before we even got there.

But she was sure right about the club. It was definitely *the* place to be. Wall-to-wall kids. The music was hammering, and the dance floor was packed.

I was really excited that so many people were there. But I was on a mission: I had to find the guy from the beach.

Marissa sort of elbowed her way through our little crowd. "Follow me," she ordered.

So we did. She seemed to know her way around the place, and we scooched along behind her. Somewhere in there she disappeared. The rest of us didn't know what to do, so we just kept going until we came out on the other side of the crowd and found ourselves in an open area that faced the beach.

There was no back wall, and the crowd spilled out onto this big deck that extended all the way into and over the water.

There was a juice bar set up on the deck, so we

headed for it. The guy behind the bar was a babe with black hair, long on top and shaved up the back and sides. He had earrings in both ears and a killer smile. He winked at me and said, "I already know what you want."

"No, you don't," I said with a laugh.

"OK," he agreed. "But I know what you should have. You need a drink to go with that dress. Let me make it for you. First one's on the house." He reached for the blender and started pouring all kinds of stuff in the canister.

"What's it called?" I asked, trying to watch what he was doing. His hands and wrists moved so fast, I couldn't keep track. He was like a magician. Bottles and chunks of fruit seemed to appear and disappear like magic.

He dropped some ice cubes into the mix. "What's your name?"

"Jessica."

"Hi, Jessica. My name's Carl, and this drink is called a Jessica Hawaiian Iced Jade Surprise." He hit the button and the whole thing exploded inside the blender. Two seconds later he switched it off, whisked off the top, poured the mix into a tall glass, and handed me a drink that was the *exact* same green as my dress.

Rachel clapped. "That is so cool. Can you make me something to match my blouse?"

Carl opened his arms. "You're looking at the primo blender-drink artist of the Western world. Of course I can make a drink to match your blouse." He pretended to study the color. "That is one gorgeous red," he commented, reaching for a bottle.

Half a minute later Rachel was sipping something tall, icy, and crimson.

"Where's Marissa and Mandy?" Kimberly asked as the bar guy went to work on something for Ellen.

"I think we lost them," Rachel said. "Ohmigosh, look!"

I looked and nearly fell over. The bar guy had actually made a drink that was *yellow and red striped*—just like Ellen's tank top.

We all burst into applause, and he took a dramatic bow.

That's when Marissa found us. Mandy was behind her. "Hi, Carl!" Marissa said.

The bar guy straightened up from his bow and gave Marissa a wide smile. "Look who's here," he said happily. "How ya doin', sweetheart?" Then he saw Mandy. "Hi," he said, sort of quietly.

"Hi," Mandy replied. Then she flushed slightly pink.

Naturally Marissa ignored the obvious chemistry going on between Mandy and Carl. She flashed us a big metal smile. "I see you met my friends. Guys, this is Carl. When he's not working here, he works for Pippa at the Surf Shop."

"Busy, busy, busy," he joked, managing to tear his eyes off Mandy.

"What do you do in the shop?" Rachel asked.

"Actually, I'm a clerk and surf instructor," Carl answered, turning back to Mandy, even though it was Rachel who had asked the question. "If people buy their equipment from the shop, they can book lessons with me."

"Can you make a drink to match my dress?" Marissa challenged.

We all laughed since her dress was black and white.

"How about I make a drink to match your eyes instead?" he suggested—which I thought made him sound very gallant.

After he had handed a drink to Marissa, he smiled at Mandy. "I knew there was a reason I stocked up on raspberries."

Mandy smiled shyly while Carl made her a frozen raspberry drink to coordinate with her outfit. I love a man who can accessorize.

By then there was a line forming behind us. So when we all had our drinks, we had to move on—even though I could have spent the whole night talking to Carl and watching him make those drinks.

"I think he likes you," I heard Rachel whisper to Mandy as we moved toward the dance floor.

Mandy giggled. "Really?"

Before anybody could say anything else, Lila gasped. "Oh, no!"

"What?" I asked.

"Oh, nonononono!" Lila groaned, turning quickly so her back was to the crowd. She pulled me slightly aside. "There's Peter Feldman."

"Who?"

"Peter Feldman. He goes to Sweet Valley High. Correction. He *rules* Sweet Valley High. And he knows Wiley." She pointed to this guy who was standing over by the rail with some older-looking kids.

"So let's go say hi," I suggested.

Lila grimaced. "Are you kidding? With Marissa around? No way. I don't want him to see me hanging with her. Let's just try to get past them and keep from being seen."

"Lila! If he's here, we're going to run into him sometime!" I argued.

But Lila had already scooted away into the main part of the club. Rachel, Ellen, Marissa, and Kimberly were standing by the opposite rail, looking down at the water.

I started to go over to them but decided I'd rather go into the club and see the sights.

Inside the club it was dark and really crowded. I walked around, smiling at people who looked friendly. But I was really looking for the guy I'd seen earlier. I had a feeling about him. Like I was just supposed to see him again.

I was still looking all around when somebody tapped me on the shoulder. I turned and sucked in my breath. It was him. The cute guy from the beach. He had on khakis and a bright yellow polo shirt. With his long hair and big blue eyes, he looked like the perfect combination of clean-cut and hip. My kind of guy.

"Hi!" he shouted. "I'm Jason Landry. I saw you on the beach yesterday."

"I saw you too. My name's Jessica Wakefield," I shouted back.

"Do you want to dance, Jessica Wakefield?"

"Sure!" He took my hand, and we somehow

found a place on the dance floor. We moved back and forth, but it was so crowded, people kept bumping into us.

After about the third time he backed into somebody and I did too, he just threw up his hands—like he was giving up—and then he put his arms around me so that we were dancing close instead of apart.

It was the most romantic thing that had ever happened to me. He put his arms around me like it wasn't any big deal at all, and I felt totally comfortable putting my arms around him.

We danced—swaying back and forth—until the music was over, then we left the dance floor. He took my hand and pulled me toward the deck. "Let's go outside so we can talk," he shouted.

I nodded and followed him. As we walked outside we passed the whole group. Lila's mouth opened slightly, and Rachel put her hand over her mouth to hide her smile. Ellen gave me a thumbs-up.

I felt just totally great. I—Jessica Wakefield—had snagged a babe. "That's better," he said, leaning back against the rail. "I can hear again."

"Are you here for vacation?" I asked him.

"Yes and no. I spend every summer here. My folks are divorced, and my dad lives in one of the condos on the beach. I've been coming for so many years, it feels like a second home. I've got a whole set of friends here. Activities, all that stuff. During the school year I live in Vermont. What about you?"

"I'm here visiting," I said. "From California."

Just then two other guys came up. "Hey!"

"Hey!" Jason said. "This is Jessica. Jessica, this is Rafe and Larry." Jason grinned at me. "Didn't you have some friends too?" he asked me.

I laughed, turned, and motioned the gang over.

They came over, giggling. Everybody introduced themselves, and pretty soon even more guys found their way over. Almost all of them were staying near Pippa's condo.

Everybody was talking, laughing, and flirting. Then all of a sudden, along came Marissa.

She went right up to Jason and said, "Hi. I saw you playing Frisbee yesterday."

"I saw you too," he said with a smile. "You're a good bodysurfer. You took some big waves."

Marissa smiled and giggled. "I guess it comes naturally. I'm in the surfing business."

"Oh, brother," I heard Kimberly sigh.

How typical. Marissa had helped Pippa out in the surf shops, and now she was acting like they were *her* shops.

"So how does everybody know each other?" Rafe asked.

I started to answer, but before I could even get a word out, Marissa jumped right in. "We're all friends," she told him. "We're having a house party. I got here early so I could scope out the scene and get ready to be the hostess with the mostess."

Kimberly glared at Marissa, but she wasn't paying any attention. Even if she'd seen Kimberly glaring, it wouldn't have fazed her. It would have taken an elephant to squash Marissa.

I didn't blame Kimberly for being mad. Marissa was making it sound like it was *her* house party and we were all *her* guests and *her* friends.

Then, as if she hadn't been nervy enough, she turned to Jason and said, "Oh! This is my favorite song in the whole world. Come on. Let's dance." Then she grabbed his hand and practically dragged him into the club where the dancers were.

I couldn't believe it. I couldn't believe that here I was getting this great thing going with Jason—and Marissa—*Marissa with her stupid braces and hee-haw donkey giggle*—had just kidnapped him.

"He's just being nice," Mandy whispered to me. "Don't get bent."

I tried to relax. Mandy was right. Obviously Jason was a really sweet guy. It was probably clear to him that Marissa was younger and didn't really fit in with our crowd—so he was going out of his way to be nice to her.

Handsome *and* a good personality. My favorite combo.

The next thing I knew, the whole gang was headed for the dance floor. All of us girls and about six guys, including Rafe and Larry.

We joined Marissa and Jason in the middle of the floor. Once we started dancing, it was impossible to figure out who was dancing with who. It didn't matter. We just danced in one big group and had a fabulous time.

Finally after about an hour Jason opened the collar of his shirt, pushed back his hair—which was damp with sweat—and took my arm. "Let's get some air," he shouted.

I was ready. Not only was I hot; the muscles in my legs and arms were turning to rubber. We went out on the deck and over to the juice bar. Carl wasn't there anymore. There was another guy behind the bar, and Jason got us a couple of orange juices.

"Let's walk on the beach," he said.

We walked down the wooden steps to the sand. I took off my sandals and hid them under a log. He took my hand, and we walked to the water.

"Marissa's got a great house party going," he said.

I was just about to set him straight on the Marissa thing when he put his arm around my shoulders. "You know, I really like the way all of you have so much fun together. At my school, hanging in a group can be impossible. Some of the kids are such backstabbers, it's scary. The minute you start talking to someone, he'll start bad-mouthing the others. You guys don't do that. Marissa had nothing but nice things to say about you and everybody else."

I shut my mouth and groaned inside. What could I say now? That Marissa was a little pest and we couldn't stand her? And have Jason think that we were worse than the kids back in Vermont? I think not.

So I just smiled and changed the subject. "Tell me about your friends."

The water came up and lapped around my ankles, cooling me off. We started walking along, kicking up little sprays of water. "Rafe comes every summer—like me. Both his parents live here. His dad was transferred here by his company, but Rafe wanted to stay at his school back home, so he boards there during the school year. Larry is Rafe's cousin, and he's here to visit for the summer. The rest of the guys are sort of a pickup crew. You know, guys that are here with their families for vacation or visiting relatives. They're all nice. That's one good thing about being here during the summers—there's no shortage of people to hang with. For the past two summers I've been a camp counselor, but this year I'm taking the summer off to have fun. I love hanging out in a big group of people."

He snapped his fingers. "Hey! I'm going camping with my dad for a couple of days, but I'll be back Wednesday. Let's have a beach party Thursday night. We could make a bonfire and cook out. Play music and dance on the beach."

"Sounds great! What can we bring?"

Jason and I walked back to the club, planning who would do what. The guys would bring soda, ice, hot dogs, and buns. We would bring dessert, CDs, and a boom box. We'd all meet just before the sun went down to gather wood for the fire.

I took another moment to retrieve my sandals from under the log, and by the time we got back to the club, everybody was out on the deck. Jason and

I told them the plan, and they were psyched.

"Wait a minute," Kimberly said. "I'm not sure Pippa's got a boom box."

Marissa held up her hand. "Leave it to me," she said in this know-it-all voice. "I've got connections."

"Who?" Kimberly challenged.

Marissa gave her a Cheshire cat grin. "Carl! He keeps one at the shop. He said I could borrow it when my friends came. And now here you are."

She turned and stared directly at Jason, who looked impressed.

Believe it or not, it made me jealous.

It also made me determined that at the beach party, I was not going to share Jason with Marissa.

Marissa needed to learn that she was a seventh-grader. She was a kid. She could get away with some things, but not with everything. Such as dancing and flirting with *my* guy.

And so, Dear Diary, that brings us up-to-date.

A lot of good stuff is happening. But there's been a lot of stress and turmoil too. So I'm not going to sign off with any predictions about how wonderful things are going to go at the party. I don't want to jinx it.

Six

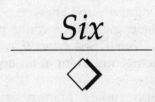

Dear Diary,

Unbelievably, I'm actually starting to like Marissa. When she's not cranked up to hypergab, she's a lot of fun. She knows a lot of jokes. She asks everybody questions about themselves. And she loves hearing us talk about Sweet Valley Middle School. It's like she just can't get enough stories about the school and the clubs and the people.

That's really how we started to be friends. Marissa loves hearing stories about me and Elizabeth. And I like to tell them. I'm missing Elizabeth. A lot. Talking about her makes me feel closer to her even though she's a million miles away in the rain forest somewhere.

Marissa and I were sitting at the breakfast table laughing about one of those stories this morning when the phone rang. It was Wiley, for Lila.

The whole time Lila was on the phone, she kept giving me funny looks—like she was sizing me up. It was really starting to irritate me. So I turned my back on her.

Then Pippa came in. She had on a black vinyl shirt and low-cut blue jeans. She looked fantastic—but not like any grown-up I knew.

I couldn't help giggling. I could just hear Mr. Haver yelling, *"Nuts!!! She's nuts!!!"*

I tried to picture my mom in an outfit like that. No could do!

Anyway, Pippa asked Marissa and me if we wanted to run over to the Surf Shop with her. Marissa said she would go, but I was happy hangin'. Besides, I wanted to get caught up on my diary.

Lila was still talking on the phone, and I could see that Lila's phone fixation was working Pippa's nerves big time. Even though Lila was on her mobile and not Pippa's phone, the point was that Lila was being rude. When Lila was on the phone, she ignored everybody. She didn't say "good morning," "good night," "hello," or anything else. She didn't come to the table if we were eating. When Lila was on the phone, the rest of us might as well have been invisible.

But the worst part was that she wanted us all to be quiet. If we made any noise or interruption, she gave us dirty looks and shushed us.

Pippa and Marissa were on their way out, and Lila didn't even acknowledge they were leaving. She didn't wave or mouth the word *good-bye*. She just kept murmuring into the telephone like she and

Wiley were exchanging national secrets or something.

So Pippa marched over to the sofa where Lila was sitting and leaned over the back of it so that her long hair hung over Lila's head like a curtain.

Lila let out this little croak of surprise.

"Good-bye, Lila! Good-bye, Wiley!" Pippa shouted. "No! No! Don't get up. I wouldn't want to interrupt you." Then giggling like Marissa, she threw back her head and ran out the door.

I cracked up. I'd never seen an adult correct somebody's manners in such a hilarious way.

Lila still didn't appreciate it, though. She took the phone and stomped out of the room.

Half an hour later Kimberly came and told me we were having a meeting in Lila and Rachel's room.

I took what was left of my raspberry tea and followed her down the hall to the back bedroom. Lila, Rachel, and Ellen were all sitting there, looking really serious. So serious, I actually got worried. "What's wrong?" I asked. "Is somebody hurt?"

Lila shook her head. "No. But I talked to Wiley. He said that he's already starting to get invitations to some of the Welcome to Sweet Valley High parties."

"Goody for Wiley," I said. "What's that got to do with us?"

Lila folded her arms. "If you could cut the sarcasm for two seconds and let me finish, I'll tell you."

"Listen to her," Rachel said. "This is serious stuff."

"Wiley said that there are a lot of cute ninth-grade guys who don't have dates. And while they're not thrilled with the idea of taking an eighth-grader, they might be willing to ask an eighth-grade girl—*if*—she *measured up*. Know what I mean?"

I did. And I felt butterflies of excitement in my stomach. Actually going to high-school parties with high-school guys was just . . . I couldn't even think of words to describe it. And the best part was that it would *kill* Steven. He *loves* making me and Elizabeth feel like underlings. He'd just eat his heart out if I actually wound up at a high-school dance with a guy who might even be on the basketball team with him.

Suddenly I felt really bad about all the things I'd written about Lila in my diary. She didn't have to set all this up for us. She could have been the only Unicorn at the high-school parties and then gloated about it until we wanted to kill her.

For Lila Fowler, this was the ultimate generous act.

"I don't think we'll have any problems measuring up," I told her, sitting down on the bed. "We look great. All of us. We've got the hair. We've got the clothes. We've got the personality and the poise. We totally measure up."

"There's a problem," Mandy said in a flat tone.

"What?"

"Marissa," they all said at once.

Rachel looked at me. "I'm betting that the beach party is going to be huge."

"So?"

"So it means that Peter Feldman will probably be there," Lila explained. "Wiley says Peter Feldman has very high standards. If Peter's at the party, he'll see us with Marissa. And Marissa will probably collar him and tell him how the Unicorns are all her very best friends, and Peter will think we're the Nerd Patrol. By the time we get back to Sweet Valley, we'll be total laughingstocks. Believe me, Wiley's friends won't want to hang with the Unidorks."

I felt really torn. I resented letting Wiley Upjohn tell me who I could or couldn't hang with. And I was really starting to like Marissa. On the other hand, I didn't want her ruining my chances of social success in the eighth grade.

"So what can we do about her?" I asked. "Pippa made it pretty plain we have to include her."

Kimberly nodded. "Yeah. Pippa made it clear we have to include Marissa. But what if Marissa didn't want to hang with us?"

"Huh?"

"We're going to make *her* drop *us*," Rachel explained.

"How?"

Ellen giggled. "We have a plan."

When she told me about the plan, I had mixed feelings about it. But I realized if I didn't go through with it, I'd wind up dateless in eighth grade.

So tonight Operation Ditch Marissa goes into action. We will, of course, keep you informed as this story develops.

TUESDAY, 10:00 A.M.

Dear Diary,

Now, short sheeting isn't the worst thing in the world that could happen to you. But it's nothing you want to deal with on a regular basis. So when Marissa climbed into bed last night—and discovered she'd been short sheeted—we laughed and told her to get used to it. We told her that the Unicorns *loved* practical jokes, and we played them on each other all the time.

She laughed and tried to be a good sport about it. But when we turned off the electricity in the condo (Rachel found the circuit breakers) while she was trying to remake her bed—she got upset and went running to Pippa. (Pippa was already asleep, which is why she didn't notice the unusual power outage.)

Pippa appeared with a flashlight. "What's going on?" she asked sleepily. "Marissa said you guys screwed up her bed and turned off the electricity." Pippa didn't sound angry. But she didn't sound very amused either.

"It was just a joke," Rachel said. "We didn't mean to upset her." Rachel's tone somehow managed to sound concerned while also implying that if Marissa weren't such a baby, Pippa's sleep never would have been disturbed. That Rachel—she's good.

Pippa took the flashlight out into the utility room, found the circuit box, and flipped the appropriate switches. The lights came back on. After that, Pippa found another sheet for Marissa. She handed it to Kimberly. "Fix Marissa's bed tomorrow morning, will you, Kimberly?"

"Where is she?" Kimberly asked.

Pippa pressed her lips together. "She's going to sleep in my room tonight. We'll talk more tomorrow. OK?"

We all went back to our rooms. "Think Pippa's mad?" I asked Kimberly.

Kimberly flopped down on her own bed. "Probably not. She's probably more irritated with Marissa for waking her up than she is with us. But we've got to be careful. We can't look like we're singling Marissa out for the treatment."

This morning Kimberly and I went into action. "*Kimberly!*" I yelled, pretending to be mad as I chased her into the living room.

Kimberly ran into the living room, jumped over the couch, laughing hysterically, and "hid" behind Ellen.

"What's going on?" Ellen asked.

I held out my hairbrush. "Look!"

"What happened?"

"Kimberly cut all the bristles off!" I yelled.

Kimberly snorted. "That makes us even," she said. "Remember the time you put peanut butter in the toes of my shoes?"

Rachel threw up her arms. "Sometimes I am so sorry I joined this stupid club! *When* are you guys going to outgrow these practical jokes?"

"Never," Ellen told her with a big grin. "They're waaaay too much fun."

I flopped down on the couch like I was too tired to chase Kimberly anymore. And Kimberly came out of "hiding." She smiled at Pippa. "You wanted to talk to us?"

Pippa stood in the kitchen behind the counter, holding a cup of coffee. She took a sip and stared at us all, like she was thinking hard. Trying to put last night's short-sheeting episode into perspective.

Finally she smiled. "I just wanted to tell you guys to leave the circuit breakers alone. I've got some computer equipment in my room, and you could mess it up. Now I want everybody to get dressed. We're going on an outing. All of us. I'll tell Marissa." Pippa left the room, and we all froze for a moment, then we silently pumped our fists.

The plan is working.

I've been ready for the last twenty minutes. But Marissa's still in the bathroom getting ready, and so is Lila.

I wonder where we're going? Pippa won't tell us. But she's standing in the living room, yelling at us all to, "Move it! Move it! Move it!"

TUESDAY, 8:00 P.M.

Dear Diary,

Did I say Pippa was cool?

Talk about an understatement.

Not only does she have a Suburban, several surfing trophies, and her own chain of surfing shops, she has *a plane!* And a pilot's license!

We went out to this little private airport where a bunch of small passenger planes were lined up ready to take off. Over to the side there was a small building that looked more like a hut. We went inside, and Pippa introduced us to Mr. Hajit.

Mr. Hajit is a pilot, and he flies people from island to island. Pippa's plane only seats four, so she had arranged with him to help her transport us all to Maui for the day.

Kimberly, Marissa, and I went with Pippa. Everybody else flew with Mr. Hajit.

I'd never been on a little plane before, and I expected to be scared. But I wasn't scared a bit. I felt even safer than I do in a big plane. I guess because we were flying close enough to the ground that we could see everything—all the islands and roads and houses. It felt more like gliding than flying.

I couldn't help imagining what would happen if the engine blew out. In my imagination, we were so light that we circled down like a gull and skimmed along the surface of the water.

We landed at another little airport on Maui. This guy named Steve met us with a van.

Pippa is going into the gift shop business, and she's opening a store in a fancy hotel on Maui. Steve's dad is managing the shop for her. They're still getting it ready.

I'm beginning to think it's Mr. Haver who's "nuts." Pippa's no surf bum. She's a big-time businesswoman.

Anyway, Steve is sixteen and very Polynesian looking and has straight black hair down to his waist, practically. He wears it in a loose braid. Talk about gorgeous!

Lucky Kimberly. She got to sit between him and Pippa in the front seat. He and Kimberly hit it off great. She even asked him to the party Thursday night. Unfortunately he said he had to work. He and his dad are doing some renovation.

Anyhow, he drove us all over the island. Maui is made up of two volcanic mountains. Between them are lots of sugarcane and pineapple plantations.

Steve had brought a picnic lunch, and we ate it in the Haleakala National Park—where we saw the crater of an actual volcano. It's inactive—so we didn't have to outrun any lava—but it was very cool.

We spent the whole day driving over the island. Up and down winding roads and mountain peaks. I've never seen so many gorgeous and romantic views.

After that, we stopped by the hotel where Pippa's shop is going to be. Talk about plush! Wow. It's a high-rise with sprawling grounds and gardens.

The gift shop area is still full of lumber and dust, but I can see that it's going to be very nice when it's finished. We met Steve's dad. He looks a lot like Steve—but older of course.

He seemed very happy to meet Kimberly and Marissa. When Pippa said they might be coming back to help out, he smiled and said he would be delighted to have them. Then he made a point of taking Kimberly on a tour of the renovation and showing her stuff. He even asked her advice about whether or not to use mirrors as shelves.

I could tell Kimberly was flattered to be asked for her opinion.

Soon it was time to be heading back. Steve drove us all to the airport. Mr. Hajit was waiting for us. We all climbed back in the little planes and went buzzing back to Oahu. As I looked down I wondered what it was like in the old days, when people got from island to island in long canoes.

We got home about an hour ago. Kimberly is sitting on the balcony, staring at the water with a very introspective look on her face.

Ellen and Rachel are trying to figure out if Larry and Rafe are interested in them. And if they are— which guy is interested in which girl?

And Lila is . . . what else? . . . on the phone with Wiley.

She's hanging up. She's motioning for everybody to meet her in her room.

Bye.

TUESDAY, 9:40 P.M.

Dear Diary,

Lila just called us into her room and gave us the rundown on the big social lineup taking place back in Sweet Valley.

Come September, it's going to be parties, parties, and more parties. Wiley is talking to some of his friends about us as potential dates. But Lila says he's very nervous about this middle-school/high-school dating thing.

According to Lila, all hinges on making a good impression on Peter Feldman. He's leaving Hawaii and going back to Sweet Valley soon. And he's going to be running the orientation program for the new freshmen!

It's absolutely, positively "imperative" (according to Wiley) that we get the Peter Feldman seal of approval. Which means phase two of Ditch Marissa goes into action tomorrow.

Kimberly held up her hand. "Hold it," she said. "I'm beginning to think this is not the greatest idea."

Lila frowned. "What do you mean?"

Kimberly bit her lip. "It's just not a great idea. Marissa's not so bad. She hasn't done anything to us. And Pippa's been really cool. I don't want to let her down."

Rachel nodded. "Kimberly's right. Pippa's really rolled out the red carpet. If she wants us to include Marissa and be nice, isn't that the least we can do?"

Mandy nodded, and so did Ellen.

Lila stood up and put her hands on her hips. "Kimberly, you're going to be in high school this coming year. Don't you see what that means? It means you have more at stake here than any of us! We all have a year to make our reps before high school. You've got *maybe* a few weeks. Remember, you're going in there alone. No backup. We won't be there to sit with at lunch. We won't be there to talk to between classes. If Janet thinks you've slipped—she won't even acknowledge you exist."

Kimberly swallowed nervously.

It was brutal, but everything Lila was saying was true.

I looked at Ellen, Mandy, and Rachel. Their eyes were big and scared.

"So I'm telling you guys," Lila continued. "If you want to be players in September, you're going to have to do it my way."

I watched Rachel's face. Rachel is just as rich

and spoiled as Lila. Just as used to getting her way. She was the one Unicorn who could usually be counted on to challenge Lila.

She looked like she was thinking things over. Trying to decide whether or not to let Lila push her around.

"Do I have to remind you guys that only one of us here is dating a guy in high school?" Lila asked. That was the clincher, and she knew it.

Rachel blew out her breath. "OK. Tell us what to do."

"Just act cool. Like you're not impressed with anybody or anything. We've been there, and we've done that. We're over it. We're over *everything*. Got it?"

Mandy chewed a nail and nodded. So did Ellen.

"That's just dumb," I said. "Jason and his friends didn't dance with us because we looked bored. They danced with us because we looked friendly."

"Friendly is for dorks like Marissa," Lila snapped. "And speaking of Marissa . . ."

Forget it. I just can't write anymore. Maybe I'll feel different about everything tomorrow.

WEDNESDAY, 7:00 P.M.

Dear Diary,

I woke up this morning feeling sick to my stomach. At breakfast I said I didn't feel too good and didn't want to go. Lila gave me such a dirty look, I changed my story and said I felt great and was ready to roar.

The plan was that we were all going to go snorkeling at Malaka Cove and play another "joke" on Marissa.

Pippa said she was going to be out most of the day and wouldn't be back until late that night. But

she said it was fine for us to go snorkeling at
Malaka Cove as long as we stayed together, and
she wrote down directions for how to get there.

On the bus to Malaka Cove, Marissa sat next to
me and talked nonstop. It was a long bus ride, and
sitting next to Marissa made it seem even longer.
The bus was cold too. They must have had the air-
conditioning turned up full blast.

Finally we got to the cove. We all took off our
cover-ups and shoes and laid them on our towels.
Then we put on the masks and fins and headed out
into the water.

I'll say this for Marissa. She's irritating, but she
is a really good swimmer. She's very brave too.
She checked out stuff that I was way too chicken to
approach.

I wish I were a better writer so I could describe
everything I saw. When I read this diary twenty
years from now, I'd like to be able to remember
how beautiful it all was. Schools of fish like flower
gardens swam around us. Their fins were like
angel wings—so clear and graceful and delicate.
They had personalities too. Some of them were
quick and excitable—like squirrels. Some were
slow and looked very bored—like they saw
snorkelers every day and didn't think it was any
big deal.

I was having such a good time looking at the
fish and the coral, I forgot about what was happening back on the beach. So when Marissa and I
swam back to the shore and walked up to get our

stuff, I was almost as surprised as she was to see that her cover-up, towel, and shoes were gone.

Then I remembered.

The others were already on the beach toweling off and getting their stuff together.

"Where's my stuff?" Marissa asked Rachel.

Rachel looked surprised, like she had no idea what Marissa was talking about. "What stuff?"

"My cover-up," Marissa told her. "My shoes. My towel. All my stuff."

Rachel shrugged. "I don't know. I haven't seen it. Lila? What about you?"

Lila toweled her hair. "Nope. Haven't seen them." The tone of her voice made it clear that she couldn't care less about the whole situation.

Marissa was starting to scamper around in circles, looking at the ground like maybe her stuff would turn up in a clump of grass or behind some driftwood. "Guys! This is serious. Where is my cover-up and towel? I need my shoes."

Nobody expressed any concern. Nobody expressed any surprise. Nobody expressed any sympathy. In fact, nobody said a word.

Finally Marissa got it. She froze for a second. Then her eyes went from one face to the next. "You guys hid my stuff, didn't you?"

Lila opened her eyes really wide. The picture of fake innocence. "Why would we do that?"

Marissa gave Lila a weak smile. "I don't know. But can I please have my stuff back?"

"We don't have your stuff," Rachel said, buckling

her sandals. "It's getting late. Let's go, or we'll miss the bus."

Everybody started walking up the beach to the road. Nobody looked back. We acted as if we didn't care if Marissa was with us or not.

"*Guys!*" Marissa shouted. "I can't leave without my stuff."

Nobody paid any attention.

"Why are you doing this?" Marissa shouted, her voice breaking. "This isn't funny."

"Think she's getting the message?" Rachel asked Mandy.

"I think she's getting it," Mandy answered.

Marissa came running up behind us, her arms folded across her chest, barefooted and in her bathing suit. "If you guys don't give me my stuff, I'll . . ."

The bus pulled up right then. The door opened, and everybody got on. Marissa hesitated outside the bus, shivering. The bus driver frowned. "Come on, kid. Are you getting on or not?"

Marissa came running up the stairs, and Kimberly dropped some coins into the box for her.

Everybody sat down. Marissa started to sit down next to me, then she stopped. She gave me a hurt, angry look and threw herself into the seat across the aisle.

She turned her face to the window and didn't say one word on the way back. The only thing I heard was the sound of her teeth chattering in the cold.

I felt bad. But then I pictured her grabbing Jason's

hand and dragging him toward the dance floor. I wasn't about to let that happen at the beach party.

I didn't feel bad after that.

When we got back to the condo, Marissa stormed into our room, shut the door with a slam, and locked it.

"Oh, well," Kimberly said. "We can use the bathroom in the hall to shower. She can't keep us locked out forever."

We all took showers, changed into shorts and T-shirts, and found some hamburger meat in the fridge.

"Should I make one for Marissa?" Rachel asked, starting to make the patties.

"Yeah," Kimberly told her. "If she doesn't want it, I'll eat it. I'm starving."

I actually wasn't. I had a heavy feeling in the pit of my stomach. I pictured Marissa in the bathroom, sobbing her eyes out.

I was beginning to wish we hadn't done it. I was beginning to think I might even go into the room and apologize. I was beginning to think that Marissa wasn't nearly as bad as I thought.

But then Marissa came out of her room.

Her eyes weren't red. She didn't look like she had been crying. In fact, she looked like she had just spent the last two hours primping. Her hair was clean, and she'd styled it with hot rollers. Her makeup was perfect, and she had on a cute outfit. "OK," she said. "I just want to tell you guys that I am sooooo sorry."

Huh? I thought. We all looked at one another.

Marissa rolled her eyes upward, like a movie star accepting an award, and then let out this breathless little laugh. "I don't know what my problem is." She smacked her head. "I'm just dense, I guess. There I was all mad and worked up, when I should have been thrilled to death."

I looked at Lila. Lila looked at Mandy. Mandy looked at Ellen. Ellen looked at Rachel. And Rachel looked at Kimberly. Kimberly looked at me, and I shrugged.

Marissa ran over to me, threw her arms around me, and kissed me on both cheeks. "Thank you so much!" she said. "This is the best thing that has ever happened to me. I should have known. I mean everybody *knows* that hazing is part of club initiation."

She twirled around and flopped into a chair. "I can't believe it. It's a dream come true. *I'm a Unicorn!*"

I thought Lila might just faint right there and then. But all she did was give Marissa a thin smile.

I was wondering who was going to burst her bubble when the door opened and Pippa came in. "Hi! We got through early, so I came on home. How was Malaka Cove?"

Marissa jumped up, ran over to Pippa, threw her arms around her neck, and cried, "Oh, Aunt Pippa. Congratulate me. I'm a member of the Unicorn Club."

Pippa looked over Marissa's head at Kimberly and gave her a proud smile. "That's great," she said quietly. "Really, really great. I'm proud of you." But when she said it, she was looking at Kimberly—telling Kimberly she was proud of *her*.

Kimberly flushed. Talk about an awkward situation.

"I think I'm going to take a walk," I announced.

And I escaped.

I probably walked about two miles down the beach. It was nice being by myself—which I really didn't understand at all. I usually don't like to be alone.

But I had some thinking to do.

It had seemed so important to me that we all be together on this trip. I had been looking forward to having a last blast with my best friends before eighth grade started. But we weren't having as much fun as I thought.

The problem was Marissa, I decided. Marissa was bringing out all our old, mean, competitive, manipulative personalities. We were all so afraid that her nerditude would rub off on us, we were acting like sharks.

The sun was going down, and I realized that if I didn't get back to the condo, the others might get worried. So I turned around.

When I got back, I found everybody sitting around the living room, pretending to be busy.

Right now Pippa is stretched out on the sofa, watching a movie.

Marissa is sitting on the floor between Ellen and Rachel with a bowl of popcorn. She's chattering away about what a great time we're all going to have at the beach party.

Mandy is in the kitchen, organizing the cereal boxes or something.

Every time I look at Lila, she gives me this series of eye, mouth, and head signals.

Now she's doing the same thing to Kimberly.

Now Kimberly is doing it to me.

Looks like they're trying to tell me to meet them in Lila's room. Should I pretend I don't understand?

Oh, well. What's the use? Might as well go in and get it over with.

Seven

Dear Diary,

Here's what happened when Kimberly, Lila, and I finally managed to have a little private chat—in Lila's bathroom.

"Well?" Lila demanded. "What are we going to do?"

Nobody spoke up.

"She thinks she's a Unicorn!" Lila yelled, like she was reminding us that we had an emergency on our hands. "Tomorrow night there are going to be about a hundred kids on this beach, including Peter Feldman! And if I know Marissa, she's going to be sure she tells everyone that she's a Unicorn."

"OK! OK! Chill out!" Kimberly said. "I know it's a problem. I just don't know what to do about it."

"I vote we just tell her flat out she's not a Unicorn," Lila said.

"No way," Kimberly said.

"Why not?" Lila demanded.

Kimberly sighed. "Look. Pippa's cool. But she plays hardball when she has to or when she feels like something's not fair. She refused to accept a trophy once because she thought one of the judges had penalized another surfer for no good reason."

"So?"

"So she's already told me how proud of all of us she is for including Marissa. If we act like jerks and tell Marissa she's not a Unicorn, Pippa might get peeved enough to put us all on a plane back home."

"OK, then," Lila said. "What if the 'club initiation' somehow prevented her from going to the beach party tomorrow night?"

Kimberly lifted her eyebrows. "What do you have in mind?"

Lila reached into her bag and pulled out her little mobile phone.

"Who are you calling?" I asked.

"Janet," she answered.

For once I was glad she had that stupid mobile phone.

THURSDAY, 4:00 P.M.

Dear Diary,

Tonight's the night.

Party night!

Right now I'm resting up for the big event.

Today we all went shopping. I bought a salad bowl for Mom and Dad, a poster for Steven, and a beautiful book on Hawaiian history for Elizabeth.

I bought myself a new bathing suit—with boy-cut legs. *No, not because I thought my thighs looked fat.* I got it because it's a totally cool style and it was on sale.

The mall looked pretty much like the malls at home except that it opened onto outside courtyards in various places and all these exotic birds came flying in and out.

It was totally cool. Like shopping at the zoo or something.

The only cloud on the horizon was the Marissa thing. Janet had come up with a plan for a "prank" that would keep Marissa from attending the party.

But I felt bad about doing that to her. And frankly, I was sick of Lila and Lila's rules.

So I volunteered to play a major role in the "prank." But my plan was to make sure the "prank" didn't happen.

After we shopped, we had lunch at this little café with an outdoor patio. I was thinking about Jason and how I couldn't wait to do some close dancing—when suddenly Marissa piped up.

"I can't wait to see Jason," she said. "I wonder if he's been thinking about me as much as I've been thinking about him."

I had a hard time keeping my jaw from hitting the table.

What was she talking about?

Then she talked about how she planned to dance the night away with Jason! *My guy!*

My memory suddenly flashed on the moment

when she asked Jason to dance and dragged him onto the dance floor—leaving me in the dust! Well, that did it. I *couldn't* let Marissa get between me and my guy! Not when I'd been looking forward to this party for *days*. So I decided to follow the plan *as written*.

I made an excuse to come back to the apartment a little earlier than the others. When I got back, I slipped green food dye into Marissa's toothpaste. Here's how:

I snipped the end off an empty tube of lip gloss. Then I washed out the tube and shoved the nozzle down into Marissa's toothpaste tube. That way I could use the empty lip gloss tube like a funnel. I poured the green dye into the lip gloss tube and squeezed it down into the toothpaste. Then I squished the toothpaste around in the tube so that it would be more or less an even color.

When Marissa brushes her teeth, she's going to look like she's been munching a seaweed salad.

All I know is that I wouldn't go to a party with green teeth for a million bucks. We're betting Marissa won't want to either.

Uh-oh!

I just heard the front door.

They're back.

THURSDAY, 11:30 P.M.

Dear Diary,

Well, what can I say? Things didn't exactly work out the way I had planned.

The somebody I'd heard coming in wasn't the

gang. It was Pippa. She asked me where everybody was, and I told her they were still out shopping. She said OK and that she had to make some phone calls.

I think it was the first time I had ever been in the condo alone with just one other person. No TV. No music. No conversation in the background.

Suddenly I realized it was so quiet, I could hear sounds I'd never noticed before—like the hum of the refrigerator and the birds chirping outside the sliding-glass door to the patio.

I could also hear Pippa talking on the phone in her room.

It sounded like she was talking to Marissa's mom. She was saying stuff like, "Oh, yeah, Marissa seems to be fitting in just fine. The other girls are being very friendly." Things like that.

Then I heard her say . . . "Yes. A practical joke or two. No. No. I don't think there will be any more. . . . No, I don't think they're picking on Marissa. . . . Well, I'm just not going to let them. . . . How? . . . I'll take them all straight to the airport and send them home if I have to. . . . I don't care what Jack and Anne think." (Jack and Anne are Kimberly's parents.)

Then she went on. "I've never cared whether they approved or not. I do what I think is right. And if the girls can't accept Marissa, they'll have to clear out. . . . Well, if their parents don't like it, they should teach their kids better manners."

Kimberly had told us that Pippa had pretty definite ideas about how people should behave. People like us. If we didn't play by her rules, she would have no problem kicking us out.

Did I want to be packed up and sent home?

No way.

Not only would it make the Unicorns look bad, it would make *Pippa* look bad. Mr. Haver had said he didn't think she could handle us. He had said she would wind up sending us home.

I didn't want him to be right.

Besides, I still had spent hardly any time with Jason!

I was on my way into the bathroom to throw the toothpaste away when the others came in. Before I could say anything, Lila turned to Marissa. "Marissa. I can really smell those onions you had for lunch."

Marissa giggled and put her hand over her mouth. "I'm going to go brush. I don't want onion breath tonight of all nights."

"Mind if I use the bathroom first?" I asked, trying to head her off so I could throw out the booby-trapped toothpaste.

But naturally Marissa's such a kid, she thought I was challenging her to some kind of race. She broke into a giggle and ran in front of me, cutting me off. "You're first—after me!" she yelled. The next thing I knew, she had run into our bathroom and shut the door with a bang.

I drifted back into the living room. Everybody sort of pretended to be busy putting their things away. Lila had a strange, crooked smile on her face.

Suddenly we heard this wail come from the direction of our room.

Ellen started to laugh and had to cover her

mouth. She ran out of the living room and into the back bedroom. Mandy followed her.

Two seconds later Marissa was standing in the middle of the living room. "Look at me!" she wailed. "Look at me!"

She took her hand away, and Rachel choked on a laugh. Marissa's mouth and teeth were stained green.

"It won't come off!" she cried. "What is it? What did you do to my toothpaste?"

"You said you wanted to be a Unicorn," Lila reminded her.

Marissa's face was just . . . I can't describe it. I could see she wasn't sure what she was supposed to be feeling. Happy or sad? Humiliated or proud?

"How do I get this off?" she asked in a small voice.

"You don't," Lila snapped.

Marissa's face crumpled. Her mouth began to tremble, and her head began to shake. She looked just miserable. "I can't go to the party looking like this," she cried, tears running down her cheeks.

Marissa threw herself facedown on the sofa and sobbed. Great big heaving, heartbroken sobs. "I've tried to be a good sport," she wailed. "Why are you doing this to me?"

Lila looked like she could hardly keep from laughing.

I wasn't laughing. I was on the verge of crying too—I felt really awful. I knew what it was like to have people be mean to me because they thought it was funny. I knew how cruel the Unicorns could be.

Janet had made me do things like carry her books

for her. And kiss Randy Mason! (Ugh!) And partici-
pate in mean jokes on people like Lois Waller.

And I had hated it!

Suddenly I felt furious. With Janet. And with
Lila. With Rachel and Kimberly. And even Mandy.
What did we think we were doing?

I looked up and saw Pippa standing in the living
room. She was obviously furious. And when she
looked at Kimberly, her expression turned to disappointment. Then to disgust.

"What happened?" she asked quietly.

Marissa sobbed that she had tried to be a good
sport, but now she had green teeth and couldn't go
to the party.

Pippa leaned over, put her hand on Marissa's
back, and whispered to her to go into *her* room.
Pippa's room.

Marissa threw us all a hurt look, then got up and
ran into Pippa's room, slamming the door behind her.

Pippa told Kimberly to get everybody into the
living room. That she had something to say to us
and would be back in a couple of minutes. Then
she went after Marissa.

My heart sank. I knew that she was going to tell us
all to start packing our bags. I didn't want to leave. I
didn't want our last summer of the Unicorns to end—
especially not like this. I didn't want to leave Jason. I
didn't want to go home feeling like a Janet Howell
clone. I didn't want Mr. Haver to say *I told you so.*

All this was going through my head in about
two seconds.

Then I had an idea. A way to save the situation. I ran into the bathroom, grabbed the toothpaste, and brushed like crazy until I had a big green smile myself.

I ran back out into the living room just as Pippa was clearing her throat. She looked at me and did a double take.

Everybody looked at me and did a double take. Rachel's mouth fell open.

"Your turn, Kimberly," I said, trying to sound totally relaxed. I grinned at Pippa. "We do this at parties back home. It's kind of a California joke. I guess we should have explained it to Marissa."

Pippa shook her head. "I never heard of this."

"Oh, it's a new thing," I said, giving Kimberly a long, steady look.

I could tell from Kimberly's pale face that she knew we had come very close to getting booted. "Yeah," she said, playing along. "It always makes people laugh. Kind of a conversation starter, you know? We're *all* going to the party with green teeth." Kimberly clamped her hand on the fleshy part of Lila's arm. "Aren't we, Lila?"

Before she could argue, Kimberly and I had shoved Lila into our room and shut the door.

"Never," Lila whispered. "Not in a million years."

"If you don't," I said, "I will personally introduce Marissa to Peter Feldman and tell him that Marissa is your very best friend."

Her eyes snapped. "You wouldn't," she challenged.

"Oh, yes, I would," I said. I went into the bathroom,

grabbed the toothpaste, and plopped it into her hand. "In fact, if *everybody* doesn't have green teeth by the time we leave, I'll do it."

Lila looked at me like she just hated me. "This is . . . blackmail."

I nodded. "That's right."

Lila took the toothpaste and marched out of the room. I plastered a big smile on my face and went back out into the living room.

Marissa was standing in the kitchen. Pippa had made her an ice pack to hold over her eyes. "I'm sorry," she said, her voice hoarse. "I know you guys think I'm a big baby. I shouldn't get so upset. You're just trying to be my friends."

"Well, you'd better go start getting ready," I said, trying to sound happy and perky. "We need to be out on the beach in another hour."

Marissa hiccuped and smiled—her braces and gums a big green mess.

Then I realized mine were a big green mess too.

That's when it hit me.

Lila was all worried about what Peter Feldman was going to think.

What was *Jason* going to think when he saw my green teeth???

(Note: I am turning into a pretty good writer, I think, because if this were a novel, that would be a perfect way to end this chapter. Sort of a cliff-hanger. I think I'll leave it there because I have to go to sleep. I'll finish the story about what happened tomorrow.)

Eight

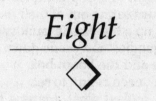

Dear Diary,

It turns out that nobody is speaking to me today. They're not making it so obvious that Pippa or Marissa would notice. But they're giving me the silent treatment.

And guess what?

I don't care!!!

Why don't I care?

Here's why.

Before we went down to the beach party, Lila made everybody brush their teeth with the green toothpaste.

Then . . . she made them all promise they wouldn't smile in case Peter Feldman was there. She figured that if nobody smiled, nobody would notice that we had green teeth.

All things considered, she told them, it wasn't the worst thing that could have happened. According to Wiley, guys like girls who are distant and sophisticated. If nobody smiled, they would look very distant and sophisticated and probably have all the guys eating out of their hands.

We loaded up a big plastic laundry hamper with the bags of goodies and went down to the beach with our CDs and the boom box. It was still light. The sun hadn't even begun to set.

Everybody looked great. Marissa had on khaki shorts and a sleeveless blue denim shirt tied at her midriff.

Lila had on a bright blue bathing suit with a matching long skirt slit all the way up the side. She looked like she stepped right out of a magazine.

Mandy had on some baggy shorts and a halter top. Kimberly wore black shiny bicycle shorts and a bathing suit top that showed off her athletic figure. Ellen wore her bathing suit and cutoffs.

I wore my tie-dyed dress. I guess I was just feeling sort of defiant.

Anyway, when we went down to the beach, we could see about thirty guys and girls already gathered. A bunch of them were piling up driftwood for the bonfire.

We got closer, and I saw Jason.

Jason, Larry, and Rafe all came running over to help us carry our stuff.

We all just kind of mumbled "hello" and kept walking with our heads down—except for

Marissa, who grinned and chattered away.

Jason gave her a sort of funny look. But Marissa seemed oblivious—I guess she had forgotten all about her teeth. She giggled and began talking to Jason about our shopping trip. He asked her all kinds of questions, and she got started talking about her collection of carved animals.

Just as I was beginning to think Jason was going to spend the whole beach party talking to Marissa, Carl showed up. He had a couple of surfboards with him and invited anybody who felt like it to take them out.

"Hey, Mandy," he prompted. "Want to give it a try?"

Mandy looked up and smiled (with her lips together). But Lila gave her a little nudge, and Mandy's smile immediately disappeared. "No, thanks," she said, turning her back on him and walking over to where the drinks were.

"I do," Marissa shouted. She grabbed one of the boards and started running toward the waves. She jumped in with her clothes on and started paddling out.

Jason watched her go. "Wow! Marissa's really enthusiastic, isn't she?"

Carl, Kimberly, and a couple of other guys followed Marissa out into the surf. They looked like they were having fun. I couldn't help thinking Mandy had made a big mistake.

"Hey, Jason. How about you guys go see if you can find some more firewood?" Rafe said.

Jason nodded. "OK. We'll be back. Come on, Jessica."

I was hoping Jason would take my hand, but he didn't. Oh, well. The night was young.

"Let's walk down to the pier," he suggested. "We can collect wood on the way back. That'll give us a nice walk while the sun sets."

"Brilliant idea," I said, thrilled that this wood collection trip was sounding so romantic.

We walked about half a mile. At one point I turned and couldn't even see the group anymore. But as we walked, kids kept passing us on their way to the party. Lots of people had blankets and bags of food. Lots of them knew Jason and said hello.

Overhead, the sky was turning a gorgeous pink and orange as the sun began to set.

"It doesn't matter how many sunsets I see," he said. "They always amaze me." He put his arm around my shoulders.

I felt this shuddery feeling between my shoulder blades. Then I put my arm around his waist. I felt him turn slightly toward me, and my heart began to pound. Was he going to kiss me? He leaned toward me and—

Suddenly we were attacked by munchkins!

We broke apart as three little boys danced around us, whooping and hollering. I was sort of embarrassed and extremely annoyed.

Who *were* these little sand rats?

Jason's face was red, but he didn't look angry. He was laughing. The smallest one jumped up, and Jason lifted him up on his shoulders. The kid was so thrilled, he screamed.

Jason began to gallop.

"Me too! Me too!" the other two cried, chasing behind them.

Jason gave all of them a turn riding on his shoulders. Finally he swung the last kid down. Two of them ran off, but the third grabbed Jason's arm. "I want another ride," he demanded.

Jason shook his head. "Not now, Hal. Maybe tomorrow."

"Now!" Hal insisted, stamping his foot.

"No," Jason said gently but firmly. "It's time for you to go home. The sun is almost down."

Hal looked up at Jason's face, like he was trying to decide whether or not to throw a tantrum. Then he pointed at me. "Who's that?" he asked.

Jason gently pushed Hal's finger down and stooped so that he was face-to-face with Hal. "It's not polite to point," he whispered.

"I don't care," Hal said.

"Yes, you do," Jason said with a smile. Then he put his hands on Hal's shoulders and turned him to face me. "Hal, this is Jessica. Jessica, this is Hal."

"Hi," I said, flashing him my winningest smile.

Hal stared at me for a long time without saying anything. Then he made this horrible face and gagging noise. "Spinach mouth!" he groaned.

"Hal!" Jason said sharply. "That's not nice."

Ohmigosh!

I had *completely* forgotten about my teeth. There I'd been—all puckered up like I expected Jason to kiss me, and he'd probably been totally grossed out by the idea.

Hal stubbed his toe around in the sand. "I'm sorry," he muttered. Then he turned his eyes toward Jason. "I don't like her. Will you come and make a sand castle with me?"

Jason shrugged an apology at me and sighed. "I'm playing with Jessica right now. Why don't you go play with Rick and Jeffrey?"

Hal kicked the sand, obviously bummed. "I don't want to play with them."

"Why not?" Jason asked softly.

"Because they don't want to play with me."

"Why not?" Jason asked again.

"Because they don't like me. But I don't care because they stink. *And so do you!*" he yelled at me. With that, Hal turned and ran up to a beach house and disappeared.

"How do you know Hal?" I asked, trying not to look insulted.

"Hal goes to the camp where I used to be a counselor."

"The camp is in Hawaii?"

Jason nodded. "He's home this weekend because he takes medication for an illness and needs to see the doctor. He'll go back to camp on Monday."

"I feel sorry for his counselors," I said.

Jason flashed me a sideways glance, and I remembered that I was supposed to be the sensitive, caring type.

"They must miss him," I added quickly. "He's such a character."

Jason smiled. "Poor Hal. He's just one of those

kids who has a hard time fitting in. He can be a total pain. I don't know if he doesn't have any friends because he's a pain or if he's turned into a pain because he doesn't have any friends. But I figure, hey, maybe all it takes is one friend to break the cycle. So I'm trying to be that one friend. Listen, about that remark he made . . ."

"I guess I'd better explain about the teeth," I said, terrified of what he would think when he heard the truth.

I told him the story. Most of it. Not all of it. I just said that a couple of the girls had played a prank on Marissa and she had gotten upset. So we had all turned our own teeth green to make her feel better.

He just stared at me with these big, puppy-dog eyes. Shaking his head like he couldn't believe it.

"I guess we're not as nice as you thought we were," I said unhappily.

"No," he said. "You're not as nice as I thought you were. You're nicer." Then he kissed me. Unfortunately it was on the cheek. But it was a start.

After that, the night got better and better. We spent most of the beach party dancing or sitting together by the fire.

And guess who showed up? Steve. He talked his dad into letting him fly over with Mr. Hajit. Steve and Kimberly danced the night away. And Carl boogied with Marissa.

Mandy was nowhere to be found. Ditto for Lila, Rachel, and Ellen.

Know why?

Because they didn't stay for the party, that's why.

The others had gone back up to the condo even before Jason and I got back with the wood.

I was the last one of our group to leave the party, and I figured that everyone would have been asleep for hours by the time I came home.

Kimberly and Marissa had gone to bed.

But Lila, Mandy, Rachel, and Ellen were sitting up waiting for me when I came in. They looked like a bunch of gargoyles perched on a wall.

"Whose side are you on?" Lila demanded.

"What do you mean?" I asked.

"How could you do this to us?" Rachel asked, giving me a green-toothed snarl and pointing to her mouth.

I sat down. "I knew that if we didn't do something, Pippa was going to send us home. I heard her telling Marissa's mom so on the phone."

Lila folded her arms across her chest. "So?"

"So I don't want to go home," I protested. "Neither does anybody else. Right, guys?" I looked at Ellen and the others. But nobody said anything.

My heart started thudding. Uh-oh.

"Wiley says there are a lot of parties going on back home," Lila said. "Maybe we should all go back to Sweet Valley and—"

"No!" I yelped. "No way. I'm not leaving Jason."

Lila's mouth fell open a little. "Jessica," she said in this really superior tone. "Just because you've danced with somebody doesn't mean he's your boyfriend."

"He is too my boyfriend," I insisted. It was *almost*

true. He seemed to like me a lot anyway. And everyone was ready to do whatever Lila told them to do just because she had a boyfriend. Well, two could play that game.

"He kissed me," I told them. Technically this is true. Why muddy the waters with details?

Lila lowered her eyelids. "Yeah, right."

Mandy and Ellen chewed their cuticles like they didn't know what to believe.

"Personally," Rachel said, "I have a very hard time believing that any guy would kiss a girl with green teeth."

"I don't care what you guys think," I retorted. "If you'd stayed, you would have seen for yourself." (Boy, was I glad they hadn't.)

"Why would we have stayed?" Rachel asked. "Nobody even talked to us or asked us to dance. It wasn't like the teen club at all."

"They didn't talk to you or ask you to dance because you looked like total snots," I pointed out. "You guys didn't smile or talk to anybody."

"How could we smile with these green teeth?" Lila practically screamed.

There was a thumping on the wall. It was Pippa, signaling us to keep the noise down.

"Look," I said. "We can have just as much fun here as we would in Sweet Valley. Come on, guys."

I got, like, a zero-degree enthusiasm reading.

"Suit yourselves." I stood up and started to saunter out of the room. "But Rafe and Larry sure will be disappointed."

"What!" Ellen and Rachel both said at once.

"They like you," I said. "Can't you tell? They asked about you."

Rafe and Larry hadn't exactly asked about Ellen and Rachel *specifically*. But they had asked me where everybody was. So technically they had asked about them.

"OK," Rachel asked eagerly. "But who was asking about who?"

I shrugged. "I'm not sure. And I guess the only way to find that out . . . is to stick around and see what happens."

Nine

Dear Diary,

Even though people aren't talking to me, the balance of power seems to be shifting. Lila Fowler is no longer the supreme dictator. Everybody has a stake in staying now.

Kimberly likes Steve. Mandy likes Carl. Rachel and Ellen like Rafe and Larry (or maybe Larry and Rafe?). And I like Jason.

Usually it's Lila who's sitting by the phone waiting for it to ring. But today it's me. I just know Jason is going to call me and ask me out to lunch or something. And I cannot wait to see the look on Lila's face.

Dear Diary,

Jason never called yesterday. I took four walks,

hoping to see him, and he wasn't on the beach. I'm trying not to get worried. Maybe he thought it was uncool to call so soon after the party. That's it. He'll call today for sure.

SUNDAY, 6:30 P.M.

Dear Diary,

It's almost dark. I haven't seen him, and he hasn't called. Lila has asked me six times where my "new boyfriend" is. Thankfully my teeth are no longer green.

MONDAY, 11:00 A.M.

Dear Diary,

I wish I had never come to Hawaii.

MONDAY, 3:00 P.M.

Dear Diary,

It's now been four days since the beach party. Jason never called, and I haven't seen him.

Today we went down to the beach and Lila almost had a cow because Peter Feldman—*the* Peter Feldman— actually came over and sat down with us.

He and Lila talked about all these people at Sweet Valley High, and Lila was name-dropping like they were all her incredibly close personal friends.

She was acting, like, *so* Marissa.

The rest of us felt kind of shy and nervous. It was one thing to flirt and giggle and goof with guys who you met in a club. It was another thing to flirt and giggle and goof with a guy who was a sophomore at Sweet Valley High.

If you made a fool of yourself, people back home would hear about it. So everybody was a little subdued.

Fortunately Marissa was out in the surf with Carl and Kimberly. He had wandered down with a couple of boards.

While I listened to Lila and Peter talking, I watched Marissa. She was lying flat on a board, waiting for a wave. After letting a couple go by she started paddling, getting her board into position.

The wave got bigger and bigger. Marissa managed to get up on her knees.

The wave started to curl.

Marissa started to stand.

I sat up and leaned forward. It looked like she might actually get up on her feet.

"She's doing it," I heard Mandy breathe. "She's doing it!" Mandy sat up too, watching.

Suddenly that wave looked about a thousand feet high. It was an unbelievable curl.

I realized I was holding my breath, watching her.

She was actually doing it! She was up on her feet, and she was *riding the wave!*

I jumped to my feet and let out this big shout. *"Yes!"* I screamed.

Mandy had jumped up beside me. She had her hands over her mouth. "Look at her!" Mandy choked. Her eyes were actually full of tears. I felt a lump in my throat too.

Marissa's arms were out, and she was teetering. But she was surfing. I couldn't help running down to the water. I heard Mandy's feet slapping the sand behind me.

Finally the board slipped out from under her feet. It flew up into the air, smacked the surface, and floated off.

A few seconds later Marissa surfaced, wiped her face, and looked around for the board. When she saw Carl grab it, she grinned and started jumping up and down and shrieking.

By this time I was about knee deep in the water. Marissa saw me and ran toward me and Mandy. "Did you see?" she yelled. "Did you see me surfing?"

"I saw! I saw!" I shouted.

"You did it!" Mandy shrieked. "You did it. You did it. You did it."

The three of us held hands and danced around—splashing with our feet to celebrate. Carl came over with Marissa's board and lifted his hand. Marissa smacked his palm.

He dropped the board and hugged her. "That was fantastic," he said.

"It *was* fantastic," Marissa agreed. "It was the most fantastic feeling in the world. I'm hooked."

Carl smiled at Mandy. "What about you, Mandy? Want to try?"

I hoped she would say yes. Her eyes were shining. She looked friendly and open. She looked like Mandy. She opened her mouth—

"Mandy!" Lila called. "Come over here."

In an instant Mandy's face had shut down. "No,

thanks," she told Carl. "I'm happy for Marissa, but I'm not really into surfing. You guys have fun." She turned back toward the beach.

I hurried to catch up. "Mandy," I whispered. "What's going on? I thought you liked him."

"Jessica! Think how stupid I would look if I couldn't do something and Marissa could," Mandy said. "I'd look like a total fool in front of Peter Feldman. Besides, Lila's calling me."

I felt like somebody had just dumped a bucket of cold water on my head. This was getting scary.

When we sat down, I could tell from Lila's face that Mandy and I had just made a major gaffe.

"Who is that girl?" I heard Peter ask Lila. He pointed to Marissa.

"That's Kimberly Haver's cousin," Lila said. "Nobody you would know."

Peter didn't seem to get that Lila was not interested in talking about Marissa. He leaned forward, watching her paddle back out into the ocean. "Looks like she's learning fast," he commented. "Surfing's hard. I've been trying for weeks and I can't stand up."

"Her aunt is a champion surfer," I volunteered. "Maybe it runs in the family."

Peter's eyes opened wide. "Cool! What's her aunt's name?"

"Pippa Haver," I said.

"I've heard of her," he said. "That's her niece? What's *her* name?"

If looks could kill . . . I wouldn't have lived to be writing this diary.

Lila was trying to put as much distance between us and Marissa as possible, and here was Peter Feldman wanting to know all about her.

"Her name is Marissa," I answered, ignoring Lila's glare. What was I supposed to do? Refuse to tell him her name?

He looked out at her and nodded. "She's cute. What grade is she in? Eighth? Ninth?"

"Something like that," Lila said, like she had no interest at all in talking about it.

Peter stared out at the water for a while, then he stood up. "I'll see you guys around. OK?"

"I'll tell Wiley you said hello," Lila told him brightly—just in case he had forgotten that she was dating Wiley Upjohn.

"Great," he said.

Then he started jogging away down the beach.

Lila bit her lower lip. Then she turned to me and said, "Let's take a walk."

MONDAY, 10:00 P.M.

Dear Diary,

Lila Fowler is insane with power.

It's hard to believe that this is the girl who has been my best friend since the second grade.

As soon as we started walking she said, "Jessica, I can make your life wonderful. Or I can make your life totally miserable."

I swear. That's exactly what she said. The dialogue could have come right out of some cheesy TV movie. I decided to call her bluff. "OK. Make it wonderful," I challenged. I folded my arms, tapped my foot, and pretended to look at my watch. "Well? I'm waiting. It doesn't seem any better to me."

"This is serious, Jessica."

"What do you want from me?"

"I want you to figure out whose side you're on. Stop sticking up for Marissa. Who's your best friend?"

"Gee, Lila. I was just wondering that myself."

Lila's face turned a little pale. "OK. I guess it's really hard for you to accept that I've matured lately. I have a boyfriend. I have an image that I have to protect. And you're too jealous to deal with it."

I felt my own face get kind of pale. She'd hit a nerve. I *was* jealous. But what did that have to do with Marissa?

"Don't you want to be popular next year? Don't you want to have dates? Don't you want to be cool?"

"Of course I do," I said. "What's your point?"

"My point is that if you don't stop acting like Marissa's big sister and best buddy, the Unicorns are going to go one way and you're going to go another."

My hands were shaking. A big lump rose up in my throat. I looked at Lila and I was filled with *rage*.

Who did she think she was—telling me who I could hang with and who I couldn't hang with? It was like having Janet Howell back in charge.

"Think about it, Jessica," she said in this real threatening tone.

She turned on her heel and started walking away.

I walked in the other direction. I was crying. I couldn't help it. I was so miserable. This trip wasn't turning out the way I wanted it to at all. Lila was acting horrible. And Jason hadn't even called me.

I had started out thinking that we wouldn't be having these problems if Marissa weren't here. But now I think we wouldn't be having all these problems if *Lila* wasn't here.

Maybe Wiley will call her and tell her he can't get along without her. Maybe we'll get lucky and she'll book herself a flight back to California and leave the rest of us alone.

Alone.

Boy, oh, boy. I am just bummed beyond words. Here I am with all my best pals—and I have never felt so lonely in my life.

Right now I'm sitting in the bedroom. Everybody else is in the living room, watching a rental movie. Lucky me. I can cry myself to sleep in peace.

Ten

Dear Diary,

This morning Kimberly and Marissa went off with Pippa to visit some family friends. Ellen, Lila, Mandy, and Rachel all went down to the beach.

I said I had some stuff to do and didn't go down with them.

"I wouldn't spend too much time waiting for Jason to call," Lila told me in a nasty voice as they left.

I sat down on the sofa with the phone in my hand. I was seriously considering calling my parents and asking them if I could come home early.

But I knew they would start asking me all sorts of questions. If I told them what was going on, it would sound totally lame. They'd tell me not to be ridiculous. They would tell me it would be rude to leave the house party. And they'd finish up by telling me that as soon as I got home, I'd beg them to send me back to Hawaii.

How can I tell them that something more important is going on? Something I can't really express.

I have this weird feeling that I don't know who I am. I don't feel like Jessica Wakefield anymore.

I don't feel confident or pretty or anything.

I don't feel comfortable with my friends. I don't like the way they're treating me. I don't like the way they're treating Marissa.

But I don't want to be on the outs with everybody. I don't want to wind up with geeky Marissa as my only friend.

Marissa has no clue what's going on. She still thinks she's being put through Unicorn membership initiation. She acts like we're best pals.

I hate her. I hate everybody.

I want to go home.

There's the phone.

Maybe it's Jason.

TUESDAY, 2:35 P.M.

Dear Diary,

It wasn't Jason. It was Pippa. She forgot to give some envelope to Carl and asked me to take it down to him at the shop.

I said I would.

TUESDAY, 9:30 P.M.

Dear Diary,

OK. Things are looking better. Not great. But better. The Surf Shop is at the very end of the beach.

There are benches out front where people can sit, drink sodas, and hang out.

I went inside the Surf Shop, and Carl was sitting behind the counter with another guy. Carl looked really glad to see me and introduced me to the other guy, whose name was Trey.

I gave Carl the envelope, which had some information about stuff they were supposed to order. They looked over the info and talked for a couple of minutes, then Trey got on the phone with the manufacturer.

Carl stretched and took some keys out of a drawer. "OK. It's quittin' time. I'm gonna catch some waves." He looked at me and cocked his head. "I can't believe that anybody as pretty and blond as you doesn't know how to surf."

I blushed. "I'd like to. I just never learned how."

"Want a lesson on the house?" he asked.

Under the circumstances, I couldn't really say no. This might sound really conceited, but I thought he might be flirting with me. Since Jason had done a fade and Mandy had made it clear her loyalties were with Lila, I figured, *Why not take Carl up on the offer?*

I had my suit on under my shorts, so I said sure.

Carl and I went outside and examined the boards that were leaning against the side of the shop. "These are for people to have fun with," he said. "Pippa figures that even if a few get broken or stolen, it's still good karma because somebody out there is surfing."

He found one for me and carried it under his

arm. We waded into the water. The waves weren't very big, and when we were about waist deep, he told me to get on the board and lie on my stomach.

I got on my stomach and paddled around for a little while.

As the little swells rose he told me to practice getting on my knees. I tried it and wiped out.

When I came up for air, Carl didn't laugh or make fun of me. He just smiled and told me to try it again.

I was starting to wish I hadn't accepted his offer of a lesson. I felt like an enormously clumsy dork.

He held the board steady while I climbed up on it again.

"Now just try to move with the board. You skate?" he asked.

"Sure," I answered.

"Well, this isn't that different. You just have to keep your balance over the motion."

We waited while some small waves passed underneath me, then Carl started saying, "Go . . . go . . . go . . ."

I paddled hard, trying to catch the wave as it rose beneath the board. Suddenly I was just into it. The wave, the board, and I were all moving together.

I got on my knees. I got one foot on the board beneath me. I was starting to stand when I heard this screech from the shore. I looked up and saw Marissa. She was jumping up and down, cheering. Pippa and Kimberly were with her. I was so surprised, I fell off the board with a big splash!

WEDNESDAY, 7:30 A.M.

Dear Diary,

In our last entry, our heroine had just done a total and complete splashdown in front of Carl, Kimberly, Marissa, and anybody else on the beach who happened to be watching.

I guess I should be grateful nobody had a video camera.

Carl and I headed back to the shore, and when I got there, Marissa was all over me. "Jessica! I didn't know you were interested in learning to surf. I'll help you. Pippa's got tons of boards down in the basement and . . ."

Argggghhhh! Just what I needed—Marissa teaching me to surf. Luckily she went into the Surf Shack with Pippa and Kimberly. I had a few moments alone to try to regain a little dignity.

That's when I saw Rafe and Larry!

Double arrggghhhh!

Could life possibly get any worse?

There I was, looking like a waterlogged geek. Mascara down to my chin. No lipstick. Hair plastered to my forehead.

Had they seen my ridiculous wipeout? And would they tell Jason?

They waved and hurried over. "Hey!" they said. "Learning to surf, huh?" Larry asked.

I tried to smile and make a joke. "Just trying not to drown."

It was kind of lame, but at least I was able to say something besides "uhhhhhhh."

I was so embarrassed. And I couldn't decide whether to ask about Jason or not. He hadn't called me, so it was pretty obvious he wasn't interested in seeing me.

"Listen," Rafe said. "Let me get your number. Jason wanted to call you, but he lost your number and he couldn't remember the name of the lady you're staying with."

"Jason wanted to call me?" I gasped.

Larry nodded. "Yeah. Jason was a counselor last year at a camp for special kids. Anyway, when he got home from the party, there was a message that some of this year's counselors had gotten food poisoning. They wanted Jason to come fill in. We went with him and came back today. Jason's staying on till tomorrow."

Suddenly life didn't seem quite so bleak.

In fact, it looked pretty darned sunny.

That was yesterday.

Which means Jason is coming back today.

All right!

WEDNESDAY, 8:40 A.M.

Dear Diary,

After breakfast I'm going down to the beach with the other girls. I didn't tell anybody about Jason. I'm just going to sit there and wait for him to come find me. If he's missing me the way I'm missing him, he'll sweep me into his arms, lay a big passionate kiss on me, and then *Lila Fowler can eat her heart out.*

I hope Peter Feldman is sitting there watching too so he can tell Wiley Upjohn that Jessica Wakefield has a boyfriend *who is taller than she is unlike someone around here whose name happens to be Lila.*

WEDNESDAY, 8:00 P.M.

Dear Diary,

Things didn't go exactly the way I scripted them, but they came close.

After breakfast we went down to the beach. I made sure I had on my new suit—*not because my legs are fat or even close to being fat.* It just made me look cool, that's all.

I lay on my stomach, wearing some new shades, and tried to ignore Marissa, who was lying next to me, reading from some book of surfing poems Pippa had on her shelf.

"Listen to this." Marissa cleared her throat.

> "A ball arcs through the air—
> Leaves no trace.
> A bird flies across the sky—
> Leaves no sign.
> I soar across the water—
> The sea swallows my evidence."

"Oh, give me a break," I heard Rachel mutter.

Marissa didn't hear her. She let out this long, dramatic sigh. "Oh, Jessica, once you've ridden the waves, you'll understand. I want you to have what

I had. I want you to experience what I have experienced. It's just indescribable happiness."

I saw Lila look at me over the tops of her sunglasses. "You asked for it," she sang under her breath.

I opened my magazine and ignored both of them. I pretended to read, but my eyes were scanning the beach, searching for Jason.

After a little while I spotted him. He was still pretty far off, walking toward us.

I closed my book and stood up. "I think I'll go get my feet wet," I said with an elaborate stretch.

I started toward the water, pretending I hadn't seen him. My heart was pounding, though. I kept imagining him getting closer and closer. It took a lot of self-control not to turn. But I was going to wait until he called my name.

Then I'd turn and let out a cry of surprise.

We'd run toward each other with our arms out.

The water would splash around our feet.

The sun would light up our hair.

It would be just like a shampoo commercial. Lila would gnash her teeth with jealousy.

I waited.

And waited.

And waited.

Finally I heard someone call my name.

But it wasn't Jason.

It was *Marissa!*

I turned around and there she was—standing with Jason and calling me over to say hello to him—

like she didn't get that he had come to see *me*.

Under the circumstances, I couldn't exactly go running toward him with my arms out. I walked over, trying to smile. But inside, I was wondering how to drown Marissa and get away with it.

I could feel Lila and the others watching. Trying to figure out if there was really anything romantic between me and Jason.

When I got to where he and Marissa were talking, he gave me a big hug.

That was something.

Of course, he might have hugged Marissa too for all I knew.

Jason put an arm around Marissa and an arm around me, and we all walked over to join the others. "Hi! Sorry to have been out of touch. We had sort of an emergency, and I left the island before sunrise the morning after the party."

Everybody asked him where he had gone, and he told them all about this camp for special kids. "Four guys are too sick to stay on. It looks like I'm going to be a counselor there for the rest of the summer," he said. "Rafe and Larry are going to fill in here and there. But I'll get three days off every weekend, so we'll definitely have some time to hang out."

He looked right at me when he said it.

SATURDAY, 7:05 P.M.

Dear Diary,

Well! Guess who's getting a little more respect these days?

Jason, Rafe, and Larry hung out with us for the past couple of days. We did a lot of group stuff. We played volleyball and took walks. Jason's dad, Mr. Landry, took us out on a boat one day.

Then it was time for them to go.

It's pretty clear now that Rafe and Larry are interested in Ellen and Rachel.

It's still not clear, though, who's interested in who.

I think it's actually pretty funny. But Ellen and Rachel are going slightly nuts. Since we never pair off and we're always in a group, it's impossible to get an accurate reading.

I'm feeling pretty confused myself. Jason hasn't made any romantic moves. But we have an understanding. At least I think we do. I wish he would kiss me—a real kiss—so I could know for sure that he was my guy.

SATURDAY, 9:00 P.M.

Dear Diary,

Jason called late this evening. Guess what? He asked me out. Here's what he said, word for word: "I'd like to take you on a day trip. To someplace special. There aren't a lot of people I could share it with, but I think you would really love it."

We're going to take a private plane. On Tuesday. Three days from now.

When I dropped *that* little tidbit of news at dinner, Jessica Wakefield's stock went up and Lila Fowler's stock went way, way, way down.

SATURDAY, 10:45 P.M.

Dear Diary,

When we went to bed, Marissa came over and sat down. Then she said, in this corny *woman-to-woman* tone—that she didn't begrudge me my relationship with Jason.

She wanted me to know that—in spite of one or two things she might have said—she would never *dream* of coming between us.

(Like I was worried!)

I humored her and told her I appreciated it.

She patted my hand and left me to write in my journal. But now I'm sleepy, so I'm turning off the light.

G'night.

SUNDAY, 4:00 P.M.

Dear Diary,

It's raining, so we're stuck inside with each other and have been all day.

I spent the morning doing what any real Unicorn in my shoes would do—rubbing it in.

Every time Lila mentioned Wiley, I mentioned Jason.

Every time Lila said she missed Wiley, I said I missed Jason.

Every time Lila said Wiley was in high school, I made some remark about how *tall* Jason is.

Finally Lila had had enough. She decided to challenge me.

"You know, Jessica," she said as we were all playing cards after lunch. "Guys aren't like girls."

"You noticed," I said.

Lila gave me this sympathetic smile. "Jessica. That's not what I meant. What I'm trying to tell you is that you might be reading Jason wrong. He might not be as serious about you as you are about him."

Marissa piped up, "Lila's right, Jessica. Guys are like that."

I wanted to grab both of them and knock their heads together. Here was Lila acting like some big relationship expert. And Marissa—who probably knew less than zero about guys—butting in like she knew everything too.

"Now that I'm in a relationship with a guy in high school," Lila started in, "I've had a chance to really see what goes on in a guy's head, and—"

"Don't compare Wiley and Jason," I said angrily, throwing down my discard.

Marissa picked it up, compared it to her other cards, and then smiled happily. (Good thing we weren't playing poker.)

"You're right," Lila said in a snooty voice. "I shouldn't compare them because there really is no comparison. Wiley is in high school, and . . ."

"Game over," I said, folding my cards.

That's when Mandy came in. "Anybody want to take a walk? If I don't get outside, I'm going to lose my mind."

I jumped to my feet. "I'll go." I didn't care that it was raining—I would have gladly headed into a monsoon—as long as I could get away from Lila and Marissa.

Mandy fished her shoes out from under the couch

and I grabbed a rain slicker out of Pippa's front closet.

Pretty soon we were walking along the road. It was too wet to walk along the beach.

"Lila Fowler is driving me nuts," I said. "How come you're letting her get away with pushing you around?"

Mandy sighed. "I want to stay on her good side so she'll fix me up when we get back. Plus who wants her as an enemy? Don't forget, she's Janet Howell's first cousin. They're not all that different."

I felt a little flicker of fear. Once we got back to Sweet Valley, I wouldn't have Jason. What if Lila got dates for everybody but me? What if everybody except me had this great social life? What if Lila decided to ruin me? She could do it.

The rain had slacked off to a drizzle. I looked at the beautiful purple mountaintops and the misty sky and felt totally dismal.

"Jessica," Mandy said. "If we do wind up at different schools next year, we'll still be friends, right?"

I looked at Mandy. Was she sincere? Or was she just trying to hedge her bets, trying to be Lila's friend *and* mine? "Of course," I said, wondering if it was really true. I didn't think it was. I was mad at Mandy in a way I couldn't really explain. She was going against everything that she believed—just to stay on Lila's good side.

On some level I just couldn't respect her anymore.

Before I had time to think about it, we were at the end of the beach and there was the Surf Shack. I realized that's where Mandy had been heading all along. "Want to go in?" she asked.

I started to say something snotty like—*Did you get a permission slip from Lila?*—but I stopped myself in time.

We stepped inside. Carl was sitting behind the counter, reading a magazine.

When he looked up, he gave both of us a big grin—but something incredible happened. He looked right at *me* and smiled. An intimate kind of smile. Like there was something between us. "Hi!" He sounded really glad to see me. "I was just thinking about you."

Talk about ironic! Finally Mandy gets up the nerve to talk to Carl, but Carl's more interested in talking to . . . me.

I hate to say this—but it made me feel *great!*

I remembered what Lila had said on the beach. *"If you don't stop acting like Marissa's big sister and best buddy, the Unicorns are going to go one way and you're going to go another."*

Well, I thought suddenly, *maybe it's time.*

Maybe we've all outgrown one another.

I loved my old friends. But my old friends didn't really seem like my friends anymore. And I was sick of the whole "Lilapalooza."

I realized something—I didn't care anymore. Suddenly confidence was pulsing through my veins. Who cared about Lila? About Janet? About Peter Feldman? About Wiley Upjohn?

And who cared about the Unicorns?

Not me anymore.

If Lila didn't get me dates, I'd get my own.

If my old friends ditched me, I'd make new ones.

In spite of the rain outside, in spite of the dark clouds overheard, in spite of the fact that Jason hadn't really kissed me, I suddenly felt great. I wasn't afraid anymore.

Eleven

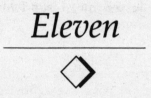

Dear Diary,

Life has never looked better.

Kimberly and Marissa left early this morning with Pippa to go to the new Maui gift shop.

Ellen and Rachel went to the mall.

So it was just me, Mandy, and Lila in the apartment when Carl called. For me.

He said it was his day off, and did I want another surfing lesson? Then he said I had natural talent, and it would be a shame not to develop it. I told Carl I'd meet him in half an hour, then I hung up and started gloating.

I turned to Lila. "Can I borrow your waterproof eye shadow?"

She raised her eyebrows. "What for?"

"Carl just invited me surfing."

Mandy's mouth fell open. She stared at me like I was the biggest traitor in the whole world. I pretended not to notice. Lila looked like she didn't know what to say. "But what about Jason?" she asked.

"What about him?" I asked in this innocent voice.

"Y-Y-You said you guys had something going," she sputtered.

"And you told me it was all in my head," I countered in this fake gullible tone.

Lila threw down her magazine and left the room in a huff. Mandy gave me a hurt look, then followed Lila.

I went into the room I was sharing with Kimberly and Marissa and started to get ready. I washed and dried my hair even though I knew I'd be going into the ocean. And I gave myself a full makeup job with all the waterproof stuff I could find.

Lila came in. "If I did this to Wiley, he'd break up with me."

"Did what?" I asked.

"Cheated on him."

I rolled my eyes. "Get a grip, Lila. You're not engaged to Wiley. You can surf with somebody, can't you?"

She pressed her lips together, trying to think up a comeback. I had her right where I wanted her.

I gave her a real patronizing smile. "Look at it this way," I told her. "It'll be good practice for next year."

She frowned. "What are you talking about?"

I opened my eyes wide. "Next year I have no intention of letting one guy take up all my time. So this is a great way to learn how to juggle more than one boy."

Lila's eyes narrowed. "Jessica Wakefield, you are really pushing your luck."

"At least I've got luck to push," I quipped. "I don't see anybody else trying to juggle two guys."

And with that, I grabbed my tote bag and strutted out of the apartment.

I met Carl down by the water, and we had a great time. In spite of acting like hot stuff in front of Lila, I was worried that I would feel shy and awkward with him. Carl looks sixteen. I wondered if he knew how old I was. People always say I look older.

But once I got to the beach, I didn't feel awkward at all. In fact, it was more like being with Steven than being with a boyfriend. Carl didn't act like a guy with a crush or anything. He seemed serious about teaching me to surf. Too serious! Long after I got pooped, he was still making me paddle out and try to stand up. I did manage to ride one wave all the way in on my knees. But I never could stand up.

After that, Carl asked if I wanted to get something to drink, and we walked down to the teen club. He got us a couple of sodas, and we sat outside on the deck.

"So tell me about life in California," he said.

I told him life in California was pretty great. Turns out Carl is a native of Hawaii. He lives here all year, and his family has been here for as long as anybody can remember. He's part Chinese and part Pacific Islander.

Also, it turned out he's not sixteen. He's fifteen

but very tall for his age. We talked and laughed and goofed, and then he walked me back to the condo.

He didn't try to kiss me or anything. I was glad. Because really and truly, I wouldn't want to hurt Mandy. Besides, my heart belonged to Jason. But I couldn't help feeling totally cocky when I got back upstairs.

Here's the score.

> Mandy—0
> Kimberly—1
> Rachel—0
> Ellen—0
> Lila—1
> Jessica—2

Numbers don't lie.

I rule.

MONDAY, 10:00 P.M.

Dear Diary,

Here's an excerpt from tonight's conversation about tomorrow's *"big date"*:

"So Jason won't tell you anything at all about where you're going?" Ellen asked me.

I shook my head. "Nope. It's a surprise." I gave my hair a last shot of spray.

"And it's on a different island? Which island?" Ellen pressed.

"Does it matter?" Marissa gasped. "It's another island. They're going away together. It's the most romantic thing that's ever happened to any of us."

I heard Lila let out this little squeak of irritation.

"Watch that 'us' stuff," she warned Marissa. "You're not a Unicorn yet."

But Marissa was unsquelchable. "OK, then. It's the most romantic thing that's ever happened to any of *you* guys. I won't even include myself because for all you know, I've had dozens and dozens of romantic adventures."

"Stifle yourself," Kimberly told her.

Marissa just giggled.

Everybody was in our room, watching me get ready for my big day of total romance, which starts tomorrow morning.

I'm doing my hair tonight because Jason is picking me up at 7 A.M.

Lila is eating her heart out. She even tried to get my date canceled by telling Pippa about it.

I guess she thought Pippa would forbid me to go. Instead Pippa waited until everybody but me was out of the condo to ask me if I would mind her calling Jason's family and touching base.

I said it was OK. (Did I have a choice?) Pippa phoned Jason's dad. I guess Mr. Landry got the Pippa Haver household seal of approval. After they spoke, Pippa said it was cool for me to go and never even mentioned to anybody that she had checked up on everything.

In a way, it was even cooler that things turned out like that. As far as Lila knew, I was making all my own decisions just like a real grown-up while *she* still has to ask permission to go to a movie with Wiley.

Am I riding high or what?

Twelve

Dear Diary,

I should never have written that "Am I riding high" line. It's right up there with . . . *"All our problems were over."*

As planned, Jason and his dad picked me up at 7 A.M. Mr. Landry drove us to the little airport where Pippa keeps her plane.

Jason's dad took us inside, and there was our old friend, Mr. Hajit. He and Jason joked around a bit—it was pretty clear they knew each other well. Mr. Hajit told Jason's dad he would bring us back around 6 P.M.

Mr. Landry said he'd be back to pick us up this evening and told us to have fun.

Mr. Hajit told us we were the only passengers on this run, so we might as well get started.

The flight only took about fifteen minutes. The little island we landed on had just a tiny airstrip. No airport—no building at all! Mr. Hajit told us to be back around 5:30 and opened the door. We hopped out, and Mr. Hajit taxied to the end of the airstrip and took off again, soaring away over our heads.

As the noise of the engine died away I began to hear the sounds of the island. The birds, the wind, and the surf.

Suddenly there were only two people in the whole world. Me and Jason, alone on an island paradise.

I felt nervous but excited. What would we do next? Go explore some romantic forest? Climb to the top of a volcano? Swim in some incredibly romantic cove?

That's when the Jeep pulled up.

And guess who was sitting in the front seat next to the driver, wearing a cap that said Camp Aloha and a big grin?

Hal, the sand rat.

I wanted to groan.

Jason turned to me and put his arm around my shoulders. "I wanted you to see Camp Aloha," he said. "It's Bring a Special Friend Day. All the counselors are supposed to bring someone who might be interested in volunteering. You're so patient and caring—I knew you'd love it."

My heart sank right down into my shoes.

This was my big surprise!!!

No *way* did I want to spend the day at some stupid summer camp for obnoxious kids.

The Jeep came to a stop. I spotted Rafe and Larry,

sitting in the back with a couple of little boys and girls. I noticed that one of them had on leg braces.

"Hi, Jessica!" Rafe and Larry smiled and waved like they were really glad to see me. "We think it's great you came," Rafe said.

"We came yesterday to help out," Larry added.

What could I do except smile and say how thrilled I was to be there? I had to act gracious. But it was a major effort not to burst into disappointed tears.

Jason helped me into the Jeep and climbed in himself. Hal stared hard at me. "I know you. You're the girl with the spinach mouth. Show everybody your green teeth."

I wanted to smack him. Instead I smiled, showing him my pearly whites. His face fell. "What happened?" he asked in a disappointed tone. Obviously he thought a girl with green teeth was much better than a girl with regular teeth.

"It wore off," I said.

"Can you make them green again?" he asked. He looked at me hopefully.

"Nope," I said. "Sorry."

Hal wasn't thrilled with that answer, but he seemed to accept it.

I was so bummed out that I hardly noticed the scenery as we drove to the camp. I'm sure under more *romantic* circumstances I would have come back with a lot of very poetic descriptions.

But I wasn't there on a date. Basically I was there to baby-sit.

When we pulled into the camp, I saw a lot of

people around my own age. I recognized a few
kids from the beach. Some of them recognized me
and came over to say hello.

One guy said that Jason must think a lot of me
or else he wouldn't have invited me here. That
made me feel a little bit better.

Jason took my hand (which made me feel a *lot*
better) and said he wanted to show me around.

"Most of these kids are recovering from cancer,"
he said in a soft voice. "Last summer I suggested
that we start trying to get kids like Hal—kids with
emotional problems—involved. I think it makes
them feel better about themselves. I know helping
other people makes *me* feel better about myself.
And you're just like I am. I can tell."

I felt my cheeks flush because I knew the truth. I
wasn't like Jason at all. His image of me was all
wrong, and I felt ashamed. Let's face it, I spend
most of my time thinking about myself. I wish that
weren't true—but . . .

Oh, well . . . let's not go there. I feel rotten enough.

Back to the story.

Jason showed me the cabins and the physical
therapy center. He showed me where the kids who
were still getting chemo had their own cabin attached to a medical building.

Then it was time for activities.

Jason, Rafe, Larry, and I were supposed to help
a group of kids make puppets and put on a show
for the other kids.

I was not thrilled. *But* . . . I do know a thing or

two about entertaining kids. (The Unicorns did a lot of volunteer work at a day care center last year.)

The group of kids we were assigned to work with were actually pretty cute. (Hal was not one of them—thank goodness!) There were four little boys and three little girls.

Rafe suggested that we put on a show about Martian invaders.

The little boys all thought that was a great idea.

The little girls weren't thrilled.

Jason suggested a fairy tale. Something everyone knew already, like *Cinderella*.

The girls smiled and the boys groaned.

I suggested a compromise. *Cinderella in Outer Space*. That got everybody excited.

Step one was making puppets. We used empty coconut halves for heads and all kinds of seashells, plants, and bark to make ugly Martian stepsisters.

Our fairy godmother had mother-of-pearl eyes, gorgeous ferns for hair, and a palm frond for a wand. The stepmother was a big octopus. We made an octopus head out of a sack of sand. It flopped around in a very realistic way.

Cinderella was a bromeliad—which is a huge pink exotic flower. She went to a ball on the planet Jupiter, where she fell in love with the prince, who was a big conch shell.

Hey! I know it doesn't make sense, but it was set in outer space, so anything went.

The horrible stepmother (from planet Day-Old Fish Sticks) was hoping to take over the planet

Earth so her ugly daughters (giant sea monsters) could eat all the earthlings.

It was pretty hilarious. The more outrageous our story got, the more creative the guys became. And the more creative the guys became, the more fun the kids had.

By the time we put on the show, our story had almost nothing to do with Cinderella. Nobody cared. They roared with laughter and thought the puppets were great.

I actually had so much fun, I forgot how angry and disappointed I had felt when we arrived.

At lunch we all sat at long picnic tables and had fruit salad and peanut butter sandwiches. Some of the kids needed help eating, and Rafe and Larry seemed very cool helping out with that.

Hal wanted to sit on Jason's lap during lunch. I sat by Jason—so that meant I had to make conversation with Hal.

First thing out of his mouth: "Do you have a boyfriend?"

Jason blushed, and so did I. Fortunately some other kid tried to take Hal's cookie, and that gave him something to think about besides me and my love life.

Did I *have* a love life? I wondered.

I looked at Jason.

He was mopping up soda where Hal had spilled it, but his cheeks were flaming.

During the afternoon we took some kids on a nature hike. We used trails that Jason had marked last summer.

When it was finally time to leave, there were a lot of people going back. Not just me and Jason but other visitors who had come from other islands.

We didn't even get to sit together on the plane. Jason's dad was waiting for us at the little airport. When they dropped me back at the condo, Jason gave me a good-bye kiss on the cheek. I wondered if he would have kissed me for real if his dad hadn't been sitting in the car.

The truth was—I had no idea. I had everybody else convinced that Jason was my boyfriend. How could I convince *him*?

Jason said he and his dad were going to a family thing tomorrow and then he had to go back to camp tomorrow night. But he would see me the following weekend.

Then—*poof*—he was gone.

TUESDAY, 10:40 P.M.

Dear Diary,

I know it's wrong to lie, but I'm not sure that what I'm doing is actually lying.

When I got up to the apartment, I'd already decided how I would handle the Unicorns. I would just refuse to answer questions. Anything anybody asked me—I'd just smile like I knew something they didn't.

So that's what I did.

"What island did you go to?" Kimberly asked.

I told them, and they all ran to Pippa's maps to look it up. "Wow! It's really small," Mandy commented.

"But big enough to get lost on, I bet," Marissa said with a giggle. "Was it gorgeous?"

I smiled.

"Did you guys take a walk?" Rachel wanted to know.

I smiled.

"Did he kiss you?" Ellen blurted out—asking the question that I knew everybody was dying to ask.

"Ellen!" I exclaimed. I just smiled again—like I *really* knew something they didn't. Then I said I was going to take a bath. I acted like I was embarrassed that they were asking me so many personal questions.

I went into the bathroom, ran a hot tub, and sank down in it to think.

All in all, I'd had a fun day. But it sure wasn't the romantic getaway day I'd envisioned.

Then I had a horrible fear. Maybe Jason thought I was gross. Or maybe he thought I was a big nerd for hanging with Marissa. A nice nerd who would enjoy volunteering. Too nerdy to be crushworthy. Not anybody he'd want to date.

The thought was so horrible and scary, I sank down into the water and wished I were a fish so I could stay down there and never have to come up and face him again.

When my lungs felt like they might burst, I came up for air.

What was I going to do? The only way that I could keep Lila in check was through this boyfriend thing. Without Jason, I had nothing.

Then I remembered Carl.

So, Dear Diary, Jessica's plan for image recovery is to make a big play for Carl tomorrow.

Wish me luck.

WEDNESDAY, 1:10 P.M.

Dear Diary,

This morning I got all dolled up and ready to work my charms on Carl. We all lay out on our towels after breakfast as usual.

For once I was really grateful that Marissa was there. She was tooting my horn so loud, I didn't have to.

"I wish you had taken a camera with you," she said. "I keep picturing you and Jason together— standing on a high cliff, looking out over a water-fall. Was it like that? Was it?"

I did my smile thing, and she flopped over on her back and groaned. "Oh, I'm sooo jealous. Jason is so adorable. So nice. So . . . everything a girl could want."

"Jason isn't all that," Lila snapped—really peeved that everybody was more interested in my romance than in hers.

I swung into action. "I think I'll walk down to the Surf Shack and see Carl," I said, trying to sound casual.

I stood up, pulled some shorts on over my suit, and started down the beach. I could hear them whispering about me as I walked away.

Down at the end of the beach I saw Carl out waxing the boards. He smiled and waved. "Hey! I'm working today, but you can keep me company."

I sat down on the bench and dug my toes down

into the sand. "I'll be officially off duty in an hour," he told me. "Want to surf in a little while?"

"You mean *try* to surf?"

He chuckled. "All it takes is practice. You'll get it. You've got the gift."

"I'll bet you say that to all the girls."

"I do," he admitted. "To all the guys too. Anybody who really wants to surf can surf. All you need is confidence."

He went inside to answer the telephone, and I watched the gulls circling over the ocean.

Confidence was all anybody needed to do anything—if you believed what magazines told you. But this whole trip has been like a confidence seesaw.

One day I'm confident. The next day I'm terrified.

Carl came out of the Surf Shack with a piece of paper. "Hey! That was some guy trying to get in touch with Marissa. He tried to call Pippa, but she's got an unlisted number. He said he saw her surfing with me, so he called here."

I took the piece of paper, and my eyes almost fell out of my head.

Message for Marissa
Call Peter Feldman

WEDNESDAY, 5:00 P.M.

Dear Diary,

After Carl gave me the message, he and I went out and goofed around in the surf. I rode in on my knees again. I still can't stand up, but Carl says it's only a matter of time.

Again he didn't really act romantic. I think he doesn't have a crush on me after all. He just likes me as a friend.

Is *anybody* ever going to like me as a *"girlfriend"*?

Mandy's still under the impression that Carl and I have a thing going. She's been giving me the cold shoulder all afternoon. Do I care?

I thought I didn't, but now I'm not sure.

I keep "forgetting" to give Marissa the message from Peter. It's horrible, but now I'm just as worried as Lila about what Peter might think. Marissa seems to think I'm her very best friend in the whole world. If Peter asks her out—(a) he'll find out she's a seventh-grader, (b) he'll realize within ten minutes that she's a motormouth nerd and not a cool surfer chick, and (c) she'll tell him that she considers Jessica Wakefield her very best pal.

By the time I get back to Sweet Valley, I'll be at the top of the dork list and nobody in the *eighth* grade even will ask me out—never mind guys in high school.

So that piece of paper is still in the pocket of my shorts.

I feel guilty. But I'm so used to feeling guilty, it doesn't faze me that much anymore.

WEDNESDAY, 7:00 P.M.

Dear Diary,

Today Lila comes in after taking a walk and says, "Jessica, I want to see you in my room."

Just like that. Like she's the school principal or something.

I started to tell her to jump off the balcony, but something about her face scared me. She looked really mean. And really serious.

As a compromise, I went to her room, but I took my time, yawning and stopping to get a soda first.

When I went in, she told me to close the door— she had something private to tell me.

Let me tell you, she was really starting to work my nerves. Still, I closed the door.

"I was out on the beach, and I had a very interesting talk with Rafe and Larry."

My heart sank. Uh-oh.

Lila smiled. "They told me all about your fabulous romantic date."

Uh-oh.

"They told me how it was just you and Jason, and a hundred other camp counselors, and little kids."

I sat down on the end of Rachel's bed and didn't say anything.

Lila crossed her arms. "I think you owe me an apology. For lying. And for actually comparing your pathetic little friendship to my relationship with Wiley."

I took a sip of my soda. "Forget it."

"No way. If you don't apologize, I'm going to make your life miserable. I'll tell the others. And furthermore, I'll tell everybody when we get back home."

I put my hand down into my pocket and pulled out the little piece of paper. "I don't think so," I said, staring at Lila through narrowed eyes.

"What do you mean?"

"I mean if you don't back off, I will give Marissa the message that Peter Feldman called her and wants her to call him back."

The color drained from Lila's face. "That's a lie."

"No lie. If you don't believe me, ask Carl. But that probably isn't a good idea. Because Carl might mention it to Marissa and . . ." I shrugged. "Well, we all know how thrilled Marissa is to be considered for Unicorn membership. She'd probably love calling Peter to tell him about it."

"This is total blackmail," Lila sputtered.

"What did you think it was when you were threatening me?" I shot back. "How come there's one set of rules for Lila and another set of rules for everybody else? If you mess with me, I'll make sure that Marissa and Peter Feldman have the dream date of the summer." I stormed out and slammed the door behind me. Then I went into my room, feeling sick and ashamed and angry.

I don't understand what is happening. Somewhere along the line Lila has gone from being my best friend to being my archenemy.

WEDNESDAY, 10:00 P.M.

Dear Diary,

I keep waiting for Lila to make a move, but she hasn't. Nobody is acting strange, so I don't think she's told anybody. But I'm *watching my back!*

THURSDAY, 3:40 P.M.

Dear Diary,

Today I went down to the Surf Shack to see Carl. He asked me if I remembered to give Marissa the message. I told him that I had, but Marissa wasn't interested in Peter and was embarrassed about the attention. I made Carl promise not to say anything to Marissa about it.

Am I good or what?

THURSDAY, 6:50 P.M.

Dear Diary,

Later Carl came down to where we were hanging on the beach. Mandy clammed up and wouldn't talk at all.

Carl was friendly to everybody. He and I went for a walk, and he told me he was going to be working the bar at the teen club tonight and said we should all plan on going.

I thought about it, but I realized if we went, Peter Feldman might be there. He might see Marissa and go talk to her, and the whole ugly truth would come out.

So I said we had other plans.

I am getting *so* sneaky.

FRIDAY, 10:00 A.M.

Dear Diary,

Jason called. He got back today and will be here for the weekend. He asked me to go to the teen club. It's a date. A real date. I'm so glad I didn't tell the others it's teen night. Now I'll be the only one to go. Take *that*, Lila Fowler. Ha-ha-ha-ha!

FRIDAY, 1:00 P.M.

Dear Diary,

Foiled! Kimberly found out it was teen night at the club. Now they're all planning to go as a big girl group. What am I going to do?

FRIDAY, 5:00 P.M.

Dear Diary,

I have such good luck: Marissa's got an earache! Pippa took her to the doctor this afternoon. The doctor put her on antibiotics and told Pippa she should stay in bed for a few days. Yay!

Kimberly went with Pippa and Marissa to the doctor. When they got back, Pippa called Marissa's mom and stayed on the phone with her for a long time.

Mandy and I were in the living room with Kimberly. We could hear Pippa's voice through the wall. It sounded like Pippa was doing an awful lot of reassuring.

"Wow," Mandy said. "Marissa's mom must really be worried."

Kimberly stretched out on the sofa. "Marissa's mom is real protective. Marissa's got some heavy-duty food allergies, and her mom is always worried that she might accidentally eat something she shouldn't."

"What's she allergic to?" Mandy asked curiously.

"Mainly she's allergic to peanuts—which doesn't sound like a big deal until you start thinking of all the stuff that has peanut oil in it."

"Jessica," Pippa said, coming into the room. "Marissa would like to see you."

I got up and went into the bedroom. Marissa was lying there, looking miserable.

"Does it hurt much?" I asked.

She shook her head. "No. I'm just bummed because I want to go with you guys tonight."

"We'll miss you," I lied.

She smiled at me. "Thanks, Jessica."

"I'll get out and let you sleep. Kimberly and I will use the hall bathroom so we don't wake you up."

"No," she said. "Get dressed in here. Even if I can't go, I'll at least get to listen to you guys talk while you get ready. It's not as good as going myself, but it makes it easier knowing somebody will be out having fun even if I can't."

Sometimes Marissa really surprises me. If I had been sick, I wouldn't have wanted anybody to have fun if I couldn't go along.

Then she blinked at me. "My birthday is coming up."

"Really?"

She nodded into her pillow.

"Know what I want?"

"What?"

"To be a full-fledged Unicorn," she murmured Then she closed her eyes and drifted off to sleep.

Thirteen

◇

Dear Diary,

What a night!

I'm sleeping in the living room with Mandy and Ellen. Kimberly is sleeping with Pippa. Pippa said Marissa is running a fever and needs her rest—Marissa has a room to herself. That's why we're not sleeping in our regular beds.

First of all, let me write down what I learned tonight so I don't forget it.

Guys like girls who are enthusiastic!

I really need to remember that. Because Lila's got it all wrong.

Anyway—where was I? Oh, yeah. Jason picked me up, and we walked together to the teen club. When he found out Marissa wasn't going, he was very bummed and made me promise to tell her hello from him when I got home.

When we got to the club, we went to the bar, and Carl was doing his blender-drink thing. Rafe and Larry were there, and they had on matching purple polo shirts with the camp logo on them. They asked me if everybody would be coming. And they looked happy when I said they were. And that Rachel and Ellen were looking forward to seeing them. (Hey! It couldn't hurt.)

Larry and Rafe grinned, then exchanged a quizzical look and a shrug. I put my hand over my mouth to hide my smile. It was pretty clear that Ellen and Rachel weren't the only ones who were confused about who was interested in who.

I decided the four of them were in for an interesting evening.

Carl made all the guys purple drinks to go with their shirts. He made me a bright pink drink to go with my sundress and matching sandals. I looked great even if I do say so myself.

Jason said he was going to talk to the DJ and make some requests. He went inside with Rafe and Larry. I stayed near the bar so I could watch Carl until they came back. He asked me where Marissa was, and I told him she was sick.

Carl said it was too bad that she wouldn't be coming. Then he told me that Peter Feldman had come by and asked about her.

"Hey," I joked. "I'm starting to get jealous. Why is everyone so eager to see Marissa?"

Carl grinned. "Seriously?"

"Sure," I answered, curious about what he was going to say.

"Marissa's a cute girl," he said, cutting up chunks of pineapple for a drink. "But mainly she's the kind of person who makes you feel good about yourself. She doesn't seem like she's making judgments all the time. She's just . . . I don't know . . . friendly. That's probably the biggest beauty secret in the whole world."

A whole bunch of people came up to ask for drinks, so I wandered into the club to find Jason. On the way in, Peter Feldman came over to me and asked where Marissa was. I told him she was sick, and he said he was sorry to hear it.

The other Unicorns got to the club about half an hour after Jason and I did. It was a little weird at first. But then Rafe and Larry asked Ellen and Rachel to dance. Peter Feldman asked Lila. And two other guys challenged Kimberly and Mandy to a game of darts.

Once everybody had somebody to dance with, flirt with, or hang with, it was almost like the last time we came to the teen club. We were a tight group again. Friends. All for one and one for all.

How long would it last? I wondered.

SATURDAY, 10:00 A.M.

Dear Diary,

Marissa is feeling a lot better. Her birthday is Tuesday. Pippa said she would take us all out to dinner at a fancy restaurant to celebrate. It would have to wait until Thursday, though, because she's busy trying to get the gift shop ready for the opening. She's spending all day, every day, at wholesale gift shows.

She's so busy, she sent Kimberly to Maui for a few days to help out. Kimberly's going to stay with Steve and his folks. Lucky Kimberly!

Since we knew we had a fancy dinner coming up, we decided to hit the mall. Rachel, Ellen, Mandy, Lila, and I all headed over on the bus. Marissa didn't want to go. She was still tired from being sick.

It was at the mall that Lila made her move.

We were all sitting in a café, eating avocado, pineapple, and mango salads when she got this cat-that-swallowed-the-canary look on her face.

"Peter Feldman is going back to Sweet Valley today. He's probably on the plane right now," she said.

"Oh?"

"And since Marissa's birthday is coming up, I think we should give Marissa a surprise party," she said.

"Really?" I wondered what the catch was.

"I think we should surprise Marissa by inviting all the guys she knows to the party—and making sure she eats enough peanuts to cover her with splotches from head to toe."

I lifted my spoon. "Wait a minute!"

Lila raised her eyebrow. "Do you have a problem with this?"

"Yes," I protested. "That's a horrible thing to do. We

don't know what happens when Marissa eats peanuts."

"My cousin has an allergy to peanuts," Ellen said. "Whenever she eats them, she gets hives."

"Yeah, but that doesn't mean Marissa will get hives. She could have a serious reaction." I looked around the table. Every face looked stony. None of my "friends" were rallying to my side here. Not even Mandy, who is usually the first to vote "nay" on stuff like this.

Maybe she was so angry with me about Carl, she couldn't think straight. I cleared my throat and tried to sound as reasonable as possible. "If we do something that mean, Pippa will probably send us all home."

Mandy shrugged. "So?"

Wow! Mandy really was furious!

Rachel leaned forward. "We've only got another week. What's the big deal if we wind up going home early? Lila says Wiley's friends all need dates starting this week anyway."

Lila nodded. "There are picnics and parties and even a dance at Janet's house. Don't you get it, Jessica? We're just wasting our time here."

I sat back. *Were* we wasting our time? This was our last summer together, but it wasn't making us closer. It was driving us apart.

Lila leaned over and whispered in my ear, "Peter Feldman is gone. That means you've got squat on me. But Jason is still here, and I could tell everybody the truth about your 'romantic day.' I could also tell *Jason* how disappointed you were."

"You wouldn't," I growled.

"Oh, yes, I would," she whispered. Then she sat back and calmly finished eating her salad. "The party is on. Day after tomorrow."

"Ellen can take Marissa shopping or something while we get everything ready," Rachel said.

Lila took a little pad out of her purse and started making a list. "Things to buy. One. Peanuts. Two. Peanut butter. Three. Peanut oil."

I realized then that I am the biggest coward in the world. I knew I was going to go along with it. Because when we all got back to Sweet Valley, Lila was going to be calling the shots. And I needed to be on her good side.

I really hate myself.

I hate myself almost as much as I hate Lila Fowler.

SUNDAY, 10:40 A.M.

Dear Diary,

Jason called, and Lila picked up the phone. She invited him and Rafe and Larry to the surprise birthday party for Marissa.

He said they'd be there. When I got on the phone, he said he was really looking forward to the party and asked me if I wanted to go help out at the camp tomorrow. I could spend the night there, and we could come back together the next morning.

I said yes. I didn't really want to go help out at the camp, but I didn't want to be here either.

When I hung up the phone, I realized that I was going to have to explain where I was going. "Jason invited me to a party at the camp where he works.

I'm going to spend tomorrow night there. We'll come back together Tuesday morning."

"A camp?" Ellen said, wrinkling up her nose. "That doesn't sound very romantic."

"This isn't that kind of date," I huffed.

"Unlike your *other* date with Jason," put in evil Lila.

I shut up. I really don't need Lila making me feel any worse than I already do.

SUNDAY, 11:11 A.M.

Dear Diary,

Marissa is up and around. Talking a mile a minute and minding everybody's business.

I hate to say this—but things were a lot nicer when she was sick. We didn't have her tagging along and acting like a big know-it-all. I feel horrible knowing what the other girls are planning. On the other hand, I'm glad I'm going away tomorrow because it'll give me a break from Marissa.

Ellen is telling everybody to get their stuff together so we can hit the beach.

More later.

SUNDAY, 7:00 P.M.

Dear Diary,

We were hanging down at the beach when Carl came over with five surfboards on his head. He invited everybody to take one and give it a try.

Of course, Marissa grabbed one and ran out into the waves without looking back. I took one, Rachel took one, and Ellen took one.

"So, Mandy," Carl said. "Want to come out?"

Mandy didn't even smile. She just examined the end of her extension. I could see that her face was flushed and she was nervous. "No, thanks," she said in a flat voice. "Surfing isn't my thing."

"Mine either," Lila volunteered.

Both of them sounded completely disinterested.

Carl and I walked out into the water together. "Am I making a pest of myself?" he asked me.

I laughed. "No way. Why do you ask?"

He shrugged. "I don't know. Lila and Mandy looked like they wanted to get rid of me. I thought maybe I was intruding."

I shook my head. "No. They're afraid of looking stupid."

"I can relate," he said with a grin. "But anybody who sits on a beach when they can be out on a board looks stupid to me."

With that, he jumped on his board and paddled out. "Come on!" he shouted.

I got up on my board and paddled after him. Pretty soon we were all bobbing on the waves— me, Carl, Rachel, Marissa, and Ellen.

We felt the ocean swell. A big one was coming. A really big one.

"Get ready," Carl said, turning his board so that it pointed toward the beach.

We staggered ourselves so we wouldn't collide.

The swell picked us up, lifting us higher and higher.

"*Go!*" Carl shouted.

All of us started paddling in, trying to catch the wave.

To my right, I saw Ellen try to climb up. It was too soon. There wasn't enough momentum. She fell off the board before she had even managed to get to her knees.

Rachel was on one knee and trying to stand.

Bam! She wiped out.

Suddenly the wave grabbed me and the board. We were hurtling toward the beach. The thrust steadied the board underneath me.

I got up on my knees. The board didn't even teeter.

I got up on my feet—in a crouch.

The board was still steady underneath me and moving forward in a smooth path.

I stood up.

I'm not kidding.

I actually stood up! *I was surfing!*

I had my arms out for balance, but after a few seconds I felt so at ease I let them hang loosely at my sides. It was like skateboarding, only better.

When I looked over and saw Marissa and Carl surfing side by side, I felt like we were sharing something incredibly special.

Finally the wave played out. We were almost to the shore. I jumped off my board, and so did Carl and Marissa. Carl grabbed me and twirled me around. Marissa jumped up and down, screaming like a maniac. "You did it!" she yelled. "You did it! You did it!"

I looked over to see if Lila and Mandy had been watching my big moment. Both of them were staring at their books, paying no attention whatsoever.

Carl's face fell. After all, this wasn't just a big moment for me; it was a big moment for him. He was a surfing instructor—and I was living proof that he was a good one.

"I guess they're right," he said in this disappointed tone. "Surfing really isn't their thing."

Rachel and Ellen came paddling in on their boards. "Nice going," Rachel said to me.

Ellen gave me a high five.

"Come on," Carl told everybody. "Let's try it again."

We all went back out and spent the next two hours having a ball. I managed to get up four times. Marissa got up so many times, I lost count. Ellen rode in twice on her knees. Ditto Rachel.

By the time we came out of the water, Lila and Mandy had already gone up to the condo. Carl collected the boards. "I'll see you guys tomorrow?"

"Not Jessica," Marissa told him. "She's going to help Jason at that camp."

Carl looked disappointed. "Too bad. But I'll see you at the—"

He caught himself just in time. I knew he'd been about to say "at the party." Marissa's surprise party.

Marissa didn't notice. She was too busy telling Kimberly how the Haver women were born to surf.

Carl winked at me and made a funny "that-was close" face. He stepped nearer to me and lowered his voice. "You'll be back in time for the party, right?"

I nodded. "Definitely."

He smiled. "OK, then. See you there."

He walked off with the boards balanced on hi

head. I watched him go and had another incredible insight. Life is a lot like surfing.

It looks easy.

But it's not.

MONDAY, 8:00 A.M.

Dear Diary,

I'm sitting out front waiting for Jason to pick me up. I'm actually looking forward to going back to the camp. I've got some ideas for new puppet shows.

Here comes Jason with his dad. Gag! Hal is with them.

MONDAY, 11:40 P.M.

Dear Diary,

I can't sleep. I've got a *real* problem.

Mr. Hajit flew us to the island this morning, and the camp director picked us up in his Jeep. When we got to the camp, they were having a field day. Only instead of stuff like relay races, the competitions were all silly things. Things like—who could keep a straight face the longest when Jason was doing his chimpanzee imitation.

Good thing I wasn't competing. I couldn't keep a straight face for six seconds. Who knew Jason was such a comedian?

After that, we all took another nature hike and competed to see who could name the most flora and fauna. I was way out of my league there—so I just kept an eye on the stragglers and made sure we didn't lose anybody.

Before I knew it, it was time for dinner. We

cooked hot dogs over a fire. Jason cooked mine for me and asked me what I liked on it. He brought me a plate and a soda and was really polite about making sure I had everything I wanted.

In a funny way, this felt more like a date than anything we had done so far. I ate my hot dog, but I didn't have much appetite.

I couldn't stop thinking about what was going on back at the condo. Maybe Marissa would see all the peanut stuff they had bought. Maybe Mandy would break down and call Kimberly and Kimberly would put a stop to it. Maybe . . .

Jason noticed that I hadn't eaten much. He asked if I felt OK. I told him I felt fine, I just wasn't very hungry.

Somebody got out a guitar, and we all sang along. Jason sat next to me and put his arm around me. But I couldn't relax. I felt stiff and self-conscious. I know he sensed it, and he took his arm away.

After the kids all went to bed, the counselors sat around talking for a while. They seemed like a nice group of people. Really nice.

When the fire died out, it was time to go to bed. Jason introduced me to a girl named Natasha and told me I would be sharing a tent with her. When he told me good night, he squeezed my hand, but he didn't kiss me.

There *were* a lot of people standing around. It wouldn't have been totally appropriate. But I really wanted to know what was going on. Did he want to be my friend? Or my boyfriend?

Natasha and I walked up the path to her tent. I noticed she was eating a cheese sandwich. "Didn't you get enough dinner?" I joked.

She smiled. "I'm allergic to hot dogs," she said. "Something in the preservatives. I can't eat any cold cuts or stuff like that."

Suddenly I felt light-headed. "What happens?" I asked. "Do you break out in hives?"

She shook her head. "I *wish*. No. I have a really horrible reaction. My throat swells up, and I can't breathe. Twice I've had to go to the emergency room and get injections of Adrenalin. I was lucky to be near a hospital. I could have died."

When she said that, my feet went numb and my hands felt icy cold. Could Marissa have a violent reaction like that?

I've been trying to sleep for almost two hours. But I can't. I'm too anxious. I have to get back first thing in the morning and stop Lila.

Fourteen

Dear Diary,

It's almost 2:30. Lila and the others are setting up the peanut-laced refreshments. I can't stand the suspense. Pretty soon the party is going to start and there's not going to be any birthday girl.

I don't know what's going to happen. All I know is that Marissa won't be eating any peanuts.

I guess I did finally fall asleep last night, but I jerked awake as soon as the sun was up. I pulled on my clothes, grabbed my duffel bag, and hurried to the main lodge.

Jason was there, helping set up for breakfast.

"Jason, I have to go back," I told him.

"We're going back on the eleven A.M. flight," he said.

"I can't wait—this is an emergency. Can you take

me down to the airstrip? I have to be on the first plane back."

Jason took me aside. "What's the matter? What's wrong? Did something happen?"

I shook my head. "I can't explain. I just have to go back."

He looked hurt. "Does it have anything to do with me?"

"No!" My voice broke. "But I have to go back. I have to go back now." I was close to panicking, and I guess he heard it in my voice.

"OK," he said quietly. "I'll get somebody to take us."

I don't know what Jason told the camp director, but he didn't try to argue with us and we were at the airstrip when Mr. Hajit landed for the first relay.

Half an hour later Mr. Landry was dropping me off at the condo.

"I'll see you at the party," Jason said when I jumped out.

I nodded. "See you there." Then I ran upstairs.

It was so early, nobody was even awake yet. I barged into Lila's room and shook her. "Wake up!"

Lila's eyes jerked open. "What? What?"

"Did you find out what Marissa's allergic reaction to peanuts is?"

She shrugged. "No. I'm sure it's hives. What other kinds of reactions are there?"

"Lots!" I shouted. "You don't know what could happen. She could have a heart attack for all you know."

Lila rolled her eyes. "Get *out!*"

"I'm serious."

Rachel sat up in bed. "What's going on?" she asked sleepily. "What are you guys arguing about?"

"Jessica is chickening out," Lila said.

"I'm not chickening out. I'm just trying to keep you guys from making a huge mistake."

Lila narrowed her eyes. "The only person who is making a huge mistake is *you*," she said threateningly. "We have gone to a lot of trouble to make sure this surprise party gives Marissa the surprise of her life. So don't blow it. Or else."

"Does Kimberly know?"

"No," Lila said. "And if she gets wind of it, we'll know who ratted."

I went into the living room, trying to think what to do.

If I told Kimberly, it would put Kimberly in a horrible position. She'd have to put a stop to it, and that would make all the Unicorns furious with her.

If I told Marissa, she probably wouldn't even believe me. She was convinced that the Unicorns were all her close pals.

And if I told Pippa, *nobody* would ever forgive me.

I picked up the phone and dialed—hoping Jason was home already.

He was. "Listen," I said. "I need you to be my friend. I need you to do something that's going to seem very weird, but I need you to do it and not ask me why."

"OK," he agreed softly.

"I need you to come get Marissa as soon as possible and take her away for the day. Don't bring her back until late tonight."

"But . . . today is her party," Jason argued.

"Jason! I'm begging you. Just do it."

"Can't you tell me what . . ."

"No. Just please do it."

Jason let out a long sigh. "OK. I trust you. I trust you a lot. Let me see if my dad can drop me off."

I hung on for a few minutes, then he came back and told me he'd be waiting downstairs in twenty minutes.

I went into Marissa's room. Kimberly was still asleep. I put my hand over Marissa's mouth and shook her gently.

Her eyes flew open. I put my finger to my lips and gestured to her to come with me into the bathroom.

Marissa blinked and followed me. I closed the door and started whispering to her. "Jason wants to take you on a special day trip for your birthday," I said.

"Me?" she squeaked.

"Shhh!" I warned. "Don't tell anybody. Just throw on your clothes, grab your bathing suit, and go. He'll be waiting downstairs."

"But . . . but . . ."

"Don't ask questions," I warned her. "If you do, you'll ruin the surprise."

Marissa hugged me and grinned from ear to ear. "I just know this has something to do with being a Unicorn, doesn't it?"

"I can't answer any questions," I said, frowning. "But if you want to be a Unicorn, you've got to do what I tell you."

She nodded, closed her lips, and made a locking

motion. I emptied out my duffel bag and gave it to her to use.

Five minutes later we sneaked through the condo and took the elevator down. When Jason and his dad drove up, Marissa jumped into their Jeep and blew me a kiss good-bye.

I could tell that Jason was dying to ask me questions, but there was no way I could answer. So I just told them to have a great time and ran back into the building.

I was munching my cereal with a blank look on my face by the time everybody was out of bed.

"Where's Marissa?" Rachel asked sleepily, stumbling into the living room with Lila.

"She said she was going shopping," I said through a big mouthful of cereal. "She said she's looking for the perfect outfit and isn't coming home until she finds it."

Rachel and Lila looked at each other. "She knows about the party," Lila said in an exasperated voice. "Who told her?" She stared at me.

Luckily Rachel covered her face. "She must have heard me talking about it with Rafe," she groaned. "I was talking to him on the phone when she came through the room yesterday."

Lila chewed the inside of her cheek. Then she shrugged. "Doesn't matter. She thinks it's a surprise party. She just doesn't know what the surprise really is. Everything is cool."

I wonder how cool Lila's going to be when she realizes there's not going to be a birthday girl at the party.

TUESDAY, 7:00 P.M.

Dear Diary,

The guests started to arrive around three. Lila was in a total tizzy. "Where is Marissa?" she kept asking everybody.

Nobody could answer.

Rafe arrived with Larry. Both of them brought Marissa a present. Ellen took the gifts and stacked them on the coffee table. Pretty soon Carl and a bunch of girls we had met at the teen club came. They had presents too.

By three forty-five the penthouse was bulging with people, and they all wanted to know where the birthday girl was.

Lila circulated around with this frozen smile plastered on her face. "She'll be here," she kept telling everyone. "She'll be here any minute."

Rafe put on some music, and we all danced.

I danced like I have never danced before. I really let loose. I felt like it was the end of the world or something. Once the party was over, I knew I was dead meat.

By six o'clock it was pretty clear to everybody that Marissa wasn't going to show.

"Golly," Lila told people, laughing, "I guess the surprise is on us. Do we feel stupid or what? We thought of everything—except making sure that Marissa was going to be here. We kept the secret too well!"

Carl, Rafe, and Larry just laughed. "I guess Jason forgot about it too. Funny. He said he was definitely going to be here," Rafe put in.

That's when they all started to smell a rat. Every pair of Unicorn eyes turned toward me and glared. Finally the guests were gone. There was nobody to protect me. It was just me and Ellen, Mandy, Rachel, and Lila.

"I don't know what you did," Lila told me as soon as she closed the door on the last guest. "But you are going to pay for this. From now on, we are not friends. Got it? From now on, we're not even speaking to you."

I lifted my chin and reminded myself that I had done the right thing. "I don't care," I told them defiantly. (Even though I did.)

The door opened and Marissa came floating in, humming to herself. She looked like she was in a complete and total daze.

"Where have you been?" Lila demanded.

Marissa smiled—a distant, foggy smile. "Let me change, and I'll tell you all about it." Then she sort of wafted into her bedroom.

I ran out of the condo and punched the elevator button. I wanted to tell Jason what had happened. I wanted somebody to tell me what a heroine I was. How brave I was. How much better than everybody else I was.

The elevator came right away. Luckily it didn't make any stops on the way down. I ran out of the lobby and looked around for some sign of Jason.

I didn't see anything.

Then I heard someone call my name. I turned and saw Jason standing in the shadows. "I hoped you would come down," he said in a husky voice.

I ran toward him with my arms out. I knew that when I told him what I had done, he would take me in his arms and kiss me for real. Kiss me like a boyfriend.

He caught me in his arms and hugged me. "Thank you," he breathed. "Thank you for the most wonderful day of my life."

"What?"

He let go of me and held me away from him so he could look at my face. "You are incredible." He shook his head as if he were overwhelmed with admiration. "I guess you're just one of those amazingly insightful and perceptive people."

Insightful? Perceptive? *Me?*

What was he talking about?

"I'm just blown away. You knew what I didn't know. How? How did you know that Marissa and I were perfect for each other?"

An invisible fist punched me right in the stomach.

I didn't know what to do, so I just listened to Jason moon over Marissa until I couldn't stand it anymore. Finally I made some excuse and stumbled back into the building. I somehow found my way into the elevator.

Maybe this is a dream, I thought. *A nightmare.*

Maybe I would wake up and still be at the camp.

Upstairs, when I walked into the living room, Marissa was sitting there telling them all about how she and Jason had fallen madly in love and wasn't it the most wonderful birthday present in the whole world?

When she saw me, she threw herself into my arms. "Oh, Jessica. You are so sly. All this time you were just waiting for the perfect matchmaking opportunity. Fooling us all by pretending Jason was your boyfriend when you *knew* he was perfect for me."

I was so numb, so flabbergasted, and so heartbroken, I couldn't even speak.

"Well," Lila snarled when Marissa let me go. "We were so worried about you. You missed your own surprise party."

Marissa's mouth fell open. "You planned a party? For me? Oh, wow!" She opened her arms and whirled in a circle. "What a birthday! A boyfriend! A surprise party!" She gave us all a watery smile. "I'm sorry I missed it. But . . . does this mean I'm a Unicorn now?" She held up a hand. "No. No. Don't tell me. I've already had so many wonderful things happen to me today. Let's save *something* for tomorrow."

A tear trickled down her cheek. "Excuse me . . . I . . . I . . . ." Her lip trembled. "I think I need to be alone for a while." She blew us all a kiss and floated back into the bedroom.

There was this long, stunned silence, then Lila threw back her head and began to laugh. "So I guess the truth about Jason is finally out."

I ran into my room. I wished like crazy that I didn't have to share it with Marissa anymore. But there was nothing I could do. I threw myself down on the bed and buried my face in my pillow to muffle my sobs.

Marissa flew over to me. "What's the matter?" she gasped. "Jessica! Talk to me."

"Nothing," I choked. "Go away."

"I'm not going away," she argued. "You're my best friend. You have to tell me what's wrong so I can make you feel better."

That did it. I sat up and just let her have it. "I am not your friend. I *hate* you!"

Marissa was so startled, she sank onto the bed.

"I hate you!" I told her again. "Get it? *Everybody* hates you, but you're just too dumb to know it."

Marissa's face turned a sickly white. "That's not true. They like me. They planned a party for me."

I shook my head. "They were planning to humiliate you. Do you know what was in that cake and in those cookies? Peanuts! They wanted you to break out in a rash in front of everybody. So I asked Jason to take you away for the day. To protect you. Ha! I should have been protecting myself. Because you stole Jason from me! And now I don't have *any* friends!"

I threw myself back down on the bed and cried some more. "I hate you, I hate you, I hate you," I said over and over into my pillow.

I don't know how long I lay there, bawling. It seemed like forever. Finally I was all out of tears. Too exhausted to cry anymore.

When I sat up and reached for a tissue, Marissa was still sitting on the end of my bed with the box in her lap. Wordlessly she handed me a tissue.

I took it and blew my nose.

We sat there for about ten minutes. Neither one of us said anything.

"Are you finished crying?" she asked finally.

I nodded.

"OK, then I have to tell you something." For once her voice sounded totally serious.

I stared at my lap, afraid to look her in the eye.

"You *are* my best friend whether you realize it or not," she told me, "because you probably saved my life."

I blew my nose again and met her gaze.

"I could have gone into a coma," she said quietly. "I might have died."

I didn't know what to say to that. I couldn't believe I had let things go as far as they had. Sure, I tried to stop it, but not hard enough.

I should have nipped the prank in the bud the minute Lila suggested it. I should have told Marissa, Kimberly, and Pippa.

I should have told the people at the camp. I should have called the police if necessary. I should have done everything humanly possible to stop it. So what if my friends got mad at me and somebody got into trouble?

You didn't risk somebody's life to keep your friends from getting into trouble!

I started to feel dizzy. To black out.

Marissa told me to lean over and hang my head between my knees. I did. Finally my chest started to relax. The dizzy feeling passed, and I could sit up. But I was hiccuping.

Marissa went into the bathroom and got me a glass of water. "Here," she said curtly. "Drink."

I took long gulps. I could feel Marissa's eyes studying me. But I couldn't look her in the face. I was too ashamed. "I am so sorry," I whispered after I finished the water.

Marissa took the glass from me. "Did Kimberly know about this?" she asked.

Now I did look at her. I looked her in the eye because she had to know that I was telling the truth. "No. They made sure Kimberly didn't know."

Marissa's face was pale. "*That's* a relief. I thought maybe my own cousin was trying to murder me."

Murder!

I started shaking. I couldn't stop. I just shook and shook. Marissa put her arms around me. "It's OK," she told me. "It's OK."

"No, it's not," I sobbed. "It's not OK. Nothing is OK. We're not having fun. Everybody including me is being horrible. And we almost killed you. How can you say everything is OK?"

She gave me a crooked smile. "I don't know. In spite of everything, I feel great. I'm in love with Jason, and he's in love with me. OK. Maybe it's not *love*, but it's a mutual crush. My first! And this summer has been great for me up until now. You just don't understand what it's been like for me. Nobody knows what the real story is."

I sat back and leaned against the pillows. "What is the real story?"

"This food allergy thing has taken over my

whole life. I've had to be so careful. And my mother is so conditioned to be overprotective, she doesn't know when to turn it off. She's never let me go to regular school. This year will be my first year to go to school with other kids."

"You're kidding!"

"No. I always had home tutors. But I told my mom I really wanted to go to regular school next year. That I had to. That I was just dying of loneliness. She said absolutely not, and we had this huge fight about it. I wound up running away, and the police brought me back home. That's why I'm spending the summer with Pippa. Mom and I agreed we needed some time apart. And it was a good way for me to prove I could make friends and take responsibility for my diet."

"I had no idea," I whispered.

Marissa looked shamefaced. "I didn't want you guys to know. Kimberly knew, but she promised not to tell anybody."

I looked at Marissa and suddenly saw her the way Rafe and Jason and Peter saw her. I saw someone with a lot of courage and spirit. Somebody who always had a smile for everyone. Somebody who wasn't too cool to care.

"So what do you want to do about this peanut ambush thing?" I asked her.

She bit her lip. "I want to sleep on it."

Fifteen

◇

Dear Diary,

It's a gorgeous day, but I don't think I'll ever feel happy again. I woke up this morning with a horrible headache from crying. My guts were in a total uproar over all the ugly stuff that had been said. And my heart was breaking.

Marissa got up early to meet Jason for a swim and a walk on the beach.

I stayed in the room. I was too humiliated, angry, and disgusted to face the others.

After a little while Kimberly came in. Pippa had picked her up, and they were both home. She was holding a note that Rachel had left on the refrigerator. The note said everybody had gone snorkeling at Malaka Cove again.

"How come you didn't go?" Kimberly asked me.

I shrugged and doodled in the margin of my diary.

"You guys all had a big fight, didn't you?" She rolled her eyes upward. "Is that why your eyes are all red?"

"Yeah," I admitted. "We did have a fight. The usual stuff. Lila trying to make me miserable and succeeding." I didn't tell Kimberly about the surprise party. She would have gone through the roof.

Kimberly flopped back on the bed and stared at the ceiling. "I'm glad this stuff is over for me," she said finally.

That surprised me. "What do you mean?" I asked.

She sat up and ran her hand through her hair. Kimberly suddenly looked a lot older than the rest of us. I can't explain it, but she seemed to have grown up over the past few weeks. "Don't get me wrong. I'm glad everybody could come on this trip. But I'm losing interest in being part of a group. I think I'd rather be myself."

I drew in my breath. "That's exactly what I've been thinking."

"I'm going to high school!" Kimberly exclaimed. "Why am I worrying about what Lila or Janet Howell or Peter Feldman thinks? I don't even like them. What's the point of getting older if you're not going to grow up?" She grinned. "Guess what I realized over the weekend?"

"What?"

"I'm really pretty. And guys like me."

I smiled. "Oh, yeah? Like who?"

Kimberly batted her eyelashes. "Steve. I hope you guys don't mind, but I'm probably not going back with you. I'm going to stay on until the day before school. I already asked Pippa. That way I can spend some quality time with Steve."

I knew where Kimberly was coming from. She was feeling confident, so she didn't need our approval. She was pulling away from the Unicorns.

If she could do it, I could do it. I took a deep breath and sat up. "There's something I haven't told you."

"What?"

I gave Kimberly the rundown on how the Unicorns planned a surprise party and laced everything with peanuts.

Kimberly's face turned purple. I swear. I have never seen anybody look so angry in my whole life.

"That does it," she fumed, standing up and pacing. "They're out of here. All of them. That's the most irresponsible, cold-blooded, evil thing I have ever heard in my life. I'm going to tell Pippa and—"

"Wait! I have a better idea. I tried to tell Lila that food allergies could be dangerous. She wouldn't listen. Some people you can't tell. Some people you have to show."

I told her what I had in mind.

She began to laugh.

"Think Marissa will go for it?" I asked.

Kimberly nodded. "In a big way. She's your number-one fan, Jessica. I think she'll do whatever you think is right."

I couldn't help feeling proud. I've never had

what you would call—"leadership quality." But knowing somebody looked up to me made me want to stand tall.

THURSDAY, 11:40 A.M.

Dear Diary,

Tonight's the night. Marissa's birthday dinner! We're going to a fancy luau.

Let the games begin.

THURSDAY, 10:00 P.M.

Dear Diary,

Tonight was actually a lot of fun. We were all dressed up, and Pippa hired a stretch limo to take us to the restaurant—a gorgeous place high up on a mountainside.

Under the circumstances, it was impossible to keep up the grudge match. So by the time we hit the restaurant, we were all laughing and talking just like nothing had ever happened.

Pippa told us we could invite whoever we wanted. So Kimberly asked Steve. Marissa asked Jason. I asked Carl.

And Ellen and Rachel asked Rafe and Larry. *But they still didn't know who was with who!* It was pretty funny when we tried to sit down. There was a lot of hesitating/lurching/sitting/standing-back-up-and-saying-"oops" stuff.

Larry finally wound up sitting at one end of the table—next to Pippa. And Rafe wound up sitting at the other end—next to Jason.

Aside from Pippa, the only two people who didn't have dates were Mandy and Lila. Lila kept checking to make sure her mobile phone was on "in case Wiley called." (I guess she thought the phone counted as a date.)

If I hadn't known what was coming, I would have teased her about it. But I knew she was going to get a big shock later. (Turns out she got an even bigger shock than I planned—but I'll get to that.)

Dinner was *fantastic*. Afterward we danced on this big black-and-white forties-style dance floor. While Carl and I were dancing, I noticed that his eyes kept wandering back to the table. He was looking at Mandy.

Mandy sat at the table, staring down at her lap. I realized that she was miserable. Not about Carl. But about the whole situation. Mandy wasn't naturally cruel, but she'd somehow let herself fall under Lila's evil spell.

I decided to see if I could break that spell. When Carl excused himself to go talk to the DJ, I went over to the table. Lila, who was still making a point of not speaking to me, left and went to the ladies' room.

"Mandy," I said, "I probably shouldn't be sticking my nose into anybody else's business, but I think Carl is interested in you."

Mandy's eyes lit up, and her face looked happy for the first time in days. "Really? But . . . I thought he liked you."

"He does. As a friend. But I think he may have a crush on you. You like him, don't you?"

Mandy bit her lip, hesitating. I guess she wasn't

sure whether she should confide in me or not.

"If you do, you've got to act different. Every time he tries to talk to you, you act like he's invisible."

Mandy blushed. "I'm trying to be cool."

"Don't," I told her bluntly. "Smile. Ask him about surfing. Quit acting like you couldn't care less if he lives or dies. Here he comes." I waved him over.

"Jessica! No!" Mandy hissed.

Carl came toward the table, smiling uncertainly. "Mandy wants to dance," I said with all the tact and subtlety of, say, Marissa.

"Jessica!" Mandy practically shrieked.

Carl's eyebrows flew up. "With me?"

"Sure, with you," I answered.

He looked at her. "Do you?" he asked uneasily, as if he half expected her to angrily refuse.

Mandy's face was bright red, but she couldn't help smiling. "OK," she said.

I kicked her under the table.

"I'd love to," she corrected herself.

Pretty soon she and Carl were boogying away. Lila came back to the table and sat way on the other side so she wouldn't have to talk to me.

I smiled behind my hand. Pippa had gone to another table to visit with some friends, but now she was on her way back. Her friends were leaving the restaurant. We were the last table of people left.

It was time for the floor show.

The music came to an end, and Pippa signaled everybody to come back to the table. When they had taken their places, she tapped her water glass and stood. "A toast. To Marissa on her birthday."

Everybody lifted their water glasses and clinked them together.

Kimberly stood up. "I just want to say a few words about Marissa and how special she's made this house party."

Marissa smiled and gave Jason a pleased nudge with her shoulder.

"I know that everybody feels the same way," Kimberly continued, addressing her remarks to Marissa. "They tried to show you before by giving you a surprise party. But you missed it. Fortunately I found the cake, and I saved a piece of it for you." Kimberly opened a silver box that she had brought from Pippa's new gift shop. She took out a small plate with several broken pieces of cake on it.

I looked around the table. Every Unicorn face was frozen.

"I say let's all take a bite for luck and to seal our friendship. Marissa, the first bite goes to you."

Mandy half stood. "Wait!" she yelled.

But it was too late. Marissa had snatched a piece of the cake from the plate in Kimberly's hand and popped it into her mouth. She chewed with a big smile.

Two seconds later her eyes bugged. Her hand flew to her throat. She staggered out of her chair.

"Marissa!" Pippa shouted, lurching toward her. "What is it? What's the matter?" She sounded so concerned that for a moment I forgot she was in on the whole thing.

Marissa made some horrible choking, gagging noises and fell down on the floor. Her eyelids fluttered, then closed.

Jason knelt beside her. He felt her wrist. He felt her neck. He leaned over and listened to her heart. His face registered shock. "She's dead," he croaked. "She's *dead!*" He lifted Marissa's limp figure and buried his face in her shoulder. "Marissa!" he sobbed. "Marissa, come back!"

No one said a word. No one moved. Then Ellen's hands flew to her face. Mandy's knees wobbled, and she collapsed into her chair. Rachel burst into hysterical tears.

I stood up and pointed at Lila. "Murderer!" I accused.

"*No!*" Lila shrieked. She was positively green.

"You killed her," I said through gritted teeth. "I told you she was allergic to peanuts. But you wouldn't listen."

Pippa glared at Lila. "You did this on purpose?" she raged. "On *purpose?* You're a killer!"

"We all did it," Mandy wailed, pulling at her braids. "We're all guilty. Oh, my God! How could we do this? How?"

"That's what I want to know!" Marissa said angrily, miraculously coming back from the dead.

Every single Unicorn screamed. Ellen and Rachel thumped right into Carl and Rafe. They fell over their chairs and tumbled to the floor.

On the way down Rafe tried to grab the edge of the table and got the tablecloth instead.

Crash!

The whole cloth came sliding off the table, complete with dessert plates, water glasses, and what sounded like a thousand knives and forks.

Larry tried to keep the big silver water bucket from falling over but wound up spilling it. Icy water poured right into Lila's lap. She let out a scream that could have awakened the dead but instead startled Mandy, who fell backward in her chair so that she lay on the floor with her feet pointing straight up in the air.

It was pandemonium!

I started laughing so hard, I fell out of my own seat.

Marissa and Jason were both hysterical with laughter, and Pippa was pounding the table.

Just then the phone rang. The phone in Lila's purse. She snatched it out of her bag. "Hello?" she said in a faint voice.

It was Wiley.

And guess what?

He was calling to break up!

Could life get any better than this?

No way.

And so, Dear Diary, by the time we all got back to the condo, everybody had apologized to everybody. Everybody agreed that Marissa was an incredible actress. Everybody agreed that it was a night they would never forget.

And everybody agreed that since we only had two days left—we should devote ourselves to having fun and stop torturing each other.

Can we actually do it?

I'll find out starting tomorrow.

Sixteen

◇

Dear Diary,

I'm sitting on the beach. I only have two more pages left in this notebook and today is our last day, so I guess I'll come out even.

We did have a good last few days. We had a lot of parties and group outings. But talk about ironic! Lila and I were the only two Unicorns who didn't have a guy of our own.

In fact, we're the only two Unicorns sitting on the beach right now watching the sun go down. Everybody else is saying a romantic good-bye to someone special.

I guess Rachel, Ellen, Rafe, and Larry finally got things figured out. Because I saw Rachel and Larry walk off in one direction and Ellen and Rafe walk off in another.

Lila cried for a whole day about Wiley. But she'd

learned her lesson. We didn't see any more Janet Howell behavior. She was also good and ashamed of herself over what she tried to do to Marissa.

School starts in a week.

I hope we don't all get split up. But if we do, I know now that it'll be OK. I'll make new friends if I have to. I sure learned how to do that this summer.

And if I have to let some old friendships go, well, I can do that too. I still love Lila. But I'm not sure I like her, if you know what I mean. I'm not sure she likes me either.

But I guess if I learned anything at all, it's this: I'd rather like myself than be liked.

No more room left.

Just the margin.

Aloha!

Good-bye and hello!

Created by Francine Pascal

Have you read the latest Collections in this super series?